"Hello."

Startled, she turned toward the person who hailed her. She smiled as she was joined by the figure who had been sitting back from the path, enjoying the sunset.

"It's beautiful, isn't it?" she asked easily.

"Is it only the sunset you never tire of?" her companion questioned with a laugh.

There was something chilling in the laughter, a wildness that was out of place in these magical moments suspended between light and dark. She turned toward her companion and thought she saw knowledge in the eyes, but they slid away. Below them, she heard the waves breaking ruthlessly against the coast, devouring the narrow beach that lay at the foot of the cliff.

She smiled; it was a nervous, halfhearted gesture. "You aren't planning to fish tomorrow, are you?"

"No, but sometimes I like to see what the tide has left on the beach. Or what it has washed away."

"Do you find many things of interest?" she inquired, making conversation to fill the uneasy silence.

"Not on the beach. But sometimes, back among the sand dunes, I come upon things of great interest . . . things that should stay dead and buried."

She froze. "You know, don't you?" she asked, looking in the eyes once more.

"Oh, yes. I know. . . ."

"Christina Dair has crafted a compelling novel of intrigue, love, and revenge. Her scenes are painted with vivid colors that leave the reader hungry for more. I couldn't put it down."

—Debbie Macomber, bestselling author

DEADLY DESIRES

◆ ◆ ◆

Christina Dair

HarperPaperbacks
A Division of HarperCollinsPublishers

This is a work of fiction. The characters, incidents, and dialogues are products of the author's imagination and are not to be construed as real. Any resemblance to actual events or persons, living or dead, is entirely coincidental.

HarperPaperbacks   *A Division of* HarperCollins*Publishers*
10 East 53rd Street, New York, N.Y. 10022

Cover illustration by Michael Sabanosh

First printing: July 1994

Printed in the United States of America

HarperPaperbacks, HarperMonogram, and colophon are trademarks of HarperCollins*Publishers*

❖ 10 9 8 7 6 5 4 3 2 1

For Marjorie Miller . . . a gifted teacher who knows how to nurture beginning writers and new ideas. This book was always yours.

For Pat Teal . . . an extraordinary agent and friend who kept the faith even when I forgot what to have faith in. Thanks for taking a chance on me all those years ago.

Author's Note

The northern California coast from San Simeon through Big Sur and up to Carmel and Monterey contains some of the most beautiful scenery in all the world. It has drawn William Randolph Hearst, Henry Miller, John Steinbeck, Robinson Jeffers, and Clint Eastwood, to name only a few. If there is no one area within this stretch of coast that contains all the scenic wonders within easy walking distance as I've described them, I hope I will be forgiven for taking literary (and geographic) license. Nor is there a Santa Lucia Inn and Resort as I have described it. The Point Lobos State Reserve exists, as does the effect the area's natural beauty has upon the soul. If you visit once, your heart will indeed be lost. You will be drawn back again and again.

PROLOGUE

Autumn 1991

Pushing aside the drooping branch of the gracious old willow tree, she stood a moment longer in the deep shade to watch the shimmering orange sun dip toward the horizon. In less than an hour, it would ease itself past the horizon and another day would be gone. But there would be no regrets for another passing day, for at the age of fifty-three she still retained the ability to live each day—each moment, even—to the fullest.

She smiled. It was foolish to say that she loved life *even* at her age; she would rather say *especially* at her age. God knew she'd had her share of tragedies, yet now, as each precious moment flew by faster than the one before, she still retained that gift of finding joy in each and every day. It was a trick she had perfected during her unhappy childhood and her even more miserable marriage—to horde those few glorious moments and cast out the dark ones. It had served her well, this gift of hers.

She glanced toward the path that led home and then back the other way. All seemed clear, yet she was careful, as was her habit. No, it was more than habit; it was a way of life. She and her lover had always been careful, so careful that in thirty-four years no one had ever known of his existence or guessed his identity. No one, that is, except her husband.

She looked back over her shoulder, back toward the place where she and her lover had secretly dug his shallow grave among the sand dunes and scrub. Not content with a blanket of dirt, they had added a canopy of rocks and living plants whose roots had clung tenaciously to the fresh soil and grown quickly to cover the raw gash upon the earth.

Ashes to ashes; dust to dust . . .

The thought flitted through her mind. She shivered. Thirty-four years later she still skirted the area, fearing a bony hand would work its way free to grab her ankle as she passed and pull her down into the cold, dark earth.

She shook her head. This wasn't the time for such thoughts; she should be happy. She smiled, thinking of her peers placidly sipping sherry and playing the day's last hand of bridge. What would they think if they saw her now? Would they see the youthful, laughing girl she felt herself to be?

The breeze ruffled her short hair, revealing waves of gray, and the setting sun illuminated the delicate lines at the corners of her eyes; but in her mind it was long, sun-kissed hair that swung freely in the wind and flawless skin unmarked by the years. In her heart she was nineteen again and breathlessly, heedlessly in love.

She put her hand up to her head and brushed the newly trimmed hair back from her face; she saw the blue-veined hand that rested on the trunk of the willow. The illusion fled; she was growing old. And she wondered, as she so often did, if their passion would have burned as brightly had they married. Would the day-to-day cares have strangled their love, as it had done to so many of her friends? She thought not.

Still standing in the shadows, she witnessed the sun's first tentative touch of the horizon; she beheld the lengthening of its reflection into a shimmering, salmon-colored path that beckoned across the Pacific. Glancing left and right once more, she stepped boldly onto the footway and started home. Still smiling, almost blushing like a new bride, she trod the footworn trail.

"Hello."

Startled, she turned toward the person who hailed her. She smiled as she was joined by the figure who had been sitting back from the path, enjoying the sunset as she had been.

"It's beautiful, isn't it?" she asked easily as she gestured toward the dying sun. "I never tire of the sunset."

"Is it only the sunset you never tire of?" her companion questioned with a laugh.

There was something chilling in the laughter, a wildness that was out of place in these magical moments suspended between light and dark. She turned toward her companion and thought she saw knowledge in the eyes, but they slid away. Below them, she heard the waves breaking ruthlessly against the coast, devouring the narrow beach that lay at the foot of the cliff.

"The tide is coming in," she said when the silence proved uneasy.

"Yes. High tide will be at nine thirty-seven tonight."

She cast a quick, anxious look at her companion. It seemed odd to know the exact moment the tide would turn, even for someone who lived at the ocean's edge.

She smiled; it was a nervous, halfhearted gesture. "You aren't planning to fish tomorrow, are you?"

"No. But sometimes I like to see what the tide has left on the beach. Or what it has washed away."

"Do you find many things of interest?" she inquired, making conversation to fill the uneasy silence.

"Not on the beach. But sometimes, back among the sand dunes, I come upon things of great interest . . . things that should stay dead and buried."

She froze. She had been right; there was knowledge in those eyes.

"You know, don't you?" she asked, looking in the eyes once more.

"Oh, yes. I know."

"What do you want?"

"For my silence, you mean?"

"Yes. For your silence," she whispered, realizing how many other lives could be ruined by her deceit.

"I want you to leave. To catch a plane to the farthest corner of the earth and never return."

She turned again to look at the diminishing sun, to watch its luminous shadow lengthen, as she tried to imagine life elsewhere . . . life without him.

"I can't," she finally said, more to the sun and the wind than to her adversary.

"I gave you a chance," her companion muttered. "Remember that I gave you a chance."

She felt something rip into her back, heard thunder reverberate close by her shoulder. Her legs trembled, faltered. The sand and rock ground roughly against her face. Feeling her own warm blood flow over her shoulder to puddle under her face, she tried to touch the place where pain gripped her . . . where she felt her life seeping into the earth.

Not me! a voice inside her cried. *Not now. Dear God, not now!*

Wildly, she tried to recall the moments of happiness. The shy, secret glances they'd exchanged. The first time he'd touched her. The nights she'd lain warm and safe within his arms. The moments of love . . . so many, so bright.

A foot kicked her, but she saw only the darkening sky and the final wink of the sun as it slipped over the horizon, pulling its long, shimmering tail into the night.

1

Spring 1994

For Jessica Martinson, life was simplest when seen through the viewfinder of her camera. Whole forests were reduced to individual leaves. The strength of the sun mattered only as it glinted off a single raindrop. The myriad passions of a human being could be reduced to one simple emotion. Not that she was focusing on anything that important at the moment. Simply a small yellow-and-black bug trudging its way around and around the lip of an orange wildflower. She wondered how long it would take the insect to discover that if it kept retracing its steps, the only thing it would create was a rut. She understood there was a great deal to be said for the safety of predictability and just as much to be feared in the sand, but she also understood that too much safety could steal the joy from your soul. She was living proof.

Not that she hesitated for even a moment as these thoughts flitted through her mind. Instead Jessica wiggled her body even farther into the sand where she lay on her stomach, her camera lens only a few inches from her quarry. She was so intent upon photographing the insect that she wasn't aware of anything but her subject.

She concentrated on the light as she viewed it through the camera lens. Cursed or blessed it as the wisps of fog altered the way it reflected off the sand. She even whispered encouragement to the little bug as it plodded along, as unaware of her as she was of the man observing her.

Her eye never left the viewfinder as her fingers turned the focusing ring and adjusted the aperture. Light and dark, depth of field, and shutter speed were adjusted with nimble fingers as she squeezed off frame after frame. There was no time to lose if she was to capture the tiny insect before it decided to take that leap of faith, to leave safety behind and take its chances in the sand. Only when her subject fell off the flower to land on its back, its tiny legs flailing in the air, did she take a greedy gulp of air. She wondered how long she'd been holding her breath in an effort to keep body and camera movement to a minimum.

"I hope," she heard a masculine voice say, "that your view is as interesting as mine."

She looked over her shoulder, and her first impulse was to smile at the tall, dark-haired man and jokingly tell him that he couldn't possibly get a good shot from where he stood. Even with the newest and most sophisticated lens, there was no way he could come close to the vivid shots she'd just captured with her dated but dependable Nikon. But when she realized that he had no camera and that she was the view he referred to, her smile faded and she retreated behind her emotional barricades, as her sister Marty so cleverly termed it. Of course, if Marty had been around, Jessica knew that the stranger wouldn't have glanced twice in her direction.

"I'm not interested in your 'view'!" She tossed her head so that her cap of brown curls danced in the morning light. Her chin jutted forward naturally. "And I don't like people looking over my shoulder."

The man shook his head as he smiled down at her in a flash of white teeth and one unexpected dimple. "Fair's fair. You were watching the bug; I was watching you."

Not about to be lured into a ridiculous discussion, Jessica turned her attention back to the capsized insect, only to discover that it had somehow managed to right itself and go exploring. She hoped the stranger would take the hint and do the same.

But he didn't, and she hated the thought of turning around and facing him again. She was willing to admit that her greeting had not been particularly friendly, but she didn't care; she'd long ago given up any desire for coy flirtation—especially if the man was overbearing and conceited. And there was no doubt that the stranger was guilty on both counts. It was there in his manner and in his carriage, in the way he spoke and in his indolent stance as he stood patiently waiting for her to come to her senses and throw herself at his feet. It set her teeth on edge.

He was still standing behind her as she began to pack her equipment into her tattered camera bag. A quick glance over her shoulder revealed that he was still watching her—and that he still had that tantalizing gleam in his eye, the one that said no woman in her right mind would turn her back on him.

Jessica had to admit that he was good looking. Somewhere in his late thirties, he was tall with dark hair and blue eyes—bedroom eyes, Marty would call them—and he was wearing a jogging suit of deep blue that accentuated the effect of his outrageous black lashes. His good looks plus the effect he was having on her pulse rate only made her more wary. She'd learned the hard way that men were not to be trusted, especially men that handsome.

So, when all of her gear was carefully stowed, she got up, brushed the sand from her faded jeans and sweatshirt, and walked away as though he didn't exist. That would be the end of it, she told herself, but in only a few seconds she heard him call after her.

"Miss," he said with that perfect note of sincerity.

But she didn't turn around; she'd been burned by feigned sincerity before. That's when she found him blocking her path. For such a big man he moved with surprising speed.

He held out a pair of well-worn tennis shoes. "These are yours, I believe."

They would have been hard to deny since her bare toes were peeking out of the sand and there was no one else nearby. "Yes. Thank you."

She took the shoes from him and started forward, but he put out a hand as if to detain her. "It wasn't my intention to annoy you."

Her eyebrows rose under the brown curls that had fallen over her forehead. "You know what they say about good intentions."

Still she made no move to get away. She just stood there looking into his incredible blue eyes and wondered if abandoned resolutions paved the same roadway. Evidently he took her moment of hesitation for invitation; he was undoubtedly used to feminine entreaties.

"My name is Brandon. Brandon Roarke. My uncle and I own the Santa Lucia Inn," he said with a nod indicating the grand Spanish-style resort perched upon a nearby bluff. Its great white wings reminded Jessica of the birds that circled lazily on the misty air above them.

"It's beautiful," she said simply.

There was no need to say more, for everyone who drove up the California coast stopped there, at least to look around. And she knew at least half the people in the country would recognize the name. With an eighteen-hole golf course that was an annual stop on the pro circuit, a whole slew of tennis courts complete with viewing stands, a stable of Thoroughbred horses, and a chef imported from the Cordon Bleu, it was straight out of "Lifestyles of the Rich and Famous."

Jessica and her sister, Marty, had stopped for an exorbitantly priced cup of coffee and the breathtaking view only two days ago. She was impressed, but she wasn't about to show it.

"Are you by any chance staying there?" he asked.

Knowing that even the broom closets would be out of her price range, Jessica smiled and shook her head.

"But you are staying somewhere around here?"

"Yes. With friends."

"Perhaps you'd join me for lunch one day?"

"No, thank you. I'm not here strictly for vacation, so I find that my time isn't always my own." This was stretching the truth just a bit. Her sister was here on business; Jessica was tagging along.

"Dinner, then?"

She awarded him points for persistence but shook her head nonetheless. "No, really. I haven't the time." She started to walk around him.

"You're certain?"

"Look, Mr. Roarke," she said evenly, "I'm sure you aren't used to being turned down. But consider me a first, if you have to. I'm not interested."

She could tell by the way he cocked his head to one side

and looked her up and down that she'd made her point.

As she started to walk off, he said, "Won't you at least tell me your name? I make an effort to remember all my 'firsts.'"

Her immediate reaction was anger; she resented his belittling of her hard-won self-assurance. But she felt her chin go up, almost of its own accord, and she was grateful that words no longer had the power to paralyze her.

"Jessica. Jessica Martinson. But most people just call me Jess. It's been interesting, Mr. Roarke," she said in the most offhand way she could manage. "But I really must be going."

With that she turned and walked away, and this time he made no attempt to stop her.

It wasn't until she was well out of his sight that Jessica was able to analyze just how much Brandon Roarke had affected her. Oh, there had been anger, but there had been another emotion almost as strong. For beneath his good looks and the banter there was a quality she found both formidable and irresistible. Some people might call it arrogance, in fact, that was what she'd first thought. But to be honest, Jessica had to admit it was nothing more than confidence. The kind of inbred self-assurance so taken for granted that people like Brandon Roarke didn't realize others struggled a lifetime to achieve it. More than his easy manner or his obvious wealth, she envied him that self-confidence.

And she had to admit that she was attracted to it.

The Watcher sat upon the cliff, back where bushes and rocks screened the view. Sat and watched and wondered. Was this the one? The woman who would help punish Brandon Roarke?

The Watcher had never doubted that one day she would come into his life. Come bringing sunlight and laughter and hope. When a man was as handsome as Brandon, women just naturally flocked to him; sooner or later he was bound to find one who could heal his heart. And so the Watcher had waited. Waited for the woman who would make Brandon laugh and forget the darkness. For the woman who would make him care once again.

The woman would have to be sacrificed, of course. That was the only way to hurt Brandon.

Killing him would not suffice. If it would, the Watcher could have had revenge a hundred times over. What was sought was Brandon's suffering, not his release. And Brandon could be hurt only through the people he loved.

He thought himself immune to love, incapable of that emotion. The Watcher smiled, knowing that had been part of the plan as well. To let him think he'd escaped. To let him think himself too wise to trust. To watch as he learned to love again.

And then to kill.

So the Watcher sat. And waited. And planned.

Jessica didn't return to the Kendall house until early afternoon. By that time, the last wisps of fog had burned away and she was again entranced by the rugged beauty of the northern California coastline. She and Marty had been there only two days, but already the rough, rocky coast had a hold on her soul. The artist in her couldn't help admiring the modern home of glass and redwood that sat upon a promontory overlooking several miles of black, craggy coast and deep blue ocean.

There was no doubt that Jason Kendall had used all

his artistic talent in planning his house. She realized again how fortunate she was to have come with Marty to visit the Kendalls. Oh, not just because of the natural beauty or luxurious surroundings they were enjoying, but because Jason Kendall was *The California Photographer*. His work was internationally known; he was the idol of every photographer she knew—and *he* had taken an interest in her work.

She knocked on the door, but no one answered. That meant Marty and Jason were still in the small town of Luz, talking to whoever would listen to them. It was what Jess had expected since that was the reason Marty was here. Her sister was, strictly speaking, on vacation from the law firm of Dougall, Dougall, and Jones, but she was donating her time to a "good cause." Marty had always been the political activist of the family, and, as always, she'd been a pushover for a good cause. This time she was trying to block the construction of a campground on a particularly beautiful and as yet untouched section of coast just north of the Kendall home.

Jess was the first to admit that Marty was quite good at what she did. Marty and Jason Kendall had first met four years ago while waging a successful campaign against the construction of a nuclear power plant farther north. When Jason launched his campaign against a public campground that was to be built within twenty miles of his own secluded home, he had naturally called upon Marty for some legal advice. And Marty had responded with great enthusiasm. Naturally.

This time, however, Jessica had encouraged her sister to throw herself into the project and had wangled an invitation to come along. For Jess, that had been proof as nothing else had been that she was indeed turning over that new leaf.

She let herself in with the key that Jason had insisted she take. She went through the entryway, the living room, the dining room with its huge windows overlooking the rocky shore, and into the kitchen. There, on the antique French chop block, she found the note from Jason's wife, Florence. She'd taken little Megan for a hike along the coast and urged Jessica to make herself at home. There were sandwiches in the refrigerator, and, of course, Jason's darkroom was at her disposal. Jess skipped lunch and headed straight for the darkroom like a pilgrim making for Mecca. While it wasn't a huge laboratory, it was well planned. Everything was neatly labeled, and it was a simple matter for Jess to find all the materials and chemicals she needed. Instead of feeling inadequate, as she had expected to in Jason Kendall's darkroom, she was elated. After all, Jason had been suitably impressed with her work or he wouldn't have offered her the use of his facilities. She began to measure the chemicals and set out the trays.

Whenever anyone asked why she wanted to look at life through the lens of a camera, Jess was quick to point out that photography was an exciting and challenging art form. First, she would say, there is the search for the proper arrangement of line, form, and color in the viewing screen. Later there is the thrill of watching the image emerge from a blank piece of paper. For Jess the moment when the picture first materialized would always be magical. Each and every time it happened, she gave in to the illusion that Merlin was standing at her elbow, waving his wand. No matter how often she was reminded that it was a simple chemical reaction, the magic never faded.

But Jessica also acknowledged that in between the magic there remained the uninspired tasks. If pressed, she'd grudgingly admit that a great deal more time was spent on the mundane chores than on the magical ones. For her, this remained the worst part of photography, for it was the time when all those fears and hurts that she managed to ignore in her busier moments came unbidden to her mind. It was the time she was forced to face her past and all her inadequacies.

Jess had always felt photography was the perfect hobby for her. Perfect because she could remain on the side of the camera where the viewing was done. It had always been Marty who needed to be center stage and Jessica on the sidelines, capturing images of others. She didn't resent this, never had, in fact. Marty took after their mother . . . beauties, the both of them. Tall, willowy blondes with clear blue eyes.

Jessica hadn't understood when her father walked away from all of it twenty years earlier, for she'd been only eleven, still trapped in a stick-thin body but grappling with the mysterious feminine changes that were about to happen. She hadn't understood how he could leave any creature as delectable and exciting as her mother. But leave her he had.

She hadn't understood then, but she did now. He'd been unable to live with his wife's superficial beauty and unwilling to satisfy her need to be center stage. And he'd possessed too much pride to live in her shadow. It had taken Jess over two-thirds of her life to realize that she'd inherited her father's ordinary looks but none of his pride. Eric Lambert had been proof of that.

Had she possessed even a vestige of her father's confidence, she would never have been content with one of Marty's cast-offs. Jessica was always quick to say in Marty's defense that it wasn't her fault men lost their self-control where her sister was concerned. Marty couldn't help being born beautiful, witty, and brilliant any more than Quasimodo could help having that hump on his back.

Jess knew in her heart that if she'd had any sense at all, she would have sent Eric trotting home as she had all those others who'd been in search of a shoulder to cry on. But she hadn't. And, like a fool, she'd actually begun to think it was her he loved. Not Marty and certainly not "Marty's kid sister," but Jessica Elaine Martinson. At the time, she'd been convinced they had a chance. And they might have—if they'd gone forever from Marty's sphere of influence . . . say, to the North Pole or the Cape of Good Hope.

But they hadn't. Eric had been adamant about that. No heartless female was going to drive him away. No manipulative legal mind would make him turn tail and run. He'd been so clever that Jess hadn't even realized he'd taken control of her life. Then there had been the inevitable slip of the tongue. It was only the wrong name whispered in Jessica's ear at a time when Eric's mind should have been strictly on her. He hadn't even realized that he'd called her by her sister's name, and she could have let it go. But she hadn't. It was the one time she had mustered any of her father's pride. Thank God.

That had been Jessica's first and last grand passion. There'd been the requisite number of crushes and dates before that, all ending the moment the boy laid eyes on Marty. But Jess decided that Eric was the end of the line for her. She'd been hurt too deeply, and she wasn't willing to risk her heart again.

Perhaps, if the right man had come along, she would have changed her mind. But she'd yet to meet a man for whom she'd risk the rock-steady love that existed between her and her sister. So, for the last four years, she'd avoided emotional entanglements like the plague they obviously were. If anything, the hurt only cut deeper now, and where men were concerned she was wary.

It was odd under such circumstances that Brandon Roarke's image should keep popping in and out of her mind. But it did. Had she not been in the midst of turning over that new leaf, she would probably have persuaded herself that it was because he was so photogenic. That the artist in her was interested only in those dramatic eyes, those angular cheekbones, and that sensual mouth. But she was being honest these days, and she had to admit that she was attracted to him the way any living, breathing female would be. She wondered why it was her fate to be attracted to men who were completely unsuitable. What she needed was some colorless bookkeeper, not a man who hobnobbed with the rich and famous. A man who'd be content to watch TV in the evenings, not one who played host to presidents. What she needed was a man who would be content with the plain Martinson sister.

Nevertheless, Jess found herself wishing she'd accepted his luncheon invitation. It might have been fun to have lunch where the rich and famous played. Besides, there was no reason he had to meet Marty.

By the time everyone returned and they finally sat down to dinner, Jess was starving. And, since she shared none of Marty's political fervor, she was content to let the others carry the conversation.

She listened just enough to know that Marty and Jason were giving a play-by-play of their day's activities in Luz: whom they'd talked to, whether they'd signed the petition, and what effect that would have on the attempt to stop construction. Florence, as could be expected, hung on their every word. Jess and Megan were the quiet ones. But then Megan had an excuse, being only six years old.

Then, as the conversation cascaded around her, Jess found herself wondering why she always managed to seat herself among beautiful women. She was used to being overshadowed by Marty, but now she realized that Florence Kendall, in her own way, put even Marty to shame.

Florence had that fine fragility that made her look like a work of art. She was tall and thin, with rich brown hair that fell in small waves to her waist. Her brown eyes were oval in shape, almost exotic, and her rather fine patrician nose was perfectly formed. Florence looked as though she couldn't be more than twenty, though Jessica had gathered from the conversation the night before that she was closer to thirty.

That's why the smile was so arresting in her youthful face. It gave the impression that she knew more than the ordinary mortals around her, that she could see a world others only dreamed of. It was the smile of a martyred saint ascending to heaven or of Aphrodite stepping out of the ocean's foam. Jess was wondering how she could capture that on film when she realized that the topic had shifted.

It was Megan who held center stage now as she related her adventures at the tide pools. She was almost a pint-size copy of Florence except for those startling blue eyes that set her apart from either parent. She was a fortunate child, Jess thought, for having inherited her father's intensity and her mother's intriguing beauty.

After dinner Megan begged Jess to play a game—some silly thing where you toss a die and move the number of spaces indicated. Jessica found it impossible to turn down the childish pleas, then could only watch in amazement as the kid beat her three times straight. Megan was well on her way to trouncing Jess a fourth time when Jason came to the rescue.

"Bedtime, princess," he announced. "Put the game away and tell Jess good night."

Jason Kendall was a great bear of a man with a thick, full beard and rather shaggy hair. He was of an intimidating size, but any fear one might have was quickly put to rest after one look into his eyes. They were brown, and the corners seemed creased in a perpetual smile. He was grinning now as he bent to pick up his daughter and set her on his shoulders.

"Oh, Jess," he said casually as he headed for the stairs, "why don't you get out those pictures you took today? I'd like to see what you've done."

Jessica's heart stopped. Even after she had rushed upstairs to the room she was sharing with Marty and was back down in the living room, she wasn't sure it had returned to a normal rhythm. Sitting on the sofa that separated the living room from the dining area, she heard little of the conversation that Marty and Florence conducted in hushed tones at the dining table behind her. She concentrated instead on the sun as it set just outside the sweep of window.

Jessica shuffled and reshuffled her photographs, all the while worrying about how simple and childish her work would appear to Jason Kendall. It sounded melodramatic to say that her whole life might change if Jason was impressed, yet that was the truth. If he was just interested enough to write a letter of recommendation or even let her use his name as a reference, it could make the difference between photography as a hobby and as a way to earn a living. And Jess desperately wanted to turn her art into her livelihood.

She wasn't sure just what she'd expected. She'd told herself that Jason would be honest; he was too good an artist to hand out unmerited approval. But in no way was she prepared for the praise he lavished on her work. Oh, there were ways to improve the photos, but they were minor. On the whole, he commended her for her choice of subject and composition.

"It's easy to see how you've won all those contests your sister's been bragging about. These are good . . . very good. This one's my favorite," he said, passing a photo of the little yellow-and-black bug to Marty and Florence, who had moved down to join them in the living room. "This should definitely go in your portfolio."

For the moment, Jess ignored the reference to a portfolio. Only professionals needed that.

"I was lucky to get that one! While I was taking it, one of your locals sneaked up on me and scared me half to death."

She gave a shortened version of her little adventure. It wasn't terribly exciting, but they listened anyway.

Jason chuckled. "That's one professional problem I've never had. But I have to admit that the local men have good taste. Any fresh face as pretty as yours is bound to attract attention."

Jess laughed with him and thought how kind he was to say that—and she didn't even mention that it wasn't her face that had been the attraction.

"Did you get his name?" Florence asked as she gave her husband a conspiratorial glance. "If it's someone we know, we might have him over for dinner."

"No, please don't bother. But, yes, I got his name. Roarke. Brandon Roarke."

The effect couldn't have been worse had she said Jack the Ripper. Jason and Florence just sat there with their grins frozen sickeningly on their faces. Marty looked the way she had the day Jessica had informed Mrs. Wooley, their third-grade Sunday school teacher, that she wanted to have a dozen children but wasn't ever going to get married. Jessica had obviously made another social blunder.

"Not him," Florence whispered.

There was such emotion in her voice that the vision of Mrs. Wooley's reddened face disappeared from Jessica's mind.

Florence's eyes had never wavered from Jessica's. "Stay away from him. He's—"

But before she could finish her sentence, Jason leaned across and grasped his wife's wrist. Florence stopped and stared down at her husband's hand, then looked into his eyes. She was struggling for control, but it wasn't a fight that was easily won.

"What Florence means," Jason cut in smoothly—too smoothly? Jessica wondered— "is that Brandon isn't welcome in our home."

There was such intensity in his dark eyes, such pain, it seemed, that Jessica could think of no answer.

"Jess, dear," Marty said, coming to her rescue as she had all those Sundays ago. "Weren't you listening at all during dinner?"

"Yes . . . well, no. Not really."

"Your Mr. Roarke is our worthy opponent." When Jess still looked bewildered, Marty added, "The man behind Seaview Enterprises. He's the one who's trying to build that ridiculous campground."

"Oh, my God." Jess looked from one stricken face to the other. No wonder he wasn't welcome in this house.

"It's a good thing I turned down his dinner invitation. What would the punishment have been for consorting with the enemy?"

"It's not a hanging offense," Jason assured her with a smile. He let go of Florence's wrist and leaned back on the sofa. "Besides, it might have helped if you'd done a little spying for our side. He's been one step ahead of us all the way."

With that statement, Jason steered the conversation away from Brandon Roarke and his campground. After a few moments, Jessica gathered her pictures and headed for the stairs. There was a tension that lingered in the room, and she hoped it would vanish if she left. She had her foot on the first step when Florence intercepted her.

"I hope you won't mind a little friendly advice." She spoke in a low voice, almost a whisper. And it was obvious from the way she glanced over her shoulder that she didn't want anyone to overhear her. "Brandon Roarke is . . . well, he's not a very nice man. I'd stay away from him if I were you."

"Don't worry," Jess assured her, touched more than she liked to admit by Florence's almost maternal concern. It seemed to Jess she'd had little enough of that in her life. "I'd already decided that."

All Florence said was, "Good," and then, "Good night," but there seemed a bit more to it than that. It was obvious that she was relieved, but there was something more in her eyes. However, Jessica was too excited by Jason's praise of her work to dwell on a situation that didn't involve her.

Jessica was still awake when Marty slipped quietly into the room they were sharing.

"It's okay," Jess said. "You can turn on the light." Marty

did, and Jess blinked several times before focusing on the little travel clock on the chest of drawers. "Two-thirty! My God, don't you think you're carrying your war councils a little to the extreme?"

"Maybe," was all Marty said, but she sounded rather vague, so Jess snuggled into the bed and kept her mouth shut as Marty slipped into the bathroom. When she emerged, she was squeaky clean and much prettier than anyone had the right to be without makeup. When she sat down and began brushing her pale hair, Jessica could see both their reflections in the mirror. Marty's profile revealed a flawless beauty.

Jess, on the other hand, couldn't avoid her own rather unremarkable image. The mirror reflected a face that looked at least five years younger than its thirty-one years, a fact everyone assured her she'd be grateful for in her old age. It also showed a cap of loose, naturally curly brown hair that had remained the same for the last two . . . no, three years. Wash and wear, Marty called it, because Jess never curled it or tried to force it into a style. The eyes were brown: not dark enough to be called black and not light enough to remind anyone of fine sherry. Just brown and very round so that they always managed to look just a little startled. Her nose was slightly uptilted, and her mouth was full. For the millionth time she realized that there was nothing arresting about her face and that, compared with Marty, she was definitely the ugly duckling. But life was no fairy tale, and she knew she was never going to turn into a beautiful swan.

"We discussed more than our battle plans, you know."

"What?" With a jerk Jess forced herself to focus on what Marty was saying. "Really? What else?"

"You. Jason is quite impressed with your work. He

wants to know if you've ever considered working as a professional photographer. Have you?"

"Yes, of course. But it's . . . well, it's very difficult to break into and rather dangerous financially."

"But if you had the chance, you'd take it. Right?"

"Yes, I guess so, but—"

"Good! I told him you'd be interested, and he said he'd make some contacts for you."

"But Marty," Jess wailed, forgetting in her panic that this was her dream, "I'm not sure I'm ready."

"Then you'd better get sure." Marty slapped the brush on the dresser and turned to face her younger sister. "I didn't come up here for my health. This is your big chance, and I'm going to see that you take it. Do you hear?"

Jessica nodded mutely. Being the little sister to someone as determined as Marty was a hard habit to break.

"I've had enough of your working at that stupid accounting firm that you absolutely hate. You have such talent; it's time you used it."

Her sister was really whipping herself into a tirade. Jessica was suddenly grateful that she'd never have to sit across a courtroom from her.

"If you don't take this opportunity, you're going to end up buried beneath the floorboards with the computer wires. So you're going to jump at this. Do you hear?"

"Yes, Marty."

"Good." She stood and snapped out the lights . "Now go to sleep."

Jess lay there for several minutes before she had the nerve to speak. For thirty-one years she'd been the follower to Marty's leader. The only time she'd blazed her own trail had been a disaster.

"Marty?"

"Uh-huh?"

"What did you mean about not doing this for your health? I thought you came up here to give Jason some legal advice."

"Oh, that." She gave a delicate yawn. "I don't think there's much anyone can do about that. Brandon Roarke seems to have things pretty well sewn up. He has the land, and it looks like he has the necessary financial backing. And the Environmental Impact Report doesn't help us at all. We only have two long shots left. First we pray that he turns up the remains of an Indian village or dinosaur bones. That would stop him dead in his tracks."

"Or?"

"Or we make one last-ditch effort to contact the people who own land around the proposed site. The people in Luz and the surrounding area are pretty evenly divided. They're either artists—writers, actors, painters, that sort of thing—or they're employed by the Santa Lucia. The artists, of course, are behind us; they value their privacy. Those employed by the inn are another story; they know who butters their bread. So we need to contact the absentee owners. If we can get enough signatures on our petition, we might convince the state agencies to take another look at our concerns. But if the absentee owners bought the land as an investment—which I have every reason to suspect they did—then they'll welcome your Mr. Roarke's project with open arms. In that case, this all becomes an exercise in futility."

"So you did this mainly for me?"

"It seems so." She sounded sleepy now.

"Thanks."

"You'd better appreciate it," she said with a soft laugh.

"It wasn't easy cashing in my round-trip ticket to the Bahamas."

Jess snuggled under the covers and smiled. It made her feel good to know that her sister still worried about her. And it proved she'd been right; she had never met the man for whom she'd risk that rock-solid love.

"Marty?"

"Uhm."

"He's not *my* Mr. Roarke, you know."

2

There was a knock on the door as Brandon Roarke hung up the office phone. Smiling at his uncle, he settled back onto his leather chair. Judging by the casual clothes and the cap embroidered in the green-and-silver logo of the Santa Lucia Inn, Brandon decided the older man had already squeezed in a round of golf this morning.

"Any luck?" Stewart asked.

Brandon heaved a sigh and ran his fingers through his hair. "Not yet."

The older man closed the door and settled onto the chair across from his nephew. "Bran, you asked for forty-eight hours. They're up."

Brandon picked up the Mont Blanc pen and turned it in his fingers. The worst part of this was that he'd thought it was going to be a terrific week. Monday morning had started off great. He'd gone for his usual morning jog along the beach and stumbled across the cutest little feminine backside he'd seen in a lot of years. He'd waited patiently and been rewarded by the kind of natural beauty he rarely saw at the inn—brown curly hair streaked through with blond highlights; big, brown eyes; freckles across an impertinent nose; and the kind of smile that could chase away shadows. But it had been the eyes that had captivated him, the eyes that haunted and tantalized him.

Then it had all fallen apart. His usual charm hadn't worked on the very intriguing Jessica Martinson, and he'd returned to his office to discover that the photographer he'd hired six months before had been injured in a car accident leaving Los Angeles. Brandon should have remembered that he no longer lived a charmed life. That he no longer deserved to.

Stewart dealt with the silence as long as he could. "Do you want me to phone Jason?"

"No, I'll call him."

"Hell, you make it sound like I'm asking you to walk the plank." Stewart rose to pace the office. "You two grew up together. You were like brothers. I don't get it, Bran. I haven't understood it for the last several years. I don't believe there's any problem too big for the two of you to sit down and work out."

"Who said there was a problem?"

Stewart only grunted in reaction to the cold, glittering stare he felt leveled in his direction.

"The two of us just don't have much in common these days. And with the campground—"

"To hell with the campground!" The glass in the office door rattled, and Stewart fought for his usual calm. "This has been going on a lot longer than your damn campground. If you can't talk to Jason, can't you at least talk to me?"

"We can talk any time you want. I just don't have anything to say about Jason." Brandon tossed the pen on

the last two days combing through the county records. It reminded her too much of the job she hated for it to be the least bit enjoyable.

Just exactly how or when she'd been drawn into Marty and Jason's "campground war" she wasn't sure, but since being ordered to the trenches, she'd allowed herself to slide into such an emotional abyss that all the excitement and pleasure of her vacation had slipped to the back of her mind. She set her pen on the desk, rose, and stretched before stepping out into the sterile hallway. A few steps down the hall and around the corner was a water fountain.

As she rounded the corner she heard the heavy door at the other end of the courthouse open and slam, then she listened to the steady tap of someone marching down the hall. Her sneakers were silent as she made her way to the drinking fountain and back. The footsteps ceased just as she rounded the corner, where she suddenly stopped and stood rooted to the floor. As she watched, Brandon Roarke put his hand on the door knob of the assessor's office.

Her first cowardly impulse was to stay hidden until he left, but then she remembered all of the information she'd so patiently copied into her notebook. Gathering her meager courage, Jessica started forward.

"Why, Mr. Roarke!" she called out as she sauntered in his direction. "What a surprise to run into you!"

But Brandon Roarke didn't look the least surprised. "Not really," he said. "I was just going in to look for you."

Her body jerked involuntarily to a stop, and she stood looking at him. He didn't look like the same man she'd met on the beach. Maybe it was the business suit, but he seemed colder and just a little threatening. Or maybe

Florence's opinion was coloring her reaction this time, for she suddenly had visions of him commanding her to get out of town—and to take her nosy sister with her. "There's no room for outsiders in this war," he'd say in a John Wayne sort of drawl. But of course, that only happened in the movies, so she stood mutely and waited.

"Jason told me where to find you."

"Jason?"

"Jason Kendall."

Jessica realized he was speaking to her the way people did with children and the mentally deficient. She stuck her hands in the pockets of her jeans and rocked back on the heels of her sneakers. "I'll just bet. And you came tearing down here to help out, did you?"

"Look, I called Jason this morning about a photography job at the Santa Lucia. He said he couldn't squeeze it in, but that I should talk to you."

"To me?"

Brandon crossed his arms. "You," he said with a nod.

"Why?"

"To see if you'd like the job. You do take on freelance assignments, don't you?"

Jessica fought the urge to swallow hard. "Time permitting," she said with what she hoped was just the right note of nonchalance.

Oh, my God, she thought. Jason had really meant it when he said he'd try to throw a job her way! She discovered that her heart was pounding at the mere *thought* of working as a photographer.

"Well, as it happens, we're in a hurry about this, so Jason told me where I could find you. He even insisted that I come rushing down here to see you before your calendar was too full to bother with our insignificant little job. Now," he said, his smile indicating that he could see the truth as plainly as if it were a flashing neon sign, "will that do or must I come up with a written letter of introduction?"

"No. That's fine. After all, how else would you have known where to find me?"

"Bright girl! And very trusting, too."

He was mocking her, and her first instinct was to tell him she wasn't interested in anything he had to say. Then she admitted to herself that she was interested—very interested—and decided it wouldn't do to antagonize him any further if there was even a possibility that she might be working for him. And she realized that she wanted the job, desperately.

"Why don't we go somewhere for a drink," Brandon suggested. "And I'll explain the whole thing to you."

She eyed the door that he was blocking. All her notes were in that room, and she didn't dare go off and leave them.

"I see," he said. "You no doubt have all sorts of secret documents in there. Tell you what, I'll wait here while you go in and tidy up. Then we can go for that drink. Okay?"

She simply nodded and went in to put the microfilm back in its proper place; she wasn't going to leave any clues lying around in case he should check in here later. Then she folded her notes and stuck them in her oversize purse. Now she was ready to listen to whatever business proposition Brandon Roarke had to offer.

In less than twenty minutes Jessica found herself settled in a plush red booth in a dimly lit, tartan-plaid bar. She thought the place rather crowded for early afternoon, but then she wasn't a serious drinker and so rarely found herself in bars at all—let alone in broad daylight.

Most of the occupants were men dressed in business suits. The few women were attired in neat outfits and had packages scattered on the seats around them; for them it was the end of a shopping trip, a break before going home to fix dinner or joining their husbands for dinner out. Jessica felt incredibly conspicuous in her jeans and sweater. She even thought the barmaid eyed her strangely. But she decided to take no notice of that and tried to act as if these business conferences were part of her normal routine.

"The proposition is a fairly simple one," Brandon said after their drinks arrived. "We're coming up on the Santa Lucia's fiftieth anniversary. It's an important milestone, and we want to capitalize on it in a new travel brochure to send out to travel agents from here to Madagascar. In order to get them printed up and delivered in time for Christmas—which is a very brisk business—and for the anniversary, we must have the pictures ready in two weeks."

"It seems to me," Jessica interjected, "that you would have done better to arrange for a photographer some time ago instead of waiting until the last minute."

"Of course." He was using that patronizing tone again. "And that is just what we did. Only he got into a car accident on his way here and won't be of any use to us."

"I'm sorry."

"It wasn't a very serious accident. Just enough to keep him from working for a few weeks. That's why I phoned Jason. I'd hoped to presume on our friendship . . . or at least what was once . . ."

Brandon's voice drifted off, and it struck Jessica as something completely out of character. Those piercing blue eyes lost their sharpness, and that self-confident smile just seemed to fade. It made Jessica wonder what emotions swirled beneath that handsome facade.

"Jason was unavailable," Brandon said at last.

As Jessica sat silently, he made an obvious effort to cast off whatever mood had settled upon him. "So I'm afraid I'm reduced to making a personal plea for your help. What do you say?"

"But you haven't seen any of my work."

He gave a dismissive wave of his hand. "If Jason says you're good, that's all I need. His professional judgment is unimpeachable."

Jessica knew she would be a fool to turn down such an opportunity. Still, she had enough sense to know they needed to come to an understanding on several items: fee, deadlines, artistic freedom, the usual mishmash of things that went into a "gentleman's agreement" in the absence of a written one. Luckily enough, she had another fifteen days of vacation coming, and after Marty's lecture of a few nights ago, she wasn't about to pass up this opportunity. So, of course, she accepted his offer.

"So," Brandon concluded sometime later as they stood in front of the courthouse where Jessica was to meet Marty, "I'll see you at the Santa Lucia tonight after dinner. Say, eight-thirty or nine."

"Tonight?"

"Oh, didn't I tell you?" His look of innocence was obviously feigned. "The one thing we insist upon is that our photographer stay with us. Otherwise, it's hard for him—or I should say her—to develop a 'feel' for the place."

"But I'm already staying in the area," Jessica protested after making a few quick mental calculations and coming to the conclusion that after paying for room and board at the Santa Lucia, her fee—which had seemed like a gold mine—would be barely enough to buy her a bus ticket home.

"It's all part of the deal," Brandon explained as though reading her mind. "Completely gratis. So indulge in all the steak and lobster you want."

With a quick handshake, he was off. A few yards down he passed Marty, who had just come out of the post office next door. Jessica kept watching, expecting him to look over his shoulder at the gorgeous blonde; but he didn't. For some ridiculous reason, she was quite pleased by that.

When Jess and Marty arrived back at the Kendalls', it was evident that not everyone was pleased with Jessica's job. The atmosphere was charged with anger and some other emotions that seemed to lie just below the surface.

Jessica found Jason in the kitchen. He and Florence were carrying on a quiet but strained conversation that ceased the moment the sisters entered the room.

"Oh, Jason," Jess cried as she threw her arms around his neck and gave him a hug. "I don't know how to thank you for getting me the job at the Santa Lucia."

"Don't thank me." He held her at arm's length. "It fell right into my lap, as though it were meant to be."

"I appreciate it anyway. I never would have gotten a job like this without your help."

"Just do your best work. I know you'll make me proud of you," he said over Florence's rattling of pots and pans. The look she shot her husband was both angry and hurt. "Now, what did you find out about the property owners?" he asked Marty, effectively changing the subject. "Think we can sway them to our side?"

When Marty and Jason wandered off to refine their

battle strategy, Jessica volunteered to help Florence with dinner. She was given the job of chopping vegetables for the salad while Florence fussed over the spaghetti sauce simmering on the stove.

"You shouldn't take this job," Florence said after a few moments of distracted silence. Still holding the lid in her left hand, she stirred the sauce. "Brandon Roarke is a dangerous man."

"You mean that fatal attraction of his, do you?" Jess asked with a laugh. Though she didn't want to hurt Florence's feelings, she wanted to keep the moment light.

But before Florence could answer, the lid slipped from her hands and landed with a clang, sending a wave of blood-red sauce onto the stove top. She spent several silent moments cleaning it up, but when she finally looked over at Jessica, her brows were drawn together in an uncharacteristic frown.

"This isn't a joking matter. You don't have any idea what you're getting into."

"I'm only going to take pictures," Jessica promised. "Nothing more than that."

"You don't know *him*."

Jessica didn't even pretend not to know Florence was talking about Brandon. "He's not my type. I like a man who's open and honest. He isn't either of those."

"He has a way with women. Young . . . old . . . middle-aged . . . it doesn't matter. He has looks, charm, and money. It's a combination most women find irresistible."

"Not me! I fell for someone like that before. I've learned my lesson."

"Remember I warned you," Florence whispered as Megan skipped into the kitchen.

"Hi, Jessica," the child said, hopping on one foot and then the other. "Want to play a game after dinner?"

"Sorry. I can't tonight."

"I'll let you pick the game."

Amused that a six-year-old was so adept at negotiation, Jessica reached over to give the child's pigtail a gentle tug. "I won't be here tonight."

"Are you going home?"

"Not yet. But I'm going to stay at a hotel for a while."

A frown puckered the child's forehead. "Don't you like it here?"

"I like it just fine," she assured the child, "but this is work."

Jess watched as the little girl thought about that. Evidently going to work was something she understood.

"Did you go to work today?" Jessica asked.

Megan giggled. "I don't work."

"Did you go to school?"

An emphatic nod of her head sent Megan's pigtails flying.

"Well, that's *your* work. Now I've got to go do mine."

The child sighed and looked up at Jessica with those big blue eyes. "Will you come visit me?"

"Of course."

"Promise?"

"Cross my heart."

Megan nodded. "I drew a picture in school today," she said, looking up at her mother, who still hadn't spoken. "Do you want to see my picture, Mommy?" the child asked with a tug on her mother's pant leg.

But Florence's eyes didn't waver from Jessica's, and suddenly Megan threw her arms around her mother's legs and cried, "Why aren't you answering me, Mommy? Don't you want to see my picture?"

"Of course I do," Florence murmured, dragging her eyes down to her daughter's upturned face. Smiling at the child, she said, "Let's go see it now," and followed Megan out of the kitchen.

After their exit, Jessica stood staring out the window for several minutes, wondering why Florence made Brandon Roarke sound like an ax murderer instead of a man who'd been born devastatingly handsome and was undoubtedly used to having his way with women.

It was almost nine o'clock by the time Marty dropped Jess at the Santa Lucia Inn. With her cardboard suitcase and battered camera bag, Jessica made a startling contrast to the couple who pulled up in their red Lamborghini with coordinating Gucci luggage strapped to the top. She'd resisted Marty's suggestion to buy new luggage, maintaining it was a waste of money since she rarely traveled. Because she still thought it was the logical decision, she held her head high while dragging her bags up the tiled steps and into the foyer. Still, she had to give grudging admiration to the doorman; he was obviously a professional who knew where he would earn the bigger tip.

The effect of the interior of the hotel was not what a visitor would expect. Instead of heavy Mediterranean furniture, the room was dotted with groupings of wicker chairs, lots of potted greenery, and lazy ceiling fans. Several guests sat there enjoying an evening drink and the muted music coming from the crowded bar down one of the corridors.

"Oh, dear," the woman at the desk said when Jessica gave her name. "I think we just rented your room." She punched several keys on her computer and stared into the screen. "We did. Just a few minutes ago. I'm ever so sorry," she said earnestly. "But when you called in about your reservation, we just naturally released the hold on the room."

"I don't think you understand. I didn't make the reservation. Mr. Roarke made it for me. I'm the photographer he hired this afternoon."

"Yes, Ms. Martinson. I know. He told me all about it. But when you phoned in your cancellation earlier this evening, he authorized me to release your room." Then, drawing herself to her full height, she informed Jessica with all the withering disdain she could command, "Mr. Roarke wasn't at all pleased with your abrupt change of heart."

"I could understand that," Jessica agreed in a tone of voice that put her in mind of her own mother. "Except that I did not call to cancel my reservation."

"I took the call myself."

"That may be, but *I* didn't make it. So why don't you try to find me another room somewhere in this big hotel."

The desk clerk did just that, pressing buttons and staring into her computer screen before she announced, "We don't seem to have any vacancies, Ms. Martinson. May I suggest a small hotel farther up the coast until we have a room available?"

"That won't do. I had a friend drop me here, I haven't any transportation, and Mr. Roarke is expecting me to stay at the Santa Lucia while I'm working for him. Why don't we let him straighten this out," Jessica said with sudden inspiration. She didn't feel the slightest twinge of remorse when the woman went a little pale before picking up the telephone.

"I'm sorry," she told Jess after trying several numbers. "He isn't in his apartment or his office. If you'll have a seat, I'll send someone to find him."

She paused and waited for Jessica to answer, as though expecting her to back down. Jess didn't.

"That's fine." Jess nodded toward a nearby chair. "I'll wait over there."

Once more she dragged her baggage across the cool tiled floor. Things certainly weren't going as she'd expected, and Florence's final warning was suddenly ringing in her ears.

"Be careful," Florence had whispered as she'd enfolded Jessica in a farewell hug. "Watch out for yourself. Don't take anything for granted. And remember you can't believe anything *he* says."

Could Florence be right? she wondered. *Could Brandon have suffered second thoughts about hiring her?*

As she sat there considering the possibility, the desk clerk summoned one of the bellmen. Jessica watched as he headed down the hall and disappeared into the bar.

But despite all Florence's warnings, Jess didn't believe Brandon would play these kinds of games. After all, she had no written contract. If he wanted out, all he had to do was say so—or deny the deal altogether.

But when Brandon emerged from the bar, the determined set of his jaw and the grim look in his eyes had her wondering if there might not be a little of the ax murderer in him after all. And she had the horrible feeling that the ax was going to fall on her neck.

"I see you've changed your mind," Brandon commented as his gaze took in the suitcase and camera bag at Jessica's feet. "Again. Do you always have such a hard time living up to your deals?"

"I think there's been some sort of a mix-up."

If he hadn't been so angry, he was certain the wide, innocent look in her eyes and the catch in her voice would have gained his sympathy. But he was angry—

surprisingly so, when he considered that he rarely lost his temper.

"So you're saying that my people at reception lied about your call."

"No! I'm not saying that. I'm sure they received a cancellation from someone. Maybe there's another Martinson with reservations for tonight; it's not all that unusual a name. Maybe someone called the wrong hotel. I can't even begin to figure out what happened. All I know is that I didn't call. And now I'm told there isn't a room left in the place."

It was a very believable performance, Brandon decided. The wide eyes, the rising voice, the way she made herself out to be the victim. So good, in fact, that he was afraid he was about to be taken in again. He'd certainly believed her this afternoon, but he considered himself a lot smarter now. He should have remembered that most women had hidden agendas. The bottom line was that he needed a photographer, so he'd play along, because women liked you to believe. But he would keep his eyes open.

"I'm glad it wasn't you who called," he murmured. "You wait right here, and I'll take care of everything."

He noticed a puckering of her forehead, but she sat and waited for him to handle the details. He spoke to Roberta at registration and arranged for a suite.

Maybe that was Jessica's game, he thought. Guests were always trying to get some sort of free upgrade, maybe she was just playing the same game. If so, she'd probably get some satisfaction out of knowing that she was the first photographer to stay in a suite while working at the Santa Lucia. Just so he could keep an eye on her, he arranged for a suite close to his private apartment.

After taking a key from one of the mailboxes, Brandon

had a word with the doorman. He couldn't help smiling at his employee's obvious distaste for the cardboard suitcase. Then, dangling the room key between thumb and forefinger, he gave Jessica his most charming, anything-to-keep-the-customer-happy smile. "Everything is taken care of."

She took the key but seemed careful to avoid touching him. "They did find a room, then?"

"Unfortunately they'd given yours away, so you'll have to make do with a suite. You don't mind, do you?"

Her eyes became huge as she looked up at him. "A suite?"

He nodded. "Two bedrooms, a sitting room, a small balcony, and an ocean view."

She smiled. "I think I can force myself."

"Good. Now that we've got that settled, suppose I take you to meet my uncle. He owns half of this place, and he's anxious to meet you."

Not waiting for Jessica's acquiescence, he took her arm and ushered her through a small door and down a hallway lined with private, glassed-in offices. They passed his door and stopped before one that read "Stewart Roarke, President." Brandon knocked and then opened the door without waiting for an invitation.

"Stewart, I've brought our photographer for you to meet."

Brandon noticed that his uncle was bent over the computer printouts, something he usually avoided. The older man smiled as soon as he saw Jessica. Rising, he brushed the white hair back from his forehead as he came around the desk to take her hand.

"Jessica Martinson?" he questioned as he drew her fingers to his lips for a kiss. It was an affectation his uncle had picked up from their European guests. "I'm glad you managed to find her," he said to Brandon. "But how did you know she'd be so pretty?"

Brandon was surprised to see Jessica blush in response to the compliment.

"We actually met a few days ago," Jessica explained before Brandon could decide how to answer. "On the beach. I can't tell you how surprised I was when he offered me a job this afternoon."

Stewart gave Brandon a questioning look. "I don't think you mentioned that, Bran."

Brandon leaned one shoulder against the doorjamb and smiled. "I don't tell you about all the beautiful women I meet." To Jessica he said, "Every woman who stays here falls head over heels for Stewart. Don't be taken in by that innocent look in his eyes."

Stewart put a hand over his heart. "I'm wounded. Don't believe the boy. If he's half as smart as I think he is, he's the one you need to keep an eye on."

"That's exactly what I was told," Jess said with a laugh.

Brandon raised an eyebrow at the comment, but Stewart rushed on before he could question it. "I trust you're settled in," the older man said.

"I am now."

Stewart looked at his nephew. "Now?"

"There was a small glitch with the reservations, but that's all been handled."

"I look forward to becoming better acquainted over the next few days," Stewart said to Jessica. "But if you two will excuse me, I'm trying to make sense of all this computer information." He waved toward his desk. "My nephew insists that I be able to read the computer printouts. He says it will make life so much easier. It seems to me that the easiest thing to do is ask one of the employees to make sense of it for me."

"Oh, no," Jessica assured him. "Once you get used to it, you'll wonder how you ever got along without one."

"You sound very sure."

"I work with computers. They're wonderful once you get used to them."

"You mean when you're not taking pictures?" Stewart questioned smoothly.

Jessica looked slightly flustered, Brandon noticed.

"Well, yes," she murmured. "I'm afraid I can't make a living with my photography yet. But I'm quite good."

Stewart only smiled. "I'm certain you are, or Jason would never have recommended you. And it's easy to see how computers would fail to nourish the artist in you." He glanced at his desk again. "It certainly takes the romance out of being an innkeeper. You two run on while I get back to work."

Stewart watched as his nephew escorted Jessica out of the office. He could barely restrain the urge to rub his hands together. He understood now why Brandon had rushed out the door to contact their photographer. Yes indeed.

He smiled as he settled back at his desk. Something interesting was going on there. She was just the sort of woman he would have conjured up for his nephew if he'd been able to—sweet, honest, maybe even a little shy. And maybe, if she was a friend of Jason's, she might even be able to heal the rift between those two hardheaded boys.

He only hoped that Brandon's cynical streak didn't mess things up. Perhaps he'd have a word with the boy tomorrow.

Jessica followed Brandon back to the lobby. She wondered if it was too early to plead fatigue and go to her room. This charade of being artistic and sophisticated was wearing on her nerves. And the attention of two handsome men was just plain unnerving. Unfortunately, Brandon chose that moment to suggest a nightcap.

"Thank you, Mr. Roarke," she said in her most businesslike voice. "But it's getting late."

"It's still early. And if you persist in calling me Mr. Roarke, no one will know who you're talking to." He gave her a grin that didn't quite reach his eyes. "Are you really tired or are you simply being on your guard, as you were evidently warned to be?"

"I don't have any idea what you're talking about, Mr. Roarke."

"Brandon," he corrected. "And you admitted to my uncle that you'd been warned about me."

"The warning was quite unnecessary. You tried to pick me up on the beach, if you'll recall."

"I also recall that you managed to brush me off."

She smiled at the compliment. "I'm not in the habit of making dates with perfect strangers."

He was obviously amused by that. "The nice thing is that we're no longer 'strangers.' We have at least one acquaintance in common, and you've met my closest relative. Besides, you're out from under everyone's thumb, and you can afford to be just a little bit reckless tonight."

That got to her as nothing else had. He made her sound cautious and dull. She resented the implication no matter how close to the truth he was. "How do you know I'm not usually reckless?"

He just laughed and reached for her hand. "One little nightcap can't possibly hurt," he said as he tugged her toward a staircase marked PRIVATE.

She offered no resistance but followed behind him, wondering where he was leading her. By the time she realized it was his private apartment, it was too late to protest. She certainly wasn't going to admit that the idea of spending time alone with Brandon Roarke made her want to turn and run, so she reminded herself that this was the new, improved Jessica Martinson, who was grabbing life with both hands. She stepped into his lair, trying to appear nonchalant about the whole thing.

"What will you have?" he asked as he crossed to a well-stocked bar. "Brandy? Drambuie? B and B? If I don't have it, the bar downstairs will."

"Nothing that strong. A little white wine if you have it."

Jessica crossed to the sofa and sat, silently assessing the room. It certainly wasn't what she'd expected. Nothing flashy or dramatic. No leopardskin pillows or black leather chairs. Instead the room was done in rather subdued blues and grays, very modern and peaceful.

He turned on the sound system that dominated one wall, and jazz floated from hidden speakers. It was cool and relaxing and filled the silence. By the time Brandon handed her the wine, she'd sunk back into the sofa and felt more at ease than she'd expected to. She closed her eyes as a mellow saxophone had her mentally floating.

"You know," he said as the last notes hung in the air, "I was angry when I thought you'd backed out of this job."

Jessica opened her eyes. "I'd never do that." His eyes, as he gazed at her, were a richer blue than she'd remembered. She pulled her gaze from his and stared into the depths of her wine. "It's my first professional job," she admitted. While he sat there studying her silently, she acknowledged to herself that she had a problem with truth; it just seemed to pop out of her mouth even when she'd be smarter to keep quiet. "I think it's only fair that you know."

"I'd guessed as much."

"But, as I told your uncle, I'm very good," she put in

quickly. "Jason even said . . . You knew?" she asked as soon as his statement sank in.

Brandon only nodded.

"Then you should have known I wouldn't pass up this opportunity. Any professional photographer would kill to get it, especially a novice."

"I was afraid our first meeting might have alienated you. I was pushy." He set his glass on the cocktail table. "I assure you it's not my usual style. Have I been forgiven?"

She nodded and smiled, relieved to have gotten through a sticky situation so easily.

"Good," he said simply as he took her empty glass and set it beside his. "I want us to be friends. You intrigued me the first moment I saw you with your nose stuck in the sand, and I'd hate for you to slip away before I've satisfied my curiosity."

It was then that she realized she'd gotten out of one sticky situation and into another. She got to her feet, knowing this was no time to worry about looking foolish. It was time to escape. But he rose and blocked her path.

The music had become softer, hinting at emotions both dark and sensual. She took a step closer as something turbulent and mysterious in her responded to the music— and to the man. He took her hand in his and grazed his thumb across her knuckle. She shivered.

"You're a mysterious woman, Jessica."

She laughed at that; it was so preposterous. But she knew it wasn't one of those sophisticated, throaty laughs. She hoped it wasn't a nervous giggle. "I've never been called that before. My sister tells me that my expression gives away exactly what I'm thinking."

He gazed into her eyes. "Not possible," he said at last.

"What does that mean?"

"No woman is that open and honest."

"That sounds rather cynical."

He brought her hand to his lips. "It was meant as a compliment."

She didn't want to respond to the warmth spreading through her body. She tried to stand up straight, tried to keep her bones from turning to water at his touch. It appeared to be a losing battle.

Brandon decided that a man could get lost in those big brown eyes, lost and never found again. If he had any sense, he'd back away from her. Instead he tugged her one step closer so that her body tantalized his. He kissed her then—gently at first. He wanted only to taste and tempt, he told himself. But her reaction was so much sweeter than he'd anticipated that he couldn't help deepening the kiss.

He pulled her even closer, and she tilted her head, allowing him better access to her sweetness. Her arms came up, but her hands remained clenched. He realized that he wanted to feel her touch, needed her hands to grasp as greedily as her lips. But instead her hands opened only to push against his chest. He fought for control, but it seemed an eternity before he was finally able to pull his mouth free of hers.

"Stop it, please," she whispered. "Mr. Roarke."

He rested his forehead against hers. "Brandon," he corrected her. "I think we're past the point of formality."

"Mr. Roarke," she said with emphasis, "I'm grateful for this opportunity, but not *that* grateful."

He froze. What she was suggesting had never entered his mind. Grasping her by the shoulders, he held her at arm's length. "Our professional relationship has nothing to do with this."

"I think it does. And I won't remain unless you promise this won't happen again."

He couldn't believe what he was hearing—or seeing. Her big brown eyes were almost liquid. Her cheeks were stained pink. Her lips had thinned with the effort to keep them from quivering. He took a deep breath and dropped his hands.

"You're good," he finally said. "Damn good. You almost have me believing you."

"Believe it," she told him with a quick nod of her head. "Now, if you'll have someone show me to my room . . ."

"That won't be necessary." He could be strictly business if that was what she wanted. At least for now. "I think I can manage that."

He led her into the hallway, through a connecting door, and down two doors. Holding out his hand palm up, he waited patiently. "Your key?" he said after a moment.

She handed it to him and followed him into the suite. In the larger of the two bedrooms, they found her suitcase sitting at the foot of the bed and her camera case upon the dresser. Brandon turned on the bedside lamp and closed the drapes. "Will I see you in the morning?" he finally asked.

"I doubt it. I usually skip breakfast."

He set the key on the dresser. "Pleasant dreams, then," he murmured before closing the door quietly behind him.

But two hours later he was still sitting on his couch nursing a snifter of brandy. This wasn't exactly how he'd expected to end the evening. Nor had he planned for her to spend the next morning hiding in her room.

He swirled the brandy and took another sip. How, he wondered, was he going to smooth things over this time?

He pulled a piece of stationery from his desk drawer. "Jessica," he wrote, "I couldn't stand the thought of you starving in your room while trying to avoid me, so I sent up a tray. In the envelope is a copy of the proposed layout for the brochure. Read it over and meet me in my office at ten-thirty."

He'd have the note delivered first thing tomorrow morning with breakfast. It wasn't an apology—he didn't think he had anything to apologize for—but it was the sort of gesture that might make her comfortable. He'd even have one white rose added to the tray, he decided.

The Watcher liked the night best. People thought that the night helped to hide their secrets, but the Watcher knew better. People became careless when they thought the darkness hid them. It was the Watcher's favorite time.

The lights in Brandon's apartment were still on at two in the morning. If he'd been successful with the woman, the lights would have been turned off long ago.

The Watcher smiled and looked out at the few stars winking through the morning fog. The time for revenge was drawing near.

3

Jessica arrived five minutes early; she knew that punctuality was one of her most annoying habits, but she had no intention of changing. Clutching the envelope Brandon had sent her, she smiled at the young woman working at the front desk. "Nancy," read the name tag pinned to her efficient-looking blazer. When Nancy informed her that Brandon wasn't in his office yet, Jessica found herself occupying the same chair she'd sat on the night before.

Reduced to shuffling through the notes and questions she'd scribbled on the proposed layout, Jessica admitted that she dreaded facing Brandon. She would have avoided it, had it been possible. Still, she wasn't sure if she was angry or relieved at being left to cool her heels in the lobby.

She could tell by Nancy's growing distress that this sort of thing was not the norm. At ten forty-five, Nancy was apologizing; at eleven o'clock she was upset; and at eleven-fifteen she was almost apoplectic.

"I'm so sorry," she said once again. "It simply isn't like Mr. Roarke. He jogs along the beach most mornings, but he's usually back in his office by ten. Ten-thirty at the very latest."

Jessica was about to go back to her room and ask Nancy to ring her once Brandon had returned, when she glimpsed him coming along the terrace. She pointed this out to Nancy.

"Oh, I'm so relieved," the woman said with a sigh. "I had visions of him lying on the beach with a broken ankle or something."

Jessica could barely suppress a smile, for she couldn't imagine Brandon Roarke simply lying on the beach waiting to be rescued. But then she saw that he wasn't alone and almost wished he'd broken a few bones—only his neck would have been more to her liking. His companion was about a foot shorter than he, with blond hair and a vibrant smile. She, too, was decked out in running regalia—lots of spandex that hugged her curves and bare spaces where her muscles stood out. She looked like an ad for one of those health spas. They separated just inside the lobby, and Brandon came toward her.

"Jessica, I'm sorry about our appointment, but I got held up with some problems."

Jessica didn't say anything; she just smiled.

"I need to get cleaned up," he continued, ignoring the chilly silence. "Why don't we discuss business over lunch. Say, twelve-thirty on the terrace." Then, without waiting for an answer, he turned and bounded up his private staircase.

Jessica had about an hour on her own, so she decided to put it to good use by looking over the grounds. She walked out the massive double doors and across the circular drive that swept under the giant porte cochere.

Mounds of luggage stood on the walkway as bellmen and guests went through the ritual of departure.

After threading her way through the confusion, Jess followed a little brick path that cut across the expansive green lawn until she stood beside the railing at the cliff edge and looked down at the foaming ocean.

Below her, the blue-green water was dotted with froth where the waves beat against submerged rock. Now, as the tide ebbed, she could see the narrow fringe of sandy beach littered with seaweed and inhabited by seagulls and sandpipers. It was nothing like the lazy, sun-kissed beaches of southern California where she'd grown up. Here one would never spread a towel and doze peacefully at the water's edge; there was nothing tame about the waves that undulated just offshore.

Nevertheless, she noticed several trails of footprints and wondered how anyone could have descended the steep rocks. They certainly couldn't have come from the south, for at the headland, the bluff on which she stood tumbled into the ocean in a jumble of deadly, jagged rocks. Then, just to her right, she noticed a wooden stair-case that etched an intricate pattern down, among, and over the rocks. The descent appeared treacherous, for the staircase clung precariously to each turn and curve of the rocky promontory. Although there were numerous land-ings with benches on which to rest, it was clear that only the fittest and bravest of the Santa Lucia's guests would follow this route.

She gazed again at the Pacific and at the land that bordered it. From its southern tip on her left, the crescent-shaped cove swept around to the right and became gradually less forbidding, diminishing into rolling sand dunes that merged grudgingly with the green inland areas before once again forming steep cliffs at the far side of the inlet. At the extreme northern tip of the cove, on a less imposing bluff than the one on which she stood, nestled Jason Kendall's home. Jessica was surprised to realize that she missed the relative security of that house and its inhabitants.

Turning her back on the thundering ocean, she surveyed the Santa Lucia. In contrast with Jason's home, which sat within the gentle embrace of the coast, the Santa Lucia appeared to thrust itself into sight. Yet it belonged here as surely as the gulls that glided and circled on the wind above her.

The central portion of the chalk-colored hotel stood three stories high with a bell tower on top, reminding Jessica of those found on the missions the Spaniards had scattered throughout California when they first arrived. The two-storied wings of the building spread out and back, gently imparting the illusion of a soaring bird. It seemed to her imagination that only the red-tiled roof kept the building from rising into the lapis sky. To the back of the hotel, the green lawn sloped gently down to join the rolling golf course, and beyond that the brilliant blue of the Pacific stretched to the horizon.

To the left of the building, a path curled along the edge of the cliff and led to what looked like a formal garden with neatly trimmed hedges. Jessica followed it and eventually found herself in a quiet garden, shaded by an old and gracious willow tree.

The first delicate colors of spring were everywhere. She recognized the roses and azaleas and fuchsias, but there were a great many other plants whose names she didn't know. The effect of the place was intimate, rather English, and completely out of character for the Santa Lucia. But, more important, it offered the solitude she so badly needed. She took a seat on one of the white wooden benches and tried to sort through her confusing reactions to Brandon Roarke.

She was attracted to him, but she didn't trust him. More to the point, she didn't trust herself; her track record with men left a lot to be desired. But this was not a subject she liked to reflect upon, and she was almost relieved when a tall man dressed in khaki pants and work shirt invaded the private bower. With his sharp features and well-worn straw hat, he reminded Jessica of the Scarecrow in *The Wizard of Oz*. He carried a small gardener's spade and an old metal bucket, which he set down with a clatter.

"Oh, I'm sorry, ma'am. The garden is usually deserted this time of day." His voice was softly southern and a little wheezy. The apologetic smile was genuine as he bent to pick up the bucket once more.

"Don't go," Jessica said quickly. "I can only stay a few minutes more."

"Thank you, ma'am. I like to put in my full time here 'cause if things aren't just right, Mr. Brandon gets real upset."

"Mr. Brandon? You mean Brandon Roarke?"

"Yes'm. But I knew him when he was just a mite. He'll always be Mr. Brandon to me."

"He's a hard taskmaster, is he?"

"Hard but fair, ma'am, and that's the truth. But this place here," he said as his eyes swept over the garden, "this was Mrs. Roarke's favorite, and he likes to see it kept up just right."

"Mrs. Roarke's?"

"Mr. Brandon's mother. Kathleen Roarke. She was a pretty little thing. Came all the way from Ireland, and sometimes she got real lonely for home. So I helped her plant this . . . oh . . . almost forty-five years ago. It was just after Mr. Robert—that was her husband—had brought her back from Europe. Just me and her," he said with a genuine sadness.

"It's still beautiful," Jessica assured him.

"When she passed away, it was Mr. Brandon and me who kept it goin'. Why, he was only a little tyke when his parents was killed in a plane crash. Barely ten years old. I came out here the next week and found him trimmin' and cleanin' up. I says to him, 'Mr. Brandon, what're you doin' here?' And he looks at me all grown up and he says, 'This is my mother's garden, and I'm goin' to keep it just the way she wanted it.'"

Jessica looked around the garden and tried to imagine Brandon as a little boy tending to the flowers while he clung to the memory of his mother. The picture the gardener painted was far different from the one she'd have imagined.

"'Course now, Mr. Brandon doesn't have time to work out here, but he still visits it. 'George,' he'll call me. 'George, I want you to take care of this garden 'cause you know just how Mother would've wanted it.'"

The old man looked around him lovingly. "So I take good care of it for Mrs. Roarke and young Mr. Brandon."

"Rather like a sacred trust?"

"Yes'm. Just like that."

Kneeling before the bushes bordering the entrance, he began carefully scooping up large clumps of dirt with his hand trowel.

"Time to pull up the daffodil bulbs," he explained quietly. "They've done their job already." He brushed the dirt off a bulb and then placed it in his pail. "Time to add new color." He worked steadily, digging up bulb after bulb, while he whistled a familiar tune.

"There must have been a lot of them," Jessica commented when his bucket was almost full.

"Daffodils aren't at their best when they're alone," he explained. "You need lots of them to get the full effect. I always think of Wordsworth's poem, the one that talks about ' . . . a crowd, / A host, of golden daffodils; / Beside the lake, beneath the trees, / Fluttering and dancing in the breeze. . . .'

"Miss Kathleen, she said we didn't have a lake, but we had the space and the trees, so we just naturally needed a whole 'host' of daffodils."

"That's lovely," she murmured. "I don't think I've heard that since I graduated from high school."

He looked up and gave her a sheepish grin before turning back to his work. "Miss Kathleen loved poetry. I always think of it when I'm working here."

"It must have been a terrible loss," Jessica said after several moments of silence. "It must have been especially hard for Brandon."

"'To live in hearts we leave behind is not to die.'" His sharp eyes came up to assess her. "I suppose it was hard, but the boy had his uncle. And he had Jason. That seemed to get him through the hard times."

"Jason Kendall?"

He gave her a sideways glance. "You know Jason?"

Jess nodded. "My sister and I were staying with the Kendalls. But Jason and Brandon aren't friends. They're barely on speaking terms."

The gardener turned back to his work. "They were best friends then. More like brothers. They helped each other through the tough times."

"But they were only children."

"'The Child is father of the Man,'" the gardener said with quiet certainty.

Jessica wasn't certain what he meant by that. She would have asked, but it was time to meet Brandon. Past time, actually. She rose to leave but couldn't help glancing back over her shoulder at the gardener. She'd never had the privilege of meeting a gardener-philosopher before. She doubted there were very many of them. And it figured, she thought, that the Santa Lucia, which boasted an extraordinary list of guests, would also need a better class of gardener. She could hardly wait to tell Marty about him; she knew her sister would see the humor in it. Between her thoughts and the crashing of waves, she didn't notice the young man with the wheelbarrow until he had almost run her down.

"Oh, I'm so sorry," Jessica apologized once she'd regained her balance and was no longer in danger of sprawling across the plants and bags of dirt. "I hope nothing's damaged."

"Ah, hell!" the boy muttered as he tried to catch one of the bags. But it eluded him and fell to the ground, spreading a dark puddle of dirt on the green lawn. "Ah, hell!" he repeated a bit louder this time, and gave the bag a frustrated kick.

At first glance he was a fairly nondescript teenager: brown hair, brown eyes, average height, and average weight. Only the sullen and resentful look of the eyes and mouth set him apart from a hundred other sixteen- or seventeen-year-olds.

"Don't be talkin' like that in front of the guests," the old gardener admonished as he hurried toward them. Then he surveyed the damage. "You didn't spill my tuberous begonias, did you, Danny? I told you to be careful with them."

"Nah, I didn't hurt your stupid flowers. Just spilled some dirt."

"It's my fault," Jess said quickly. "I wasn't watching where I was going, and I ran right into him. And I'm not a guest," she added. "Just a fellow employee, of sorts."

The old man smiled at her. "No harm done, miss. Danny will just clean this up, and no one will be the wiser."

"You're sure?"

"Oh, yes'm." He picked up two boxes that evidently contained his prized plants. "These're just fine."

Jessica apologized again and then quickly made her exit. But as she walked away, she heard the boy complaining.

"It's just dirt," he whined. "I don't see why we can't just leave it."

"Listen, Danny," George answered patiently. "I hired you on for your uncle's sake. He's a good man. But if you can't get the feel for workin' with dirt and plants, then you'll have to go—no matter who your uncle is."

"Yeah. All right," was the boy's sullen reply, and then the sea breeze blew away his bad-tempered words.

In only a moment Jessica was climbing the wide, easy steps that led to the terrace where lunch was being served on tables covered in bright Mexican tile and shaded by umbrellas of blue and white. Bougainvillea threw arms of vivid purple and pink over the low wall that framed the patio, and in the center was a fountain lined in the same bright tiles where a trio of sculpted dolphins glistened in the sun. Water bubbled from their blowholes and cascaded merrily down their sides, adding the rhythm of shimmering water to the conversation of the diners.

Jessica glanced around the terrace until she found Brandon in earnest conversation with the blond jogger she'd seen that morning. She wasn't about to be left twiddling her thumbs while he flirted with the guests again. Business before pleasure, she told herself sternly as she marched toward their table.

"Jessica," Brandon said as he rose. "I'd just about given up on you."

Jessica glanced at her watch. She was only five minutes late. Normally she would have considered that a heinous crime, but after his boorish manners of this morning, she was determined to treat it casually.

"I didn't realize you were such a stickler for punctuality." The smile she gave him was too saccharine to be sincere. "It won't happen again."

"Jessica, I'd like you to meet Susan Sorenson. Susan, this is Jessica Martinson, our photographer."

Brandon watched as the two women smiled at each other and exchanged greetings, but he couldn't help comparing them. Susan had to be close to fifty, although the best European spas and a talented Beverly Hills plastic surgeon had kept at least ten of those years from showing. She had on the latest designer resort wear and enough diamonds to draw the attention of most of the guests on the terrace. Jessica, on the other hand, had on a pair of snug jeans and a T-shirt. She would have his full attention as soon as he'd gotten rid of the recently widowed blonde. Actually, Jessica almost had his full attention now, and he could see that his paying guest was not pleased by that.

As soon as he thought it polite, Brandon said, "I'm afraid you'll have to excuse us, Susan. Miss Martinson and I have some business to discuss."

He thought he'd handled the situation as graciously as possible, but Susan was evidently piqued. She turned a venomous stare on Jessica, looked her up and down, then gave Brandon a look that said she'd still be close by when he'd finished his business. But the look she gave Jessica made him think the older woman would be spending a little extra time in the gym this week.

"If you can't squeeze me into your busy schedule," Jessica said in an impatient undertone, "I wish you'd just say so. I can go ahead and start taking photos based on the information you sent me."

"I'd like to discuss the brochure before you begin," Brandon said simply. He waited until they were seated at one of the tables secluded behind some dwarf lemon trees before adding, "And what makes you think I don't have time for you?"

She shrugged. "Your paying guests seem to take up a lot of your time," was all she said, but when she rolled her eyes, he couldn't help smiling at her.

"If you're referring to Susan, you might like to know that she and her husband vacationed here for almost twenty years."

Jessica spread the linen napkin on her lap. "I don't believe I've seen Mr. Sorenson."

"I doubt that you will. He passed away last year."

Jessica gave him a quick assessing look. "I'm sorry. I didn't know."

"She's lonely," Brandon said. *And looking for male companionship*, he thought. "That's one of the things about a family-owned inn. We know the guests. Many of them have been coming here for years." And they know us, he thought. Susan had ambushed him as he'd left an emergency meeting with his head gardener this morning. As though it hadn't been bad enough that he was going to have to fire a shirttail relative he'd hired as a favor to his uncle, he'd found himself waylaid by the merry and very aggressive widow as he'd headed back to the office.

Women were a curse, he decided. Then he looked into Jessica's brown eyes and wanted to believe in the honesty he saw there. Dammit—he'd just reached a point where he thought he'd come to understand women; why did she have to wander into his life and confuse him again?

"There are a few shots that we definitely want for the brochure," Brandon began. "One of the bell tower and, of course, one of the golf course."

Jessica took out her notes and began adding to them. Brandon continued, "The fourteenth hole is infamous. It's been known to give the pros nightmares."

"We'll want to avoid photographing that one, then."

"You're not a golfer, are you?" When Jessica shook her head, he laughed. "We definitely want a photo of the fourteenth."

"That doesn't make sense. Why include a hole that even the pros have trouble with?"

Brandon was fascinated by the look in her eyes, the one that said she was being absolutely reasonable.

"Golfers aren't logical. They love telling about how much trouble they had on the fourteenth. No, don't ask me why," he said when she started to interrupt. "If you want an explanation of the finer points of golfing frenzy, you'll have to ask Stewart."

The discussion continued through lunch. Brandon was pleased with some of her suggestions but even happier to find that she didn't mention the previous evening. He'd been afraid she'd rehash the situation or try to extract a promise that he wouldn't put the move on her again. And he damn sure wasn't giving her a promise like that.

In fact, the longer he was around her, the more attracted he was. There was an honesty about her that he found sexier than any amount of tanned skin or daring décolletage. More important, he wanted to know if she was real or simply the best actress he'd ever met.

"I'd like to introduce you to someone who might be

able to help," he said as he lingered over his iced tea. "His name's George, and he's been employed by the inn from day one. Before that, even. He's the head gardener, and he knows ever nook and cranny of the place. You want to know the best place to see the sunrise, George'll know. You want to know where the sunset casts its rosiest glow, George can tell you."

"Sounds like a godsend."

Brandon nodded. "The thing is that people tend to think he's a little simple at first. But it couldn't be farther from the truth."

"And does he look like the Scarecrow from *The Wizard of Oz?*"

Brandon set his glass down. "Did Jason tell you about him?" That would be like Jason, he knew. To give his protégé an inside source—and a place to turn for help should she need it. Funny, he tended to forget about Jessica's connection to Jason. Or did he simply accept it? As though his connection to Jason were still strong and vital. As though it were only natural Jessica should know his best friend. The man who used to be his best friend, he amended. Now Jason was simply a local celebrity—and a business adversary.

Jess shook her head, and her short, burnished curls bounced. "Actually I ran into him in that little garden to the north of the inn. He was quoting poetry," she said with a bemused smile. "I thought he was wonderful."

Brandon didn't understand how something so simple could fill him with joy. Most of the guests tended to dismiss George as part of the scenery. Even the ones who talked to him rarely saw beyond the serviceable clothes and dirty fingernails. But Jessica thought he was "wonderful." Maybe, just maybe, she was everything she appeared to be.

* * *

Despite a busy day, Jess dreaded having a lonely dinner, or at least a dinner alone. She was about to phone room service when Stewart Roarke saved her from her lonely fate by insisting that Jessica join him and his nephew in the elegant dining room.

Wearing the one simple cotton dress she'd brought with her, Jess was afraid she'd feel out of place. Instead she felt like a fairy-tale princess. She'd never before been the object of attention from two such handsome and charming men, and she found herself completely disarmed by them. She enjoyed herself shamelessly. She didn't contribute very much to the conversation, but she laughed a great deal and even threw what she hoped was a sophisticated smile at the blond Susan Sorenson, who glared at them from across the dining room.

Both men kept her entertained with stories about the hotel and its eccentric guests, and she lost all sense of time until she noticed that all the tables save theirs were empty and that only their waiter idled wearily nearby. So she said her thank-yous and floated up to her room on a cloud made of equal parts champagne and magic.

Oh, there was no doubt about it, Jess acknowledged as she assessed herself in the mirror; she was completely enchanted by the whole experience.

Stewart leaned both arms on the railing and looked down at the waves as they crashed against the cliff. In his hand was a snifter of after-dinner brandy, which he swirled gently. Brandon stood with his back to the sea and his eyes on the inn. On a particular window where the light still burned. On the room in which Jessica Martinson prepared for bed.

"She seems very nice," Stewart said without looking up. "Naive. Not the kind of woman who would know how to engage in a casual fling."

"I think she'd be insulted by that analysis, but I think you're absolutely right. And I doubt that she's casual about much of anything."

Stewart smiled. Brandon had known right away whom he was talking about. He took a sip of the brandy and wondered how to probe his nephew's intentions. "I would have to take exception with any man who hurt her."

Brandon took the time for a deep breath and hoped it would help ease the sharp pain his uncle's words had caused. "I didn't know your opinion of me had sunk so low."

"I have the utmost regard for you in most things, Bran. But your attitude toward women has me puzzled. Had your mother lived, you would have understood what wonderful creatures they can be." He took another sip. "Maybe it's my fault. If I'd married, perhaps you'd have more appreciation for the strength and passion to be found in such delicate packages."

Brandon had to laugh at that. "Most women today don't fit your description."

"I'm sixty-seven years old, Bran. Too old to change. I can't admire a woman for how many push-ups she can do or how many pounds she can bench press. There's a different kind of strength that women have. It's the way they have of making a man feel invincible. It's how they can hold a family together under the worst circumstances." He looked up at the stars. "Your mother couldn't lift a fifty-pound sack of flour, but she was the strongest woman I ever knew."

Jessica's light winked out, but Brandon continued to study her window. "And you loved her."

Stewart nodded. "Yes, I loved her. And knew that she loved my brother. Unfortunately, I could never find the woman who could live up to her."

"I can understand that."

"Can you?"

Brandon nodded. Oh, yes, he could understand. There was a woman he'd found once. Or thought he'd found. She, too, had spoiled him for anyone else, though not in the same way. He'd not trusted one since.

The Watcher hadn't anticipated this. Hadn't thought that Brandon's softening might heal the rift between him and his uncle. There was much to be feared in that, for Brandon knew things. Secret things. Powerful things.

If Stewart should find out, he might be able to keep the Watcher from taking revenge. That couldn't be allowed to happen.

4

"*I don't think the camera has been invented* that can capture all this on film." Jessica didn't even realize she'd said it aloud until she heard the raspy chuckle from behind her.

"Mother Nature can be overwhelming," George agreed. "But don't even think about trying to get it all in one picture. Just focus on one thing at a time."

Nodding, Jessica wondered how she could ever pick one image over another and how there could be so many marvels within view of her camera.

When she'd contacted George the day before, he'd suggested they get started before the sun was up. Jess had agreed, knowing that the magic hour, as photographers called the interval at dawn and again at dusk, was both dramatic and flattering. So, while the inn's guests still slept, she'd stowed all her equipment in a golf cart and entrusted her fate to the man who'd driven unerringly over winding paths that crisscrossed the grounds of the Santa Lucia. In those misty moments when the light was no more than a distant glow, he'd pointed out a herd of deer bounding across the natural vegetation, then racing across long open stretches of the golf course. He'd pointed out the manmade beauty where a particularly difficult hole lay nestled on a narrow spit of land, the yellow flag of the pin flapping in the incessant wind as waves crashed only fifteen feet away.

When they'd finally arrived at the southernmost tip of the golf course, she'd found no pale sand dunes in the moments just before dawn. Instead George had led her up a rocky incline to a point jutting out into the ocean where cypress trees clung tenaciously to the rugged terrain. There had been no neatly laid out path and no quaint gift shop, only rock and waves and the tang of salty water. Jess had set up her equipment and waited for daybreak. Patiently she'd watched the sky turn from gray to opalescent, though no light had actually broken through to herald the dawn.

Then, just when she had despaired of having enough light to take photographs, the sun had begun filtering through the mist, slyly at first, in little pools or twinkling shafts of light. And now, as she looked to the north where the coastline stretched like a lazy cat lolling in the first hint of warmth, light broke through the fog in dazzling columns that highlighted the sandy beach and the lacy foam that lapped at its feet. Gulls circled on the wind, their cries echoing off the rocks and mixing with the crashing of waves. Offshore the fog persisted like a walled fortress. She squeezed off several shots of the coastline, then made herself stop. There were other images to capture.

Behind Jess, the Santa Lucia Inn sat in soft shadows where the sunlight was just beginning to punch holes in the sky. The chalky color kept the focus soft and made

Jess think of an apparition that might disappear in stronger light. Farther to the south, where the coast grudgingly gave way to sand dunes and more vegetation, the fog still clung in long, pale fingers that followed the contours of the land, settling into the low-lying areas like a ghostly hand grasping an unwary victim's billowing skirt.

Jessica gave an involuntary shiver at the image and turned her camera on the inn itself. Using a wide-angle lens to capture the magical vista, she figured there was just enough time to take a few shots before the sunlight broke through in earnest, washing the building in harsh light. She hoped the subdued lighting would make the resort look like a sun-washed castle rather than a glorified, high-priced hotel.

Jessica stepped back from the camera she'd mounted on the tripod and glanced around. "I'm glad Brandon suggested you as my guide. I would never have found this vantage point."

"I know 'most every corner of the grounds." George removed his old straw hat and ran a hand through his thinning hair. "Fact is, I've probably pulled weeds or planted flowers on most every inch of the place. And I've always thought this was the best time of day." He plopped the hat back on his head and turned his face toward the light. "'Give me the splendid silent sun with all his beams full-dazzling,'" he quoted, then gave Jess a sheepish grin. "It's quiet and clean before people start wanderin' around and messin' things up. Makes me wonder what paradise must've been like before people mucked it all up."

Jessica's gaze swept the area again. "I know what you mean. I have the feeling that if I wandered off into those sand dunes, I'd feel like the only person on the earth as soon as the fog cut off my view of the inn."

"You mustn't do that," George said with an emphatic shake of his head. "There's things out there that you don't expect to find. Things better left alone. It's no place for a woman by herself."

Jessica couldn't help laughing. "You don't have to worry about that. My sense of direction is so bad that I can get lost going around a city block, let alone wandering out in an uncharted wilderness like that. I'd have to leave a trail of bread crumbs."

"Now that wouldn't do you a bit of good. All those little critters that make their home in the underbrush would make short work of your bread crumbs."

"Okay, you've convinced me. I'm not going anywhere there are scurrying little animals." She loosened the bolt on the tripod and swung the camera around to face south. "Especially if those scurrying animals have beady little eyes and sharp, jagged teeth."

"Grew up in the city, did you?"

"Guilty as charged." Jessica adjusted the aperture and considered a time exposure. It would make the fog seem even thicker, almost like a living, breathing entity. "I'm afraid I wasn't an adventurous child. I enjoyed watching the world from the safety of my very civilized front yard." And most of her adult life she'd spent watching life through the lens of a camera, but she didn't tell George that.

"You missed a lot, then. This is a great place for kids. I remember Brandon and Jason when they were just tykes. I used to take them on overnight campin' trips. Used to go where Brandon is plannin' to build his campground, actually. When I couldn't go with them, they'd pack a lunch and be gone all day."

Jessica noticed his wistful smile and wished she could turn the camera on him. That craggy face and distant look would make for a great character study.

She set the camera for a time exposure and attached the shutter cable. "So those little animals in the under-brush didn't scare them off, hmm?"

"Truth is that they had a tendency to bring those little critters home. Scared Jacqueline half to death."

"Jacqueline?"

"Jason's mother," George explained. "She wasn't pleased to find animals runnin' loose inside her house. Many's the time Stewart sent me over to the Kendall home to flush out some critter that had taken refuge under a bed or behind a sofa."

Jessica looked up and rolled her eyes. "Oh, that must've been fun. And what did you do with it once you'd caught it?"

"More often than not, the boys talked me into buildin' it a cage out back of my place. We'd keep it for a while, then I'd go with the boys to turn it loose. Wild things need to be put back where they belong."

"You live close by?"

"In a little house on the edge of the inn's property. Came with the job," he said as though he needed to explain why he lived on the grounds.

After a moment of silence, Jessica looked up to find him studying the Kendall home, which was barely visible in the fog. "I haven't been back there since Jacqueline died."

Jessica was surprised that Jason's mother had lived there, but she only said, "It's a beautiful place. You can tell it's an artist's home; everything is arranged to please the eye."

George nodded. "Always was. The boy inherited his mother's eye for beauty." He looked away, then back again as though drawn to the structure. "I never see him anymore, either." His gaze came back to rest on Jessica. "You stayed there for a while, didn't you? How is he?"

"He's wonderful—very kind and encouraging. I would never have gotten this job without his help."

George nodded, but whether it meant he knew or wasn't surprised, she couldn't tell.

"Sounds like him," the gardener finally said. "Always willin' to help others. Always wantin' to make things right for other people. He's the one used to bring injured animals to me, askin' me to make them better. But I couldn't always do that. There's a whole bunch of little grave markers out back of my place where he buried them. He had such a soft heart."

Jess pondered the image of Jason as a child while she broke down her equipment. "Where to next?" she asked when everything was packed up.

George put the largest case in the back of the cart. "Thought you might like to see the inn from up closer. You know, with the ocean in the background."

Jess nodded as her gaze swept the area once again. The sun was skimming off the ocean, making it a perfect time to take the kind of picture he suggested.

"Do you take many photographs?"

He guided the cart in a tight U-turn and started back toward the inn. "Not much. Why do you ask?"

"You just seem to have a knack for knowing when the lighting is right."

"Just a matter of lookin' around. Lookin' at the world. I can't do nothin' fancy with a camera. When I take pictures, it's usually of people. I like the ones where you can see straight into the soul."

Jess couldn't help smiling. "Those are my favorites, too. I like to capture a personality or an emotion. It's never going to happen just exactly like that again, and I'm compelled to preserve it on film."

George stopped in the lee of a tree as a foursome teed off not far away. "You didn't happen to take any pictures of the little girl, did you?"

"Megan?"

George watched the last of the foursome hit a ball that landed only a few feet on the other side of the tree. While the golfer muttered to himself and stalked the errant ball, George set the cart in motion once more. "I remember when she was born. She was beautiful."

"She still is."

George nodded. "Just wondered if you'd taken any pictures of her."

Jess shook her head. "I'm sure she'd be a great subject, but I never got around to it." She thought of how Jason doted on her. "I'll bet she's posed for hundreds of pictures for her father."

"What's she like?"

"Sweet," Jessica answered without hesitation. "And quiet. Kind of shy, I guess, though she can play games like a demon."

She explained how the child had suckered her into playing and then proceeded to beat her every time. Surprisingly enough, George seemed fascinated by the little hustler. Jessica supposed that even a confirmed bachelor like George would be interested in a child as beautiful and sweet as Megan Kendall.

It was well after noon by the time George dropped Jess at the front door of the inn. She'd taken several rolls of film and was anxious to develop them. She hoped they were as good as she thought, but what if they weren't?

Knowing she wouldn't get over her jitters until she'd developed them and made proof pages, she phoned the

Kendall home as soon as she could. When Megan answered and told Jess that her daddy was gone, Jessica decided that since Jason wasn't using his darkroom, she would. She slipped the exposed rolls of film in her backpack and, at the last minute, included her camera, which held a partially exposed roll. If she found a few good shots on her walk to the Kendall home, she could develop this roll, too.

George had pointed out the path that led from the Santa Lucia across the cliff overlooking the beach and almost directly to the Kendalls'. He'd assured her that once she was on it, she couldn't possibly get lost—but Jessica knew better. Her sense of direction was so poor that under other circumstances she would have waited for someone to guide her, but this time she was just too anxious to see the pictures. Setting off across the expansive lawn, she headed to the area George had pointed out. If she could just keep the Pacific Ocean on her left, even she should be able to find her way.

She was almost at the path when she heard her name. Looking over her shoulder, she saw Brandon and his uncle striding toward her. When her heart skipped a beat, she told herself it was only because she was annoyed at the interruption. Nevertheless, she feared it wasn't annoyance that Brandon saw in her eyes.

"How are you doing?" Stewart asked. "And where are you off to?"

"I thought George was going to show you around this morning," Brandon added before she could respond to the older man.

"I'm doing just fine," she informed Stewart. "And George spent the morning with me. He's incredible," she added. "He knows the area like the back of his hand. He showed me places I would never have found."

Stewart chuckled. "I sometimes think he knows more about the inn than I do. I'm glad he could be of help."

"He was terrific. Now I'm headed to Jason's to use his darkroom. I'm anxious to see if I captured even a fraction of what I saw on film."

"I was hoping we could spend the afternoon together," Brandon said. When both Jessica and Stewart turned to look at him, he explained, "For the interior shots. You'll need several of those, and I'd like to help you select them."

He hated seeing the way her smile faded at the thought of spending time in his company. He'd obviously over-played his hand before, been too pushy. But all he needed was a little time to show her he could be charming.

Jessica looked over her shoulder at the path leading to the Kendalls'. "I really need to develop these first, if you don't mind."

Brandon fought down a flash of annoyance. "It seems to me that you'd want to take all the shots first. Then you can develop them all at once."

He watched as she chewed on her lower lip for a few seconds. "Actually, I'd like to develop these first. Just to make sure that the equipment is working. I'd hate to take all the pictures and then find out that the light meter had malfunctioned. If it's off by even a little bit, it could make the difference between good pictures and great ones."

Before Brandon could even form an argument, his uncle spoke up. "You're the expert, my dear," Stewart assured her. Brandon watched Jessica's smile blossom again. "I'm sure my nephew can show you around tomorrow. If not, I'll be happy to do so myself."

"Thank you," she said to Stewart with that incredible smile, the one Brandon wanted turned in his direction. "That really would be better."

Before Brandon could think of any way to stop her, she was gone.

"You're pushing too hard, my boy," Stewart told him as soon as Jessica was out of earshot. "She's man shy. A woman like that will run if she thinks she's cornered."

Brandon stuck his hands in the pockets of his slacks and started back toward the inn, unwilling to give his uncle the satisfaction of seeing him gaze after Jessica until she faded out of sight. "And just what is that supposed to mean?"

Stewart's chuckle grated on Brandon's nerves. "That you usually show more finesse when you're trying to make a move on a woman. And that this one is special. You do remember what I told you last night, don't you?"

There it was again, the inference that he wasn't a man to be trusted. And it hurt just as much this morning as it had last night.

"She's a grown woman. She doesn't need you running interference for her."

"No, but evidently you do if you're not going to mess this up."

Brandon stopped and turned to face his uncle, who had stopped as well. "I can't see that you've had such incredible success with women that you can go around giving advice."

"This has nothing to do with my experience with women. It has to do with you. You're becoming pushy and unreasonable."

Brandon turned and strode off. Stewart came after him. "I mean it, Bran. You're not handling Jessica very well. And you're being completely unreasonable about this campground."

"The campground? What the hell does that have to do with Jessica?"

"Nothing. But it has to do with you." Stewart placed a restraining hand on his nephew, who stopped at last to face him. "You seem to be running roughshod over everyone's feelings. Jessica's. Jason's. Mine. I thought last night that we were starting to communicate again. Perhaps I was wrong."

Brandon went cold. "I have no idea what you're talking about, Stewart."

"You don't? Then why is it you seem to be driving everyone away? You just sent Jessica running off. You haven't really talked to Jason in years. And you and I have lost the closeness we once enjoyed. What's happened to you? Why are you so angry? And why are you holding everyone at arm's length?"

"You must be imagining things."

"Oh, Bran. I raised you, remember? What are you going to do about Jessica?"

"I believe that's my business."

"Then what about the campground? How can you let that come between you and Jason? You don't need the money it might bring in. Besides, it will take several years to recoup your original investment. And mine."

"It's not about turning a profit. And if you feel that way, you can damn well keep your money. I don't need it. I can find other investors."

"And what about us?" Stewart asked quietly. "What happened to the closeness we once had?"

"I'm thirty-six years old, Stewart. I don't need a nursemaid anymore," he said before turning away.

And he knew that he didn't deserve the friendship or love of a man of such honor. Not after what he'd done.

*   *   *

By the time Jessica reached the Kendall home, she had almost forgotten the meeting with Brandon and Stewart. She'd taken a few shots on the walk over, and she was so excited about seeing the results of her morning shoot that she was impatient with the time it took for Florence to answer the door. After ringing the bell, she knocked on the door, wondering if Florence and Megan had left. She still had the key Jason had given her but hesitated to use it since she was no longer staying there.

When no one came to the door, her impatience to see the pictures overcame her reluctance to intrude. Using the key, she unlocked the door and stepped inside.

"Hello," she called. "Anyone home?"

"Jess?" a small voice answered.

"Megan? Is that you, sweetie?"

"Jess!" Megan called, louder this time.

Jessica just had time to look up to the walkway overlooking the living room before the child burst into action, running down the stairs and speeding across the living room to hurl herself into her arms.

"You said you'd come visit, and you finally did," she said, squeezing Jessica with all the strength of a six-year-old. After releasing her hold on Jess, Megan leaned back and looked up into her face. "I've missed you."

"No one to beat at games, huh?" She smoothed a hand over the child's hair as she spoke. Funny, but she'd missed the little bundle of energy. She hadn't even realized how much until the child had hugged her so fiercely. How, Jessica wondered, did such a little person manage to worm her way into my heart so quickly? "How come you didn't open the door?" she asked.

"Mom's outside working in the garden. I'm not supposed to answer the door when I'm here alone."

"You're all by yourself?" She had to stop herself from

asking how often that happened. Jessica thought six was too young to be left alone, but then she was hardly qualified to make that kind of decision. Besides, this was a rural area, not the crime-ridden big city.

"Can you play a game with me?"

Responsibility warred with Jessica's heart. Responsibility—and curiosity—finally won. "I can't play right now. I need to develop some film."

"Oh."

How could one little syllable sound so disconsolate? "Do you want to keep me company in the darkroom while I work?" she asked the child.

Megan gave a forlorn shake of her head. "Mommy says that's off limits."

That was probably a wise rule. Too many chemicals. Too many things to get into where she could get hurt.

"I got a new doll yesterday. You want to see it?"

Jessica could at least spare time for that. "I'd love to."

"They're special dolls," Megan informed her as she led the way up the stairs. "'Cause they're sent to me by my secret friend."

"Secret friend? Who's that?"

Megan giggled and turned to face her at the top of the steps. "If I knew who it was, it wouldn't be secret, would it?"

"Silly question, I guess."

Megan nodded, then took Jess's hand and tugged her along the passage. When the child swept open her door, Jessica was absolutely astounded. The child's room looked like something out of a magazine. A canopy bed dominated the pastel-pink-and-green room. Butterflies flitted across the wallpaper and soft Priscilla curtains framed the window seat. The view encompassed coastline and ocean and even the Santa Lucia. A perfect place to sit and read, Jess thought. And dream. She wondered what six-year-olds dreamed about these days.

To one side of the window stood a large telescope. From here Megan could watch the migration of the whales or the stars at night. A large dollhouse took up one corner. A child-size desk and easel filled another corner. Across one wall was a series of shelves filled with books and toys, and lining the top of the shelf at Megan's eye level were the most wondrous dolls Jessica had ever seen. They weren't take-me-to-bed-and-cuddle-with-me dolls. Instead they were made of delicate porcelain and wore gorgeous period costumes.

"Do you recognize any of them?" Megan asked, her big blue eyes gazing up at Jessica.

"I've never met any of them before. Will you introduce me? Have you given them all names?"

"They came with names, silly."

"Does your secret friend give them names?"

Megan shook her head, exasperated as only a child could be by an adult's obtuseness. "They're real people. Or at least they're made to look like real people."

Jessica looked at the dolls again and realized that she did indeed recognize some of them. "Let me see if I can guess them. Is this one Cleopatra? And Queen Elizabeth? And Mary, Queen of Scots?" Megan nodded enthusiastically. Jessica stopped at one in lavish eighteenth-century dress and elaborate hair. "Who is this?"

"Marie An'tonette," Megan informed her. "People cut off her head 'cause they didn't want to eat cake."

"And this?"

"Ann Bowlin'. Mommy says they cut off her head 'cause she didn't have any little boys. Daddy says her husband must have been really stupid, 'cause little girls are the best."

Jessica laughed at the six-year-old's version of history and thought how wonderful it must be to have parents who loved her so much. The dolls were obviously expensive—too expensive for a "secret pal" to be sending them. Jess wondered if her parents sent them and talked about her secret friend to add a little mystery and excitement to the child's life. "You're very lucky to have a secret friend who sends you these."

Megan nodded. "Mommy tells me I'm a lucky little girl. When she was little she didn't have any dolls. She didn't even have a mommy who wanted her. This is my new one." She pointed to a doll dressed in the white costume of ancient Greece. Her long dark hair was crowned with a wreath of delicate silk flowers. Megan held out the doll for Jessica's inspection. "Her name is Helen."

Jessica wiped her hands on her jeans before taking the proffered doll. "Helen of Troy. And what did she do?"

"She started a war," Megan informed her solemnly. "Daddy says wars are bad things. That people get hurt in them. Sometimes they get killed."

"Your father is absolutely right. But if I remember my history, Helen didn't actually mean to start a war. She just wanted to be happy. The problem was that she didn't care who got hurt in the process." Jessica crossed to the window seat and held the doll in the light. "She's very pretty, isn't she?"

Megan nodded. "She has blue eyes. Just like mine, Daddy says."

Jess held up the doll. "Come here and let's see. . . . Well, you two could be sisters," Jessica decided when she'd placed the doll next to the child's soft cheek. Megan giggled.

"I've got an idea," Jess said as she removed her backpack

and began to dig in it. "Let me take a picture of you and your sister."

"She's not really my sister."

"Okay, then, you and your doll."

Megan nodded. "Where do you want us to stand?"

"How about in front of the other dolls," Jessica suggested.

As she posed Megan and her doll, Jessica decided she'd been right about Jason taking pictures of the child. Megan knew just how to tilt her head and smile for the camera. Jess was just squeezing off the last shot when she heard Florence calling her daughter.

"In my room," Megan called.

In only a moment Florence was up the stairs. "Jessica," she said, breathing hard as though she'd run a long distance. "I didn't realize you were here. I've been working in the garden."

"She's been taking pictures of me and my dolls," Megan whispered.

Jessica suddenly felt like an intruder. "I came to use the darkroom, if that's okay."

"Of course."

"Megan was showing me her dolls." She wondered why the child was suddenly quiet and still. "They're wonderful."

Florence crossed the room to take Helen of Troy from her daughter. "You're not supposed to play with them unless your father or I are here."

"That's my fault," Jess said when she saw Megan's small shoulders slump. "I said she looked like the doll and suggested taking a picture of her with it. I didn't realize that I'd be getting her in trouble."

"She's not in trouble." Florence placed the doll back on the shelf, where the pristine white dress caught the light from the window. "Would you like anything to eat or drink before you use the darkroom?"

"No, thanks. Well, I'd better get busy." Jess picked up her backpack and started toward the door. "I have lots to do." To Megan she said, "Thanks for posing for me. I'll make you a copy of the picture if you'd like."

Megan only nodded shyly in answer to Jess's offer.

The darkroom was, once again, a haven for Jessica. Here she was, locked away from the tensions between Brandon and herself and the odd impression that she was trespassing in the Kendall home. Though the negatives had been developed and were hanging to dry, she was reluctant to go out into the house, and she found herself sitting on the stool leaning against a bank of file cabinets.

She shouldn't snoop, she told herself. But somehow she just couldn't help herself. The opportunity to look at the pictures Jason had filed away was just too tempting. They were in chronological order. The first ones were obviously snapshots taken when he was very young. There were several pictures of a dog, some with a young boy not much older than Megan was now. Was that Brandon? Jess looked more closely. Certain it was indeed Brandon, she wondered how he had gone from this smiling, open child to the man he was today. She found more pictures of Brandon, this time with his parents. Stewart looked very much like his brother; no wonder Brandon bore such a striking resemblance to his uncle.

Determined not to dwell on her enigmatic employer, Jess kept going through the files. There were pictures of a young Jason with a beautiful woman, evidently his mother. Then there were pictures of Brandon and Jason, in baseball and football uniforms, with fishing poles, and even at a prom, looking young and self-conscious and very chummy. Stewart and George appeared, too, but no one that Jessica could identify as Jason's father. Jess was fascinated. She didn't even hesitate before going onto the next drawer.

There were a few college pictures, and then there were Jason's earliest published photos. Photographs of death and despair and horror that had captured the world's attention. The faces of war. She remembered so many of them. Faces of young soldiers cradling their fallen comrades. Faces of children sitting in the dirt beside dead or wounded parents. Pictures of death and destruction and even the noble acts of self-sacrifice. Pictures taken all around the world, wherever man decided that his political or religious beliefs gave him the right to wreak destruction upon others. It was hard for Jess to believe that the kind and gentle man who'd taken her under his wing could have witnessed these horrors. If anyone knew enough about that glorified insanity to tell Megan that war was bad, it was the child's father.

Interspersed with the dramatic photos were scenes of normalcy. Pictures of Jason at home with his mother. Pictures of Brandon and Stewart and George. Finally there were the first pictures of Florence. She'd had the kind of youthful delicacy that must have been enough to stun someone with Jason's appreciation of beauty. Eventually baby pictures of Megan abounded—with her mother, her grandmother, even with George. Mixed in with the usual baby pictures was a photo that stopped Jessica's progress. Megan was obviously young, only weeks old, and Jason sat holding her. He looked too frail to stand with the child, too haggard to be the robust man she called friend, too haunted to be the man the world knew. Next was another snapshot of the baby taken at about the same time, but the photo had been torn to eliminate the person holding her. Jessica could just make out the sleeves of a jacket, but nothing more about the person who'd been ripped from the picture.

She went back to the photo of Jason, drawn to the haunted image. She remembered reading about his captivity, of course. It had been big news. As a famed photojournalist on assignment in war-torn South America, he'd been caught in a bloody battle. She remembered that another journalist had been killed and someone else was wounded badly enough to be helicoptered out.

Jason had been presumed dead, his body supposedly buried in a mass grave. Instead he'd been taken by the guerrilla forces. For months he'd lived in captivity while the world had mourned his death. Then, somehow, he'd managed to escape and make his way to civilization. The news of his survival had been all over the newspapers and television. Once he recovered, he'd turned his camera on the California coastline. Now the man who'd made his reputation recording acts of inhumanity was renowned for capturing images of natural beauty.

Indeed, that was what made up most of the other pictures, along with photos of his family. There were almost as many images of his daughter as there were of the coastline, but there were no more photos of Brandon and few of George or Stewart. Pictures of Jacqueline ceased abruptly when Megan was three. After that there were mostly pictures of Megan, sometimes with her mother but more often alone. And photographs of the California coast. And a sense of being alone. Isolated. Hidden behind the camera. It was an emotion Jessica understood.

By the time she closed the last file drawer, Jessica felt

as though the man who'd taken these photos was not the man she knew. Deciding she would have been better off if she hadn't snooped, she began to concentrate on completing her proof pages. When at last she emerged from the darkroom, her one thought was to escape the Kendall home. But Jason was there, looking every bit the lovable bear of a man she knew, so she took the time to show him her work.

"I knew you'd make me proud," he said after shuffling through the proofs.

"They're okay, then?"

"Better than okay. They're terrific." He took the magnifying glass to study one of the photos she'd taken on her walk over. It was a distant shot of the inn from an unusual angle. "There's someone in this picture using the side entrance. If they're recognizable when the photo is enlarged, you might want to get a release. Otherwise, I'd suggest sticking to pictures without people. Clothing tends to date a photograph."

"I've certainly got plenty of those."

Jason nodded as he thumbed through the proof sheets once more. "You took all of these today?"

Jess laughed. "I took the pictures, but George showed me where to stand."

"That figures. How is George these days?"

"A genuine character. Probably the only poetry-quoting gardener west of the Atlantic." Jessica couldn't help thinking Jason's question was an echo of George's. What was it about men that kept them from just picking up a telephone and chatting once in a while? "He certainly knows all the scenic spots—and the perfect time of day to get there."

"I'm glad that hasn't changed." He handed the proofs back to Jessica. "He gave me my first camera."

"George?"

Jason nodded. "I couldn't have been much older than Megan is now. It was Christmas, and he had identical presents for Brandon and me. The next day he took the two of us out to take pictures. He always spent the day after Christmas with us. Mom loved it. Said it gave her time to recover, but all Brandon and I cared about was that we were going to get outside and do something exciting." He shook his head at the memory. "The camera just seemed to get in Brandon's way, but I can hardly remember going out of the house for months afterward without it in my hands. George knew all the right places then, too. When I look back, I marvel at the amount of time he spent with me that year."

"You were fortunate. He has a unique way of seeing the beauty that's around him."

Jason nodded and walked to the window overlooking the coast. "People think that's easy to do, but it isn't. I spent years taking pictures of death and violence, but it wasn't until I was locked up that I learned to appreciate the beauty that's all around."

When he looked back over his shoulder at her, Jessica thought his eyes had that haunted look she'd seen in the photograph. There was no sense pretending she didn't know what he was talking about. "How long were you held captive?"

"Almost six months." He gazed back out at the ocean. "It seemed like six years."

"I can't imagine. . . ."

"Don't even try to," Jason warned. "I spent years trying to forget."

"But you survived."

"Sometimes I wonder." He shook his head and smiled at her over his shoulder. "It was the first time I noticed the little things. The things that George had always taken time for. I'd be ready to give up, and then I'd see the morning dew on a spiderweb and I'd remember George showing me a spiderweb when I was just a kid.

"And I'd think about everyone back home. About George and my mom and Florence. And I'd decide to hold on just a few more days. Then there'd be another spiderweb or the kind of sunset that could make you weep.

"I didn't know they thought I was dead." He shrugged and looked back at the ocean. "Brandon had gone with me that trip. Said he was tired of being cooped up at the inn—that he wanted to see the world.

"The last thing I remembered seeing was my friend diving for cover. I assumed that if Brandon was alive, he'd tear up the countryside looking for me. If it had been me, I wouldn't have rested until I found his body. I assumed he felt the same.

"It wasn't until I escaped and arrived home that I realized he'd just let it go. He'd even delivered my eulogy." Jason laughed, but there was no joy in it. "And he'd gone back to the inn and picked up the threads of his life while I was rotting in a jungle thousands of miles from here, believing he was looking for me."

Jason straightened away from the window and looked at Jessica. "Ancient history, of course. But it taught me to see the beauty of little things. To appreciate life each day. Be sure to take the credit for your own vision in these pictures. If George had taken me there at your age, I wouldn't have seen it the way you did. I couldn't have captured this the way you have. You have incredible talent. I'm only glad I could help out a little in the beginning of your career."

Jessica looked at the photos in her hands. She was unused to praise and wasn't quite sure what to say.

"Thanks," was all she could manage. "I hope I can live up to your expectations."

"Daddy. Daddy," Megan cried as she came tearing into the room. "You're home."

Jason caught his daughter as she launched herself into the air.

"Jessica's here," she announced after planting a noisy kiss on her father's cheek.

"I noticed."

"Can she stay for dinner?"

"Not tonight, kitten. I thought I'd give Mommy a break and take my women out to dinner."

Megan gave him a stern look. "What are we eating?"

"What do you want?"

"Hamburgers," Megan decided. "With French fries and lots of ketchup."

"I think we can manage that."

"Can Jessica come to dinner tomorrow night?"

Jessica laughed. "That's not necessary."

"Why don't you go ask Mommy," Jason urged.

But instead the child threw her arms around her father's neck and pressed her cheek to his. "Pleeeease, Daddy," she wheedled.

Jessica smiled. It was easy to see that Megan had lots of experience in negotiating with her father, and that her father would give in without too much of a fight.

Jason smiled at Jessica. "Can you make it tomorrow night? . . . Well, that's settled, then," he said when Jessica nodded. He looked at his daughter. "If Mommy can't cook, will you make boiled snails for Jessica?"

Megan only laughed. "You ask Mommy to cook. She'll do it for you."

Jason heaved a great sigh. "I don't stand a chance; I'm always outnumbered two to one."

Jessica couldn't help laughing when Megan gave her father another big kiss.

"Before I leave, I'd like to say hi to Marty."

"You're out of luck. We drove into town separately, and she said she had an errand. I don't expect her until later this evening."

"Tell her I asked about her." Jessica picked up her backpack and slipped into it. "And I'll see you tomorrow for dinner." But before she could turn to leave, Megan squirmed out of her father's arms to give Jess a hug good-bye.

Jess would have preferred a leisurely stroll back to the inn, but it was getting dark even as she left the Kendall home, and George's words about the animals that lived in the underbrush had her hurrying along. By the time she stepped into the lobby, the sun was poised just above the horizon. She was surprised to find Marty there, talking to Brandon. Surprised and disappointed, she wished she'd taken Brandon up on his offer to spend the afternoon with him. Now that he'd seen Marty, the plain Martinson sister would hold no interest for him.

Marty enveloped her in a hug, and Jessica couldn't help comparing her own jeans and sweatshirt to her sister's tailored pantsuit.

"I thought I'd missed you," Marty informed her.

Brandon smiled. "I told her you'd gone to Jason's."

Jessica forced herself to look only at her sister. "And Jason just told me that you had an errand and wouldn't be back until after dinner."

"As it happens, you are my errand," Marty said with a laugh. "I thought I'd drop by and have dinner with my little sister." She glanced at Brandon and back at Jessica. "You don't have plans, do you?"

Jess shook her head. "No."

"Good." She smiled and turned to Brandon. "It was nice to meet you," she said as she extended her hand. "I hope you realize how lucky you are to have Jessica doing the pictures for your publicity."

Brandon took her hand and smiled, but his eyes slid back to Jessica. "Yes, I think I do. It was nice to meet you, too. And please enjoy your dinner on me."

"That's very kind."

"My pleasure. Jessica, if you'll just sign both dinners to your room . . ."

"That's not necessary."

"No, of course not. But I'm trying to make a good impression on your sister." His eyes were still on her, and she felt herself starting to blush. "Ladies, please enjoy your meal," he said as he finally glanced at Marty, then turned to leave.

Marty snaked her arm through Jess's and led her toward the dining room. Jessica resisted the urge to look over her shoulder at Brandon's retreating form and instead kept her eyes focused on Marty.

"How do you do that?" she asked her older sister. "I usually have a terrible time getting rid of him."

"Why would you want to? He's gorgeous. And very interested in you."

"What makes you say that?"

Marty laughed. "Female intuition. Besides, he asked questions about you."

"He's probably regretting giving me the job. Maybe he's looking for a character reference."

"They weren't those kinds of questions."

Jessica ignored the flip-flops in her stomach and asked for a table by the window. They were barely seated before Marty whispered, "He wanted to know if you were involved with anyone at home."

"He asked that?"

"Actually he asked if you'd been terribly inconvenienced by extending your vacation. He wondered if anyone in L.A. would be upset that you were staying longer."

Jessica made a study of her menu. Finally she said, "That's not the same thing."

"You've got to read between the lines." Marty, too, pretended to study her menu. "What's good here?"

"Everything. This place is a dieter's nightmare."

Jessica decided on the fresh salmon Cajun style and set aside her menu. Turning her attention to the lingering sunset, she couldn't help wondering if Marty was right. What if Brandon's interest in her was genuine? Did she dare risk her burgeoning independence?

Marty set her menu on Jess's. "You might be interested to know that under cross-examination he revealed that he's never been married and isn't involved with anyone."

"You didn't!"

"Of course I did. It's my duty as your older sister. Besides, it's my job as an attorney. Don't worry. My questions were clever. I'm good at cross-examination." When Jess rolled her eyes, Marty shrugged. "Okay, maybe I wasn't terribly subtle. But I showed more finesse than he did."

"You had no right. Besides, I've spent the last three days trying to stay away from him."

"I don't think your hard-to-get act will be a deal breaker. It might even have heightened his interest."

After a few thoughtful moments, Marty asked, "Why were you running from him?"

Other than the fact that she'd been running most of her life? Jess wondered. Aloud she said, "I didn't think it would be a good idea to mix business and pleasure.

Besides, Florence said some unflattering things about him."

"I know, but I think she's mistaken."

Jessica pointed a finger at her older sister. "Aha!"

"What do you mean, 'Aha'?"

"Just that. I mean, 'Aha, that's why you're here.'"

Marty had the good grace to look slightly embarrassed. "Florence had me worried that you'd fallen into the clutches of a serial killer or something. But I think she's wrong," she added before Jess could say "Aha!" once more.

"So now that he has your seal of approval, do you suggest I just go up to him and tell him I've changed my mind about dating my employer?"

Marty shook her head. "Something much more subtle."

Jessica gave her sister a hard look. "Well?"

"Don't run so fast. A man that determined is bound to catch up."

The Watcher reveled in the old man's pain. Though Stewart was wandering in the darkened shadows of the inn, the Watcher knew that Stewart's blue eyes—eyes like Brandon's—were dim with the hurt that only the rift between him and his nephew could cause. And the rift had been obvious when they'd argued this afternoon. But the real satisfaction came in knowing that Brandon suffered, too. Mingled with the satisfaction was relief. Relief at knowing the two Roarke men weren't really talking. Weren't sharing the information that might lead to the Watcher's identity.

Of course, there was still the problem with the woman and her camera. If it was true that one picture was worth a thousand words, then the one Jessica had snapped that afternoon might prove invaluable, for it would prove that the Watcher wasn't where everyone had thought.

When the Watcher whispered, "I must have that picture," the small, bright-eyed night animals went on their way undisturbed. Creatures of the dark respect the urge to hunt.

5

The next morning Jessica realized that the time she'd spent with George had been a godsend. Whereas yesterday the sunlight had fought its way through the cloud cover, today the fog still clung tenaciously to the land, even at midmorning.

Jess had hoped to spend these early hours taking pictures of the local beach, a place George hadn't been inclined to go. Now she was ready to admit that if she'd had any sense, she would have stayed indoors instead of trudging around in three layers of clothes—all feeling quite damp by now—trying to take pictures when all she could see were shades of gray. Stopping, she tried to decide if the fog was as thick as it had been an hour before.

"Pea soup is pea soup," she muttered to herself. What did it matter if it was made from fifteen peas or fifty? It was still too thick to photograph through.

Settling onto the crest of a nearby sand dune, she

decided it was time to stop running and admit that the reason she was wandering around in the fog had two legs, dark hair, and gorgeous blue eyes. If she hadn't been so intent on avoiding Brandon, she would probably be snugly indoors, sipping hot tea. Sighing, she picked up a handful of sand and let it slide through her fingers. *Like her life?* she wondered.

Maybe Marty was right; maybe Brandon was interested in her. Maybe it was time to take a leap of faith and believe in herself and all her possibilities. The problem was, she'd been running for too long. She'd made a habit of sitting on the sidelines while others enjoyed life. The only time she'd made an exception had proven to be disastrous. Oh, hell, maybe she should quit "maybe-ing" and admit that she was attracted to Brandon and was scared of getting hurt again.

There. That was infinitely more honest. And cowardly. The same kind of thinking that had kept her working in an office she hated when she should have been pursuing a career in photography. After settling her elbows on her knees, she dropped her chin into her hands and wondered what she should do. Was it smart to break a lifetime habit of keeping people at arm's length on the remote possibility that at thirty-one she might still have a chance at life?

For some reason the image of the little bug she'd photographed not too far from here came back to her. It had kept going around and around on that flower, creating its own rut—just as she'd done in her own life. Well, she'd already taken one leap of faith when she'd grabbed at this photography job. What was the point of leaping once if you didn't have enough faith to leap again? Maybe it was time to leap into life and grab hold with both hands. Maybe it was time to really live.

When she raised her head to look out to sea, she decided that too much introspection wasn't good. She was obviously hallucinating, for the object of her thoughts was running right at her. She had to stop herself from laughing out loud. What had ever made her think she could escape Brandon by wandering around on the beach where she'd first met him? Sometimes, she decided, her subconscious was miles ahead of her conscious mind.

She watched him as he jogged easily along the beach. His sweatshirt was damp, and his skin and hair glistened from exertion, but he seemed utterly relaxed, as though he hadn't a worry in the world. He looked like the boy she'd seen in Jason's old photographs. Youthful. Happy. Uncomplicated. Suddenly it was easy for her to rise and wave to him. She was relieved when he waved back. Relieved to find that she could surprise a smile from him and delighted to feel a similar smile on her own face.

"We're going to have to quit meeting this way," she said when he came to a halt before her.

Brandon shook his head. "I don't care how we meet, as long as we do. What are you doing out here this morning? Surely not thinking of taking pictures in the fog."

"I'd hoped it would clear up."

"Not today. If we're lucky, we'll see a bit of sunshine by midafternoon."

"Maybe it's a good day to do those interior shots, then."

His smile dimmed. "I left a message at the desk for you."

"Yes?"

"I have some appointments this morning and a commitment in town this afternoon. I asked if you'd wait until tomorrow to do those pictures so I could accompany you."

Jessica shrugged, feigning an indifference she didn't

feel. "It's your decision. After all, you're the one paying the bill."

"And if I say yes?"

"Then tomorrow it is."

"Good," he said, and turned to go. He took a few steps, then turned back. "I will be back in time for dinner. I don't suppose you'd consider dining with me?"

"I'd love to," Jessica began. His smile came back. "But I've already made plans."

He took a step toward her. "Break them."

Jessica thought about it. She even found that she wanted to, but then the image of Megan's disappointed face came to mind, and she just couldn't.

She shook her head. "I'm sorry. The Kendalls are expecting me. I promised—" She was about to say she'd promised Megan, but Brandon didn't let her.

"I wouldn't want you to break any promises you made to Jason." He turned as if to go, then turned back just as abruptly. "Tell me, are the rules about consorting with a mentor different from those about your boss? Is it okay to give in to the whims of the man who recommended you for the job—even when he's married—but not acceptable to spend time in the company of your employer? Who, I might add, is not married and seems determined to make a fool of himself over you. I seem to be unclear on the etiquette here. Are there some rules down in L.A. that we don't have up here? . . . Well, are there?"

Though Jess could hardly believe what she was hearing, she held out one hand to stop him. "Don't say anything more foolish than you already have. I'm going to have dinner with all of the Kendalls—and with my sister."

"You had dinner with your sister last night. At my expense, I might add."

She raised one eyebrow. "You can bet that will be changed as soon as I get back to the inn."

"Surely the Kendalls would understand if you told them you were working late."

Jess thought of her promise to Megan. "There is one Kendall who wouldn't."

"Jason always did love a house full of beautiful women. With you and your sister there, he must be as happy as a pasha with a harem."

"I'm not going because of Jason. I'm going because of Megan. She's only a child—and I don't break promises I make to children." With that she picked up her camera case and started back toward the inn.

Brandon made no attempt to stop her, only called out, "We're still on for tomorrow. Be in my office at ten."

After what seemed like thirty minutes of walking, Jessica decided that her sense of direction had thrown her off again. If she'd been headed for the inn, surely she'd be back by now. Instead she found herself lost amid sand dunes and fog, where the slightest rustling of the underbrush brought to mind the sharp-toothed animals George had told her about.

She stopped and listened, thinking she could determine her direction by the sounds of the ocean, but in the heavy air, the waves seemed to be crashing all around her. She'd lost sight of the Pacific several minutes before, and for all she knew she could be walking around in circles. She supposed that she should retrace her footsteps in the sand until she found the ocean, then either keep going the way she was or turn back the other way. As long as she kept the ocean in sight, she'd know she wasn't completely lost. Logic was a wonderful thing, she decided; unfortunately, it couldn't replace of a good sense of direction.

She'd walked only a few more steps when she heard voices. She saw nothing more than the faint outline of the couple when she called to them. The pair was obviously startled, and she thought at first that they were going to turn back into the fog, but when she called out that she was lost, they stopped where they were.

"I can't tell you how glad I am to see you," Jessica called out as she hurried in their direction. "I'm a guest at the Santa Lucia Inn, and I've gotten completely turned around in this fog. Which way . . . why, Danny!" she said when she recognized the young man. "You may not remember me. I was in the garden the other day when you were working with George. I almost tripped over the wheelbarrow," she continued when he didn't acknowledge her greeting.

"I remember."

Jessica decided that his disposition wasn't much improved. She smiled at the blond teenage girl who accompanied him and hoped he treated her with more courtesy than he did others.

"I went out for a walk this morning and can't find my way home. Could you point me back toward the inn?"

Danny pointed in the direction she'd come from. "That way."

It wasn't until he'd stuck out his arm that Jessica realized he was carrying a shovel. Danny, too, had a comical look of surprise when he saw the tool at the end of his arm.

"It's about a ten-minute walk," the girl volunteered. "We'd give you a ride, but we're gathering wildflowers."

She held up a stack of empty burlap sacks. "For my botany class."

Jessica shook her head. "It's nice of you to offer, but I'm sure I can get back now that you've pointed me in the right direction. The inn is too big to miss."

"It sure is," the girl agreed with enthusiasm. Jessica was certain the girl would have continued talking if Danny hadn't grabbed her by the arm.

"We don't have all day," he told the girl. Jessica wondered what a cute, outgoing teenage girl could see in a kid with such a bad attitude. "Let's get this done."

Jessica thanked them for the directions and started back the way she'd come from, thankful to be away from the sullen young man. She couldn't help wondering what it was about the tortured James Dean type that attracted teenage girls. Then she remembered that youth still believed in the redemptive powers of love.

Jason hunkered down in the sand dunes and watched Brandon as he jogged up the beach. The fog was beginning to clear, but it still gave the entire scene a surrealistic feeling. How many times in their youth had the two of them run together along this same stretch of beach? He remembered that summer between their sophomore and junior years when they'd been determined to make the jump to the varsity football team; they'd run this stretch of beach every day. How many times had they collapsed, exhausted, in the sand to discuss the great philosophical issues of their teen years? Life. Death. What they wanted to do when they finished school. How to get girls—especially that cute little cheerleader with the big pom-poms—to give it up in the back of Brandon's new car. If anyone had asked at the time, Jason would have sworn that he and Brandon would be friends till their death. Of course, if anyone had asked, he would also have sworn that either one would give his life for the other. He'd been only half-right.

When Brandon was within a hundred yards, Jason rose and started down toward the water. Down to where he could intercept Brandon. The wary look on Brandon's face when he saw his old buddy made Jason realize just how difficult this was going to be.

Brandon came to a stop when he was still three or four yards away. "Well, isn't this is a coincidence?"

Jason shook his head. "Not really. I wanted to talk to you about the campground." And this seemed like the best way to do it. If Florence or Marty or his attorney knew. . . .Well, any one of them would tell him what a fool he was. But he had to make one last effort. Had to try to talk some sense into Brandon.

"That's a bit of a change, isn't it? I seem to recall a time when I suggested that, and your response was to hire an attorney to do your talking for you. He hasn't resigned, has he?"

"No, he hasn't quit. But our attorneys don't seem to be getting much accomplished. I thought that if we could talk—just the two of us—we might be able to iron things out."

Brandon laughed at that. "What you mean is that your attorney hasn't been very successful. Mine, on the other hand, has accomplished a great deal. He's finalizing the contracts even as we speak. I'm signing them this afternoon. Did you know we're planning a ground-breaking ceremony in thirty days?" He started past Jason. "I'll see that you get an invitation."

Jason grabbed his arm. "I don't want an invitation. I want you to stop that damn campground."

Brandon stared at where the other man's fingers gripped

his arm. Once Jason let go, Brandon looked him in the eye. "I have no intention of stopping it. And it seems you've been unable to."

"You don't need it," Jason reasoned. "You have plenty of money. Why do you want to ruin that particular stretch of beach?"

"How do you figure it will be ruined?"

"Traffic. Cars and campers. Trash. Wherever people go there's trash. And noise. Lots of noise."

"Traffic will be kept to one road, and recreational vehicles won't be allowed. Just people who are willing to hike in and camp out on the beach. Like we did when we were kids."

"Yeah, sure. With their kids and their trash and their noise."

"As opposed to two or three homes like your own? Designed by an internationally known architect with walls of glass so the residents can enjoy the view without stepping out of the house?" Brandon let out a quick bark of a laugh. "Jason, I do believe you've become a snob. You need to spend more time out with the masses."

"Like you do in that big, fancy hotel of yours? I fail to see how operating a resort featured on 'Lifestyles of the Rich and Famous' qualifies you to speak for the masses."

"The nice thing about the inn is that we have all sorts of visitors. Admittedly, they can't all afford to stay the night, but they can browse through our shops for free. And for the price of a cup of coffee they can sit in one of our restaurants and take in the view. You'd be surprised what I've learned by talking to people."

"I'll just bet. Did you do a survey to find out how much they'd fork over to stay the night on a rough piece of beach? Did you figure out how much you could bilk them for and how little they'd expect for their money?"

"You've got a bad attitude, Jason. You've never gotten the hang of dealing with people since you returned from San Bernardino."

"Returned from San Bernardino?" Jason echoed. "You make it sound like I was on vacation instead of rotting in a jungle prison in a South American country where guerrilla warfare is the favorite outdoor sport."

Brandon raked a hand through his hair. "I thought you were dead. How many times have I told you? They said you were buried in a mass grave."

"They who?" Jason practically snarled. "The same guys who gave us the war in the first place? Why would you have believed them?"

"I found your camera." He'd discovered it amid the exposed bodies and the stench of death. Just the thought of it could still make him ill. "I couldn't believe you would go off and leave your camera."

Now it was Jason's turn to laugh. "A camera isn't a helluva lot of protection against men with guns." This time it was Jason who ran a hand through his hair. They'd had this argument before, lots of times. He hadn't meant to get into it again. But it was always the same. The anger. The frustration. The feelings of abandonment. He had never come to grips with Brandon's desertion— or his betrayal. "This isn't what I wanted to talk about," he finally said.

Brandon let out a weary sigh. "It doesn't matter what we talk about. We always end up arguing."

"And whose fault is that?"

"Don't start. I won't be the scapegoat for everything that's gone wrong in your life."

"And I won't stand by and watch you build that damned campground. You're going to parade hundreds of cars right past my door. You're going to destroy my privacy."

"Don't you mean your isolation? There's a difference, you know."

Jessica was still trudging along fifteen minutes after she left Danny and his girlfriend. It seemed she'd been walking forever. She couldn't think of any reason they would have pointed her in the wrong direction, but if she didn't see or hear sounds of life soon, she was going to sit down and wait for the fog to clear. When she heard the voices she took it as a sign that she had rediscovered civilization. When she realized they were raised in anger, she decided that civilization was probably overrated. She could barely make out the two figures in the distance, and she was wondering how wide a berth she should give them. The last thing she wanted was to eavesdrop on someone else's misery. Then she recognized Brandon and Jason.

Jessica stopped. She definitely didn't want to get stuck in the middle of this argument. Edging off to the side, she sought the safety of the deeper sand dunes and wondered if she could slip by them undetected. She'd begun to pick her way through the brush when she realized that being discovered this way would be even worse. Stopping, she dropped down into a sheltered area and decided to wait them out. But now she could hear them more clearly, and what she heard she didn't like.

"I won't let you do it!" Jason shouted. "I won't let you destroy that stretch of beach, and I won't let you destroy my life."

"You don't need any help destroying your life. You're doing a great job all by yourself. But you can't stop me from building the campground. Not you or all your high-priced, snooty attorneys. Hell, I even have my own high-priced lawyers now—though I'll admit none of them are as attractive as the last one you brought in."

Well, Jessica decided, so much for the theory that Brandon hadn't noticed Marty. What could possibly have made her believe Brandon Roarke would be interested in the plain Martinson sister? Between her own self-pity and a set of strong waves, Jess missed part of the conversation. Just as she was wishing that she'd missed all of it, the voices grew more urgent. Even the crashing of the waves couldn't conceal Jason's threat.

"I'll see you in hell before I let you build this campground."

She heard Brandon laugh. "I've been to hell, buddy. You'll have to find something else to threaten me with."

"I'll stop you. You just wait and see."

"I'll be waiting," Brandon promised. Then, even louder, he yelled, "I'll be waiting," so that Jess poked her head above the sand dune to see what was happening.

She was surprised to see Brandon smiling—and alone. In the distance she could just see Jason stalking off into the fog. She watched as Brandon jogged away. She waited a little longer before coming out of her hiding place. All she wanted was the safety of the Santa Lucia and the privacy of her own room.

Tired after walking up and down the beach for the last two hours and still emotionally off balance after witnessing the argument between Brandon and Jason, Jessica decided she'd never been so grateful to see a building in all her life. The sun had just begun to peak through the fog, and the Santa Lucia Inn stood on the hillside, looking for all the world like the fabled city of gold. So much for her decision to grab life with both hands. All she wanted now was to hide out in her room.

Still shaking after her flight through the lobby, she jammed the key in the lock and threw open the door, only to discover that instead of a quiet place to sit and think, her room had become the center of a storm. At least that's what it looked like.

Instead of a neat hotel room with beds made and pillows fluffed, she was faced with the aftermath of a violent assault. The bedcovers were ripped off, and the mattress had been slashed. The pillows had obviously been cut as well, for feathers covered every surface and even floated nearby, where the breeze from the open door had them dancing back and forth like sea anemones on the ocean floor. The closet door hung open, and the drawers were dumped on the floor. Her clothes—her rather unremarkable wardrobe of jeans and sweaters and shirts—were scattered about the room. They, too, had been hacked at so that the sleeve to her blue chambray shirt hung from the top of a nearby lamp while the rest of it lay at her feet.

A quick look in the bathroom revealed that her toiletries had been given the same treatment. A jar of cream lay broken on the floor. Dusting power had been thrown about, and her comb and brush were broken. Her lipsticks had been opened and smeared on the counter—and on the mirror, where someone had left her a message.

"You don't belong here, Jessica. Go home," she read.

This was a mistake, she decided. Some terrible mistake. Why would anyone seek her out and do this to her few possessions? Who could hate her enough to do this?

She crossed to the phone, knowing it had to be reported, knowing Brandon would deal with it competently—only to discover that the phone, too, was covered in something gooey to which feathers were stuck. She picked up a piece of her nightshirt and used it to lift the receiver.

"I need to speak to Brandon Roarke," she said when the operator answered. "It's an emergency," she insisted when she was informed he was unavailable. "Have him paged or send someone to look for him. My room has been ransacked. Room two oh four," she told the woman, then hung up.

She'd barely cradled the receiver when she remembered her photographs. After yanking open the desk drawer where she'd stored them, she found them intact. Relieved, she replaced them in the drawer, then leaned back against the desk with her eyes closed and breathed a prayer of thanks.

That was how he found her, leaning against the desk, eyes closed, skin so pale he was afraid she would pass out.

"Jessica." Her brown eyes flew open and seemed even larger and darker in her pale face. Instinctively he held out his arms, his only thought to hold her close and feel her heart beat. When she flew into his embrace, he held her tighter than he'd meant to. Her arms snaked around his waist and held him close. Brandon just stood there, his cheek resting on her hair, until she stopped shivering.

"What happened?" he asked, still holding her tight.

Jessica pulled out of his embrace just far enough to look up at him. "It was like this when I returned." She cast a look at the room, then quickly burrowed against his shoulder again.

"Why would anyone do this?"

She shook her head. "I don't know."

Brandon heard footsteps in the hallway and turned in time to see his uncle enter the room.

"What the hell happened here?" Stewart demanded.

Brandon gave a quick shake of his head and glanced down at Jessica, who was still nestled against his heart.

"Are you all right, my dear?" Stewart asked. "You weren't hurt?"

Jessica shook her head.

"She found the room like this," Brandon explained. Pulling back so that he could look down at her, he was relieved to see that some of the color was back in her cheeks. "I'm going to take you to my apartment. You can rest there while we sort this mess out and get the room straightened up. Come on, now," he said when she struggled to get out of his arms.

When he realized how determined she was to break free, he released his hold. She went to the desk where he'd first found her.

"My pictures," she explained as she opened the drawer and pressed the stack of photos to her chest. "As far as I can tell, they're the only things that weren't damaged."

"Bring them, if you want," Brandon said. "But I want you out of here while someone deals with this."

"Yes, come on, my dear," Stewart added when she stopped to look around. "You don't want to stay here."

When Stewart offered his arm, Brandon stepped between them. If anyone was going to offer support, he'd be the one to do it. To his surprise, she refused them both and walked out on her own. He glanced at Stewart and caught the question in his uncle's eye; he decided to ignore it for now.

"Maybe it was a mistake," Jessica suggested as she wrapped her hands around the mug of tea room service had delivered. "Maybe whoever did it got the wrong room."

Oddly enough, it wasn't the actual destruction of her

property that bothered her as much as the idea that someone could hate her that much. Even Eric's cruelty had really been aimed at Marty. Jess couldn't recall anyone ever hating her before. She'd always been too nondescript to attract any kind of strong emotion—let alone that kind of violent hatred.

"Your name was on the mirror," Brandon said quietly. The expression on his face hadn't changed since he'd returned from a careful search of Jessica's room. Or perhaps it would be more accurate to say there wasn't any expression. There was no anger or surprise, only a coldness that reminded Jessica of a face carved in marble. Considering his first reaction, the way he'd gathered her to his warmth and buoyed her with his strength, this coldness was even more frightening.

Jessica pulled her legs up under her and settled even farther back into the couch, but she found no warmth there. What she needed was Brandon's arms around her, but she didn't know how to tell him.

"We'll see what the police say when they arrive," Stewart suggested from where he stood beside the window.

"They won't be coming," Brandon said evenly.

"And why the hell not?"

"Because I didn't call them. Think of the publicity," he said before his uncle could speak. "Think of the mass exodus we could have on our hands if people thought they weren't safe."

"And what if they aren't?"

"I called security. They'll be sending over extra personnel tonight. We'll have the place covered."

Stewart shook his head. "I don't see how we can guard against one person in a place this big."

"Jessica's name was on the mirror," was all Brandon said. But the implication was clear enough. He didn't expect the intruder to be after anyone else. Jess couldn't suppress a little whimper of fear. Why would anyone wish to harm her?

"We'll replace everything that was destroyed," Stewart assured her. "Just go down to the shops and pick out anything you need. Tell them to bill the hotel."

Jessica looked up at the older man. "I couldn't do that."

"Of course you can, my dear. After all, we take full responsibility for the damage."

"You'll move into my apartment," Brandon informed her when she would have argued with Stewart over the prices in the hotel shops compared with the cost of her simple wardrobe. "I have an alarm system that can be activated on my private apartment and video cameras in the hallway outside the door."

"And a separate bedroom with a lock on the door?"

He smiled at that. "Of course. Though there isn't a lock at the inn that I don't have the key to."

"Then I'll have to ask for your word of honor."

"About what?"

Jessica hesitated. What exactly did she want? "That you won't enter uninvited."

Brandon nodded. "You've got my word."

Jess let out a breath she hadn't realized she was holding. "Okay." She was surprised by the relief she felt. She simply didn't want to be alone. "Now let me see if I can salvage anything from my room."

"No."

Startled by Brandon's emphatic reaction, she looked over at him, and in his eyes she saw the truth. There was nothing to be salvaged. Someone had ruined all that she'd brought with her. And he wanted to protect her from the violence of the act.

But he couldn't, and she knew that something more precious than her belongings had been destroyed: her belief that because she was incapable of hate, no one would hate her. The loss of it had her closing her eyes against the tears. She didn't open them again until she heard Brandon on the phone. She listened as he issued orders.

"That's correct," he said. "Everything a lady needs for overnight from a toothbrush to a nightgown. And add whatever creams and potions you think necessary. Maybe some pants and a sweater. No, just one outfit. She'll pick out some more tomorrow when she's feeling better." He listened, then turned to study her. "About a size eight?" he asked her. When she nodded, he added, "And lingerie. She'll need that. Send it up to my apartment when you have everything. Thanks. And be sure to call me when the security supervisor arrives. I want to go over some things with him."

Jessica squeezed her eyes shut when he hung up the phone. "Maybe I should just go home."

She felt the couch dip when he sat on it. Felt the warmth of his hands as he took hers. "Don't leave," he said, and she opened her eyes to gaze into his.

"I don't want you to take any unnecessary risks with her safety." Stewart's voice startled Jess. She'd forgotten the older man was there.

"I'll keep you safe," Brandon promised, never taking his eyes from Jessica. "Give me a chance."

And because he seemed to be asking for more than a chance to guarantee her safety—or because she hoped he was offering more than a chance to complete her first professional work—she nodded. "If I'm staying, I guess I'd better check out the accommodations."

Brandon pointed to a door beside the wet bar as she

rose. "I'm going to have to ask for your word of honor," he said, stopping her in her tracks.

Jess turned to face him. "About what?"

"That you won't wait for an invitation to come into my room if you feel the need."

Jess smiled and turned back to her room. "Don't get your hopes up, Mr. Roarke. My mother taught me better manners than that."

She heard Brandon swear and Stewart chuckle as she closed the door behind her.

The Watcher sat in the afternoon sun, leaning back against the warmth of the rock. No one passing by would guess that the unmoving body studied the Santa Lucia Inn through half-closed eyes. Studied the movement of employees in and out the side door as they carried away boxes filled with ruined clothes and a mattress covered in sheeting so that none of the guests would see the angry slashes. The Watcher was confident that with all the wanton destruction, Jessica wouldn't notice that one strip of negatives had been taken.

The Watcher smiled, knowing that inside, Brandon would be planning ways to keep the woman safe. Ways that would have no effect, for the Watcher hadn't intended to hurt the woman—at least not yet. Only to frighten her. And to make sure that Brandon's attraction to her was so strong, he wouldn't let her go.

If the Watcher knew anything, it was that Brandon had a weakness for a woman who needed protection. And right now Jessica Martinson was in need of more protection than even Brandon could imagine.

The Watcher fought the exhilaration that built up inside. Fought to keep from rubbing hands together over the knowledge that Jessica's fate had been sealed. But the laughter spilled forth anyway, scaring a squirrel that had been snuffling the ground nearby and drawing the blue-eyed child's attention from the school of dolphins that leaped like molten silver just offshore.

6

Brandon eased onto the chair opposite his uncle's desk. Though Stewart hadn't actually asked him to come down to the office where they could talk in privacy, he hadn't needed to. Brandon had known from the look on his uncle's face that there would be no escaping this meeting.

"How is Jessica?" the older man asked once Brandon had settled in.

"She has a headache. Who can blame her? She said she wanted to rest."

"And then what?"

Brandon shrugged. "I'll see if she can make a list of everything that was destroyed. That way we can be certain to replace it or pay her for it."

"That's not what I meant." Stewart's look bespoke annoyance and reproach. "Why did it happen? And how can we be sure that it won't happen again?"

"It's all my fault." Brandon could give his uncle that much of the truth, at least. Unsure of what else to say, he shoved himself out of the chair and began to pace the small office. "The intruder is trying to get at me through Jessica. I don't know what else might happen. What kind of danger she could be in."

"Who is it?"

Brandon stopped pacing. "I have my suspicions, but I'm not absolutely certain."

"And you can't—or won't—share those suspicions with me?"

Brandon shook his head. How could he tell Stewart that he was safer if he didn't know? That Stewart had been safe these last three years because of his ignorance? Knowledge had taken one life; Brandon wouldn't let it claim another.

"And yet you asked Jessica to stay?"

"What can I say? I have a weakness for beautiful women."

"Bran."

Just one word, Brandon mused. Just one. Yet in it were myriad emotions. Impatience. Confusion. Love. And Brandon was very much afraid that once his uncle knew the truth, the love would be overshadowed with disappointment.

"I have a weakness for Jessica," he admitted.

"That's been apparent for some time."

Brandon couldn't help the quick grin his uncle's comment brought. "To everyone but Jess. Half the time she looks likes she wants to run away, the other half like she doesn't believe anything I say." At least she'd taken his word that he wouldn't enter her room—until she invited him, of course. He slipped back onto the chair. "If she goes home now, that will be the end." He didn't know how or why, but he was as sure of that as he was that the sun would set over the Pacific tonight.

"Would that be so awful?"

"About the worst thing I can imagine. And yet . . . ."

"Yes?" Stewart prompted after a moment.

"What if I can't keep her safe? What if the intruder isn't content to destroy Jessica's things next time? What if Jess becomes the target?"

Jessica slowly opened her eyes and glanced at the clock at the side of her bed. The darkened room made her think it was much later than four o'clock; then she remembered that Brandon had closed the drapes before he'd left. He'd also showed her how to activate the alarm and how to work the locks. Then he'd told her to sleep. She'd doubted that she would be able to lie still, much less go to sleep. Perhaps it had been the headache medication that had done it. Or maybe her nerves had been so frazzled that she'd just short-circuited. Whatever the reason, she'd slept. She felt better now, though she still couldn't shake off the question of why anyone would hate her enough to trash her room and destroy her things. She counted herself lucky they hadn't discovered her photographs. Her clothes she could replace, but it could have taken her days or weeks to get those shots again.

She sat up and glanced over to where the proof sheets and negatives lay on top of the chest of drawers. She wasn't so worried about the actual photographs; she could make more of those. But the negatives were another thing. She'd meant to ask Brandon to put them somewhere secure, maybe in a locked office or a safe. Anywhere rather than just lying around so that they could be lost or destroyed. Because she wouldn't rest again until it was done, she threw back the covers and got out of bed.

Standing before the bathroom mirror, she had to admit

that the face looking back at her was not an especially pretty sight; there was nothing particularly attractive about oversize brown eyes in an ashen face. Grateful that the cold water put some color back in her cheeks, she searched through the bag of emergency supplies that Brandon had arranged for. She tried to tame her unruly hair with the comb she found, then decided not to bother with the assortment of cosmetics someone had thrown into the bag. Mascara wasn't as important as getting the negatives put away safely.

She felt guilty as she searched through Brandon's desk, but once she found an empty envelope she labeled it with the type of pictures and the dates. Leaving the negatives in their clear plastic sleeves, she slipped them into the envelope. Finally she deactivated the alarm system and stepped out into the hallway. Conscious of the security cameras mounted near the ceiling, she gave a nervous smile toward the lens, then headed for the office. If neither Brandon nor Stewart was there, surely someone would be able to help her.

Nancy was working the desk, as she had been that first morning. "How are you?" she asked. Before Jessica could answer, she whispered, "Everyone was very upset about what happened. I can assure you that security has been beefed up. You don't need to worry about it happening again."

Jess couldn't quite manage a smile. "I'm not worried." *Much*, she thought. "But I have some things I'd like to put in a safety deposit box, if you have one available."

"I'm sure Mr. Roarke will put it in the safe for you," she said. "He's in the office with his uncle." Just as Nancy reached for the intercom, the phone rang. And while she was handling the phone call, one of the desk clerks came over with a question.

Nancy rolled her eyes. Placing her hand over the mouthpiece, she motioned with her head toward the offices. "Why don't you go on back? I know Mr. Roarke won't mind."

Jessica smiled and stepped into the hallway. But right away she knew that Nancy was wrong. Brandon would certainly mind that she was there.

"What do you mean, 'next time'?" Stewart demanded. "And why would anyone want to hurt Jessica?"

"It's a long story—and not a particularly pretty one." When his uncle said nothing, Brandon leaned forward and put his elbows on his knees. "Part of it you know already."

"It has to do with Jason, then? About the time he was captured in San Bernardino?"

"Yeah." Brandon nodded. "But it has more to do with me. About how I failed him. About how I betrayed him."

"Bran, you weren't responsible for the civil war or for Jason's capture. How could you have pre—"

"I know that. But I'm responsible for what happened later. No," he said when his uncle tried to interrupt. "You don't know the whole story." Despite the fact that he'd intended to stay seated and calm, Brandon rose to pace the room. "I'm not a particularly religious man, but I can truly say that I have . . . sinned. Sinned against God and society and a man I love like a brother."

"Oh, Bran."

He looked over at his uncle to see confusion and pain. And love. There was still love there. He held fast to that. "I can't tell you any more because there are innocents who would be hurt. And I've caused enough pain. I can only tell you that I was prepared to make atonement for what I'd done. Resigned to the fact that I could never have the normal sort of life that most people take for granted. No wife and kids. No way for more innocents to be caught up in the retribution that I knew I deserved.

"And then I saw her." He looked at his uncle and struggled to explain it, but all he could say was, "I just saw her out on the beach taking a picture of this little bug. And when she looked up at me, I was stunned. I thought, here is my miracle. It was like a glimpse of heaven. She was so . . . real. Honest. You could see it in her eyes. And I forgot about the price of atonement. Forgot that there was this darkness in me. That I'd been touched by evil. All I could think about was Jessica. I wanted her. I pursued her." He paused and ran a hand through his hair. "And look what happened. I've put her in danger."

"Bran, did you trash Jessica's room?"

"God, no!"

"Then you're not responsible," Stewart said in his calm, rational voice.

But then Stewart didn't know what Brandon had done. He hadn't seen the evil. Hadn't stood and looked into the eyes of the devil. Stewart could still be calm and rational.

Jess stopped, frozen in the hallway outside the office where Brandon and Stewart talked abut sin and atonement and evil. Such melodramatic words. Normally she would have scoffed at them. She would have said they were the stuff of Greek tragedies and Bible-thumping preachers. But when Brandon said them, they sounded real. Like reaching out to pet the family cat, only to find yourself confronted by razor-sharp teeth and the glow of hunger in a carnivore's eyes.

But she wasn't going to look into those eyes. Wasn't

going to stand here and wait for one of them to spot her. She turned and walked quickly back to the reception area. Without pausing to return Nancy's wave, she bolted out the front door. On a run, she started across the lawn toward the English garden. Then, when she saw that George and Danny were there, she changed course and headed for the beach. Maybe her own problems would seem ridiculously small when confronted by the power and majesty of the Pacific Ocean.

Stewart looked at his nephew. "She won't be here forever. In another day or two her work will be finished."

Brandon nodded his head wearily. "I know."

"Then what?" When Brandon only shrugged his shoulders, Stewart continued. "I've been mulling over an idea—one that could easily keep her here a little longer. We're coming up on the Santa Lucia's fiftieth anniversary. I think we should do a picture book. A coffee table sort of thing, using old photographs and new ones. We could keep Jessica busy for months."

"It might work." Might? God, it had to. "That is, if I can convince her to take the job."

"How will you do that?"

Brandon brushed his hands over his weary eyes. "I'll fight heaven and hell to keep her from leaving." And in doing so, he would prove himself to be the most selfish bastard of all. Another sin. Another darkness within him. The endangerment of another innocent. He looked into his uncle's eyes. "It might be kinder to let her leave."

"You and Jason need to talk," Stewart finally said.

Brandon's laughter held only sadness. "We tried that earlier today. We only ended up yelling at each other." Besides, it would take more than talk to keep Jess safe.

"Maybe if—" The sharp jangle of the phone interrupted Stewart.

"Hello." Stewart extended the receiver toward Brandon. "It's for you. Security."

"What is it?" Brandon asked without preamble.

Stewart watched as the color drained from Brandon's face. "What's wrong?" the older man asked as soon as his nephew hung up the phone.

"It's Jess. She's left my apartment, and security doesn't know where she is."

"Is that bad?"

"If she runs into the wrong person, it could be. Security is sending some men out to look for her. I'm going, too."

"Count me in."

Brandon shook his head. "She's probably just out for a walk to clear her head. But if she shows up, I need you to keep her here. Also, it gives us someone to check in with."

"It makes me feel old and useless."

"If she shows up and you can keep her here, it will be the most useful thing anyone can do."

"Okay. But you let me know the minute you find her."

Brandon nodded, then stepped into the hallway and closed the door behind him. He took a moment to take a deep breath and run a hand through his hair, then squared his shoulders. It wouldn't do to let anyone know just how terrified he was. She was probably out in the garden visiting with George, he reasoned. Or in the shops looking for clothes.

He'd almost convinced himself that everything was all right when he saw the envelope on the hallway floor. He picked it up, looked at the writing, and held the negatives up to the artificial light. They were Jessica's, and they hadn't been there when he'd come in earlier.

That meant she'd been within earshot when he was talking to Stewart. How much had she heard? he wondered. What was she thinking? And more important, where had she gone? He pushed through the door, grateful to find Nancy on duty. She would know when Jessica had been there. She might even know which way she'd gone.

Stewart paced the office one more time and stared at the phone. It had been over an hour since security had informed them that Jessica was missing. More than fifteen minutes since Brandon had last checked in. He couldn't sit and wait any longer. He had to do the one thing Brandon hadn't tried. He picked up the phone and called the Kendall house.

"Is Jess there?" he asked when the phone was answered. "You're sure?" he persisted. "I'm coming over," Stewart said before the other person could hang up. "Now. We need to talk."

Stewart hadn't realized how late it was. He'd thought the walk over would give him time to sort things out. Picking his way along the cliff path in the twilight, he cursed himself as a fool for not driving. At least he had taken the time to put on his yellow jacket. He decided he would call the Santa Lucia to send a car for the return trip.

He hoped Jessica wasn't out in this gloom. Hoped she'd returned to her room or the office. He had asked Nancy to keep an eye out for Jess. Nancy was a sensible, dependable young woman. If Jessica showed up, Nancy would handle the situation in her usual efficient manner.

Stewart hesitated. Just ahead something moved back among the brush. No, not something. Someone.

* * *

The Watcher stood back among the shrubs and brush, studying Stewart Roarke as he picked his way along the path. The old fool just might fall over the cliff himself, saving the Watcher a bullet and the trouble of eliminating him. Such a shame that the old meddler had decided to start asking questions, but then he'd always been an unknown factor.

The Watcher felt the weight of the gun in the coat pocket. Wrapping steady fingers around the cold handle of the revolver, the Watcher felt the power. The finality. Though the old man had remained blessedly ignorant for the last three years, it was evident that could no longer be counted on. He was starting to think. And if Stewart started putting two and two together, there was a good chance he'd come up with four. So, knowing there was no other choice, the Watcher stepped out onto the path.

Stewart looked up and smiled. "Well, hello. I was just on my way to your house."

The fool was still smiling when the first bullet caught him in the chest.

7

Jessica watched as the sun touched the horizon and turned the water to molten gold. Like the Little Mermaid in Copenhagen's harbor, she watched the world from atop a rock set at the ocean's edge. When she'd first clambered up onto the large outcropping, the sun had lingered well above the horizon and the world had still been blue as far as she could see—blue ocean and blue sky, with only the whirl of an occasional seabird. And while the world had changed from blue to gold, her thoughts had simply whirled around until she could no longer be certain of what she actually believed and what she simply wished.

Though she was still certain that she'd heard Brandon call her a miracle. His miracle. And he'd said she stunned him. Stunned him? Her? She'd rarely been able to get a man's attention, let alone stun one. And a man like Brandon . . . no, that was unbelievable.

Yet she'd heard him say it to Stewart—along with other things like sin and retribution and atonement, such serious words. Maybe Brandon was given to flights of fancy. Maybe the sophisticated, cynical man-about-town was just a cover. Yeah, and maybe snails could fly.

Truth was that she was doing it again: running away. The answers would be found only by confronting Brandon, not by sitting out here on this rock. She took a moment to study the Santa Lucia Inn. That was where she would find the truth, and it was high time she went back for it. Jess stood up, brushed the sand from her pants, and took one final look at the golden world before her.

Fool's gold, she thought. Only the illusion, for it would fade in the next few moments as the sun dipped farther beyond the horizon. If she was lucky, the real gold lay back at the Santa Lucia. In a golden opportunity at life and love. If she was brave enough to try it.

But when she turned to make her way off the rock, she realized that her decisiveness might have come too late. For the rock that had set at the water's edge was now transformed into an island by the incoming tide. It took only a few seconds to realize that if she climbed down the same way she'd climbed up, she would end up in the waist-high water that swirled and slithered around the base of the rock like a hungry animal scenting food. And she was afraid the ocean was as likely to devour her as it was to toss her upon the sand.

In her frantic search for another route down the face of the rock, she discovered that it was not quite surrounded. For when the waves receded, a small sandy path opened up at the very back of the massive rock, beckoning Jessica to the shore. Even in the dim light, she could see it was a sheer drop. The only way down was to jump from the rock to the sand—probably eight or nine feet below—and hope she didn't break her neck.

She took a few more moments, hoping to find another way, then cursed her cowardice when she looked back. The sky had turned from gold to lead, and in the darkening light the sandy path was now hidden just beneath the cold, gray water. She was truly cut off, and the only way back was to jump from the rock into the surf, then wade through the water.

She took a deep breath and jumped as far as she could. She landed in water that was already surging around her feet, dragging her back toward the ocean. She fell to her knees and gasped as the cold water hit her in the face. It took her breath away, then had her scrambling forward on all fours, grateful to feel the rough sand and rocks beneath her hands. Grateful to have escaped the sea's icy grasp.

She might be cold and wet, but the sand was solid beneath her feet, and the Santa Lucia was only a short walk away. She brushed the sand from her hands and turned toward the inn, only to realize that the sandy beach, which had wound easily between the ocean and the rock, was already submerged. In order to get to the steps that led up the steep cliff, she was going to have to fight her way through the encroaching surf or climb over the rough rocks.

Already shaking from the cold water nipping at her feet, Jess chose the rocks and hauled herself up on the nearest one. Carefully she picked her way over the jagged terrain, knowing that one misstep could leave her lying injured and helpless, waiting for the tide to come in and sweep her out to sea. Even now the sea was reaching for her, forcing her away from the straightest route, herding her back toward the cliff in an effort to stay away from the cold spray and slippery footing.

If she hadn't stopped to catch her breath—to gauge

whether she would make the steps before the waves cut her off—she might not have seen it. At first it seemed nothing more than a bright spot against the dark cliffs. A splash of yellow almost swallowed up in the waning light. Even then she might have passed it by if the salt spray hadn't caught her, hadn't sent her shivering back even closer to the cliff.

A piece of trash, she decided. Something picked up and carried by the wind. But as she drew closer, she decided it was larger than she'd thought. Maybe a bright piece of clothing or a picnic blanket. Then she realized that the brightness was only part of the object. A darker part was draped over the rocks as well. And as she drew closer, the object took on a recognizable shape. Oh, God, she thought. Someone else caught by the encroaching tide. Someone else trying to make his way back across the rocks. Someone unlucky enough to fall.

"Hello," she called, hoping to get some response. No longer picking and choosing her footholds, she made her way toward the figure. "Are you all right? Can you answer me?"

And then the figure took on even more recognizable characteristics. The long, athletic body. The bright yellow windbreaker with the Santa Lucia logo. The gray hair.

"Stewart," she cried. "Stewart, are you all right? Stewart, it's me, Jessica." She crawled over the last few rocks to grasp his face in her cold hands. "Where are you hurt, Stewart? . . . Please, answer me."

But there was no answer. No smile at seeing her. No recognition in his eyes. Only the unwavering stare of the dead. Only the lifeless form of a man she'd called a friend. She laid his head down gently, as though it mattered, then pulled her hands away. Her fingers were dark and sticky, and she found herself grateful that the salty tang of the sea overpowered the smell of death. She heard a whimper over the surging power of the ocean and recognized the voice as her own.

Then she forced herself to look, really look, and she wondered how she could have missed it before. Stewart lay among the rocks like a doll that has been tossed aside, his arms and legs at awkward angles, his head at an improbable tilt. She looked directly up at the cliff and realized that he must have fallen from there.

She looked back down at where her useless hands were clenched together. There was blood. My God, there was blood on her hands. She couldn't decide what she should do. She glanced back at the ocean as it inched its way toward them. She gauged the distance to the steps. She doubted that she could lift Stewart, and even if she could, there was no way she could drag him over the rocks to the staircase. But surely she couldn't leave him to the mercy of the ocean. She would have to go for help if there was any chance at all of saving Stewart's body from being washed out to sea.

Without a final glance at his body, Jessica made her way over the rocks. Sometimes on her feet, sometimes on all fours, she fought and clawed her way toward the steps. She felt the first few cuts on her hands, then they became numb. She heard her pants rip, felt the abrasions on her knees; she pressed on. The incessant wind whipped at her clothes and stung her cheeks; she ignored it. At the foot of the steps, she didn't pause to catch her breath but started up at breakneck speed. She felt her breath catch in her throat, thought that she would not be able to fill her lungs one more time, then shuddered as the next breath ripped through her chest.

Heedless of the splinters from the railing, she used her already battered hands to pull her up one more step and then another until, aeons later, she fell to her knees at the top of the staircase. Only the knowledge that the ocean was eating up the shore, that the waves never faltered, had her struggling to stand. She pushed the damp, clinging curls from her face and used the back of her hand to brush away the useless tears, then hauled herself to her feet. Struggling for each breath, she concentrated on putting one foot in front of the other. She'd actually managed a few steps when she heard her name. She shook her head, certain that it was only the wind, then before she could force herself to take another step, she heard it again. She looked up to see Brandon racing across the lawn.

"Jessica," he shouted. "Jessica!"

The relief was overwhelming. To know that Brandon was there, that he would know what to do, made her weak. She wanted to run toward him, to throw herself into his arms, but her feet simply wouldn't move. He caught her just as her knees buckled. One moment the earth was rushing toward her, and the next she was held tight in his arms.

"Where have you been?" he demanded. "I've looked all over for you." He held her out at arm's length, took one look at her, and hauled her back into his arms. "What happened to you? I've been so worried." His embrace tightened as he brushed his lips against her hair. "Don't ever scare me like that again."

The relief in his voice made her want to weep. She couldn't let him go on when she knew that Stewart's body lay lifeless on the beach below. Steeling herself, she put her hands on Brandon's chest and pushed away from him. But instead of the brave words she intended to use, a whimper of pain was all she could manage.

"My God, what happened to your hands?" he asked.

Gently grasping her wrists, he turned her arms so that her palms were face up. "Your hands," he murmured.

She tried to pull them away. "It's nothing."

"Nothing? There's blood. I've never seen so much blood."

"It's not mine."

He released her hands and put an arm around her shoulders. "I'm taking you to the hospital."

"No."

"Can you walk? I'll carry you if I need to."

"Stop it." She stepped back when he bent to scoop her up in his arms. "I'm not going to the hospital."

"The hell you aren't. Your hands—"

"Forget my hands," she cried as she used them to grab the collar of his jacket. "We've got to help Stewart."

He went completely still. "Stewart?"

She closed her eyes and fought the sob she felt welling up inside her. "He's down on the beach."

"What the— Is he hurt?"

She just stood there looking at him, unable to speak.

"Is he *hurt?*"

She closed her eyes and leaned her forehead against his chest. "Dead," she whispered.

His hands were fierce as they gripped her shoulders and held her away from him. "What?"

She opened her eyes and stared straight into his. "He's dead." She watched his eyes go from fierce to flat.

"Not Stewart," he murmured.

Jess nodded. "He's down on the rocks. He must have fallen from the cliff. We've got to hurry if we're going to get him before the tide does."

Brandon released her and started for the stairs. "I told him to stay in his office." He looked over his shoulder to where Jessica trailed behind him. "He would have been safe if he'd stayed there. I should have told him. Oh, God, if only . . ." He fell silent with a deep, shuddering sigh and stared out to sea.

Jessica stepped in front of him. She held out her hands as if to cup his face, then saw the blood on them. She dropped them to her sides again. "We have to hurry," she said when he only stood there.

"Why?"

"The tide—"

"I'll get to him before the tide does." Gently he reached out and pulled Jessica into his embrace. "Poor Jess," he whispered. "What have I done to you?" Then he laid his cheek against her hair and just held her, as if by doing so he could draw strength for the ordeal ahead.

"Brandon—"

"Shhh. Just give me a minute."

She snuggled against his chest, content to hear the steady rhythm of his heart until he set her gently away.

"Go back and ask the desk to page George. Tell George to get a stretcher and another man and meet me here." Jess nodded and would have turned to do just that, but he held her firmly by the shoulders. "And a blanket. Have George bring a blanket. Let's at least let Stewart keep his dignity."

Then he released her and turned toward the staircase. Jess watched as he began his descent. She watched as his feet and his body and at last his head dropped out of sight, then she turned and ran toward the inn as if the hounds of hell were on her heels.

Brandon found Stewart's body at the foot of the cliff where the murderer had tossed the other body—found it lying broken and discarded as though it were no more important than the other debris that floated in and out on the tide.

He wanted to cry out that it wasn't fair, that Stewart shouldn't be the one to pay for his sins, but he knew that his cries would be lost in the pounding of the surf and that his tears would be worthless unless he could make the murderer pay.

Hunkering down beside the body, Brandon picked up his uncle's cold hand and clasped it in his and made a vow. A solemn promise to the man who raised him that the murderer would not be allowed to kill again. That there would be an end to hatred and killing—and, if he was very lucky, the beginning of love.

Then, with the salt spray at his back, he picked up the broken body and started toward the staircase. And above the crashing of the waves, he thought he heard laughter— the wild, crazy laughter that lingered in his memory and haunted his dreams.

Jessica was the first one to reach the head of the stairs. The fog was drifting in, but she could still make out Brandon in the pale moonlight. He was sitting on the bench of the lowest landing, cradling Stewart in his arms. The tears she'd fought against came streaming down her cheeks, so that instead of going to Brandon and offering him her strength, she was backing away from the scene to sit on a nearby bench and weep into her own hands.

"There now, miss." George's gnarled hand was gentle on her shoulders. "Cryin' isn't goin' to help Mr. Brandon now. He needs our strength."

Jessica used her sleeves to wipe away the tears. "I know. I just needed a minute."

"Seems like you're entitled. You've had a shock yourself."

Jessica looked over George's shoulder to where another man stood. "Are you going down to get Stewart?"

"As soon as you're ready."

Jessica stood. "I'm fine." She wiped away the last of her tears. "Really."

"Then we'll be bringin' Stewart up. You'll wait here?"

"At the top of the stairs."

George hesitated. "You won't be leavin'?"

"I'll be here as long as Brandon needs me," she assured the gardener. "I won't desert him, if that's what you mean."

George nodded. "I thought you'd be the stayin' kind."

Moving toward the stairs, George motioned for the other man to fall in behind him. Jessica stood and watched as the men relieved Brandon of his burden. She watched as they made their way up the long flight of stairs, staggering under the awkwardness of the stretcher and the dead man's weight. When they started across the grass, she fell in beside Brandon.

Grief was emanating from him in waves. She would have been afraid to intrude if he hadn't pulled her to his side, if he hadn't seemed to need her pressed against him with her arm around his waist. Together they followed the stretcher and its gruesome burden to a small door set away from the bustle of guests.

Releasing his hold on Jessica, Brandon went ahead to unlock the door. He led the way down a hall and then unlocked another door. When Jessica followed them in, she realized it was a storage room. Lamps sat on shelves. Plastic-covered chairs lined the wall. Discarded patio furniture was shoved into one corner. Jess shivered and hoped it was from the damp.

George and his helper placed the stretcher in the middle of the floor, then stood back. When Brandon knelt beside his uncle and grasped the blanket, Jess started to reach out. She wanted to spare him if she could, but George placed a gentle hand on her arm and gave an almost imperceptible shake of his head, so that Jessica's protest died on her lips.

Brandon pulled the cover back just enough to see his uncle's face, and Jessica had to close her eyes against the sight. Where before she'd seen Stewart only in the twilight, now the harsh electric light showed the scrapes and bruises on his cheek, the blood clotted in his hair and splattered on his clothing. Jess opened her eyes to find Brandon gently brushing Stewart's gray hair back from his forehead. The gesture was so loving that she couldn't stop the tears. She was wiping them away with the sleeve of her sweater when Brandon dropped the blanket over his uncle and turned back to the living.

For the first time she noticed the blood on Brandon's shirt and pants. Stewart's blood. Seeing the way it was smeared over his clothes, Jessica realized how he had struggled to carry his uncle's body from the beach to the stairs.

"George, I want you two men to guard the door. Grab a couple of chairs to sit on in the hallway. Don't tell anyone what has happened and don't let anyone in here unless I'm with them."

Once the door was locked and the men were settled in the hall, Brandon again gathered Jessica to his side. She stepped willingly into his embrace.

"We'll phone the police from my apartment," he told her. To the men he said, "That's where I can be reached if there are any problems." He'd taken a couple steps before he turned back to George. "Would you like me to send someone to relieve you?"

George shook his head. "He was my friend, faithful and just to me. Why would I leave him now?"

Brandon nodded and turned to go, only to be stopped by the old man's raspy voice. "Just promise me one thing," George said.

Brandon looked over his shoulder. "Name it."

"That along with the grief, there will be remembrance—and atonement."

"I promise," Brandon said.

Jessica couldn't help thinking it sounded more like a threat than a promise.

"The police will be here soon. How are your hands?"

Jessica looked up from the sink where she was washing her hands to see Brandon at the bathroom door. "Much better," she assured him.

The water had stopped running red, and now that Stewart's blood was gone, she could see that her hands weren't as bad as she first feared. There were dozens of cuts and abrasions and splinters, but nothing that would require stitches or a trip to the hospital.

"Let's see about getting some antiseptic on them, then," Brandon said as he stepped up to the medicine cabinet. Then he stopped as he saw, for the first time, how he was covered in blood. His eyes swept down his shirtfront, taking in the blood not only on his clothes, but also on his arms and neck and even on his cheek. In one fierce motion his swept the polo shirt up and off to toss it in the trash. Then he plunged his own hands in the water.

Blotting her tender hands on a towel, Jessica watched as Brandon scrubbed at his hands and arms, then bent over so that he could dash water on his face and neck. When he stood up again, all traces of blood had been washed from his body, but his bleak expression told her that the shock was starting to wear off and reality was setting in. As she watched, he just stood there with the water dripping from his dark hair down his face and onto his chest to glisten in the swirl of hair there. Finally she raised her towel to his cheek. Gently she blotted the water from his face and hair. With the fingers of her other hand, she brushed the damp hair back from his brow. When she took the towel in both hands and would have dried the water from his chest, he caught her wrists.

"Don't." He closed his eyes but didn't release her. She just stood there, watching, as he fought his own grief and anger. She wanted to put her arms around him and hold him, but she was afraid he would push her away. So she stood there with his fingers around her wrists and waited for him to fight the battle that waged within him. But the battle was long and fierce, and it was reflected in his grip, so much so that his fingers bit into her soft skin until she could no longer fight a whimper of pain. He released her then. Released her and stepped away from her.

"I'm sorry." He looked at the angry marks his fingers had left. "I didn't mean to hurt you." He looked her in the eyes. "I never mean to hurt the people I care about, but I seem to do it anyway."

"The marks are already fading." She lifted her wrists for his inspection. "See?" Gently he grasped her wrists and turned them so he could look at her hands.

"But these aren't fading."

He leaned down and placed a gentle kiss first on one palm and then on the other. The moment was so exquisite that Jessica forgot to breathe. How long she would have stood there with her breath caught in her throat she didn't know, but when he grasped her around the waist and lifted her onto the counter, she felt the breath rush back into her lungs.

"Let me put some medicine on those," Brandon said as he opened the cabinet.

Jessica sat quietly as he dabbed an antiseptic cream on each scrape and cut. She thought to protest only when he pulled a roll of bandaging gauze from the cabinet.

"What are you doing?"

"I can't put Band-Aids all over your hands. I'm going to have to bandage them."

"I'll look like the mummy," she protested.

"It will keep the dirt out."

"They'll be useless."

"I'll take care of you." He looked her in the eye. "I promise."

Jess rested her wrists on his bare shoulders. "You don't have to take care of me. I'm perfectly capable of taking care of myself. Why don't you let me take care of you instead?"

He kissed the soft skin on the inside of one wrist and then the other. "Jess," he whispered, his breath a soft caress against her sensitive skin. "Sweet, gentle Jess. You're a miracle."

She shook her head and tried to tell him that she was no miracle, but flesh and blood; but her voice wouldn't work.

His lips went from her arms to the side of her neck. She'd never felt so cherished in her life. She closed her eyes and gloried in the touch of his lips against her skin. In the way they trailed up her neck and across her cheek until they hovered over hers. His kiss, when it finally came, was gentle, so gentle that it seemed like little more than the caress of the summer breeze. She was so caught up in the sweetness of it that at first she didn't realize there were tears streaming down her face. Not until she felt his thumb sweep across her cheeks.

"Don't cry," Brandon murmured. "Please don't cry. I promise I'll take care of you."

"I always cry," she murmured through a tremulous smile. "I cry when I'm sad. When I'm happy. I'm a regular fountain," she explained. It was the best she could do, for how could she tell him she wasn't crying out of grief or fear? That she had forgotten about everything except the sweetness of his kiss? That her world had selfishly narrowed down to the spot where his lips touched hers? She pulled him toward her until her lips touched his once more.

He could feel it when their lips met. Not passion. Not desire. Not even love—not quite yet. But compassion and caring. The need to give and to heal. He let the gentle kiss linger, then he laid his head upon her breast and listened to the sweet song of her heart.

"Let me hold you," she whispered. "Just let me hold you."

When her arms went around him and held him tight, he sighed, content to let this miraculous moment lengthen. For compassion, to a man who didn't believe he deserved it, was the greatest miracle of all.

By the time Nancy called to say that the police had arrived, Brandon had changed into a fresh shirt and slacks. Jessica had talked him out of bandaging her hands, but he had insisted that she lie down on the sofa, and he'd even tucked a handmade quilt around her.

When she tried to get up, he exerted just enough pressure on her shoulders to keep her down. "You wait right here," he told her. "I'm going down to talk to the police. They'll want to see Stew . . . the body. And I'll point out where you found it. I know they'll want to talk to you, but let me take care of a few things first."

"I want to go with you."

"You don't trust me to handle this?"

"Don't be ridiculous. I just don't want you to face this alone."

Brandon sat on the edge of the sofa. "Jessica, please let me do this my way. It's going to be hard enough for you to give a statement, at least let me smooth things for you."

"But Stewart is your uncle. If anything, I should be the one handling this for you."

"This is the way Stewart would expect me to handle it. Please. I need to do this one final thing for him."

"Okay," she said, relenting under this final argument. "As long as you promise to call me if you need me."

He bent down to drop a quick kiss on her brow. "I can get through anything as long as I know you're here waiting for me."

Jessica smiled. "I'll be here. I promise."

She was still smiling as Brandon pulled the door shut behind him. She waited until she was certain he'd had time to start down the stairs before she gave in to the tears. And once they'd begun, there seemed to be no stopping them. She wept for Stewart, and she wept for Brandon. She cried for George, who stood guard over his friend's body, and she cried for Nancy and all the other staff members who had yet to be informed of Stewart's death. And she cried for herself, for all her lost chances and for the loss of her friend. She cried until she was so exhausted that she could no longer fight sleep.

She awoke to sunshine and butterflies. To warmth that surrounded her and the gentle brush of butterfly wings on her cheeks.

"Jess." She smiled as another butterfly touched her forehead. "Jess, you need to wake up."

She snuggled against the warmth and resisted opening her eyes.

"Oh, honey, I'd let you sleep if I could. But the police want to talk to you."

That had her opening her eyes to discover that the warmth came not from sunshine, but from Brandon's embrace, and that instead of butterflies, Brandon's lips fluttered gently over her face. And reality came flooding back. She looked into Brandon's drawn face and saw fatigue and grief. When she closed her eyes again, she saw Stewart as she'd found him, broken and dead. With a sigh, she opened her eyes and struggled with the quilt that clung to her legs. Brandon freed her, then stood back as she rose. She winced and put her hands over her eyes as the room tilted.

"Are you okay?"

Jessica nodded, then immediately regretted the action. "A headache," she whispered. Undoubtedly the result of her crying.

"Sit down." He pushed her gently back on the sofa. "I'll get you something."

She waited with her eyes closed, then took the pills he brought her. Still clutching the glass of water, she laid her head back on the couch and waited for the pain to let up.

"Jess."

She looked at Brandon through slitted eyes. It seemed he'd aged over the last few hours, though she knew that wasn't possible. She wouldn't add to his pain, she decided. She sat up. "I'm ready." But as she started to rise, he sat beside her.

"There are a few things you need to know before you see Carl Mendoza."

"Who?"

Brandon sighed. "Carl Mendoza, the chief of police for the city of Luz. We contract with the city for police protection."

Jess nodded. Luz was the small town that had sprung up beside the Santa Lucia Inn. Originally it had been the home of the inn's employees. Now the small city had its own gift shops and restaurants that attracted tourists coming and going to the inn.

"Carl will be handling the case," Brandon explained. "He and I went to school together."

"Oh." She didn't know what else to say. When Brandon raked his hand through his hair, she sat and waited. "Mendoza seems to think—" He stopped and raked a hand through his hair again. "He has reason to believe—"

But before he could finish there was a sharp knock on the door. A bulldog of a man stepped into the room.

"I was beginning to think you'd skipped town," he said to Brandon.

Brandon stood. "Don't be ridiculous. Jess was asleep when I came up."

"But she's awake now," Mendoza said smoothly with a look at her where she sat on the sofa. "I'm Carl Mendoza." He came toward her with his hand outstretched. "Chief of Police Carl Mendoza."

Jessica took his hand. "Jessica Martinson."

"I understand you had a bit of excitement this evening."

Excitement? Jessica wondered. "Not excitement," she finally told him. "A tragedy."

Mendoza pulled a notebook and pen from his jacket pocket. "It was you who found Stewart Roarke's body?"

"Yes." She took a sip of water. "I was down on the beach, and I realized that I'd been out too long. I was climbing back over the rocks when I found Stewart's body."

"And what did you think?"

"For God's sake," Brandon cut in. "She thought he was dead."

"Did you?" Mendoza asked, never taking his dark eyes from her.

"Not at first." She wet her lips and looked over at Brandon. "At first I thought it was just some bright-colored trash. A scarf or blanket or something. Then when I got closer I realized it was a person. I thought that someone had slipped and been hurt." She dropped her gaze to her lap. "As I got closer, I recognized Stewart, but I didn't realize he was dead until I reached him."

"And then what did you do?"

She looked at Brandon. "I knew the tide was coming in, and I was afraid Stewart's body would be washed out to sea. So I ran back to the Santa Lucia to find Brandon."

Mendoza paused to make some notations in his notebook. "And did you have any trouble locating him?"

"Actually, he was just coming across the lawn when I made it up the stairs."

Mendoza made another notation. "And do you have any idea what Mr. Roarke was doing out on the lawn at that time of day?"

"Why don't you ask me?" Brandon demanded.

Mendoza looked up at him. "What were you doing?"

"I was looking for Jess."

"And why was that?"

"Because it was getting dark and I hadn't been able to find her."

"I didn't realize that you kept tabs on all your guests."

"She's working for us. I explained that to you."

"Indeed you did." He slanted Jessica a searching look, then focused back on Brandon. "Neither did I realize you kept such close tabs on all your employees. She might have been resting or taking a shower. Had you left a message at the desk?"

Brandon nodded. "But she hadn't picked it up."

"Had you checked her room?"

"As I said, I'd left several messages."

"Yes, but did you have access to her room?"

"I have access to all the rooms."

Mendoza smiled. "Perhaps your reputation doesn't do you justice, then."

Brandon took a step toward the policeman. "And what the hell does that mean?"

"I'm staying here," Jessica said, drawing their attention. Both men looked as though they'd forgotten she existed. "I'm staying in Brandon's suite."

He glanced at Brandon and back to her. "I see."

"No," she told him. "I don't think you do."

"Then perhaps you'd like to explain."

"I moved into Brandon's extra bedroom because someone trashed my room."

He slanted a quick look at Brandon. "I don't believe you mentioned that, Brandon."

"We were dealing with Stewart's death. I didn't think to mention something so minor. And so unconnected."

Mendoza smiled at Brandon. "How about if you tell me everything, and I'll figure out what's unconnected." To Jessica he said, "Did you report this to the police?"

"No." When he raised an eyebrow in question, she added, "I thought it was just kids."

Mendoza nodded. "Of course kids do that kind of thing, but they don't normally break into the most expensive hotel in the area and pick out one room."

"We put on extra security," Brandon said. "It won't be happening again."

"And of course the guests were warned to take extra precautions?"

"I didn't think it necessary."

He looked up at Brandon. "Wouldn't want to scare the guests away, now, would we? What exactly was the damage?"

"They took a knife to the furniture and bedding," Brandon explained.

"Cut up all my clothes," Jessica continued. "Destroyed my cosmetics and wrote all over the mirror with my lipstick."

"Wrote? What did they write?"

Brandon spoke first. "Things like 'Go home. You don't belong here.'"

"Ah, yes, teenage vandals who don't like tourists. I hope it doesn't start a trend."

Jessica licked her lips. "It said more than that. It said my name." She couldn't look at Brandon, so she concentrated on Mendoza's dark, hard eyes. "It said, 'Jessica, go home.'"

Mendoza made a few more notations. "Teenage vandals who hate tourists and go to the trouble to find out the name of their victim are a bit more rare." He snapped his notebook closed. "I'll want to talk to you again, Ms. Martinson. I hope your plans call for you to stay a while longer."

Jessica reached out to touch Brandon's arm. "I plan to stay at least until the funeral." She was relieved when Brandon's hand covered hers.

"Maybe longer," Brandon added.

Mendoza concentrated on their clasped hands. "I see. Then there's really no rush with the questions. I'm sure you're both tired, so I'll bid you good evening."

"Let me walk you to the front door," Brandon offered.

"Want to make sure I don't hang around and make a nuisance of myself? Is that it? Maybe ask some embarrassing questions?"

"Don't be ridiculous, Carl." Brandon crossed to the door and opened it. "You're welcome to question the employees. If they know anything, they'll want to help. They loved Stewart."

Without being asked, Jessica followed Mendoza out the door. She didn't want the two men left alone since they seemed to antagonize each other.

"It was a lucky thing you found Stewart's body, Ms. Martinson. It's always difficult to solve a murder without the body. It's even difficult to prove it occurred."

"Murder?" Jessica felt her step falter.

"You didn't notice the bullet hole, then?"

"Bullet hole?" She stopped and looked from Mendoza to Brandon. "What bullet hole?"

It was Mendoza who answered. "The one in Stewart Roarke's chest. However, the coroner will have to tell us if it was the bullet or the fall that actually killed him."

She looked at Mendoza. "I didn't know." She suddenly remembered how George had demanded atonement. "You knew, didn't you?" she said to Brandon. "You and George. Why didn't you tell me?"

"I was trying to when Carl came busting into the room."

Jessica thought a moment. "But why not before? You must have known when you brought him up from the beach."

They were at the top of the stairs; Brandon took her arm to steady her as they descended. "You were already upset. I thought I'd spare you that—at least for a while."

"If Brandon didn't tell you about the bullet," Mendoza

put in smoothly, "I'm certain he neglected to mention that we had an identical murder three years ago."

Jessica was grateful that Brandon had such a strong grip on her arm, or she would surely have stumbled head-long down the stairs. "Identical?" she heard herself ask.

Mendoza stopped at the bottom of the stairs and turned to face her. "Same method. Same place. And I'd assume the same murderer. We'll know more when we get the ballistics report."

Jessica looked at Brandon as though waiting for a denial. He said nothing.

"Only the first time Brandon found the body himself. He was out walking—just like you, Ms. Martinson—and the tide was also coming in then. He managed to carry Jacqueline Kendall all the way up the steps that time. But then she was a tiny thing, wasn't she, Brandon?"

Jess swallowed hard. "Jacqueline Kendall?"

Mendoza nodded. "Jason's mother."

"And she was killed the same way?"

Mendoza nodded again. "Shot at close range, then tossed over the cliff into the rising tide. There's no doubt we've got us a smart murderer here. If you hadn't come along when you did, the body would have washed out to sea. Of course, the tides being what they are, the body might have washed up a few miles down the coast."

He started across the lobby, and Jessica followed him. Brandon kept hold of her arm. "The coroner has taken the body, and my men are cordoning off the cliff above as well as the path that Stewart most likely took to get there. But any evidence that might have been left with the body will be washed away with the tide. You see what I mean by a clever murderer. So we'll need to rely on your memory, Ms. Martinson. If you can recall anything that was on the body—anything at all—it might be helpful."

"Brandon is more likely to remember than I am," Jessica protested.

"I doubt it. You see, when he found Jacqueline's body he couldn't remember a thing. I was surprised at the time, because he'd been such a good student when we were in school together. And I figured that a man who handled the day-to-day operations for a business this size would have an excellent memory. But he couldn't remember anything. Could you, Brandon?"

"There wasn't anything to remember, Carl."

"So you said then, Brandon. It's just that most murderers leave something behind. Maybe this time Ms. Martinson can be of help"

"I'll try," Jess promised as the stopped before the big double doors.

"I'm sure you will. You get some rest, and I'll be back tomorrow."

Jessica waited until the policeman was out of earshot before she turned on Brandon. "Why didn't you tell me he'd been murdered? And why didn't you mention Jacqueline Kendall's murder?"

Brandon looked around the lobby. "I don't think this is the time or place to discuss it. Why don't you go back upstairs and go to bed. I've still got to inform the employees and decide how to notify the guests."

Jessica's anger faded when she realized the tasks that lay ahead for him. "How can I help?"

"By going back to the room and staying put. Can I rely on you to stay there this time?"

Jessica nodded.

"Good." He placed a kiss on her cheek. "Go on, then. I don't know when I'll get back."

* * *

The Watcher sat out in the cold night, observing the Santa Lucia Inn. Most of the police were gone. Only two officers remained to stand guard over the area they'd cordoned off. They'd find no evidence there. The Watcher had been very careful. The gun was safely hidden again, and the Pacific had taken care of anything that Stewart might have dragged over the cliff with him. The Watcher cursed the cold and the damp while waiting for the light to come on in Brandon's bedroom, while envisioning the lonely man who stood in his room. Would he take the time to get ready for bed, or would he simply lie down on top of the covers, exhausted and alone?

The light went out almost immediately, and the Watcher imagined the lonely figure sprawled on top of his bed, fighting the grief and guilt that fools suffer when they think they could have prevented a death.

8

Jessica fought her way out of a deep sleep. Her feet were cramped, and her legs ached; she'd been running in her sleep. *Running to or from something?* she wondered groggily. Then she sat straight up in bed and raked the unruly curls back from her face as yesterday's events came hurtling back. The fact that she wasn't in the room she'd previously occupied made her realize that Stewart's death hadn't been a bad dream. It was reality. Her first instinct was to pack and leave; old habits died hard, she decided. Instead she took a deep breath and reminded herself that she wasn't going to run from this. She would stay and face it—with Brandon.

The thought of Brandon had her looking at the bedroom door. It had been closed when she'd finally fallen asleep. Closed, but not bolted. She knew Brandon's word was stronger than any lock. The door was open now. The fact that Brandon had looked in on her when she was completely vulnerable should have made her uneasy, but it didn't. It made her worry that he'd needed her.

By the time she'd showered and dressed, Jess was again overwhelmed with all the questions that had gnawed at her the night before. Questions about Jacqueline Kendall's murder and why Brandon hadn't mentioned it. Questions about the enmity between Brandon and Carl Mendoza. Most of all, questions about who would murder Stewart Roarke. The questions she had about her relationship with Brandon, she suppressed. There would be time for those later.

At the front desk, a red-eyed Nancy informed her that Brandon could be found on the terrace, having breakfast. Before Jessica could turn to leave, Nancy's cold hand grasped hers.

"Take care of him," the clerk whispered. "He's being so strong. He says Stewart would expect him to carry on with the business of running the inn, but he's hurting. And I think you're the only one he'll let help him."

"I'll try," Jessica promised, but when she reached the terrace, she realized that might prove more difficult than she'd thought.

Brandon sat at what she'd come to realize was his usual table, off to the side and back. The tables with the best views were given to guests, and they were all craning to watch the police who were tromping around the grounds, doing whatever it was police did. Only Brandon appeared indifferent to the activity. He was studying a computer printout while he picked at his breakfast. Realizing that his studied indifference to everyone's curiosity would keep his eyes riveted to the printed page, Jessica took the time to observe him. He was drawn and tired. Dark circles shadowed his beautiful blue eyes, and deep grooves bracketed his mouth. Not that these marks took away from his good looks, but they made him appear harder, less approachable. While it might make others back off, it only made Jessica more determined to break through the grief. She walked across the patio and slipped onto the chair opposite him.

"Good morning."

Brandon's look of careful nonchalance gave way briefly to one so vulnerable and full of pain that it took Jessica's breath away. Then it was gone as quickly as it had come.

"I thought you might sleep in this morning." He'd looked in on her at first light, and after his long, sleepless night she'd looked so peaceful that only his word of honor had kept him from crawling into bed beside her. "There was no reason for you to get up so early."

"And what about you?"

"I have things to do. Arrangements to be made for Stewart. A business to run." Though what he'd really wanted to do was wake Jessica with kisses and beg her to run away with him. To run from the inn and the grief and all the mistakes he'd made. Only one thing—the fear that doing so would reveal him as the coward he really was—had stopped him. That and his love for Stewart. He owed his uncle, owed him a send-off that did justice to a man of honor and the tradition of excellence that defined the Santa Lucia Inn. Besides, he had a murderer to confront.

"How long have the police been here?"

Brandon glanced over at the search area. "They arrived about six. I hadn't realized that public servants actually started that early."

She ignored his sarcasm. "I hope they find some clues. Anything to help them catch the murderer."

Brandon looked at Jessica, saw the trust and the faith she put in these men, and wondered how she'd ever managed to get through thirty-one years with her ingenuous attitude. "I'm not absolutely certain they could find an elephant in a snowstorm," he told her. "After all, they didn't find the killer last time."

Jessica looked down at the mention of the previous murder. "We're going to have to talk."

When she looked up at him, her eyes were clouded with doubts and questions. Brandon knew he had Carl to thank for that. "We are talking."

She shook her head. "No, I mean really talk. About Stewart's death and about what happened before."

"Okay." He put his hand palm up on the table. "But not right now." He couldn't suppress his sigh of relief when she placed her hand in his.

"Okay. But soon."

"Soon," he promised as he looked at their joined hands. He was so grateful to feel her hand in his that he had to fight the urge to weep. It could have been her body at the foot of that cliff, he'd realized in the middle of the night. Her lifeless form bundled off in a bag in the coroner's van. Her smile that he'd never see again. Her sweetness and generosity that he'd never savor. And it would have been his fault. Just as Stewart's death was his responsibility. It wasn't an easy fact to live with.

He squeezed her hand in his and felt her healing touch. Felt the sweetness and faith that he'd never found anywhere else. And he thought, for the first time in years, that he might actually have a future. If she would only teach him to trust again—in himself and in love. And if he could keep her alive.

With his free hand he signaled for the waiter. "Eat a good breakfast. Then we'll go see what Carl's up to."

By the time Jessica finished breakfast, the knot of people on the lawn had grown. As they approached the group, Jess noticed that George was talking to Carl Mendoza.

"Don't know why you have to go pokin' around them plants," George was saying to Mendoza. "They've only been in the ground a couple days. If you dig up the roots, they'll never take."

Mendoza sighed, and Jessica could see that he, too, was exhausted. "We have a report from one of the guests that Stewart was seen around these plants late yesterday afternoon. Considering the time of the sighting, it may have been the last time anyone saw him."

"That's no reason to be pokin' around the plants."

"The guest reported that Stewart bent down and looked under the plants. There are footprints in the dirt. We've taken casts of them to compare to the shoes Stewart was wearing at the time of the murder."

"And just exactly what will that prove?" Brandon asked.

"Good morning, Brandon. Ms. Martinson."

Brandon didn't bother with the amenities. "Well, Carl, what will it prove?"

"It could establish the last time the victim was seen. It might also give us some clue as to where he was going."

"It might also prove that my uncle saw some trash that was blowing around and decided to pick it up. He is . . . was insistent that the grounds be kept immaculate. How is that pertinent to this investigation?"

"We're trying to establish the time and reason Stewart went out to the cliffs. We know what time he spoke to the woman working registration, but we can't be certain he left the inn at that time. The coroner can give us an estimate of the time of death. Say, between four and eight. But if we can pinpoint it more closely, by the last time he was seen and the time Ms. Martinson discovered the body, that gives us a more exact time frame." Mendoza looked at Brandon. "Then we look for people who can't account for their whereabouts during that time period."

Brandon smiled. "Carl, I've already admitted that there isn't anyone to vouch for my whereabouts. I was all over the grounds looking for Jess. And I was alone most of the time."

"You'd be surprised how many people reported seeing you. The problem is that none of them can give me an exact time."

"Which puts me on your list of suspects, is that it?"

"You there," George yelled at one of the officers before Mendoza could answer Brandon. "Quit pokin' in the dirt. There's no need to be diggin' up my plants."

The policeman in question looked up. Jessica decided that with his sun-burnished hair and freckles, he looked young enough to be in braces. He grinned at them and then went back to his digging. George muttered something under his breath, then hitched up his pants as if getting ready for battle.

Brandon laid a hand on the gardener's shoulder. "It'll be all right. Just take it easy."

George nodded and resettled the straw hat on his head. "There's no need to uproot my plants. No need at all."

"I'm sure the chief of police wouldn't dream of allowing his men to cause any gratuitous damage, would you, Carl?"

"This is a murder investigation," Mendoza explained. "What are a few plants compared to a man's life?"

"I suppose it depends on what you think you might dig up under a rosebush."

"It depends on what someone might have left there. Or buried."

Brandon laughed at that. Threw back his head and laughed so that others turned to stare at him. "Oh, Carl, you can't possibly believe that Stewart paused to plant a clue under the fifth rosebush from the left. Like a treasure map or a cryptic message. You're really reaching this time."

Carl wasn't amused. "Statistics say that nearly fifty percent of homicide victims know their killer. In a town this small, I'd double the percentage. Taking that into consideration, along with the fact that there's no sign of a struggle on the cliff where Stewart was shot, we have to assume that Stewart knew his killer. If we can find out why he was there or where he was headed, and if we can find out which of his acquaintances don't have an alibi for the time of death, we should be able to narrow the field of suspects."

Brandon stiffened. "You wouldn't have anyone in mind, would you?"

Mendoza just smiled. "When we take the list of suspects for Stewart's murder and compare them with the list from Jacqueline Kendall's, I'm hoping some interesting possibilities might turn up."

Brandon took another step toward the detective. "I'll just bet you are."

Jessica was trying to think of a way to head off what seemed like an inevitable confrontation when the young policeman called Carl's name. She was certain Brandon would have marched right through the yellow tape that separated them from the crime scene if she hadn't been there. She stepped in front of him.

"I know this is difficult for you," she said, drawing a quick glance from Brandon. She cupped his glowering face in her hands and waited for him to give her his full attention. "You can't continue to bait the police, Brandon. Mendoza is only trying to do his job."

Brandon's hands came up to cover hers. "You don't know what it feels like."

"Then tell me," Jessica said simply. "I want to understand."

Brandon placed a kiss in each palm, then, keeping her hands in his, lowered them to his chest. Jessica waited.

"It's like a nightmare," he said at last. "Like one of those dreams where you know you've been in the same situation before. And you couldn't run then, either. It's like my feet are stuck in quicksand, and I know what's coming, but I can't get away from it."

"You're forgetting something."

"What's that?"

"I wasn't here before. We're in it together this time." Brandon gathered her close so that she laid her cheek against his warm, solid chest.

"I know," he told her, but it didn't sound as though he took much comfort from her presence.

Carl Mendoza looked at the bones that Jim Miller was pointing to, then looked back at his youthful assistant.

"So?"

"They're human bones, sir. From a human hand."

"How can you tell?"

"I was in premed before I decided to pursue police work."

"I'll bet your parents weren't very happy about that, were they, Jim?"

"No, sir, they weren't. What do you want me to do with the bones?"

Well, hell, Carl thought. What was he going to do with the bones? And how the hell had this young hotshot managed to dig them up?

"You don't happen to have a full skeleton there, do you?"

Jim dropped down and proceeded to brush away the dirt.

As far as Carl could tell, they could be chicken bones, but Jim was confident. And he had to give the kid credit: he might not look old enough to drive his father's car, but he was bright and capable. It was just an annoying package, all that youth and intelligence wrapped up in one redheaded, freckle-faced body. It made Carl nervous to realize that Jim might be pushing for his job before too long. All the more reason to pursue this case, he knew. The man who could solve the murder of two well-known locals wouldn't have to worry about some pimply-faced kid taking his job.

"Well, sir?"

Carl looked at the pile of bones and wondered what he should do. That was the thing about police work; there were always surprises.

Carl looked back to see Jessica Martinson held firmly in Brandon Roarke's embrace. That was another surprise. He could hardly imagine two people less suited to each other than Brandon Roarke and Jessica Martinson. He'd been convinced that Brandon enjoyed his bachelor status and all the beautiful women who checked in and out of his life. Yet there he was, looking for all the world like a man ready to give up the single life and settle down. And with Jessica Martinson, no less. Who would have figured he'd fall for the "sweet young thing" type? Okay, so she wasn't all that young. But she was definitely sweet. And naive. One look in those big brown eyes, and you just knew that she got misty-eyed over weddings and babies and still believed in happily ever after. And Brandon Roarke was a hard-eyed, cynical soul if he'd ever known one. The fact that he hadn't always been like that made it all the more intriguing.

Carl had gotten wind of rumors at the time of Jacqueline Kendall's death—rumors about an affair between Brandon and Jacqueline, who'd been a helluva good-looking woman even though she'd been old enough to be his mother. People had sworn they'd seen Jacqueline slipping back from the direction of the inn in the early morning on several occasions. Some had even thought Brandon the murderer, though Carl had never quite believed that. But his gut instinct told him that Brandon had held back information during the Kendall investigation. He couldn't prove it, and he didn't know what it was, but his instincts had saved his life on more than one occasion.

"What about the bones, sir?"

Carl turned back to see that Jim was still digging in the dirt. "Nothing else, huh?"

"Not so far. We really need to take up some of these bushes and dig down farther to be sure."

Oh, yeah, Brandon was gonna love that. And so was that gardener who was pacing like someone in a hospital corridor waiting for news about his next of kin.

Carl nodded. "Bag the bones and send them to the Department of Justice lab. Then get a couple men to help you. Take up these three or four bushes and sift through the dirt. See if you can find anything else."

Convinced that this would stir things up, he stood back and waited for the first outcry. It was his experience that if you could get people upset, they would blurt out information they meant to keep to themselves.

He didn't have long to wait.

"You there," George called. "Leave those rosebushes alone!"

Jessica raised her head from where it lay against Brandon's solid warmth in time to see George plow through the yellow crime scene tape and storm toward the group of policemen who were wrestling with his rosebushes.

"What the hell do you think you're doin'?"

"We're looking for clues," Mendoza said.

Jessica followed Brandon to where George stood. "What kinda clues you lookin' for in those bushes, boy?"

The freckle-faced smile was polite. "Not in the bushes, under them."

When George would have gone for the nearest man, Brandon put his hand out to stop him. George refused to back up but seemed content to hold his ground for the moment.

"Carl, be reasonable," Brandon urged. Jessica was glad to hear his voice so calm and level. "Do you really think Stewart stopped to bury something here yesterday?"

"No."

"Then why are you doing this?"

"It seems my assistant has found something suspicious."

Brandon sighed. "And what might that be?"

"A human hand."

"A human . . . hand?" George asked, growing pale.

The young officer stepped forward. "Actually, part of the skeleton of a human hand."

Brandon stared at the bones the younger policeman pointed to. "How can you be sure they aren't gopher or squirrel bones that some dog buried?"

Mendoza smiled. "Jim here was in premed."

Everyone stared at the young man, who proceeded to turn a subtle shade of pink. "Forensics will have to verify it."

"What else do you expect to find?" Brandon asked the younger policeman.

"The rest of the skeleton."

"The rest of the skeleton?" Brandon grinned. "I think I can promise you that I'm not burying bodies under the rosebushes, Carl."

Carl shrugged. "Just following through. If there's a hand, there might be more."

George hitched up his pants. "Must've been in the soil."

"That's why we're digging deeper," Carl explained.

George shook his head. "I mean it must've come with the plantin' mix." Jessica was glad to see his color coming back. "I've found other things in it before. A watch once. And a weddin' ring."

Carl's eyes snapped with curiosity. "You mean you buy dirt to plant with?" He turned to the younger policeman. "It could have been an industrial accident."

"I don't think so, sir. These bones are older than that. There's no flesh clinging to them. Nothing to indicate that they were buried in the last few years, let alone the last few days."

"Oh, God," George said, his color draining again.

They were all standing quietly, staring at the bones, when the bellman arrived. "Miss Martinson?"

Jessica turned to him. "Yes."

"A message. Nancy said I should get it to you right away," he added as he handed her an envelope.

Jess opened and read it. "It's from Marty." Her eyes sought Brandon's. "She wants to see me right away." She didn't add that Marty had instructed her to pack up everything and return to the Kendall home at once. That was something she would settle with her overprotective sister on her own.

Brandon gave her a reassuring smile. "She must be worried."

Jessica chewed on her lower lip. "I should have called

her." Now, judging from the note, it was too late for a phone call. She needed to talk to Marty face to face. It was the only way she was going to persuade her older sister that she was okay. Grateful that things had calmed down here, she stuck the note in the pocket of her jeans. "I think I'll just walk over and have a little chat with her."

"No, you won't," Brandon told her.

"You don't know Marty. If I don't go to her, she'll come here. And I don't think she'll be very friendly."

Brandon smiled and reached out to push back one of her curls. "I don't mean that you shouldn't go see her. I only mean that you aren't walking over there."

"I have to agree with Brandon," Carl added. "There is a murderer running loose somewhere, Ms. Martinson. I don't think you should be out walking alone." He looked at Brandon. "I don't think anyone should."

"It's broad daylight," Jessica protested.

Mendoza shook his head. "Need I remind you that Stewart Roarke was killed during daylight hours? Admittedly it was late afternoon, but there was still enough light to see whoever lay in wait for him. And on the very path that you propose to take."

Brandon turned to the bellman. "Take one of the cars and drive Ms. Martinson to the Kendall home. And wait for her," he said before his employee could turn away. "If you value your position at the inn, you will not to come back without Ms. Martinson. Do you understand?"

"No, I do not have my luggage with me," Jess said in answer to her sister's question.

"We'll pick it up on the way home, then," Marty decided as she folded her nightgown and put it in her suitcase. "It shouldn't take you long to pack."

Jessica perched on the corner of a chest of drawers and folded her arms. "Actually, it probably wouldn't take more than two minutes. Most everything I own was destroyed when someone broke into my room."

Marty stopped in the middle of folding her silk blouse and stared at Jessica. "Someone broke into your room?"

Jess nodded. "Yesterday afternoon. They trashed everything except what I had on."

Marty sank to the mattress, heedless of the silk scarf beneath her. "Why didn't you call me? I would have driven over to get you."

"I didn't want to leave." She nodded toward Marty's open suitcase. "I don't think Stewart Roarke's murder is any reason for you to pack and run, either."

"What?" She looked at the suitcase, then focused on the blouse in her hands. That must have reminded her of the silk scarf because she hopped up. "That isn't why I'm leaving. Though it seems reason enough to me."

"Why are you leaving?" Jess asked, placing a slight emphasis on the pronoun.

"I got a call this morning from Dougall Senior." Marty didn't pause in her packing. Her hands kept moving as she talked. "It seems Junior is in the hospital with a bleeding ulcer."

"Dougall Senior could have that effect on almost anyone," Jess said. She'd met the elder Dougall on several occasions; as far as she was concerned, the man was a menace. Junior, on the other hand, was timid as a mouse.

Marty glanced around the room, looking for anything she'd neglected to pack. "Naturally I'm going to have to fill in for Junior on several cases." She checked her watch. "If we leave now, we'll be home before the five o'clock news."

"I'm not leaving."

Marty snapped her suitcase shut and picked it up. "Let's tell Jason and Florence good-bye." She picked up her purse from the bed. "Then we'll drive by the Santa Lucia and get your things."

"I said I'm not going."

Marty stopped dead in her tracks and stared at her sister. "What?"

"I'm staying here."

"Don't be ridiculous." She snapped back into action and crossed to the door. "A photography job isn't worth risking your life—not even this one."

Jess continued to perch on the chest. "I'm not being ridiculous. And I'm not leaving. The job isn't the only reason I'm staying here."

Marty turned to face her sister. "Oh God, it's those blue eyes again, isn't it? You're a sucker for blue eyes."

"It's not just the blue eyes. And what do you mean, 'again'?"

"Eric had blue eyes, and you fell for him like a ton of bricks."

Jess stood up. "Eric had blue eyes?"

"You don't remember?"

Jess shook her head. When she thought about it, she realized that she could hardly remember Eric's face. She was certain that when she'd arrived at the Kendalls' she'd had a clear vision of what the bastard looked like.

"You never really loved him, then."

"I must have. It hurt like hell."

"What hurt?"

Jess hesitated. She'd never discussed this with Marty, had never expected to. Eric had wanted Marty, like any red-blooded man. Marty had wanted nothing to do with Eric. That was when Eric had turned his considerable charms on Jessica. At first she'd thought to give him a shoulder to cry on and a pat on the back before sending him back into the world—as she'd done to so many heartbroken males who'd been sent on their way by her older sister.

But he'd continued to hang around. He'd turned the tables and started listening to her. Then he'd flattered her and courted her and gotten her to fall head over heels for him. She'd even agreed to marry the bastard. Then he'd slowly driven the sisters apart.

Jess had begun to spend less time with her family because Marty made Eric uncomfortable. Then she'd stopped spending evenings out with her sister because Eric always had something for them to do together. She'd given up phoning her sister, because everything she had to say involved Eric—and Marty bristled every time the man's name was mentioned. Soon she'd been isolated from her sister, estranged from the very relationship that had gotten her through the tough times. She'd been only a few days from marrying Eric, only a few days from committing the worst mistake of her life.

And it hadn't mattered that Marty had begged her to wait, that her mother had insisted Eric was only using her, that all her friends had said he'd taken control of her life so that they hardly recognized her. She'd been determined to marry him—and she would have, if it hadn't been for a slip of his tongue. It was in one of those moments that her mother described as the throes of passion, at a time when his mind should have been completely on her. But it hadn't been.

When Jessica found her voice, it was barely more than a whisper. "He called me by your name," she told her sister.

"He what?"

"We were in bed." She shook her head, determined to be ruthlessly honest with herself and with Marty. "We were having sex." She knew now that was what it had been: sex. Not love, just sex. "And I told him I loved him . . . and he . . . called me Marty."

"Oh, God."

He hadn't just called her by the wrong name. "He said, 'You're mine now, Marty. I'll never let you go.'"

There were tears in Marty's eyes. "I'm so sorry."

Jess was surprised that her own eyes were dry, that the memory didn't have the power to hurt her anymore. There was no need to tell Marty that he'd gotten rough. No reason to mention that he'd tried to hurt her when she'd told him to get out. That she'd turned ferocious and threatened to make sure he'd never be able to touch another woman if he touched her again. All Marty had to know was that she'd come to her senses in the nick of time.

"It was my pride that hurt," Jess admitted. "I hated that everyone else was right and I was wrong. And I hated having you stand in front of the church, telling people to go home. That there wouldn't be a wedding after all." She smiled at Marty. "I should have been counting my lucky stars that I found out the truth before it was too late. And I should have told you how much I appreciated the fact that you never once said 'I told you so.' Even though you had every right to."

"It was my fault. He knew how close we were." Marty took three long steps and put her arms around her sister. "He knew the surest way to hurt me was through you. I'm so sorry, Jess."

"Hey, look at me," Jess said as Marty dashed away tears. "Do I look like I'm still hurting?"

"No." Marty shook her head. "I'm the one who's crying."

"Then stop it." Jess looked around the room for tissues,

then handed her sister the box. "It's over and done with."

"Thank God."

Jessica watched as Marty dabbed at her face and blew her nose. Maybe there was some justice after all, she decided when she noticed that her sister's face was red and blotchy and her eyes were swollen.

Marty threw the tissues in the trash. "I'm so glad that's over." She picked up her suitcase again. "Now let's get your stuff and go home."

"I'm still not leaving." Jess had to smile when her sister threw her a bleary look of exasperation. "And it isn't just because of his blue eyes."

Marty set down her suitcase once more and turned to face her younger sister. "Then why?"

"Because I'm in love. And this time it's the real thing," she added before Marty could protest. "And I think he loves me. But if I leave, I may never be sure."

"Los Angeles is not the other side of the world. Once the murderer is caught, you can come back. Or he can come down to L.A."

Jess shook her head. "He needs me now. And he needs to know he can depend on me."

"According to Florence—"

"I don't want to hear what Florence has to say."

"Jess, this is just like before. Your family and friends tried to talk to you then, but you wouldn't listen."

"No, it's not like before. I was so blind that I couldn't understand how anyone could doubt Eric. This is different. I already know there's a misunderstanding between Jason and Brandon. It's only natural that Florence would side with her husband." Then, to prove that she knew more about the situation than Marty, she asked, "Did you know Brandon and Jason grew up together? That for years they were best friends?"

Marty shook her head. "What happened?"

"I'm not sure. I only know that their enmity goes back quite a ways. So I don't think you can necessarily believe anything Jason or Florence has to say."

"But the chief of police said—"

Jess gave her sister a narrow-eyed look. "When did you talk to him?"

"As soon as I read the morning paper. And don't give me the evil eye. I was concerned."

"Hah! If you were concerned, you should have called me. You were pulling your big sister routine again."

"So what if I was? I am your big sister."

"That doesn't give you the right to run my life."

"I'm not trying to run your life. I'm just trying to save you from making another mistake."

"It's not a mistake this time." She crossed her arms and stared right back. "This time it's love."

Marty backed up until she sat heavily on the bed. She opened her mouth, but nothing came out.

Jess had to smile despite the pain; she seldom saw her sister speechless. "You don't think a man like Brandon can fall in love with me, do you?"

Marty shook her head. "Don't be ridiculous. If Brandon Roarke is in love with you, it just shows he has good taste."

"Then what's the problem?"

"You sound so sure."

Jess went to sit beside her sister. "I am sure."

Marty looked as though she were going to start crying again. "That figures." She took her sister's hand in hers. "You've always had lousy timing."

"What does that mean?"

"In case you haven't noticed, there's a murderer running around shooting people and dumping bodies over the cliff."

"I'm the one who found Stewart's body. Believe me, I've noticed."

"Then why won't you come home with me? Just until they've caught the killer." When Jess shook her head, Marty said, "I didn't think so. Promise me you'll be careful."

"Cross my heart."

"Don't get mad when I call and check on you."

Jess hugged her sister. "I'll be disappointed if you don't."

"Oh, God." Marty drew back and gave her sister a horror-stricken look. "What will I tell Mother?"

"If you don't mention that I didn't come back with you, she'll never know I'm still gone."

"Jess!"

"It's true. Now, you'd better get a move on if you're going to get home before dark."

"I'll drop you at the Santa Lucia on my way out."

Jess shook her head. "Brandon had someone drive me over and wait for me. If I don't get back in the car, there's no telling what this guy might do. Brandon was very insistent."

"I like him better already."

Jess rolled her eyes. "That figures."

Marty rose and picked up her suitcase again. "Just promise me one thing. If you need to talk, you'll call me."

"Who else would I call? You're the only big sister I've got."

Jessica was still awake when Brandon returned at midnight. She was sitting on the couch, listening to one of his jazz records and wondering where he could be at such an hour. She hated to think that he was alone, hurting, and wouldn't come to her.

"I thought you'd be asleep by now," he said as he removed the key and closed the door. "You didn't have to wait up for me." He turned the dead bolt.

"I thought we could talk."

At the bar, he poured himself a drink and tossed it back. "I'm not up to any heavy discussions tonight." With the refilled glass in his hand, he turned to face her. "Would you like anything?"

She raised the glass of white wine she held in her hand. "I'm fine, thanks."

Brandon nodded, then stood there staring into his glass.

"We don't have to talk," Jessica finally said. "We can just sit here and listen to the music." When he still said nothing, she rose. "Or I can leave you alone if that's what you want." She started across the floor to her bedroom.

Brandon looked up and saw the hurt in her face. The best thing he could do for Jess was let her go. He knew that in his head, but his heart was a different thing.

"No." He slapped the drink on the bar and started toward her. His voice came out harsher than he'd intended, and he had the feeling that fatigue was making his actions jerky. He was afraid that when she turned there would be fear in her eyes, but he was wrong. There was only comfort—and tears. He shouldn't have underestimated her. "Don't leave."

She held out her arms, and he stepped into them. His own arms went around her and pulled her close. God, she felt good. Soft and warm and willing. When he kissed her he felt all the aching loneliness drain away, almost as if she absorbed it from him. He felt her healing hands in his hair. Felt her fingers caress his scalp, then slide down to his neck and shoulders, where she tried to massage the tension away. His hand sought her softness, felt the weight of her breast fill his palm, felt the nub of it harden beneath his thumb. He drew back and touched his forehead to hers.

"I thought I barely had the energy to make it up those stairs." He smiled. "Now look what you've done to me."

Jess glanced down at the hardened ridge beneath his trousers. "It seems things have perked up a bit."

"Unfortunately, I think it's a case of the body being willing but the spirit being too tired to do you justice."

Jess pulled back so she could look him in the eyes. "I didn't wait up so I could take advantage of you in a weak moment." That earned her a smile and a quick kiss. "I just wanted to be here in case you needed me."

He kissed her on the forehead. "I need you. It's scary how much."

"Then let's just sit here." She tugged him toward the couch. "Let me hold you."

"I'm willing to sit here." He settled his big body back in the corner of the sofa and crossed his feet on the cocktail table. "But I want to hold you." He tugged her down so that she settled across his lap and nestled her cheek just under his chin. A few minutes later he said, "The day wouldn't have been half so bad if I'd been sure it would end this way. I had the feeling your sister was going to try to talk some sense into you."

"She went back home today."

His grip tightened almost imperceptibly. "I'm glad you're still here."

"Did you make arrangements today?"

He nodded. "For the day after tomorrow, if the coroner releases the body."

"Should there be a problem?"

"I don't think so. That should give them plenty of time to perform an autopsy. But, as Carl so nicely pointed out, not even the Roarke money or name can rush that."

"It'll be fine." She pressed her lips to the juncture of his neck and shoulder. "That's just Carl's frustration talking."

"You really think so?"

"Uh-huh."

Brandon felt his body really relax for the first time since he'd realized Jess was missing. Maybe she was right, he thought as he settled more comfortably on the couch. Then, surprisingly, he felt himself give in to sleep.

It was almost dawn when Jessica stepped onto the terrace. Smiling, the Watcher noticed that she still wore the clothes she'd had on the day before. There was fatigue in the lines around her eyes, and the tired slump of her shoulders bespoke the emotional drain. She had probably never been more vulnerable in her life.

The Watcher wondered if it was time yet. Time to kill Jessica and make Brandon suffer all the more. It would be a simple matter to slip up close to the balcony. A single shot would be enough to do the job, and in the moments just before dawn, the Watcher would be able to elude anyone who might be around. Just as the fingers wrapped around the gun, just as the feet started to slip out from behind the screen of bushes, a dark figure moved in the shadows beneath the balcony. Then the shadow separated from the trees and moved out into the light cascading from Jessica's open door.

It was not anyone the Watcher knew, but judging by the stealthy way he moved, the man was not a guest out for a late night stroll. The police. Or a security guard. The Watcher smiled and drew farther back into the shadows.

Patience. All that was needed was patience. Jessica's time would come.

9

Jessica intended to steal only one last glance in the mirror but decided that the ashen face staring back at her needed brighter lipstick. After applying the makeup, she took a calming breath, picked up the jacket to her new suit, and slipped into it. Linen the color of butterscotch set off her dark hair and eyes and lent her an unusual aura of sophistication. She'd refused to wear black for Stewart's funeral, refused to look grim and stricken when she knew Brandon needed her to buoy his spirits and bolster his own flagging strength.

She'd barely seen Brandon in the last thirty-six hours. Since sitting with him on the sofa the night before last, they'd both been busy. Brandon had made arrangements for the funeral and kept an eye on the operations of the inn. Jess had busied herself answering the phone, keeping a record of the profusion of flowers, and finally slipping into a few of the hotel shops to find something to wear for the solemn occasion.

Even last night Brandon had sent her to her own

room, saying she looked tired and he needed time to himself. She suspected that he'd retreated behind closed doors and finally given way to tears. She wished he'd trusted her to hold him close while he cried, but she understood he was not a man who would willingly share his emotions. She stepped into the living room and found him sitting on the couch.

He rose. "You look beautiful. Not quite like the bohemian artist I'm used to, but beautiful."

Jess took in his white shirt against the dark blue suit he wore. The blue accentuated his eyes and lashes as well as the dark circles beneath them. "You look tired," she told him.

He took her hand and pulled her into his arms. "Honest to a fault, as usual. I wonder how I survived thirty-six years without you to set me in my place."

She looked up at him. "Just remember I'm here now."

"Stay close today. I'm going to need you." He kissed her on the forehead and then, with his hand at the small of her back, urged her toward the door.

Jess held his hand throughout the quiet ride in the dark limousine. When they finally alighted before a small, stone church on a bluff overlooking the Pacific, she was overwhelmed by the number of cars and people. She would have let go of Brandon's hand and faded into the crowd had he not kept a tight grip on her. As they made their way through the crowd, she found herself smiling at people she didn't know and intercepting curious glances aimed in her direction.

Whenever Brandon stopped to introduce her, Jess saw the shock of recognition on people's faces—probably because they connected her to the newspaper accounts. She found it difficult to smile at the openly curious faces but told herself that if Brandon could manage to be gracious under the circumstances, then so could she.

The low drone of voices was as natural as the sun and the wind, and its sudden cessation was as noticeable as the muting of the ocean. The unnatural quiet had her scanning the area. When the subdued crowd parted to reveal Jason standing at the door of the church, she found herself holding her breath like everyone else, wondering what the two men would do. But Brandon never hesitated. He kept to his course—though his body tensed as if waiting for a physical blow—until he stood less than a foot from his boyhood friend.

"He was a good man." Jason held out his hand. "I feel like I've lost part of my own family." That was when Jess felt Brandon's grip falter, as though he'd lost he ability to hold himself in check any longer. He pulled her closer to his side.

"It's good of you to come." Brandon took the other man's hand.

They stood there looking at each other while the crowd shifted from foot to foot. Jess thought they would clasp each other around the shoulders and thump each other on the back as men so often did when they need physical contact. Instead they reluctantly released their clasped hands.

"I wish I could turn back the clock," Jason finally said. "I wish I'd spent time with him during the last few years."

"He talked about you. Followed your career. He still loved you."

Jason shook his head. "My loss," he said, and when the silence became awkward, he turned to Jessica, nodded, and faded back into the crowd.

It was as though Jason's departure was the signal for people to move and talk again. The crowd shifted. Conversations resumed. Brandon made his way up the wide steps with Jess's hand still clutched in his own. As they moved slowly through the crowd, Jess saw several people she recognized. George and Nancy were there, as were many other employees. Even Danny, George's sullen assistant, was present. Jason, of course, she could see over almost everyone's head, and beside him were Florence and Megan. Even Carl Mendoza and his youthful assistant were there, though they had the good grace to stand off to one side. Jessica wondered vaguely if Mendoza's presence was personal or part of the job.

When they stepped through the side entrance into the private family room, Jess was surprised to find an older couple there. Probably in their late sixties, the couple was dressed in lavish style. The woman wore a perfectly tailored black dress with a black hat perched on her pewter hair. Diamonds glimmered at her ears and circled her throat. When she raised her hand to smooth back the flawless hair beneath her hat, more diamonds caught the light. Her lips curved in what might have passed for a smile if one didn't look into her eyes. The man with her stood erect in his charcoal suit. He was tall, with white hair, and Jess could imagine that in another time he would have led a cavalry regiment or ruled a small principality. His finger, too, glinted with diamonds when he extended his hand to Brandon.

"I can't tell you how sorry I am, Bran."

"I'm glad you could make the ceremony."

"We have been here for almost an hour." The woman's tones were as icy as the stones that glittered at her throat. "I was beginning to wonder if we'd have to proceed without you." She spared Jessica a glance, a mere stroke of the eye, that said more succinctly than words that she deemed the younger woman inconsequential. "But then you always did have complete disdain for punctuality and common courtesy." She looked back at Jessica. "I hold you directly responsible and shall certainly speak to the funeral director. How can you allow such slipshod timing? You should have secluded the family long before the crowd began to arrive."

Jessica could think of no reasonable reply.

"Jessica doesn't work here. She's with me."

The woman's gaze shifted back to Brandon. "I wasn't aware that one brought a date to funerals these days."

Brandon smiled. "Jessica, I'd like you to meet Amelia Kendall-White, Stewart's second cousin, and her husband, John White. John, Amelia, I'd like to introduce Jessica Martinson."

Amelia nodded, though her lips formed a small, disapproving pucker. John's big hand encompassed Jessica's warmly. "I'm so glad that there was someone with Brandon during this time," he said.

Amelia Kendall-White glanced at her diamond-encrusted watch. "While it's very kind of you to see about Brandon, I believe it's time for you to join the others."

Jessica tried to ease her hand from Brandon's, but he tightened the grip.

"Jessica came with me. She will remain with me." When Amelia opened her mouth to speak, Brandon said, "If your sense of propriety is outraged, I'm sure we can find you a seat elsewhere." The woman snapped her mouth shut with enough force to make her teeth click.

The small room was shrouded in silence when the funeral director entered and ushered them to the family seats. Jessica's attention began to wander. Delayed shock and the stress of the last few days, she was certain. She listened as several people, including George, spoke of Stewart's life. That Stewart had been well loved was made obvious not only by the eulogy, but by the number of mourners: the church was filled to overflowing. That Stewart had friends all over the world had been made clear to Jessica when she'd kept track of the flowers that had come from Hong Kong and New York. That he had a diversity of friends had been made apparent by the cards that arrived from movie stars and two past presidents as well as from the man who ran the local dry cleaners.

But even that hadn't prepared her for the bank of flowers that filled the front of the church and spilled down the aisles or for the line of people who filed by after the service, equally eager to extend their condolences to Brandon and satisfy their curiosity about the woman who stood at his side.

It didn't help her nerves that Brandon had planned a buffet back at the Santa Lucia and that he had invited each of the mourners to join him. What she wanted to do was go back to her room and cry. Instead she accompanied Brandon to the limousine, knowing that another difficult task lay ahead of them.

"How are you holding up?" Brandon asked almost two hours later.

Jess's feet were killing her, and her smile felt as though it were frozen in place. "Fine," she said.

He smiled. "You're a terrible liar. It's one of the things I love most about you."

Jessica felt her heart leap to her throat when Brandon used the word *love*. He could see her reaction, she knew it, and she felt herself blush.

She chanced a glance around the room to see if anyone else had noticed. Though the gathering had begun on a somber note, the food and surroundings had turned things more amiable. To Jessica's right a group of men were discussing strategy for stock market investments in these difficult times. On her other side men in equally expensive suits were comparing golf handicaps. A table full of women was showing off pictures of grandchildren, and another group was exchanging recipes.

Jessica sighed. "I don't think they'll ever leave."

"The room will start to clear in fifteen minutes."

She glanced around again. "Are you planning to set off a fire alarm?"

"Something even more effective."

She raised a questioning eyebrow.

"That's when they'll begin taking the food away. Nothing clears a room quite so effectively."

Jessica couldn't suppress a genuine smile.

"Brandon," Jason said softly from behind them. "I want you to know you can call me if you need anything."

Jessica saw Brandon stiffen as he turned to face the other man. "I appreciate that."

Jason couldn't quite look Brandon in the eye. "I remember what it felt like. It takes a while to come to terms with this kind of loss . . . with murder. It's such a senseless way to lose someone you love."

"My guess is that it made some sort of warped sense to the person who pulled the trigger."

Jason took a long drink of the amber liquid in his glass. "Then that person would have to be mad."

"How hard do you think it will be to find one madman? Because I can guarantee you that I won't give up until I do."

Jason nodded. "I felt the same way."

"Then what the hell happened?"

"Life," Jason said softly. "After a while, the grief fades and the needs of the living overwhelm the need for revenge." He nodded toward Jess. "Here is the perfect example. Do you spend your time concentrating on revenge or on the possibilities for a life? A real life, Bran. One that would make Stewart proud of you."

"I don't see that I have to choose between the two."

"You will. And in your heart you know that Stewart would want you to choose life."

Brandon put an arm around Jess and pulled her closer. "How can I choose life, as you so nicely put it, if I can't guarantee that what I love won't be next? It seems to me that the only way to choose life is to be certain the murderer won't strike again."

"What if you could be certain that this . . . person, this murderer, won't kill again? What if I could guarantee it?"

"I would have to be mad to believe that kind of guarantee. Or you would have to be mad to make it."

"To make what?" Florence asked. She stood just beside them, though none of the three had noticed her approach.

"Nothing," Jason said hastily.

Brandon took the time to study the beautiful, dark-haired woman. "Your husband was trying to cheer me up."

Jessica noticed that Jason's mouth had flattened into a thin line. Whatever dialogue the two men had begun was obviously cut short by Florence's presence. Hoping that she could give them more opportunity to talk, Jessica shook free of Brandon's arm.

"If you gentlemen will excuse me, I think I'd like to powder my nose. Florence, would you like to join me?"

Though the look Florence gave the two men revealed just how reluctant she was to leave them together, Jess had given her little choice in the matter. She could be rude and refuse the request, or she could leave the two men to themselves.

"Of course," Florence said as she turned and walked with Jessica out of the room.

Jessica gave one final look over her shoulder as she stepped into the hall. She was relieved to see that Brandon and Jason hadn't moved from where she'd left them, though she couldn't tell if they were speaking.

"I hope you know what you're doing," Florence said as they moved down the hall. "If they get into a fight, it'll be on your conscience."

"A fight? They're both grown men. I hardly think they're going to start throwing punches."

Florence stopped and let Jessica precede her into the lounge. "You don't know much about men, do you?"

Jessica slid onto the upholstered bench before the large gilt mirror and began to fluff her curls. She knew little about men but certainly didn't want to admit it. "What would they have to get into a fight over?"

"They've barely been civil since the affair with Jacqueline. At least when she was alive she could keep them in line. Since her death, they can hardly be in the same room. Jason holds Brandon responsible for his mother's murder."

"That's ridiculous. Brandon isn't a murderer."

"Oh, I don't mean that he thinks Brandon killed her, but if they hadn't been having an affair, Jacqueline wouldn't have been out by herself where the murderer could get to her."

Jess felt the blood drain from her face. "What do you mean, 'having an affair'?"

"Oh, dear. I shouldn't have said anything."

"Maybe not, but you have." Jess held Florence's gaze in the mirror. "So you might as well explain."

"There isn't much to explain, really. Brandon was having an affair with Jacqueline. Rumor has it that they'd been . . . seeing each other for quite some time."

Jess turned to face Florence directly. "But she was old enough to be his mother."

"I know. But she was beautiful." Florence shrugged philosophically. "Jacqueline knew how to manage men. She knew how to attract them and please them and . . . Well, let's just say that Brandon wasn't the first, though he was probably the youngest. As Jacqueline got older, the men seemed to get younger."

Jessica concentrated on keeping her mouth from gaping. She remembered the pictures of Jacqueline she'd found in Jason's files. She had been beautiful, and she'd hardly looked old enough to be Jason's mother, but she hadn't looked the like the kind of woman who'd lure men—who'd lure her son's best friend—into an affair. But then Jess knew that the camera was as capable of hiding the truth as revealing it.

"Are you certain?"

Florence shrugged and turned back to the mirror to fool with her own hair. "As sure as I can be without actually having seen it with my own eyes. It wasn't much of a secret." She removed lipstick from her purse and hesitated with it open in her hand. "You can ask almost anyone who was around during that time."

Jessica nodded, then dug in her purse for her own lipstick. Oh, God, how could she hope to hold the interest of a man who was used to someone as beautiful and glamorous as Jacqueline Kendall? She couldn't even find her own lipstick. Frustrated, she dumped the contents of her small purse on the vanity and rummaged through the mess. Keys. Comb. An empty tissue package. Finally, her lipstick.

What had George said about Jacqueline? She'd had an eye for beauty. He'd sounded as though he might have been half in love with her himself. When she realized her hand was shaking too much to apply the lipstick, she rose on the pretext of looking for tissue. To blot her lipstick, she explained to Florence. In reality she thought she'd need it for the threatening tears.

When she rounded the corner, she put her hands on the edge of the sink and dropped her head. What had she done? Fallen for a man who could have any woman he wanted? Risked her heart again when she should have had more sense? And yet . . . he'd called her a miracle. He'd said he needed her. He'd kept her at his side despite public curiosity and the obvious disapproval of his cousin Amelia, however many times she was removed. And she'd foolishly looked into his eyes and believed he could love her.

She raised her head and looked at herself in the mirror. Where should she place her faith, in her own instincts or in the gossip Florence was passing along? She ran her hands under the cool water, blotted them on the paper towel, then pressed the towel against her own heated cheeks. She was almost ready to face Florence when she heard the door open.

"So this is where you're hiding," she heard Amelia Kendall-White say.

Jess glanced at the entryway, as though expecting to see the woman bearing down upon her. Instead she heard Florence say, "I'm not hiding anywhere. Jessica and I came to powder our noses."

"Jessica is here?"

Jess forced herself to walk around the corner and into the lounge area. "Right here," she said as brightly as she could manage.

The older woman raked her with a glance before settling onto the bench Jessica had occupied earlier. "You're looking a bit pale, my dear."

"It's been a long day."

Florence added, "We've been discussing Jacqueline."

Amelia gave Jess a blatantly pitying look. "Don't expect me to speak well of the woman just because she's dead. She was nothing more than a cheap trollop from the wrong side of the tracks, and ensnaring my brother did nothing to improve her. You know what they say: You can take the trollop out of the slums, but . . ." She let the sentence trail off as she peered into the mirror to slick her hair back under her hat.

Jessica was aware of the way Florence was studying her, but she asked anyway, "Your brother?"

"Walter was several years my senior. He was handsome and charming and could have had any woman he wanted, but he became enamored of that dark-haired creature. She was still in her teens, but she knew how to cast her evil spell even then. Walter was determined to have her. They ran off and married. She eventually drove him to drink."

"What happened to him?"

"He disappeared," Florence said.

"Before Jason was even born," Amelia added. "The family spent thousands of dollars looking for Walter. Father hired detectives and placed ads in newspapers up and down the coast. Mother was never the same; she died convinced that Jacqueline murdered him."

Florence snapped her purse closed. "You're being melodramatic, Amelia."

"I'm only telling you what Mother believed. Besides, you lived with Jacqueline. Don't you think she was capable of murder?"

Florence rose. "Please, Amelia. Remember that you're talking about my husband's mother. Megan's grandmother. I'm hardly likely to go around accusing her of murder."

Amelia swept aside the contents of Jess's purse and

pulled a jeweled compact out of her own purse. "Well, I have no such hesitation." She swiped the powder puff over her nose. "I grew up with her. Even as a child she could bat her eyelashes over those big brown eyes and get her way." She snapped her compact closed and slipped it into her purse. "By the time she was sixteen, she had every boy in town following her around, but she wasn't content with a boy—or even a man of her own kind. Walter came home from college and fell hopelessly for her. I told him she was no good, but he had to have her. Jacqueline, of course, couldn't resist the Kendall money. The Kendall curse, actually." Amelia stood. "You'd think I would have learned from Walter's mistake."

Florence slanted Jessica an enigmatic look. "I think I'd better go find Megan. George volunteered to entertain her for a few minutes, but he's probably ready to pull his hair out by now."

Jessica stuffed her things back into her purse. "I'll go with you. I haven't had a chance to talk to Megan yet." Unwilling to be left alone with the older woman, she followed Florence out into the hallway, only to discover Amelia right on her heels. In the hall they were all brought up short by John White, accompanied by Danny.

"Three such lovely ladies make the wait worthwhile, don't you agree?" the older man asked.

Danny shrugged.

Amelia spoke to hide the awkward silence. "Jessica, I'd like you to meet our nephew, Daniel White."

"We've met," Jess told the older woman, then proceeded to explain how Danny and his girlfriend had saved her out among the sand dunes.

Rather than stay to bask in the glow of his aunt's pride, Danny excused himself.

"Stewart's death was a blow to Daniel," Amelia confided to the group, as though trying to explain the boy's abrupt departure. "Stewart had given him a job, but then Brandon fired him. I'm sure, had Stewart lived, he would have made George take Daniel back. The boy just loves flowers and plants. I know it would have been a wonderful opportunity for him."

John patted his wife on the shoulder. "Let's not worry about it, my dear. Something else will turn up."

Amelia looked at her husband. "But you had such hopes."

"It will work out," the older man said, then turned to shake hands with Jason, who had just stepped into the hallway.

As the conversation flowed, Jessica watched Amelia, whose eyes remained on her husband. There came over the woman's face a look of such vulnerability and longing that Jessica blinked to be sure it was real. But by then the look was gone, and the usual sour expression had returned. But there had been that momentary transformation, Jessica was certain. And she remembered Amelia's comment about the Kendall curse—and about how she should have learned from her brother's mistakes.

Jessica put her fingers to her temple and massaged the headache that was beginning to build behind her eyes. Too many emotions were swirling around, too many complex relationships, too many mysteries. Just as she was about to excuse herself and go in search of Brandon, she heard her name called in a childish voice.

She looked up to see Megan coming through the outside door, her small hand in George's much larger one. Jess smiled and waved at the child as Amelia continued to drone on about people not living up to their promises.

When Megan broke loose from George's grip and headed in her direction, Jessica opened her arms and waited for her to run into them. Just as the child rounded the group, Amelia made a wide gesture with her arm. The child's shoulder came in contact with the woman's hand. The purse the older woman carried was brushed out of her fingers, hit the ground with a thud, and broke open, spilling the contents across the hallway. Amelia whipped around to glare at the child, who had backed up against the wall, her eyes wide with fear.

"I'm sorry, Mommy. I'm sorry. I'm sorry."

Jessica reached the child first. She put her arms around the small shaking shoulders as the men went down on their hands and knees to gather Amelia's things. "It was just an accident, sweetie," she assured the child. "Accidents happen to everybody."

"Little girls shouldn't run inside," Amelia scolded.

Careful to stay between the child and Amelia, Jess turned to face the woman. "She said she's sorry."

Amelia said nothing as her gaze scanned the area, then finally stopped only inches from Jessica's feet. Jess looked down to see the small, deadly object that had everyone's attention. A gun . . . there was a gun lying only inches away from her. Jessica took an involuntary step backward, making sure that Megan remained out of sight. My God, she thought, it could have gone off. Someone could have been hurt—or killed.

In a move more swift than Jessica would have expected from her, Amelia bent down and scooped it up, then grabbed her purse from her husband and stuffed the weapon into it. Without another word, the older woman nodded to the group and started toward the exit with her husband in tow. Only when they were out of sight did Jess release her hold on Megan.

Megan's big round eyes were on her mother. "I didn't mean to, Mommy. I'll be more careful. I promise."

But it was Jason who bent to the child, not Florence. He scooped her up and held her against him, though the child's gaze remained fixed on her mother.

Florence reached out to stroke her child's dark hair. Megan hid her face against her father's shoulder. "It was an accident, just like Jessica said." Though Florence's voice was mother-calm, her hand shook visibly. No doubt she, too, realized just how fortunate they'd been that the gun hadn't discharged accidentally.

Jess was standing in front of Brandon's apartment, rummaging through her purse for the key, when the door was opened from the inside. Jazz, deep and dark, poured out of the room.

"There you are." Brandon smiled down at her. "I was beginning to wonder if I should start looking for you."

Jessica tossed her purse on the table. "I was visiting with the Kendalls and the Whites."

Brandon grimaced. "Poor baby. Is white wine okay?"

Jessica nodded and watched as Brandon poured her a glass. He'd tossed his jacket and tie over a nearby chair. The top button of his white dress shirt was undone, and his sleeves were rolled up. He appeared more relaxed than she'd expected, but a quick glance at his face had her wondering if it was sheer exhaustion. "How are you holding up?" she asked, echoing the question Brandon had asked her earlier.

"Better than I'd expected. Though that could still be shock." He handed Jess the wine, then returned to the sofa, hoping she would settle into his embrace as she had two nights ago. "My head knows we buried him today, but in my heart . . . it's hard for me to believe that I won't see Stewart again."

She came to him then and sat on the sofa beside him. "I don't know what to say to you." She set her glass on the table.

Instead of waiting for her to come willingly into his arms, he reached out to pull her to him. She snuggled into his embrace and laid her cheek on his chest. "I feel better when I can hold you," he said simply. He could feel her smile.

"Maybe a teddy bear would work just as well."

"No." He cupped her face in his big hands and lifted his head so he could look at her. Just look, he told himself, but her big brown eyes were filling with tears, and he used his thumb to wipe away the first one to slide down her soft cheek. "No one has ever made me feel the way you do."

He tilted his head and focused on her lips. Soft, luscious, just made for kisses. His kisses. He was amazed at how sweet she tasted. Not just sweet, he realized, but healing. He'd meant only to taste her, but he found himself deepening the kiss. His fingers sought the softness of her hair as his mouth plundered hers. He felt her hand at the open collar of his shirt. It felt like satin fire. He felt her gentle fingers stroke the skin at the juncture of his neck and shoulders before gliding up to comb through his hair. He burned where she touched him.

Then he heard her whimper, felt her body pressed closer to his, and understood the needs that had overtaken her. After releasing her lips, he held her far enough away to see the hunger in her eyes. He could have her here and now, he knew. He felt desire rip through him, like the talons of a hungry animal, but he realized just as swiftly that he didn't want Jess for just one night. He wanted her forever, and he didn't think forever could be grasped at in this kind of frenzy. He gave her one last gentle kiss before settling back against the sofa and pressing her cheek against his heart.

He felt her take a deep breath, felt her breath hitch as she did—and he hoped like hell that she wasn't going to cry in earnest. If she looked up at him with tears in her eyes, he wouldn't be able to deny what they both wanted. But, for himself, he selfishly wanted to wait. He wanted to be certain that the first time they made love it was because she wanted him, not because she was overcome with grief and needed that most basic of human contact. And not because she pitied him, but because she wanted him—forever.

He brushed the curls back from her face and dropped a chaste kiss on her forehead. "Thanks for sticking by me today."

"Was that a thank-you kiss?" There was a quiver in her voice.

"Only the last one. The others were the 'I love you' kind."

There was a moment of silence that made Brandon hold his breath.

"Really?"

"Really. What kind did you think they were?"

"The 'I want your body' kind of kisses."

He smiled down at her. "I think that all goes together."

She looked up at him, her heart in her eyes. "Then why did you stop?"

"So you'd know my intentions are honorable, but if you keep looking at me like that, you're going to push my resolve to the breaking point." He traced her lips, lips that were red from his kisses, with the pad of his thumb. "I don't want to rush this."

He saw the blush before she tucked her head back under his chin. "I think that was supposed to be my line."

He smiled. Jess would take it wrong if he told her that he could get sex anytime he wanted, that what he needed from her tonight was her sweetness and her healing powers. That most of all he wanted her to be sure, because once they'd passed the barrier of physical intimacy, he'd never let her go. The first would enrage her and the last might scare her, so he kept his mouth shut and leaned his cheek against her hair.

"Did you and Jason get to talk?" Jess asked once her breathing had evened out.

Brandon dropped another kiss on the top of her head. "That was another thank-you kiss," he told her before she could ask. "It's been a long time since we've been able to do anything but argue."

"About the campground?"

"Among other things. But today it was as if none of that existed. We talked about the 'old days.'" He gave a rueful laugh. "God, that makes me sound old. We reminisced about the Halloween we crawled up in the bell tower of the hotel and rang the damn things at midnight."

"You didn't!"

"We were only in fifth grade, and it seemed like the ultimate Halloween prank."

"What happened?"

"Let's just say that Stewart was especially persuasive when the police cars and the fire trucks pulled up." He liked Jess's soft laughter. "Then there was the time Stewart decided to discuss the birds and bees with us."

"How old were you?"

"Probably eleven or twelve. When he told us he wanted to talk about birds and bees, we took him literally. We had this injured bird, you see, and we thought he was going to help us out. We were terribly disappointed when we realized he was talking about girls. We didn't consider them very important at that point."

She looked up at him. "And now?"

He bent down to give her a searing kiss. "What do you think?"

"I think it's pretty odd that you've made it this far without ever getting married." Jess snuggled against his shoulder, afraid her eyes would reveal how important her next question was. "Haven't you ever been in love?"

That stopped him. She felt him stiffen, then consciously relax.

"I thought I was in love once."

"And?"

"I was wrong."

"How did you know?"

Brandon sat up straighter and held Jess by the shoulders so he could look right in her eyes. "I couldn't have been in love with her. She wasn't you, and I've been waiting all my life for you."

Jess felt the tears gathering in her eyes. Judging by the expression on Brandon's face, that wasn't the reaction he was hoping for, but she just couldn't help herself. The idea that anyone could feel that way about her made her want to cry.

"Shh, Jess. Don't cry, honey."

His kisses were feather light. She felt them fan across her cheek and up to the eyelids she closed in an effort to halt the tears. His lips when they found hers were gentle at first, then Jessica felt the abrupt change, as though something in him had broken loose. His mouth became demanding, and his body pressed her back against the sofa. She was surprised to find that she wasn't scared, only excited. Her hands crept up to his neck and then into his hair. Thick, silky hair with just a hint of curl. So different from the hair that peeked out of his collar.

Brandon couldn't believe that anyone would be so generous. Couldn't believe that Jess could be so giving when he'd offered so little in the way of courtship or charm. But, God, she felt good. Her whimpers of pleasure were driving him out of his mind, and the magic she could weave with just a touch had him wild. With shaking fingers, he undid the tiny pearl buttons on her blouse and pushed both blouse and jacket off her shoulder. He nuzzled the soft skin just above her collarbone while his hand cupped her breast through the lacy bra she wore. He was in the process of inching the silk down to reveal the creamy skin of her breast when the phone rang. His first thought was to ignore it, that if they couldn't reach him, they'd call Stewart. Then reality came back like a dash of cold water, and he found himself sitting up and groping for the phone.

Jessica couldn't believe that she'd want to cry for the loss of Brandon's body on hers. Couldn't believe that the abrupt cessation of all those wonderful reactions he'd caused could have her suddenly unsure of herself again. She struggled with the strap of her bra as he answered the phone. Unaware of—and uncaring of—what he was discussing, she pulled her blouse back on and struggled with the little pearl buttons that had seemed so elegant before. Lost in her own world, she was surprised when Brandon's hands came down over hers.

"Don't," he said gently.

She looked up at him, tears and hurt shimmering in her eyes.

"Don't be embarrassed by what we were doing. I was going to make love to you, Jess. Love. Not something to be ashamed of."

She managed a watery smile. "You were? I thought you didn't want to rush?"

"How could we be rushing things when I've been waiting for you all my life? And I intend to finish what we started—only not right now." He rose and pulled her to her feet. "I've got an emergency that needs handling." He kissed her. "But I'll be back as quickly as I can."

"Is this where I offer to slip into something more comfortable?"

"Only if you want to. As far as I'm concerned, you can offer to slip into my bed. That will save me the trouble of having to slip you out of anything." He grabbed her by the lapels of her new suit and dragged her to him for a hard kiss. "Just tell me you'll be here when I get back."

"I'll be here," she promised, then watched as he walked out the door. It was several moments before she could force her limbs to move. Her first thought was that the room was warm, but when she put her palm up to her cheek, she discovered that she was blushing. She opened the door to the balcony and stepped out into the cool night. The air, heavy with fog, cooled her skin, and the rhythm of the waves lapping against the shore soothed her nerves.

Love. He'd said he loved her. She smiled up at the waning moon that peeked through the fog. Everything would be just fine.

The Watcher waited for Brandon to join the woman on the balcony, and when he didn't the Watcher felt a spurt of satisfaction. Brandon had always been a chivalrous fool; he'd never known how to take what he wanted. And he did want Jessica; that had been obvious today, as obvious as the fact that there wasn't the kind of intimacy between the two that comes with hot, slick sex. If, of course, the timid female was capable of anything that lusty.

The stupid, vapid smile on Jessica's face sent a flicker of rage through the Watcher. It had the Watcher wondering how close Jessica would have to be for the gun to blow that smile right away. How would Brandon react to that? How would the fool feel when he found Jessica in a pool of blood and knew that it was his fault? That he had killed her?

It was tempting, of course. It would be easy to sneak up in the shadows. Even if Jessica saw the Watcher, she wouldn't be frightened. But that was too quick. It wouldn't make Brandon suffer long enough. And it was the suffering that the Watcher wanted. So Brandon would be allowed the illusion a little longer. The illusion that he could protect Jessica. The illusion that he could have an honorable life.

The Watcher could wait a little longer because that would make Brandon's guilt cut that much deeper. And because the Watcher had left a surprise for Jessica.

10

Jessica left the balcony door open when she came in. She loved the cool night air and the sound of the ocean as it mingled with hot jazz. She swayed to the music and wondered if she would ever again hear the sultry sounds without thinking of ocean vistas and blue eyes.

Though the combination had a way of stirring up long dormant needs, she knew she would never be able to shed both her clothes and her inhibitions and climb into Brandon's bed. However, she could slip into something a little less formal, something with fewer buttons and easier access.

She was still swaying to the music when she entered her room. She removed a nightshirt from the drawer—her only sleeping apparel since her own clothes had been destroyed—then glided into the bathroom. One look at the mirror stopped her in her tracks.

"Last chance!" was written in lipstick across the mirror. "Jessica, go home now." On the floor she saw what was left of her camera; someone had smashed it against the tiled wall.

Jess stumbled back and came up hard against the door frame. The gown slipped from her fingers as she turned and ran to the living room. Grabbing the phone, she dialed the desk.

"This is an emergency," she said in what sounded like a calm, rational voice though the hand holding the receiver shook so hard that she had to use the other one to steady it. "Have Brandon return to his apartment at once."

She slammed down the receiver and stood with her back pressed against the wall. Someone had been in her room again, someone who wanted to terrify her. She willed herself not to scream. Admittedly, this time they hadn't indulged in the frenzied violence of before. No cut-up clothes, no broken bottles and jars, just the simple message and the destruction of her camera. But that was enough. More than enough. This time just the knowledge that the mysterious intruder—most likely a murderer—had been here had her dredging up visions of the possibilities. And the fear that he might still be in the room.

Her instinctive response to that thought had her flattened against the wall as though she could sink right into solid matter. She put her hand to her mouth to keep from screaming and found she was holding her breath so that the sound of her ragged breathing wouldn't betray her position. So this is what it feels like to be stalked, she thought. To know that someone is watching your every move.

A noise had her looking frantically around the room before she realized it had drifted in through the open window with the evening breeze. Another noise startled her. Mute, frozen, she listened to the footsteps in the hallway and the rattling of her doorknob. She glanced around, frantic for a hiding place. The wind fluttered the curtains over the sliding glass door; she was halfway across the room when she heard the key in the lock.

"Jess."

She turned, her hand to her throat, to face Brandon as he entered the room. Without a word she ran straight toward him, barely giving him time to open his arms for her.

"What's wrong, Jess? What is it?" But when he would have held her away so that he could see her, she clung to him more tightly. "Okay." He held her close. "Just tell me you're all right. You are all right, aren't you, Jess?"

She nodded her head where it was buried against his shoulder. "Just give me a minute. Please."

"You can have all the time you need. Just as long as you're all right." She felt his lips against her hair, felt his hand glide up and down her back. "You're crying," he said finally. "Are you hurt?"

She sniffled. "No."

"Just let me look at you, Jess. Then I'll hold you as long as you like."

She released her grip somewhat so that he could lift her head up to meet his eyes.

He swore savagely, then hauled her back into his arms. "You're pale as a damn ghost." He started toward her bedroom, "You need to lie down."

"No." She dug in her heels. "Not in there."

He turned around and eased her down on the sofa. After placing a pillow behind her head, he held her hand until she stopped shaking.

"Whatever scared you, is it in the bedroom?" Jessica shook her head. "In the bathroom, then?" She nodded.

"Will you be okay long enough for me to look?" She took a ragged breath and nodded.

Brandon came back swearing, snagged the receiver from the phone, and punched in a number. "Carl Mendoza," he demanded after a moment. "Tell him it's Brandon Roarke." He reached out to touch Jess's cheek, then jerked back. "Yes, Carl, I damn well know what time it is. You need to get over to the inn right now. There's been another incident."

Brandon checked his watch only to discover that it was less than three minutes since the last time he'd checked. How the hell long could it take Carl to get from his office to the Santa Lucia? Jessica's cheek was nuzzled against his damp shirt, but at least she'd stopped crying. He didn't know if he could have taken many more tears. He stopped himself from looking at his watch again, then made a silent promise that if Carl had stopped off for doughnuts, it would be the last stop the man ever made as a law enforcement officer.

Jessica shifted in his arms. "Do you have any aspirin? I've cried myself into a headache," she explained when he gave her a questioning look.

He nodded, released her reluctantly, and went into the bathroom for aspirin, a glass of water, and a cold washcloth.

"We need to talk," Jessica told him when he returned.

"Take these." He waited until she'd swallowed the pills and set down the glass before he handed her the damp cloth.

Her "Thank you" was muffled by the thick terry cloth, but the sigh of relief made him glad he'd thought of the cool compress.

"We need to talk," she repeated after a moment.

"About what?"

She lifted the cloth from her face and looked up at him. "I'm scared, not stupid." Her eyes were red and puffy, but the dark irises didn't waver. "Something's going on. Something that cost Stewart his life and probably Jacqueline Kendall as well. If the message on that mirror has anything to do with the murders, I might be next. I think that gives me the right to know what's going on. And I think you know more about it than you've told."

"I don't know who the murderer is." He had suspicions. God, did he have suspicions. But even he couldn't bring himself to really believe them. He started to pace the room. "That was Stewart I buried today. The man who raised me when my parents died. The man I respected most in the world. Believe me, if I had proof, I'd turn it over to the police."

"Then why do I have the feeling you know something you're not telling?"

"Maybe you've been listening to the wrong people."

"Don't do that."

He stopped and looked at her. "Do what?"

"Go on the offensive." She shrugged. "Change the subject. Put up that invisible wall of yours. It won't work with me. You can't make me go away that easily."

"Are you crazy?" He crossed to her in three long strides and hauled her off the sofa. "The last thing in the world I want is for you to go away." He pulled her body tight against his and kissed her long and hard. "Does that feel like I want you to go away?"

She relaxed into his embrace, then shook her head. "I guess I'm just upset."

He thought he heard a suspicious sniffle. "Don't start

crying again." He stepped back and framed her face with his hands. "You have every right to be upset."

God knew he was upset. More than upset. He was furious, not only at whoever had broken into the room, but at himself. And he was terrified—terrified he'd overlooked something important and that he wouldn't be able to take care of her.

And terrified that in order to keep Jess safe, he was going to have to destroy someone else he loved. "I won't let anyone hurt you," he promised.

"And how are you going to manage that? Someone broke in here without your realizing it. Are you planning to put me in a locked cell where no one can get to me and I can't get out?"

He smiled at the idea. "You'd go crazy."

"I know. So what are you going to do?"

"For starters, I'm going to keep a security man with you."

"Oh, please." She gave a vague wave of her hand. "I'm hardly the type to be trailed by a bodyguard."

He smiled down at her. "I had someone following you today. You don't think I would have let you out of my sight otherwise, do you?"

"There was someone following me today?"

Brandon nodded. "Once we got back to the inn. You gave him a few bad moments when you stayed in the ladies' room so long. He said if the other women hadn't been there with you, he would have stormed the place."

"Oh, my God."

"In fact, that was security who called earlier. While I had someone on you, I didn't think it was necessary to monitor the surveillance cameras. But when head of security reviewed the tapes this evening, he discovered that someone had covered the camera lens outside my door for about three minutes. That must be when our message writer got in the room." He stopped to look around. "Only I told security that there were no signs of forced entry. Since the only two keys are yours and mine, I don't understand how our visitor got in here without forcing the lock. Do you still have your key?"

Jess nodded. "In my purse."

Brandon handed Jess her bag and waited patiently as she rummaged through it. When she came up empty-handed, he took the purse from her and dumped the contents onto the table.

Jess sorted through her things, then turned her puzzled eyes to Brandon. "It's not here."

"When did you last see it?"

"When I let myself in."

Brandon shook his head. "I let you in."

"That's right. When I put it in my bag, then. No, it was in the ladies' room."

"You're sure?"

"I couldn't find my lipstick, so I dumped everything out. Just like this," she said with a nod toward the jumble of items on the table. "I must not have picked it up."

"Then anyone could have found it."

"Any woman," Jess pointed out.

Brandon pulled on one of her curls so that she looked up at him. "Jess, I don't think someone who has murdered two people would hesitate to go in the wrong restroom." Whatever she might have said to that was cut off by a firm knock on the door.

"This had better be important," Carl said when Brandon let him in. The policeman's face was heavily shadowed, there were deep circles under his eyes, and his shirt looked as if he'd slept in it. Brandon explained what had happened. After a quick check of the bathroom, Mendoza asked to use the phone.

"I'll need to get some pictures and check for prints," Mendoza said when he went back to the bathroom for another look. "Unfortunately, I'm short-handed tonight. I'll have someone here first thing tomorrow. Leave everything just the way it is."

Brandon raked a hand through his hair. "Don't you think you're being too casual about this? What if this is connected to the murders?"

"We're a small police force, Brandon, with limited manpower and resources. I want to put my best man on this. Unfortunately, he's out of town. Besides, I don't think we're going to find much of anything. Anyone smart enough to cover up the security camera probably didn't leave any clues lying around."

He took statements from Brandon and Jessica, then had Brandon call security for a copy of the videotape. They watched the three minutes of blank tape twice before Mendoza admitted it wasn't any help, then he insisted on going over the details again. He was very thorough, which should have reassured Jessica. Instead she fought the urge to wring her hands.

"And when did you first realize your key was missing, Ms. Martinson?"

Jess gave him a nervous smile. "Just before you arrived."

She watched as Mendoza made notations in his little notebook. "So anyone could have found it."

Jess nodded.

"Of course, Brandon wouldn't have needed to take your key since he has one of his own."

"It is my apartment, Carl."

Mendoza nodded. "And you did have ample opportunity to create the illusion that someone else had been here before Ms. Martinson returned to the room."

Brandon sighed. "And why would I do that, Carl? Do I really look like I want to scare Jess off?"

"Looks can be deceiving."

Brandon took Jess's hand in his own. "Not this time."

Carl nodded and studied his notes in silence for several minutes. Without looking up, he said, "Brandon, I think it's time to tell me what you know. Ms. Martinson's life could depend on it."

"Damn it, Carl, if I knew anything, don't you think I'd tell you?"

Mendoza looked Brandon in the eye. "It would certainly be in your best interest. Assuming you want the murderer caught."

"What do you mean by that?"

Mendoza closed his notebook. "It means you're the only person I can think of who was intimately acquainted with both victims and had the means and the opportunity to vandalize Ms. Martinson's rooms."

Jessica jumped to her feet. "That's ridiculous. I don't believe it for one minute."

The fact that she would defend him so vehemently made Brandon smile. He would have felt even better if he'd been certain she was trying to convince Carl and not herself.

The look Mendoza gave her could only be described as pitying. "I'm sure you don't, but it's my job to protect you. To do that I must look at all the possibilities."

"Then you'd better keep looking, because Brandon wouldn't hurt me. He wouldn't," she insisted when Mendoza only looked at her.

"Don't." Gently Brandon tugged her down to the couch beside him. "If he can't see that, then there's no use telling him. It's enough that you know the truth." He wished he could be certain there wasn't a pucker of doubt around her eyes.

"It's nothing personal, Brandon," Carl assured him. "Ms. Martinson isn't a suspect because she wasn't here when Jacqueline was murdered. Otherwise I would be taking the same look at her motives and opportunities."

Brandon nodded. "If you really believe I might be guilty, I'm surprised you're willing to take my word that I won't go in the bathroom and tamper with evidence."

"If you are guilty, you were already there. And if you aren't . . ." Carl shrugged. "Then you want the guilty party caught as much as I do." He looked at Jessica. "Probably more."

"Much more," Brandon assured him.

Carl rose. "I'll be back tomorrow. Early."

"I want to be kept informed," Brandon warned Carl as he was leaving.

"Don't sit around waiting for a big breakthrough, like they have in the movies. I think our man is much too clever to have left anything behind." Carl stepped out into the hallway, then turned back. "Oh, I think you might be interested in the fact that the state lab verified my assistant's find. Those were human bones under the rosebush."

"Oh, my God," Jess whispered.

Brandon's gaze focused on Carl. "What does that have to do with the murder investigation?"

"Probably nothing." Mendoza shrugged. "Though it does make me wonder what else might be buried around here."

Brandon sighed. "Nothing that I'm aware of. Go home, Carl." He looked over at Jessica, noticed not only the fatigue, but the definite signs of worry. "You've done enough damage for one night."

Hardly noticing the door close behind Mendoza, Jessica turned back toward her room. She knew she wouldn't sleep, but she desperately needed some privacy to think. Could Mendoza be right? Could Brandon have done those things? Admittedly she'd exercised bad judgment with Eric, but surely she'd learned enough about human nature not to fall in love with a murderer. Hadn't she?

"Jessica."

She turned at the sound of Brandon's voice. "Yes?"

"You can't go in there." He pointed toward her bedroom.

She looked at the door and remembered Mendoza's edict. "I guess I'll just sleep on the couch, then. The quilt should be enough cover."

"Like hell you will."

Jess measured the sofa in a glance, then looked back at Brandon. "Be reasonable. Your toes will hang over the end."

"I have no intention of sleeping on the sofa."

"Then where . . ." She stopped when she saw the way he looked at her. There was a white hot fire simmering there. It had bleached the color from his eyes until they were almost gray. She would have stepped back from him if he hadn't reached out and grabbed her shoulders.

"Don't run from me, Jess."

"I'm not running."

"And don't lie. Not to me and not to yourself."

"I'm not. I only—"

"If you don't have faith in me, then no one does. I need you to believe in me."

There it was again: that need. It got her as nothing else could. "I know you didn't kill anyone. And I know you aren't the one who's stalking me." This time it was she who framed his face with her hands. Her skin looked pale next to his tan cheek. Her fingers looked frail set against his strong jaw. "If I thought you were capable of that, I would have left with Marty."

"You're sure?"

"Yes," she told him, and realized that when he looked her in the eye and asked her point-blank, she truly believed in his innocence. No questions. No doubts. Just an absolute faith that he was no more capable of murder than she was.

It was a heady feeling to have all that worry and doubt fade away; she wondered why she didn't sense a similar relaxation in Brandon, then she realized that the emotion that had him strung tight was different. It was passion. Desire. A physical need for her that seemed to radiate off him in waves.

She felt as though she were standing at the mouth of a volcano, and the knowledge that she wanted to leap into the flames, that she wanted to be scorched by the heat, had her wondering if she'd finally lost her mind. For once she'd been seared by his heat, she would never be the same again. She discovered that this keening desire was more frightening than the idea that he might have killed.

Brandon saw it in her eyes. Longing. And needs that she didn't quite understand. Though all trace of doubt had been swept from her eyes, he wondered if she had really—if only for a moment—believed him capable of cold-blooded murder. He knew that despite his reputation for charm and persuasiveness, he didn't have the words to explain himself to her. But he needed her to believe in him. God, how he needed it.

He had other needs as well. He needed her sweetness, her light, her love. He needed to see passion in her eyes and to hear his name on her lips. But most of all he needed her faith in him. Only that could light the dark corners of his soul.

With one hand, he tilted her face up to him. He searched her eyes for any sign of fear and, finding none, lowered his mouth to hers. His kiss wasn't gentle; he didn't intend it to be. It was filled with passion and longing and the need for her to be his. His fingers curled around the back of her neck, and he could feel her pulse scrambling beneath his thumb. He slanted his mouth over hers and plunged his tongue within. She would be his. She would. With his body he would drive any vestige of doubt from her mind. He would show her what it meant to be cherished and protected.

Is it fair to bind her to you in that way? a small voice asked. He ignored the question and used his other hand to pull her against him. It felt good to have that hard, hot part of him nestled against her softness. So damn good. It felt even better to have her arms snake around his neck, to have her go up on tiptoe as though she couldn't get close enough to him. He tore his mouth from hers so he could trail kisses along her cheek and nibble at her ear. She shuddered when his teeth closed over one lobe, then leaned her head back to give him better access to her neck.

"I need you," he murmured when he raised his head to look at her. The desire in her eyes drove him to taste her again and again. "I need you now," he whispered in her ear. "Let me show you how much."

He wanted her, Jess thought, though he talked only of needs. His physical need was all too obvious. Even if the hard, rigid strength of it hadn't been grinding against her, she would have known. But the fact that out of all the women he knew, he wanted her . . . ah, that was what almost had her weeping. She murmured his name as he pressed kisses along her throat.

The murmur of frustration when he encountered her

clothes made Jess smile. With nimble fingers he worked her blouse from the waistband of her skirt and cupped her breast; her smile disappeared. She'd never known a touch could transform her. Never thought that his hand upon her, his thumb teasing her nipple, could make her feel this way. Powerful. Irresistible. Wanted. She opened her eyes to find him studying her, and the look stole her breath away.

"Let me love you," he whispered. "Let me cherish you and keep you safe."

When she smiled up at him—a tremulous, fleeting smile that exposed her fears and uncertainties—he bent to taste her sweetness. She was everything he'd dreamed. Gentle and fierce. Innocent and seductive. A miracle. His miracle. He scooped her up into his arms and carried her to his bedroom, knowing that after tonight Jess would have the power to destroy him. Or save him. He hadn't prayed in a long time, but as his lips sought hers, as his fingers skimmed her curves and his body enfolded hers, he took the time to pray that when she saw into his darkened soul she wouldn't turn away.

Jessica fought her old doubts when he set her beside his bed. He was used to experienced women; what if he found her clumsy? He was used to beautiful, sophisticated women; what if he found her boring? But when he hesitated, his hand trembling over her breast, she knew that he was as frightened as she was. And she knew, with a certainty that astounded her, that he was as profoundly moved.

Jess smiled and placed a kiss beside the pulse that beat in his neck. She nuzzled the warm skin and rubbed her cheek against the hair that peeked out of the collar of his white dress shirt. With trembling fingers she unfastened the next button and placed a kiss there. She undid another and laid a trail of kisses farther down his chest. With each button, with each kiss, she felt his heart beat faster. By the time she reached for the fastening on his pants, she couldn't resist throwing back her head and laughing up at him. It was heady stuff, this power over Brandon. She'd never experienced anything like it before.

Brandon couldn't resist smiling down at her, couldn't resist the joy he saw in her. She was as radiant as the sun, as pure as moonbeams, and he needed her to light all the dark places in his heart. Before her clever fingers could release his pants, he turned the tables on her.

He eased off her jacket, and again his fingers worked the small, slippery buttons of her blouse. With his mouth he trailed hot kisses down her body, as she had for him. Once the jacket and creamy silk were tossed aside, he concentrated on tempting and teasing the rosy nipples that peeked through her lacy bra. The way she murmured his name and clutched at his shoulders had him wild. While he cherished the turgid peaks with his mouth, his fingers worked to divest her of her skirt. Easing her back on the bed, he removed her shoes, then eased off her panty hose, indulging in an exploration of the soft skin of her thighs and the surprising flex of the muscles in her calves. The contrast of her softness and strength had him reeling. When he would have explored further, she called his name.

She had raised up on her elbows. Her heated gaze caught and held his. "Love me," she demanded.

"I am." He intended to love every inch of her.

"Love me now," she insisted. "I've waited so long."

He detected insecurity in her eyes and wondered how she could possibly doubt he was wild for her. He smiled as he straightened and removed the rest of his clothing. The slow exploration could wait. For now he'd be content to prove that she'd driven him beyond thought. He bent down to remove the swath of lace that was her bra, then grazed his hand down her heated flesh until it came to rest on the last scrap of material that stood between them. While he teased her lips with his own, he dipped his fingers into her fire. She was hot and slick. He dispensed with her panties and fumbled in the bedside table. He tore his lips from hers and sat back on his heels as he made quick work of the foil packet. When he looked back at her, her eyes were wide.

"I promised to protect you," he murmured as he covered her body with his. "I'll always protect you. Even from myself."

Jessica opened her arms and welcomed him into her body. She'd never felt so cherished or so precious in her life. Never known that a man could smile down at her as he eased within her. Never known that giving of herself could make her feel powerful and precious. Never known that the give and take between a man and a woman could drive her from languorous to frantic in the space of a few heartbeats, could have her writhing with heat and desire, could drive her to such heights that she could come apart in his arms time after time, only to discover that the most precious moment was when he cried her name and found his own release.

Exhausted, she smiled as she held him close and waited for his breathing to slow. Smiled the secret smile of a woman in love and wondered how she could be so weary and so powerful at the same time.

When Brandon could finally move, he rolled onto his back and pulled her close so that her cheek was resting on his heart. He could feel the smile on her face, and he figured he was grinning from ear to ear. Like a kid. As though he'd been reborn without the guilt and the darkness. He raised up just enough to drop a kiss on her hair, then he collapsed back, content to hold her in his arms. Until her clever little fingers stirred along his body. Until his body responded.

When the alarm went off at six the next morning, Brandon reached over and turned it off. With his other hand, he smoothed the curls back from Jess's face and dropped a kiss on the tip of her nose. Her smile was instantaneous and made him feel as if the room were flooded with sunlight.

"Are you sure you want to go jogging this morning?" she asked between the kisses she feathered across his chest.

"What makes you think I'm going jogging?"

She looked up at him. "Nancy says you always do."

"Not this morning. I got plenty of exercise last night."

"Oh," was all she said, but the blush that started at the tips of her breasts and spread right up to her hairline had him smiling. With his fingers he circled one rosy nipple and was delighted to feel it harden beneath his touch. The blush intensified. He rolled Jess onto her back and rose over her. With his hands and his lips and his newly gained knowledge of her body, he brought her to fever pitch within moments.

"Isn't this much better than jogging?" he asked as he moved within her heat.

He smiled when all she could do was moan in answer. Now was not the time to tell her that he no longer felt he had to go out in the crisp morning air in order to feel alive. No longer needed to pound along the ocean's edge in an effort to wash away the guilt that assailed him in the dark hours of night. No longer needed to sweat out the bitterness that burned his soul like acid. All he needed was her smile, her touch. Her love.

Two days later, Jessica was still head over heels in love. Though the nights remained magical, the days were starting to drag. Brandon was in meetings or busy most of the day, and without a job or a camera, each hour seemed like two.

"I was never much of a shopper," Jess confided to Nancy over their iced tea. "Two days of shopping is a day and a half too much." Besides, without a camera she felt naked.

"Maybe I could find you something to do in the office."

Jessica nodded. "That would help."

"George needs someone to help on the grounds since Danny was fired."

"I already asked. George says it's hard manual labor. Unsuitable for a woman." She made a face. "I think he means unsuitable for the woman having an affair with his boss." When Nancy almost choked on her tea, Jessica rolled her eyes. "I'm not saying anything everyone else isn't saying." She could tell by the way people stared at her and stopped talking when she entered a room.

"They'll get used to it." Nancy stared into her tea, then smiled up at Jessica. "If anything, it should let you know how unusual this is. Brandon has never indulged in flings with the guests or the employees. He takes his friendships . . . relationships seriously."

"I'd hoped that was the case," Jess said with a nod. But even thoughts of Brandon weren't enough to keep her from losing her mind from boredom at the moment. "I need a camera, Nancy."

"You can borrow my Instamatic."

Jessica shuddered. "Where's the nearest large camera store?"

"Santa Cruz. A two-hour drive to the north," Nancy explained.

Jess made a quick decision. "Where can I rent a car?"

"Not around here. Brandon left strict orders that you are not to be allowed out of sight or off the grounds."

Jess sighed. It might be a gilded cage, but it was still a cage. "I'm serious, Nancy. My sanity is at stake."

"Better your sanity than your life." She sipped at her tea. "Or my job."

If she couldn't play on Nancy's sympathy, she'd have to resort to logic, Jess decided. "I appreciate the fact that Brandon doesn't want me wandering around the beach. After all, that's where the murders occurred. But it seems to me that I'd be even safer in Santa Cruz than I am at the inn."

"How do you figure that?"

"I don't think anyone is going to sneak up on me in a department store and shoot me. There's a kind of safety in numbers and being in a public place."

Nancy nodded. "Makes sense."

"In fact, it seems I'd be doing everyone a favor by staying out of harm's way for the day." Jess gave Nancy a bland smile. "All I need is a car."

"Walk me back to the desk," Nancy said abruptly. "I'll give you the key to one of the inn's cars. They're parked in back of the tennis courts."

Jess couldn't resist giving Nancy's hand a quick squeeze. "Thanks."

"But so help me, if you go off and get yourself killed, I'll never forgive you."

*   *   *

Five hours later Jessica was on her way back from a successful shopping trip. She smiled, remembering the horrified look on the face of Brandon's security man when she had hopped in the car and taken off. The memory of it had amused her for the entire two-hour trip to Santa Cruz.

The car was a domestic economy model in fire-engine red with more radio power than guts, so she tuned in to a station that played classic rock, cranked up the volume, and sang along at the top of her lungs as the Eagles hit the airwaves. "Hotel California" seemed like the perfect song as she sped back toward the Santa Lucia. She had the car windows rolled down so that the ocean breeze whipped through her hair and made her feel as though she were soaring along the coast.

To her left, the mountains rolled green and rugged right down to the road, and on her right the mountain fell away in a sheer drop that ended in jagged rock and rough surf. The road itself curled and curved along between the two vistas. The sky and ocean were tinted a deepening coral by the setting sun. She was tapping her hands on the steering wheel when Bob Seger started his musical ode to that old-time rock and roll.

She'd had several hours of respite from the tension at the inn, and she'd indulged in the best camera she could find, then added a powerful zoom lens and a top-of-the-line wide-angle. She knew Brandon would be furious that she'd sneaked off, but she was almost back now, none the worse for wear. Besides, the moment was too perfect for her worry about Brandon's reaction. She'd face up to him in about twenty minutes, but right now she wanted to enjoy her freedom.

She checked the rearview mirror and kept watch as a car pulled out of one of the little side roads and fell in behind her. She wanted to enjoy the scenery, but she realized that locals were usually more interested in getting to their destination than in the view. She'd already pulled over and let several cars speed on their way this afternoon. But this car held steady about fifty yards behind her over a stretch of several miles, so eventually she relaxed into the drive and the music.

Jess was so busy singing along with Linda Ronstadt about going home to the blue bayou that she didn't pay much attention to the other car. The next time she looked in the rearview mirror, it was bearing down on her at a speed that verged on reckless. Jess was looking for a turnout when she heard the screech of tires behind her. The large American car—its body tinted pink by the sun and the glass rendered opaque by the reflection of the sunset—was gaining quickly enough to make her forget about slowing down to turn off the road. Instantly she pressed down on the accelerator until the rolling hills became a blur and the ocean a shimmery pink wasteland while Jerry Lee Lewis screamed "Great Balls of Fire!"

For several moments it seemed that she would be able to keep the distance between them constant; then the other car accelerated enough to bump the back of hers.

"Damn fool," Jessica muttered as she gripped the wheel and concentrated on steadying the car.

A quick glance in the rearview mirror revealed a driver hidden behind a baseball cap and a bulky, hooded sweatshirt pulled up to hide the face. Wraparound sunglasses hid the rest of the features, so that there was not a clue as to the identity of the driver. Jess's heart seemed to stop for several seconds, then tripped into double time. She swallowed the fear, a bitter metallic taste, and concentrated on pushing the car as fast as she could. It wasn't fast enough, she realized as the other vehicle nudged her bumper again.

"Oh, my God," she whispered, then went silent as the Beatles begged to hold her hand. She struggled to stay on the road and ahead of the oncoming car. When the vehicle gathered even more speed and pulled into the north-bound lane, Jess knew it wasn't going to pass her. Praying there wasn't a northbound car around the next curve, she swung her own car to the left to keep the other vehicle from pulling up on the driver's side and pushing her off the road onto the rocks below. Immediately the big car dropped behind her and settled for a deadly game of bumper cars.

This couldn't be happening, she thought. Not to her. Not now. Not when she finally had something—someone—to live for. Fighting back tears, she concentrated on keeping the gas pedal to the floor and not letting the other car pull into the lane beside her.

She was coming out of a sharp right curve when the other car hit her rear bumper. Jess's car turned and slid sideways along the road for several yards. The tires squealed as she looked directly into the sunset. All she could do was pray that her car stayed on the road and that no one came around the sharp bend just ahead. The other driver dropped way back, not willing to risk being hit by her car should it spin out again.

Then, just when Jess was certain her vehicle was going to slide off the road and into the rocks below, the car's front bumper kissed the guardrail, shooting sparks into the darkening light. Before Jess could react, the car made a sudden two-hundred-seventy-degree turn and ended up heading south toward the Santa Lucia. But there was no time to utter a prayer of thanksgiving, no time to think that she still might make it back to the inn—back to Brandon. The other car was again closing in on her.

She pressed her foot to the floorboard in an attempt to get a head start. In less time than it took the Beach Boys to go on a surfin' safari, her lead was eaten up by the more powerful car. Jess was braced for the impact when she saw a recreational vehicle headed north only two or three curves away.

"Please, God," she prayed. "Please don't let me hit them. Please. Please."

She was still praying when the car slammed into her rear bumper. She fought the wheel and thought she had the car under control when the other vehicle slammed into it again. She was braced for the next impact when her pursuer suddenly stopped. Jessica was so amazed to see the vehicle receding in the rearview mirror that she almost missed the curve straight ahead of her. Making the turn on two wheels, she forced herself to concentrate on the road, though she couldn't help throwing a quick glance in the rearview mirror. The car was nowhere in sight. A few seconds later, she passed the Winnebago.

By the time Otis Redding finished singing about the dock on the bay, she was following the highway as it cut inland. When she turned onto the road leading to the Santa Lucia, the adrenaline had stopped pumping through her body. Her hands were icy and shaking, her legs were quivering, and she was very much afraid that when she stepped out of the car, she would crumple in an ignominious little heap on the front steps of the prestigious inn.

The Watcher sat on the side road in the stolen car and watched as the Winnebago rumbled past. Several little brats sat at the back window, their ghoulish little faces pressed against the glass. It was their fault Jessica wasn't dead on the rocks below. If it hadn't been on the road, if the Watcher hadn't been afraid the vacationers would be able to given the police vital information about the "accident," Jessica's body would be smashed on the rocks below.

"Damn." The Watcher slammed a hand against the steering wheel. "Damn, damn, damn!"

It had been close. So close. The Watcher eased the car back onto the highway and headed to where the other car was hidden. The gun would have been so much more effective, but the Watcher, afraid that the police might search for it, had buried the small, dependable pistol in a spot that had remained undisturbed for over thirty years.

When the time was right, the Watcher would dig it up. That would make quick work of Jessica Martinson. And of Brandon's hope. The Watcher smiled at the thought. And while Brandon mourned, the Watcher would laugh. Laugh and gloat and rejoice in the joy of revenge. The Watcher smiled over the fantasy while ditching the stolen car. Was still laughing when, turning down the road to home, a siren wailed in the distance. Evidently Brandon had called the police—for all the good that would do.

11

Brandon closed the door behind the highway patrol officer and turned to look at Jessica. She'd dealt with the officer's questions quietly and efficiently. Too bad Carl wasn't as easy to get rid of, but then the highway patrol had been called in to investigate a hit-and-run accident. Carl was investigating a murder.

As he watched, Jess shook her head in answer to another one of Carl's questions. He didn't know how much longer she could take it. Hell, he didn't know how much longer *he* could take it. He was tired of Carl's persistent questions and insistence that Jess must have seen something. Tired of his obvious conviction that she knew something she wasn't telling.

What Brandon really wanted to do was take Jess to bed and make love to her until neither one of them could lift a finger, just to convince himself that she was alive and his. He supposed some people would say it was a primal instinct, an urge left over from the time when men dragged women home by the hair. They might even be right since he wasn't feeling especially civilized at the moment, but the need to touch her, to reaffirm life at its most basic level, was almost overwhelming.

He dragged a hand through his hair and took the time to study Jess. She was exhausted. Her hair was a mess, she had circles under her eyes, and she jumped at the smallest sound. Her eyes were huge and dark and set in a face that was still white, but she hadn't cried. Not one tear since she'd come careening down the driveway to screech to a halt beneath the porte cochere. Not one tear when he'd wrenched open the door of a car that looked as if it had been in a demolition derby. Not even a sniffle when he'd hauled her out where he could call her a fool and hold her in his arms. Not even so much as a blush when he'd swept her into his arms to carry her past the crowd and through the lobby to his apartment. She'd just clung to him and assured him that she wasn't hurt, until at last he'd quieted down. Then she'd told him he looked terrible and needed to sit before he fell down.

Since he was used to her tears, he couldn't help being surprised at her dry-eyed response to this latest attack. He wondered if she might be in shock. He'd had the doctor in, of course. No concussion, no broken bones, just plenty of bruises from being banged around in the car and eyes that were older than they'd been that morning. Still, she was the most beautiful sight he'd ever seen. If he tried to tell her that, she'd probably tell him to sit down again, but God knew it was the truth. And he'd make certain she believed it, just as soon as Carl was finished with his questions.

"Ms. Martinson, I want you to think very carefully. I find it hard to believe that our murderer had singled you out unless there is a reason. You must have seen something."

Jessica sighed and pushed the hair back from her face. "I can't think of anything. I've been over and over it in my mind." Exhausted, she closed her eyes and leaned her head against the back of the sofa. "I wish I could help you."

Mendoza was firm. "Something you've seen or heard. Maybe even something you photographed."

Jess shook her head without opening her eyes. She was suddenly afraid she was too tired to open them again. Too exhausted to deal with Mendoza, let alone the rage and pain she'd glimpsed in Brandon's eyes. She struggled to lift her eyelids, only to have them drift close again.

"For God's sake, leave her alone, Carl." Jess watched as Brandon charged across the room. "Can't you see she's ready to collapse?"

"Yeah, and I can see she was almost dead. It's my job to find out why."

"Browbeating the victim isn't going to help. Why don't you go catch the murderer?"

Mendoza turned and squared his body in Brandon's direction. "Are you throwing me out? Interfering with an investigation can get your ass thrown in jail, you know."

Brandon only smiled. "And that could get you out of a job the next time your contract comes up for renewal. The city council is very appreciative of the taxes generated by the inn."

"Threatening a law enforcement official can get your ass thrown in prison."

"I'm not threatening, Carl. Just helping you out with some career planning."

"It sounds to me like you don't want the murderer caught. Do you have something to hide, Brandon?"

"Don't be any more of a fool than you already are."

Jessica watched as Mendoza studied Brandon. Anyone

else would have fidgeted under such close scrutiny, but Brandon simply stared back.

"Maybe I've been looking in the wrong direction," Mendoza finally said. "Maybe the murders are incidental rather than an end in themselves. Maybe someone is trying to cover something up, and the victims simply got in his way."

Brandon shook his head. "Carl, I don't have the slightest idea what you're talking about."

Neither did Jess, but she didn't like the way the chief of police was looking at Brandon. "Brandon was at the inn all day. He couldn't be the one who tried to run me off the road." When Brandon gave her a questioning look, Jess managed a wan smile. "Nancy said you'd been driving her crazy all day."

"I was worried about you, damn it. And ready to have her head for giving you the car. As it turns out, I was right to be furious." He gave her an exasperated glance and raked a hand through his hair. "You could have at least called."

He was right, of course. She should have let him know where she was. "I'm sorry. It was a stupid move."

There was neither amusement nor forgiveness in the look he settled on her. "It certainly was."

Mendoza sighed. "This is one time Brandon and I are in complete agreement. It was foolish to go off by yourself. Foolish to put yourself at risk for a camera."

"I didn't think I was putting myself 'at risk.' I thought I'd be safer away from the scene of the crime." She turned her gaze on Brandon, needing to explain not only why she'd gone, but who she was. "I was going crazy with nothing to do."

Brandon sat beside her and took her hand. "Why didn't you say something? I would have driven you to

Santa Cruz. Or I could have had the camera shipped here."

"You've had so much on your mind." Jess cupped his cheek in her hand. "You've been wonderful, and I didn't want to whine or complain. Besides, I wasn't sure what I wanted. I needed to look and fiddle." She smiled. "And compare prices."

Brandon shook his head. "Price is no object. I would have bought what—"

Jess placed a finger over his lips. "You weren't buying it. I was. And I needed to compare prices."

Before Brandon could respond, Carl cut in. "You know, Ms. Martinson, you may be correct."

"Carl, this has nothing to do with you. The inn was responsible for replacing the other items that were destroyed. I fully intend to replace her camera as well."

Carl waved a hand as though to dismiss Brandon's statement. "I'm not talking about the camera. I'm talking about Ms. Martinson being safer if she left the area. It might be a good idea for her to return to L.A."

"Jess will be safe here if she'll just stay put." Brandon slanted her a quelling look.

Carl ignored Brandon. "I know your sister would feel better if you returned home. She's very much concerned for your safety."

Jessica's eyes widened despite her fatigue. "And just how do you know that?"

"She's called twice since her return home. Just to keep abreast of the situation, of course."

"She could have called me."

Mendoza gave her a sympathetic smile. "She said she's afraid you'll gloss over things. She wants the full, unvarnished picture."

"I can assure you I'll call her and give her the full picture," Jess told the policeman. Her eyes were narrowed at the prospect of telling Marty that she was perfectly capable of managing her own life. If Marty wanted information, she would by God have to get it from the source from now on. "I promise to call her myself."

Mendoza nodded. "Meanwhile, I don't think you should be left alone, not even for a minute."

"Don't worry," Brandon told the other man. "I don't intend to let her out of my sight."

"Now why doesn't that reassure me?" Mendoza asked.

"It reassures me," Jess said. She smiled at Brandon. "Are you willing to have a shadow for a while?"

"Either I'm going to have a shadow or you're going to be locked in a room."

Jessica crossed her arms and stared right back at him. "My life. My decision."

"Your last decision almost got you killed."

"Then it would have been my fault and no one else's."

Mendoza coughed—to cover a smile, Jess was sure. "I'll leave Ms. Martinson in your capable hands, then."

"Keep me informed," Brandon said.

"I'll just show myself out."

Brandon's gaze never wavered from Jessica's. "You do that, Carl." Once the door closed behind the man, he said, "If you ever pull a fool stunt like that again, you won't have to worry about the murderer. I'll throttle you myself."

Because she was fighting the urge to throw herself in Brandon's arms and promise him she'd never make a decision without his approval, she asked, "How bad is the car?"

"Screw the car." He grabbed her by the shoulders. "You almost got yourself killed. How do you think I would have managed if you had? How do you think Nancy would have dealt with the guilt?"

She concentrated on keeping her chin from trembling

and the tears from falling. "I didn't think I was in any danger on the open road."

He gave her a little shake. "You fool. How could you think that after finding Stewart's body?"

Jess shrugged. "Terminal stupidity?"

"Almost." Brandon raised a trembling hand to brush back her hair. His gentle touch was at odds with his grim expression. "You aren't going to cry, are you?"

Jess shook her head. "No more tears," she promised both Brandon and herself. "This time I'm just plain angry."

"Angry enough to be sensible?"

Jess nodded.

"I meant what I said about being your shadow. You are not to be out of my sight until Mendoza makes an arrest."

"Be serious." Jess used a gentle touch to try to erase the grim set of his jaw. "It's been three years since Jacqueline Kendall was murdered. No one can stand that much togetherness."

"Then I'll just have to see that Carl finds the murderer this time, won't I?"

And he knew he would. This time he'd have to confide his suspicions to Carl and hope to hell the man could come up with some proof. Unless he could figure some way for the murderer to get the psychological help needed without being locked up in prison. He raked a hand through his hair and decided he needed a little time to think things through.

But not now, he decided as he pulled Jess into his embrace and kissed her. Now he needed to know she was alive and belonged with him.

"Love me," Jess whispered.

Brandon smiled as he unfastened the top button of her blouse. "I intend to."

* * *

Jess's glance swept the crowd gathered in the small conference room at the inn. Though she'd been at the inn only two weeks—in the area less than three—she was surprised to realize how many of the people she knew, how quickly she'd become integrated into Brandon's life. Oddly enough, she seldom thought of the life she'd left behind in Los Angeles. The only person she missed was Marty, and after their conversation the night before, she knew that distance could never be a factor between them. The love had been as sure and real as the flare of temper.

The distinguished man at the head table shuffled his papers, coughed discreetly, and rose. "If everyone will be seated, we'll get started."

Brandon's hand tightened on Jess's. She looked around to see George sitting with a group she recognized as employees of the inn. On the other side of the room, apart from the others, sat Amelia and John. John had come over to exchange greetings, though Amelia had maintained her distance. Jess wondered if she was embarrassed by her behavior with Megan or by the gun she carried, then couldn't help smiling at the image of the snooty Amelia as a pistol-packing danger to society. It was probably closer to the truth that the older woman simply felt they didn't deserve to be graced with her presence.

At the head table, the man settled a pair of half glasses on his nose. Looking over the tops of the frames, he said, "My name is Charles Ferris. I was Stewart Roarke's attorney as well as his friend. I've asked you here for the reading of Stewart's will, as he requested." He paused to study the crowd. "I assume the others will not be joining us, so I'll begin."

Jess cast a questioning look at Brandon. Who, she wondered, hadn't bothered to show up? Brandon shrugged and gave her hand a reassuring squeeze.

Charles Ferris began to read. "'I, Stewart Roarke, a resident of Monterey County, state of California, make and declare this to be my will and revoke all former wills and codicils made by me.

"'I declare that I am not and have never been married and that, to my knowledge, I have no . . .'" Charles Ferris stopped and looked over his glasses as the door opened. "There you are. Glad you could join us."

Jess looked over her shoulder to see Jason, Florence, and Megan. Florence took the chair closest to the exit as Jason quietly closed the door.

The attorney adjusted his glasses. "I'd given up on you. Started without you, though you didn't miss much. Would you like me to begin again?"

Jason shook his head, then scooped Megan up and sat on the chair beside his wife. Megan leaned her head on her father's shoulder and waved at Jess. Jess smiled and waved back.

Charles Ferris cleared his throat and resumed reading. "'I declare that I am not and have never been married and that, to my knowledge, I have no issue. My closest living relative is Brandon Cuthbert Roarke.'"

Jess couldn't help turning to look at Brandon, who she would swear turned a shade darker. "Cuthbert?"

"Named after Mother's father," he whispered back. "It's not a name I plan to pass on to my children."

"Thank God."

Charles Ferris cleared his throat again and paused long enough to shoot Jessica a disapproving look. When she looked appropriately chastened, he continued. "'I would declare that I love the boy as though he were my son, but if I haven't proven that to him by now, there is no use declaring it.'" The attorney looked at Brandon. "Those are Stewart's exact words." He turned his attention back to the will. "'To George Lewis, employee and friend, without whom the Santa Lucia Inn would not be the same, I leave the sum of fifty thousand dollars. Use it as you wish, my friend.'"

Jessica glanced over her shoulder in time to see George pull a pristine handkerchief from his hip pocket and swipe at his tears.

"Didn't need to do that," George murmured.

Charles Ferris read bequests to other long-time employees, though none were that large. "'To my second cousin Amelia Kendall-White and her husband, John White, I leave the antique Limoges clock in hopes that they will realize that time is fleeting and that love is a precious gift. Don't let either slip away.

"'To Megan Jacqueline Kendall, the daughter of a dear friend, I leave one hundred thousand dollars to be held in trust. The trust is to be administered jointly by Brandon Roarke and Jason Kendall. If the two of you have not made up yet, you will have to work together anyway.'"

Jess looked first at Brandon, who had gone still as a statue, then couldn't help craning her neck, as everyone else was doing, to stare at the Kendalls. Florence sat staring at the hands she'd folded primly in her lap. Jason pulled Megan more firmly into his embrace, as though to shield her from prying eyes.

"Daddy." Megan squirmed within her father's hold. "What does that mean?"

Jason looked down at his daughter and smiled. "It means you still have to pick up your toys and make your own bed."

"Oh." She settled back into his arms to think about that.

Charles Ferris continued. "'The balance of my estate, including personal items, money, bank accounts, stocks and bonds, and my interest in the Santa Lucia Inn, I leave to my nephew, Brandon Cuthbert Roarke.'" The attorney looked up. "That's it. Short and to the point, as Stewart always was. Does anyone need clarification?"

When no one spoke up, Brandon rose and thanked the attorney. "I know Stewart would be pleased with the way things were conducted."

Charles nodded and began replacing the papers in his briefcase. "You and Jason will need to come to my office to go over the details of the trust." He lowered his voice so that even Jess had to struggle to hear.

"Basically, the two of you will administer it jointly until the child turns thirty. Money is available for her education and medical emergencies, if both you and Jason agree. There are a few other provisions I'd like to go over privately with the two of you."

Brandon nodded. "I'll contact Jason and we'll make an appointment to come in."

"Very well. Nice to have met you, Ms. Martinson," he said, and started toward the door. On his way out, he passed Carl Mendoza, who was just entering the room.

Carl wore dress slacks that showed dirt around the knees and a starched white shirt rolled up at the sleeves; his usually immaculate salt-and-pepper hair was wind-blown. He was wiping his hands on a neatly pressed handkerchief. He spoke briefly to Jason and Amelia before heading in Brandon's direction. Jessica stepped closer to Brandon.

"It's fortunate that everyone is here," Carl told Brandon. "We've made a surprising discovery with the reluctant help of one of your former employees. Something I think you'll all be interested in."

Brandon took in the condition of the man's clothes and sighed. "You haven't been digging under the azaleas, have you, Carl?"

"Out in the sand dunes. But I'd rather have you all accompany me than explain it here." When Brandon didn't agree, Mendoza added, "It also involves theft from the inn. From the groundskeepers, as a matter of fact, so I'd like George to accompany us as well."

"This had better be good, Carl."

Mendoza smiled. "I think I can safely say this will be a surprise for everyone involved."

Brandon stopped in the lobby to let Nancy know where he was going. The Kendalls waited on the other side of the lobby while George spoke quietly with Mendoza. John picked up a newspaper and settled onto one of the lobby chairs, and Amelia sidled up to Jessica. The glint in her eyes reminded Jess of a rat that had scented food.

"My, my, and I thought the biggest news around here was the theft of my Cadillac yesterday. That's certainly insignificant compared to the revelation we just witnessed, isn't it?" the older woman asked.

Jess didn't like the smirk on her face. "What do you mean?"

"The bequest to Megan, of course."

"Stewart Roarke was a generous man."

Amelia's laugh set Jess's nerves on edge. "How can you say that when the child should have had half of everything?"

"How do you figure that?"

"The child is obviously Stewart's. Why else would he have mentioned her in the will?" Amelia raised one sculpted eyebrow. "It certainly wasn't from any particular fondness for the girl. He probably hasn't spoken to her more than a dozen times since the estrangement between Brandon and Jason." She laughed. "In fact, Stewart was probably responsible for the estrangement."

Jess felt her eyes go big and round. She struggled to keep her mouth from hanging open. "Are you suggesting that Florence and Stewart had an affair? That Megan is Stewart's child?"

"I'm not suggesting anything. I'm saying it."

Jess glanced around the lobby, hoping that no one else could overhear their conversation. It would only add fuel to an already inflammatory situation. "If I were you, I'd be careful about repeating your suspicions to anyone else. I believe that people have been sued for slander over less."

"You can't be sued for speaking the truth. Look at the child. Just look at her. Those blue eyes, don't you see that they're just like Stewart's? I always wondered about those blue eyes."

"I think you should take a good look at the relationship between Jason and Megan. Between Jason and his daughter. Brown eyes or blue, they adore each other. I've rarely seen a father and daughter so close." Though Jess had gotten her looks from her father, there'd been no such affection. When Amelia gave a snort of derision, Jess fought to hold on to her temper. "If I were you, I'd spend more time worrying about my own life and less gossiping about others."

Without another word Jess walked away, unwilling to trust her temper in the company of such a mean-spirited woman. With her hand in Brandon's, she walked with him to join the cluster of people around Carl.

When Carl had everyone gathered together, he spoke to the group. "It will be easier if you take your cars. Turn left off the highway at the fire road. One of my men is there to let you through. From there it's a short walk to the part of the beach where we made the discovery."

Amelia spoke up first. "I'm hardly dressed for a walk on the beach, Carl. I hope you won't mind if John and I pass on this fascinating jaunt you've planned."

"I can't force you to come, but I think you'll regret it."

"And just exactly what have you found that's so very interesting?"

Mendoza smiled. "Remember the bones we found under the rosebush? We've found the rest of the skeleton in the sand dunes. And we have reason to believe the remains are those of Walter Kendall."

Amelia paled and grabbed her husband's arm for support. "My brother?" She fumbled in her purse and came up with a linen handkerchief. "You've finally found Walter after all these years." She dabbed at her eyes, then turned a horrified look on Mendoza. "You mean someone buried Walter under a rosebush and . . . in the sand dunes?"

"No, I don't mean that, Mrs. Kendall-White. I believe your brother was buried out in the dunes."

It was John who responded. "Then how did part of the skeleton end up under the rosebushes?"

"You'll want to ask your nephew, Danny, about that. You can find him at the police station. He is presently under arrest for misappropriating funds from the Santa Lucia, falsifying records, falsifying signatures on checks and statements, and diverting company funds into his own pocket."

John's face went as white as his hair. "You must be mistaken."

"I wish I were, John. Really I do."

George stepped forward. Jessica couldn't decide which

of the older men was paler. "What has that got to do with the bones you found under the roses?"

"I'd rather explain it at the site." Mendoza looked around. "Will you all join me out in the dunes?"

Jason's hands were still sweaty when he parked on the dirt road behind the police cruiser. He could hardly believe they'd finally located his father, the man who'd disappeared before Jason was even born. All his life he'd heard abut Walter Kendall. Very little of it had been good. Mostly it had been whispers and innuendo when he was young. He'd finally confronted his mother when he'd entered his teens. She'd tried to give him the usual answers. She'd told him that his father had been handsome and charismatic and had swept her off her feet. But by then he'd heard other rumors, ugly whisperings that Walter had a temper, that he'd beaten his young wife. Jason hadn't been content with the fairy tale.

So his mother had told him the truth. Told him about his father's drinking and violence and the night he'd wandered off, never to return. The answer to her prayers, his mother had confessed, because she was pregnant. She'd been planning to run away, but with no money of her own, she'd despaired of giving her child a good life. Then Walter had disappeared, and Jacqueline Kendall had been left in peace to raise her son and live a quiet life. Until someone had killed her.

Jason leaned his forehead on the steering wheel. God, but his family was steeped in violence. Maybe that explained his own behavior, he thought, then shook his head to rid himself of the thought. He had killed in self-defense, he reminded himself. He'd choked the life out of a man who would have killed him or, worse yet, thrown him back into that pit in the ground, and he knew he couldn't have taken that. If they'd thrown him back in there, he wouldn't have come out sane. He almost laughed out loud at that thought. There were moments he wasn't sure he was sane even now.

"Daddy . . . Daddy . . . ?"

Jason looked over his shoulder to see Megan's trusting face.

"Are we gonna sit in the car all day, Daddy?"

How could a man look in those innocent eyes and then into his own darkened soul without feeling inadequate? What if he let her down? What if someday he lost control and hurt her? What if, in his cowardice, he let someone else hurt her?

He looked at Florence, who sat quietly waiting for him. There was no doubt he'd hurt her. He'd not done it with his fists, as his father had, but he'd hurt her nonetheless. He'd known about her background when he married her. Known how her own mother hadn't wanted her. How her relatives had refused her and how she'd been shifted from one foster home to another. Still, he'd gone off on assignments and left her at home. She'd seen it as one more desertion in a life filled with rejection. She'd been getting even ever since, and he'd been letting her. But how much did you owe someone for the hurt you inflicted without meaning to? How long did you pay for being young and stupid?

"Can we go, Daddy? Are we going for a walk on the beach? Can I hold Jess's hand? She's waiting for us."

He glanced at his daughter once more. Young. Innocent. Trusting. He'd do anything to keep her that way. To keep from hurting her. Only he wasn't sure he could protect her much longer. He wasn't even certain that the lies he'd fabricated were in her best interest. It might be best if he told the truth and let the courts sort it out. But he'd been too much of a coward to do even that—though today's bequest would undoubtedly stir things up.

Jason unfastened his seat belt and opened the car door. "Come on, kitten." He didn't exactly consider this a walk on the beach, but he'd be brave for her sake.

It was a nightmare, Jess decided where she sat huddled on a rock. Megan was cuddled up beside her, and she hugged the child closer not only for warmth—for the ocean breeze had stiffened, kicking up sand and prickling her arms with goose bumps—but because she thought they both needed the emotional support. Amelia sat on a rock a few feet away, her features transformed from elegant to tormented by fury and grief. With her arms folded in front of her, the older woman rocked back and forth while her husband tried to comfort her.

"There, there, my dear." John knelt in the sand before his distraught wife. "Don't take on so. He's been dead for years."

Mendoza stood over the couple. "Then you can definitely identify both the watch and the ring?"

"Yes," Amelia cried. "They're Walter's."

John patted her shoulder and made soothing sounds, though he looked decidedly uncomfortable in the face of his wife's emotional outburst. "He's been gone for years, my dear. Years."

"But I never believed he was dead. Never," she confessed through her tears. "I always believed he'd come back one day. That he'd had amnesia or decided to travel around the world. Anything but dead."

"The coroner will have to make a definite identification," Mendoza cautioned.

John rose. "But you believe that's my wife's brother, don't you?"

Mendoza nodded. "It seems very likely."

Amelia brushed away the tears. "What happened to him? Who did this to him?"

"Again, the coroner and forensics will have to make an official determination. However, my assistant did notice one side of his skull was cracked. It could have happened after his death, but it could have been the cause of death. As to who did it . . . well, it happened a long time ago. We may never know the answer to that."

"She did it," Amelia cried. Rising, her hands like claws, she gripped the policeman's shirtfront. "Jacqueline killed him. I know she did."

John grabbed his wife. "My dear." He pried her fingers loose from Mendoza's rumpled shirt. "My dear, don't do this to yourself. You'll make yourself ill."

Grief stricken, she turned into her husband's embrace as Mendoza stepped back.

Megan turned her big blue eyes on Jess. Huge teardrops clung to her thick, dark lashes. "Why is she saying bad things about my grandma?"

"She's upset." Jess smoothed the child's hair back. "Do you ever say things you don't mean when you're upset?" She waited for Megan's nod. "Well, adults do, too. I'm sure she doesn't mean it."

"Good." Megan snuggled closer. "I miss my grandma. She used to play games with me and sing me songs. Daddy misses her, too."

"And I'll bet your mommy does, too."

"I guess so." Megan mulled that over. "They used to yell a lot."

Jess thought of her last conversation with Marty, about

the flare of temper as well as the love. "That doesn't always mean you don't love someone."

Jess leaned her cheek on the child's hair and held her tight. Truth was that Amelia's hysterics didn't worry her as much as Jason's lack of reaction. He just stood at the edge of the excavation, staring down at the bones of his father. He looked up when Mendoza stopped beside him.

"How did you find him?" Jason asked.

"Luck and good police work," Carl said. "You know Danny White, don't you."

"John's nephew. His mother shipped him out to stay with John and Amelia."

Mendoza nodded. "It seems he and his girlfriend discovered a way to make a little extra money. The girl works for the nursery that supplies the inn."

Jess saw George and Brandon move closer. Even Amelia got control of her hysterics. Mendoza flipped open his little book.

"It seems George has the nursery make up a special mixture of soil and sand and special nutrients to use on certain plants. Danny was usually sent to pick up the supplies. Instead of returning the burlap sacks to the nursery to be refilled, he and the girl filled the sacks themselves—with dirt and sand and whatever was handy."

"I saw them," Jessica said. When the others looked at her, she explained. "The day before Stewart was murdered. I got lost out in the fog, and I saw Danny and the girl. They had a shovel and sacks. She said they were gathering plants for her botany class."

"That's not very likely," Mendoza told her. "The girl dropped out of school last week. She was too busy falsifying records to spend time on her studies." He glanced at his notes once more. "Sometimes George paid out of a petty cash account he kept. Other times by check." He looked at George. "The cash payments were easy. The boy just pocketed the money." His gaze shifted to Brandon. "The checks were a bit tougher, but they managed to forge the necessary signatures. I'll expect you to press charges."

Brandon nodded. "No one steals from me and gets away with it."

Mendoza closed his little book and slipped it back in his pocket. "The nursery got suspicious first. After all, they were used to the revenue from the inn. When they asked the girl about it, she caved in. Implicated Danny. He's tougher. Won't admit to anything." He skewered Amelia and John with his dark gaze. "Did you tell Stewart that your nephew had a juvenile record?"

Amelia shook her head. "No."

"Yes," John said just as quickly. He looked at his wife. "I had to. Stewart was my friend. Such a good friend that he was still willing to give the boy a chance, for all the good it did."

George, white and shaken, asked, "How did you find the skeleton?"

"I was convinced the bones had come in the dirt. The girl was willing . . ." Mendoza smiled. "Anxious to show us where they'd been digging."

Thinking back, Carl realized it was a good thing they hadn't needed to get the information from the boy. He might be young, but he was already a tough character. He wondered how many people knew the boy was John's illegitimate child. Amelia surprised him; she must truly love her husband to take in his bastard. Unfortunately, the boy hadn't taken advantage of the opportunity. But the girl . . . He hoped the girl had been caught in time.

Jason turned to Mendoza. "All this to find a man who

died over thirty-five years ago. You should have left him undisturbed." Florence stepped to her husband's side. Jason took her hand and held it. "What's the point?"

"There's no statute of limitations on murder," Mendoza pointed out. "Besides, we also found a more recent addition. A handgun, probably buried in the last week."

"How do you figure that?" Brandon asked.

"The condition of the weapon, and the fact that it's the type of gun used to kill both Jacqueline and Stewart. Ballistics is checking it out now, but I have reason to suspect that it was used in both murders."

Brandon sighed. "What makes you think that? Unless there's something special about the gun."

Mendoza shook his head. "It was wrapped in a towel from the Santa Lucia."

"Oh, for God's sake, Carl. Do you have any idea how many towels we have at the inn? How many are stolen in a year?"

"No, but I'm sure you can supply me with that information."

Brandon raked a hand through his hair. "Damn right."

"I'll want to have him buried beside Daddy and Mother," Amelia said to no one in particular.

Jason was glad to be relieved of that responsibility. He wouldn't have buried the bastard next to his mother, that's for sure. Jacqueline had been glad to get rid of her husband the first time, he certainly wasn't going to inflict the man on her gentle spirit.

He wanted to turn and leave but somehow couldn't drag himself away. So that's what we all come down to, he thought. Dust and bones. And if you were lucky, one or two people who mourn you. *Who would mourn him if he just disappeared?* he wondered. Megan. Megan would grieve. But would she be better off without him, as he'd been better off without his own father? God, he hoped not. But what legacy could he leave to her? Could he teach her about love and beauty? Or would he, too, leave a legacy of violence and death?

He turned when a hand fell on his shoulder. Turned and looked into the gentle brown eyes of George Lewis. There was a legacy worth passing on, a legacy of caring and patience.

"Waste no grief on him," George said softly. "He wasn't worth it then and he's not worth it now. You're like your mother. She was an island of serenity in a world gone mad. She found beauty all around her. Look into your heart. Look at the peace there. You owe none of it to him."

Jason nodded and wished it was true. He wished he could say that there was nothing of his father in him. But since he'd let the violence free, he'd never been able to contain it again. It seemed to lurk just under the surface, waiting to break free.

The Watcher stood over the bones of the long dead man and fought the urge to laugh. Fought the urge to call them all fools. To laugh in Mendoza's face. To shout, I'm here. Right here among you and you can't see me!

Fools! You're all fools. . . .

The Watcher had found the body years before. Of course, Jacqueline had been a fool as well and talked of Walter's death. Of sin and guilt as though they were real. Only fools felt guilt, and only the weak believed in sin. The Watcher knew that neither existed. Only victory and revenge.

And death. Yes, death was real. Just ask Jacqueline or Stewart. Of course, they couldn't answer. The Watcher had seen to that. They were dead. And death was the final reality.

The Watcher fought the urge to laugh and to dance and to kill. It wasn't time. Not yet. But the time was approaching. Oh, yes, it was definitely approaching.

12

When Brandon woke the next morning, Jessica's head was on his shoulder, her leg thrown over his. After fumbling with the clock radio, he managed to switch it off just a few minutes before it was set to ring. If he was any kind of gentleman, he mused, he'd ease from the bed and let her sleep while he caught up on some paperwork; but the way she snuggled closer to him, the way her hand lay nestled over his heart, had all thoughts of gentlemanly behavior drowning beneath a flood of sensations. Other thoughts, however, were rising—literally and figuratively.

Brandon let his hand glide over her ribs and down to cup the cute little backside that had first captured his attention. He couldn't resist kneading the warm flesh, if only to convince himself that Jess was really here. In his bed. Warm and real and so very desirable. When she dropped a kiss on his chest, he realized she was waking. And willing. He could feel it in the way she moved sensuously against him.

"What's it going to be?" she whispered. Her breath was warm against his skin. "Jogging or that other form of exercise?"

"When you're this close, I never think about running."

Her fingers trailed down over his ribs. "I'm so glad."

"However, I'm a great believer in the importance of exercise."

"Uh-oh. Is there going to be a problem?"

Brandon executed a quick move that had Jess beneath him. "I think we can work it out."

"I've never bothered much with exercise." She brushed the hair back from her eyes and smiled up at him. "You'll have to convince me."

"Oh, yeah?"

"Yeah," she told him with a laugh. The laughter turned to a groan when his lips touched hers. "I think you're making progress."

"I intend to," he told her between kisses. "Then you and I are going to run away."

Her body went still and her eyes grew wide. "Run away?"

"For one day," he explained. "I think we deserve one day." One day before he had to send her away. One day before he had to face his own ghosts. One day before he had to tell Carl about his suspicions. One perfect day to hold on to until it was safe to bring Jess back permanently. But because he didn't want the separation to shadow their day together, he said only, "We've earned one day for ourselves, don't you think?"

Jess let out the breath she'd been holding. "Yes." She smiled and trailed her fingers down his spine. "But this is my favorite way to start the day."

She was still smiling when he entered her.

* * *

Jess pulled Brandon's big jacket tighter and watched the shadowy landscape whiz by. She felt young and carefree again, as though they had really left all their troubles at the inn. Even the memory of that last desperate drive down this same road didn't haunt her now that Brandon was at the wheel.

The rugged Land Rover had surprised her. Jess had pictured Brandon in some expensive sports car. When he pointed out the four-by-four in the parking lot, she'd laughed in surprise and used the running board to scramble up onto the passenger seat while he'd tossed a big blanket into the back, along with the huge picnic basket the kitchen had prepared. Now they were speeding along Highway 1 toward the Monterey peninsula.

"Where are we going?" she asked, not because she was concerned, but because anticipation was part of the fun.

He grinned over at her. "North."

"Even I can see that." It was so much easier to know north from south when you had something as big as the Pacific Ocean for a landmark.

"Can I surprise you?"

"You generally do."

He reached over with his right hand to catch hold of hers. "I could say the same for you."

"Me?" Jess couldn't believe what she was hearing. "I'm depressingly predictable."

"Not to me. You're not predictable, and you're certainly not depressing. You're a constant source of amazement—which is one of the reasons I'm sticking to you like glue."

Jess slanted him a look. "Only one of the reasons?"

Brandon nodded. "The other being that you make me crazy."

"Well, there's a compliment I've never had before."

"Crazy, as in crazy to hold you. Crazy to touch you.

Crazy like a seventeen-year-old who just discovered a whole new world."

Jess felt herself blush and looked out the window, hoping he wouldn't notice. "You make me sound like the fountain of youth."

Brandon shook his head. "Even better. You make me believe in a world full of possibilities without the doubts of youth."

She turned to look at him. "You make yourself sound like you're fifty instead of . . ." She let the sentence trail off, not sure how old he was.

"Thirty-six. But it's not always the number of years. Sometimes it's a matter of what you've seen."

"And you've seen a lot in your thirty-six years?"

"More than you could possibly imagine." He lifted her hand to his lips for a gentle kiss before unlacing their fingers and grasping the steering wheel with both hands. "Here we are," he announced as he took the turnoff to Point Lobos State Reserve.

Jess sat quietly as he paid the entrance fee and drove into the reserve. Pine trees dominated the entrance, then thinned to allow scrub brush and wildflowers.

The fog was still heavy. It clung to the tops of trees and made Jess feel as though they were the only people in a primeval world. A few other cars were in the parking lot, but for the most part they saw and heard no one else.

Brandon pulled into one of the spots, took binoculars out of the glove compartment, and opened his door. "We walk from here," he told her.

"Will I need my camera?"

He smiled. "This is my favorite place on the face of the earth. I'll be disappointed if you don't want to take pictures."

Jess followed him along the trail. He pointed out

plants both common and romantic. Morning glories and white fairy lanterns, California poppies and soap plants. A ground squirrel scampered across the path in front of them, and then Brandon was pointing to a spot about thirty feet away.

"Deer," he whispered, and waited as Jess studied the area. They looked like shadows in the fog. There were four moving slowly, stopping to graze on the plants, then stroll along until the urge to munch had them dipping their heads to the ground again. Once they were out of sight, Brandon urged Jess along the path.

The trees and brush thinned as they made their way to the rocky area overlooking the ocean. Scraggly pine and tenacious cypress clung to the wind-ravaged granite cliffs and hard-packed earth. In the protected cove the ocean surged toward the cliff and back out to sea; no white-tipped waves beat against the rocky shore. Brandon tugged her down beside him on a rock close to where the earth dropped suddenly to the water. Jess studied the offshore area, trying to see through the fog that still shrouded both land and sea.

Brandon placed a gentle finger over her lips. "Listen. What do you hear?"

"The ocean," she answered immediately. There was something about the way it surged back and forth, almost like the soothing rhythm of a rocking chair. The cradle of life, Jess thought, and couldn't help smiling.

"What else?"

A bird soared through the mist to disappear in the distance. From somewhere close by, another called "kee-di, kee-di."

"Birds," she whispered as though she were in a place of worship.

"What else?"

Then she heard it. The tap, tap, tap of . . . what? "Woodpeckers?"

Brandon shook his head. "There are woodpeckers here, but that's not one."

She listened again. It sounded like someone pounding in a nail, then there was a moment of silence before the sound resumed. "Someone building a house?"

"Sea otter," Brandon said as he handed her the binoculars and pointed toward the ocean. "In the middle of the kelp bed. At first it will look like a log with bumps at both ends. Those are the head and feet. See it yet?"

Jess studied the area. "No." Suddenly a log turned and dove beneath the water. "Yes. It just went under."

"Keep looking. Soon he'll resurface with an abalone and a rock. Then he'll place the rock on his chest and bang the shellfish against it to get to the food. That's the tapping sound you heard. Look, he's back. Do you see him?"

"Oh, my God. It's almost like he's looking at me. There he goes again." She waited for the otter to come back up with more food. "Hungry little devils, aren't they?"

Reluctantly, she held the binoculars out for Brandon. He waved them away.

"They're voracious eaters. They were almost hunted to extinction by the abalone fishermen before the environmentalists came to their rescue."

She focused the binoculars again. She loved the quick, agile moves. The big brown eyes. "I could watch them all day."

Brandon nodded. "But I've got more to show you."

Only he couldn't seem to move. He just sat there, looking at the wonder on her face as she watched the otters.

Suddenly she turned to him and gave him a quick kiss. "So far, I love my surprise."

Just to keep her attention focused on him a few more minutes, he gave her a long, hard kiss. He'd had no idea that sharing the beauty of the coast could be so . . . stimulating. When he lifted his head, she was smiling.

"There's lots more to see." He went back for another kiss. "You're too distracting," he finally informed her. He stood and pulled her to her feet before he could be tempted again.

They walked hand in hand around Whalers Cove, played tourist in the cabin that had been built by Chinese fishermen in the mid–1800s, and studied the whale skeletons and the huge cast-iron try-pots that had been used to boil whale blubber by Japanese and Portuguese whalers. He waited patiently while she snapped pictures. She listened intently to his stories about the area. They clambered out on the rock at Headland Cove, watched great ocean waves clash with the rocky shore at Devil's Cauldron, and laughed over the antics of the seals along Sea Lion Cove.

"Point Lobos is named for the seals," Brandon explained. "The Spaniards called this 'La Punta de los Lobos Marinos,' the Place of the Sea Wolves. The name stuck."

Finally they walked back to the car and drove to a meadow overlooking the ocean, where they spread their blanket and unpacked the food. The sun had finally come out, so they shed their jackets and ate a leisurely lunch. By the time they'd finished the French pastries, Brandon had just enough energy to refill their wineglasses and settle back to enjoy the scenery and the way everything felt so right.

Lying there, with the gentle sun and the angry ocean and Jess's hand in his, he could almost believe that his world hadn't been torn apart. That he hadn't spent the last six years in his own personal hell, that people he loved hadn't been murdered, that the one gentle person who could save him wasn't in imminent danger.

In all that time, this had been his place of refuge. Whenever he felt the darkness pressing in, he'd fled here. Here, where he could watch nature and forget about the evil in man. Here, where he could savor the passing of the seasons and the rhythm of nature. Here, where, if he was lucky, he would be able to watch the human race in its best and most basic form: the family.

He'd observed fathers, mothers, and children from angelic to whining. He'd fought the urge to walk up to them and tell them they were blessed. That he'd trade all his wealth and prestige to have that little girl's pudgy, sticky fingers clutched in his or that little boy's big, amazed eyes turned up to him.

Sometimes, when he was very lucky, he could strike up a conversation with a family. It didn't matter if they were from Des Moines or Paris or Hong Kong. He would point out the otters or the sea lions or the whales in migration season. And for that moment he could get a glimpse of heaven. But now, with Jess's fingers laced with his, he felt heaven was within his grasp. All he had to do was get the murderer put away. When Jess snuggled closer and laid her head on his shoulder, he knew that tomorrow he would talk to Carl. And in doing so, he would set in motion a chain of events that might destroy the one person he loved as much as Jessica.

He dropped a kiss on the top of Jess's head. "This is my idea of heaven."

"No pearly gates? No harp-playing angels?"

"No. Just the world at my feet and the woman I love in my arms." He looked down at her startled face and wondered if he was pushing again. Maybe he'd better give her a little time to adjust. "What's your idea of heaven?"

She opened her mouth, then closed it. He waited while she dipped deep inside herself. "To love and be loved. To feel like I belong someplace."

"I'd say we're not so very different."

"I'll bet you say that to all the women."

"That we're not so very different?"

Jess raised up on one elbow and shook her head. "That you love them."

"That's not a line, if that's what you mean. I've only said it one other time in my life." Then, too, he'd thought he glimpsed heaven, only to find himself staring into the depths of hell. "I love you." He grasped her shoulders. Too hell with patience. To hell with giving her time. "I want to marry you. I want to have a home and a family. Does that sound like a line?"

"No." She shook her head. "No. But it sounds impossible."

"Why?"

"Because you're . . . you." She waved her hand in his direction, then back toward herself. "And I'm me."

"Which is exactly why I love you."

"You don't know me. Not really." She fought tears and won. "I'm not special. I'm not as pretty or as smart as other women. I'm not . . ."

Brandon shook her hard, just once, to get her to stop. "Don't say that. Don't ever say that again. You're beautiful and you're brilliant and you're the most special person in the world. Whoever told you different? If it was your sister, so help me I'll set her straight."

"Marty?" She shook her head. "Marty would never say that. My mother told me." Brandon watched her eyes fill. She wiped the tears away, and he fought the urge to shake her again.

"She said I wasn't as pretty as Marty or as smart, but that she loved me." Jess stopped and pressed a hand over her mouth until she had control. "She said that since I was her little girl, she'd love me, too. But I always knew that if I wasn't her daughter—if I hadn't been born to her—she wouldn't have loved me. She wouldn't even have bothered with me."

Appalled, Brandon hauled her into his arms. No matter what tragedy had befallen him, no matter what disasters had shadowed his life, he'd always been told that he was important. That his presence made the tragedies easier to bear.

"She should never have said those things to you. You are beautiful. And you are smart." He took the time to kiss her. To cherish her lips and her eyelids and then hold her close to his heart. "And you're the most special person in the world. No other woman has ever made me ache to love her. Your mother must have been too stupid to see what was right before her." And cruel, Brandon decided. But he'd make sure she never hurt Jess again.

Jess pulled out of his embrace. "Eric said so, too. And Eric should have known."

Brandon strove for patience. "Who is Eric?"

"He was my fiancé. But he wanted Marty first, and when he couldn't have her, he decided to settle for me. And I was too stupid to see that I was a substitute. Everybody told me, but I refused to see it."

"That makes you trusting. Not stupid." He brushed the hair back from her face and looked into her eyes. With Jess you could tell exactly where you stood, and he stood on the very threshold of heaven. "So that fiancé is in the past, right? Because I don't want to have to go punch his lights out."

Jess smiled. "Way past. Prehistoric, even."

"You're going to marry me, then? Before God and family and friends?"

Tears weren't exactly the reaction he was hoping for, but at least she was smiling through the waterworks. "If you want me."

"Honey, I've never wanted anything more," he told her as he pulled her closer for a fierce kiss.

And as he held her in his arms, he wondered how he could have fallen for two women who'd had such similar backgrounds. And how one of them, the one he held next to his heart, could have turned such misery into sweetness while the other had turned so bitter.

Carl Mendoza didn't bother to look up at the knock on his office door. "Come in."

"Hey, chief," Jim Miller said in greeting.

When Jim closed the door behind him, Carl set aside the report he was working on. "What's up?"

"You want the good news or the bad first?"

"I could use some good news."

"We found the Whites' car."

"Thank God. Maybe now that . . . woman will get off my back." Amelia had called and threatened and generally been a pain in the ass since her white Cadillac had been stolen from the inn driveway two days before. Pointing out that she'd left the keys in the ignition hadn't helped matters.

"It was discovered just off one of the private roads in a deep ravine. Less than ten miles from her home. It's totaled. A couple kids found it when they were out playing. We won't be able to haul it out of there until tomorrow, but I climbed down to take a close look at it."

Carl settled back on his chair. When Jim had something to tell, he went into detail. "And?"

"There was red paint all over the front of the car."

"Red paint?"

"My guess is that it will be a match with the car Jessica Martinson was driving day before yesterday."

"Holy shit. That means someone stole the car, then attacked the Martinson woman with it." That made him smile. "My guess is that the owner will be very disappointed her car was used for such a vulgar purpose."

"Unless she turned in a false report."

"Are you suggesting Amelia Kendall-White is our murderer? I know she can be a"—Carl searched for the right word but could find no real substitute for "bitch"— "problem. But she's not a murderer. Okay." He held his hands out palms up. "She's bitter enough to have murder in her heart, but she's the type who would hire it done. She'd never dirty her own hands. So what's the good news?"

"That was the good news."

"How so?"

Jim grinned. "Now that we've found the car, she can harass the insurance company."

Carl ran a hand through his hair. God, if that was good news, they must be in worse shape than he'd realized. "Hit me with the bad."

"Mrs. Amelia Kendall-White just remembered that she left her registered handgun in the glove compartment. It's not there now."

Carl rubbed his hands over his face. He needed a shave and a good night's sleep. He wasn't likely to get either one for a while. "Shit." There went any hope that the murderer would try to purchase another weapon. "We're not getting any breaks, are we?"

Jim shook his head. "Not so far."

"Let's go over it again. What, exactly, have we got?"

"The murders of Stewart Roarke"—Jim held up one finger—"and Jacqueline Kendall," he continued, and added the second digit. "Both locals. Both without any known enemies. Both killed with the same gun, dumped over the same cliff. The murder weapon has been found but is unregistered. We have a third murder committed approximately thirty-six years ago." He leaned forward on his chair, obviously warming to his subject. "The victim is Walter Kendall, member of a wealthy and influential family, who by all accounts was a no-good son of a bitch. No one except his immediate family mourned him. He was probably killed by a blow to the head, then buried out in the sand dunes. He would have remained there except for a bit of larceny by an ungrateful little bastard who accidentally dug up part of the skeleton."

Carl shook his tired head. "It doesn't sound one bit better when you say it."

"It's a damned mess, sir. And not getting any better."

Carl picked up the story from there. "Since the same weapon was used in the two recent murders, I think we can assume they were committed by the same person." He rose and filled his cup from the coffeepot that had been warming for hours. The jolt of caffeine wasn't going to help him think, but it might help him stay awake. "The other murder seems unconnected. The common denominator is that all three were locals and had undoubtedly made an enemy or enemies locally. Then we get a tourist." He held up a hand to forestall Jim's comment. "I know she's now an employee, but she came here as a tourist. She's been threatened, had all her belongings destroyed, and been the victim of an attempted murder. I'd consider the attacks on the Martinson woman unrelated if she hadn't discovered Stewart Roarke's body."

He sat down and rubbed the back of his neck. "My gut instinct says the attempt on Jessica has to be related to her discovery of Roarke. She's such a sweet little thing, I don't think she could make an enemy if she tried."

"But we don't know that for sure. Have you checked her background at all?"

Carl made a note on a yellow legal pad. "Might as well. We're at a dead end otherwise." He tapped the eraser on the desk. "But I say she comes out looking like Pollyanna."

"Go over the murder of Jacqueline Kendall again. I wasn't here at the time."

"I'd been back less than a year myself." Carl remembered the anger he'd felt about that one. He'd left San Francisco for a more peaceful existence, only to have a murder victim turn up a few months later. He went over the details again. Described how she'd been murdered and dumped over the cliff. How Brandon had come upon her and carried her up from the beach.

He left out the part about wanting to solve it because he'd gone to school with Jason. About how he'd come close to arresting Brandon even though he'd also gone to school with him. Hell, the three of them had played varsity football together. That case had made it clear that being chief of police in the small town where he'd grown up wasn't going to be the picnic he'd expected. "After a few months went by, I decided that it might have been a thrill killer passing through the area. I checked files up and down the state for anything similar." He sipped at the thick coffee. "I came up empty."

"Motive?" When Carl only shrugged, Jim continued. "Revenge?"

"She was well liked in the area. Did volunteer work and was a soft touch when someone was in need."

"Gain?"

"The only person who gained financially was her son. By all accounts they were close. I dug, but couldn't come up with anything there."

"Love?"

Carl smiled. "There was a rumor about her and Brandon."

"Roarke? Jeez, she was almost old enough to be his mother."

Carl shook his head. "She was exactly old enough to be his mother. Brandon and Jason are the same age. They would have been around thirty-three at the time." He knew because he was almost the same age. "Jacqueline Kendall was in her early fifties."

"That's disgusting."

Carl decided Jim had never sounded so young—or so naive. "Catherine Deneuve is fifty. Would you turn her down?"

"Well . . ."

"Jacqueline was beautiful." And kind. He remembered when he'd been young and tongue-tied around her, she'd always been careful of his delicate male ego.

"Besides, Brandon categorically denied it, and you can't throw anyone in jail over a rumor."

"Could the killer have been covering another crime? Like the murder of the dead woman's husband?"

Carl's feet went flat on the floor, his back ramrod straight. "It never occurred to me."

"You didn't have Walter Kendall's remains at the time."

"It's something to think about." The trouble was that he was too tired to think straight at the moment. "But why wait thirty-some years to kill her?"

Jim shrugged. "I don't know. I'm just thinking out loud here."

Carl tried to sort things in his tired, muddled mind. "Then how do we connect the murderer to Stewart Roarke?"

"Do we have to?"

"The weapon already connects them."

"Hell." Jim rose to pace the room. "What's the motive this time? Revenge?"

"Not that I've been able to dig up."

"Financial gain?"

"Brandon stood to gain the most. But, hell, he's got more money than he knows what to do with." Carl rubbed a hand over his face once more. "Check into Brandon's finances. See if he has any debts we don't know about. Maybe he gambles. Hell, maybe he embezzled funds from the inn."

Jim made an entry in his notebook. "How about the hundred thousand Roarke left to the Kendall kid?"

"Hell, I don't know. She's a cute kid. Maybe he liked her."

"That much money is more than 'liked.' If he'd 'liked' her, he would have given her a hundred-dollar savings bond for her birthday."

"Check into it."

Jim made another notation. "How about love?"

"I suppose you could say that he loved the kid if he left her that much money."

"I mean as a motive for Stewart's murder."

"Oh." Carl thought a minute. "Brandon loves Jessica."

"What?" Jim looked as confused as Carl felt.

"Brandon Roarke loves Jessica Martinson." As far as he was concerned, that was still the most unlikely match he'd ever seen. "That's the wild card here. It's got to be. Our murderer hasn't been heard from in three years, then the Martinson woman arrives, and pow, we've got a second dead body. And an attempt on her life. It's connected somehow." He turned bleary eyes on his assistant. "I just can't figure out how." Jim stared right back at him until Carl closed his eyes. "We're overlooking something. Evidence or a witness or something." And he was too damn tired to see it.

"Chief." Jim waited until Carl opened his eyes. "Go home. Get some rest. I'll call if anything turns up."

"Yeah." He turned off his desk light, checked to make sure he had his wallet and car keys. He was halfway across the room when there was another knock on the door. He muttered a curse. "Come in."

Millie, his no-nonsense receptionist and file clerk, entered. She closed the door behind her. "There's someone at the front desk who says he wants to confess to the murders of Jacqueline Kendall and Stewart Roarke."

Carl was in no mood for a practical joke. "Yeah, sure. Anything else?"

Millie nodded. "Also the murder of Walter Kendall."

Jim smiled. "How about the Easter bunny?"

"A flake," Carl decided. "Have someone take his statement, then send him on his way."

The woman stood solidly in front of the door. "He's no flake. I've known him almost forty years myself."

Carl smiled at his assistant. "Maybe our luck is about to change."

Jessica stopped to look in the store window. Brandon's arm stayed around her shoulder as he, too, studied the seascape. The small, picturesque town of Carmel-by-the-Sea was filled with art galleries and individual shops.

Brandon had hoped that Jess would want to stop to ooh and ah over expensive clothes. He wanted to buy her a new wardrobe. He wanted to spoil her and indulge her and let her know how special she was. Instead she'd stopped at every art gallery.

"I like your photographs better," he whispered as he bent to kiss her. He couldn't seem to keep his hands off her.

"Shh." She nudged him with an elbow. "What if the artist is here?"

"If he saw one of your photos, he'd agree."

Jess flashed him a smile and turned to resume their leisurely stroll down Ocean Avenue. Grinning, Brandon fell into step. He couldn't believe it was possible to feel so carefree. The best part was that he expected to feel this way the rest of his life. He fought the urge to laugh at himself when he found himself thinking that the sky had never been bluer and the air had never been sweeter.

"Oh, look." Jess stopped in front of another gallery. "Isn't it beautiful?"

But this time it wasn't a painting that had captured her attention. It was a small bronze sculpture of a school of dolphins. And on the back of one was a small child, her pudgy little arms clasping the animal's muscled sides, her soft cheek laid on the animal's sleek back, her long hair streaming out behind her.

"Look at her smile," Jess urged. "It reminds me of Megan."

Brandon felt his world tilt. "Megan?"

Smiling, Jess turned to him. Her smile turned to a frown with one glance in his direction. "I know you and Jason don't get along, but Megan's a sweet kid."

He tried for a reassuring smile. "You like her?"

"Actually, I'm crazy about her. She's loving and bright and funny. From the moment I met her, there was something special about her." Jess shrugged. "I don't know how else to put it except to say that I fell in love with the kid."

Brandon couldn't believe his heart could be so full. There was so much he wanted to say to her, about how she had a good heart, about how he didn't deserve her, and about how he planned to spend the rest of his life making her happy. But standing on a crowded sidewalk while tourists surged around them didn't seem the right time.

He turned his attention back to the window. This was an excellent gallery; he knew the owner, Daphne Devereaux, and bought items from her regularly. He'd even tried to interest her in opening a second gallery at the inn, but Daphne had maintained that at her age she didn't want the pressure of a second place. Just keeping first-class art in one gallery and pursuing her own craft was enough to keep the elderly woman as busy as she wanted to be.

Tugging on Jess's hand, Brandon started toward the entrance. "Let's take a closer look at the dolphin sculpture."

Once they were in the shop, Jessica took her time, studying the paintings and sculpture that were displayed around the front gallery, but she kept coming back to the little girl and the dolphins. It wasn't exactly what Brandon had had in mind when he'd decided on a stroll through the colorful streets, but it was the one object that had captured her attention. He was about to ask the young man with the flowing blond hair and earring about the artist and price when the gallery owner glided into the room in a swirl of lavender silk and flowery perfume.

"Brandon," she cried.

He dutifully opened his arms and waited for her to

step into them. She gave him a surprisingly strong hug and a kiss on each cheek.

"You did not tell me you would be coming in today. I would have been here had I known."

He smiled at the vibrant woman who, even at her advanced age, stood straight and tall enough to look him in the eye.

"It was a last minute decision."

She nodded. "I was so sorry to hear about Stewart. I was out of town at the time, or I would have attended the funeral." She sighed and shook her head. "He will be missed by many, but by you most of all. My heart is with you."

"Thank you." He fought the shadow that threatened to overtake him, then looked at Jess, who was watching him. He held out his hand, and Jess laced her fingers with his as she stepped to his side. "Daphne, I'd like you to meet Jessica Martinson." He smiled down at Jess. "Someday soon she'll be Jessica Roarke."

Brandon couldn't help grinning as Jess was wrenched from his side to be enfolded in Daphne's ebullient embrace. Just as swiftly, Brandon found himself once more in the older woman's arms. He was surprised by the tears in Daphne's eyes, but not by the way she turned to her employee.

"Champagne," Daphne demanded of the young man who was watching, bemused, from the safety of his desk. "Bring a bottle from the back. And glasses. The best crystal." She turned back toward them to cup Brandon's face in her large, graceful hands and smile down at Jessica. "This deserves a toast."

An hour later they had finished off a bottle of imported champagne and the employee had packed up the sculpture after Daphne had cut the price by several hundred dollars in honor of their impending marriage. Daphne's accent was pure Californian, but Brandon knew her heart was as French as her name and the champagne. However, even he had been surprised by her joyful excitement and the dramatic slash in price. He was just gathering Jess and the heavy box containing the brass dolphins when Daphne clapped her hands.

"Oh, I have almost finished your next order," she cried before he could make an exit. "Come see."

Before Brandon could decline, Daphne had stepped into the back gallery with Jess in her wake. He'd hoped to avoid this, but obviously even the excitement of his engagement hadn't made her forget her craft.

"It is Josephine, empress of Napoleon," Daphne announced with a dramatic flourish toward an almost completed porcelain doll. "A woman of immense power and passion."

"It's beautiful," Jess murmured.

Brandon studied it. "Exquisite, as always," was his opinion.

"I am a little slower these days. Just a touch of arthritis," Daphne explained, flexing her long fingers. "So it takes longer to complete. But I will not sacrifice quality for speed."

"A fact I always appreciate," Brandon told her.

Jessica's eyes were wide with surprise. "I've seen dolls like this before." She turned to look at Brandon. "Megan has a shelf of them."

"Does she like them?" Daphne asked before Brandon could decide how to respond.

"Yes." Jessica tore her gaze from Brandon's and seemed to focus on the room around her. Other dolls stood finished around the room—all, Brandon knew, copies of the ones Jess had seen in Megan's room. "I took pictures of Megan with the latest one, Helen of Troy."

"I would like to see it."

"I'll see that you get a copy," Jess promised the older woman.

Brandon watched as Jess walked around the room, studying the dolls. He saw her eyes widen when she glanced at the price tags.

"I can see why Megan's mother didn't want her playing with the dolls without supervision," Jess said to no one in particular. "When I consider how much the Kendalls have spent on the dolls, I'm surprised they don't have them under glass."

Jess was busy studying the porcelain figures and so missed the look that Daphne shot in Brandon's direction, but Brandon felt the reproach in it. Okay, he admitted it. There were secrets that he hadn't been brave enough to share with Jess yet. But Jess loved him. And she loved his daughter. He prayed . . . no, he believed that Jess would find forgiveness in her heart once he told her the truth.

The Watcher had tried to sleep but couldn't. Brandon and the woman had been gone all day. They'd left before the Watcher was aware of it, and they hadn't returned yet. They'd been gone hours. Hours. The Watcher peered through the telescope to study the inn once more. Brandon's car was still gone. The lights in his room were still dark.

There was no reason to huddle in the cold, waiting, when there was a warm, cozy room. The child in the bed whimpered. The Watcher ignored it. The brat was too frightened to move. Too frightened even to acknowledge the Watcher's presence. She was curled up in a tight ball with her eyes squeezed shut. She would stay that way until the Watcher left. She always did.

But what if Brandon had confessed his secret? What if Jessica knew about Megan? That was why Stewart had died. Because he'd known. Because his sense of right and wrong was bound to have him telling Jessica.

Right and wrong. Stupid concepts. Meant for fools and weaklings. The Watcher was impervious to such out-dated concepts. Revenge and power were what mattered. And the Watcher was determined to get both.

But what if Brandon told Jessica the truth? The truth as Brandon saw it. For no one saw the truth as the Watcher did. No one ever confessed to destroying the Watcher's youthful dreams. No one saw the Watcher's agony. No one cared. Well, they'd care soon enough. And they'd understand. The Watcher would make certain of that. If only they'd return.

What if Brandon had taken the woman and fled? What if they'd moved beyond reach? Could that happen? No, there was nowhere they couldn't be found. Nowhere that would take them beyond the Watcher's horrible justice.

13

By the time he and Jess started back to the inn, Brandon was as certain of his future as he had ever been in his life, and he knew that it was time to bring all the secrets to light. Only then would the innocent be free of the specters that writhed and waited in the dark.

Tomorrow morning, bright and early, he would call Jason. He would give Jason a chance to make his own peace with the past—Brandon owed him that much. But whether Jason chose to go with him to see Carl, or whether Brandon went on his own—one way or the other—by tomorrow night, the murderer would be safely locked away. And Brandon would be free of the secrets that haunted him.

He looked over at Jess where she slept on the passenger seat. She didn't look much older than Megan in this light. With her youthful features and mop of curly hair, she seemed very young and surprisingly innocent. He still couldn't get over the fact that she wanted to spend the rest of her life with him. That small voice at the back of his mind told him that she didn't know everything yet. That she might change her mind when she did. But the rational part of him said that once she'd given her heart, she would understand human frailty. He held fast to that belief as he turned into the parking lot at the inn and parked the Land Rover in his reserved spot.

He turned off the motor and leaned over to kiss her. "We're home," he whispered.

Jess's eyes fluttered open. "Home?"

"Home," Brandon repeated. It felt good to say that and let the word conjure up images and emotions that he'd suppressed for so long.

Jess smiled and turned toward him. Slipping her arms around his shoulders, she leaned in to the kiss. "I love you," she whispered.

Brandon gripped her shoulders when she would have kissed him again. "Say that again."

"I love you."

He kissed her hard. "Again."

Jess laughed, a low, throaty sound that made his stomach clench. "I love you."

"I thought you'd never get around to saying it." He rested his forehead against hers. "I've never heard anything so beautiful."

"Let's go upstairs, and I'll tell you again." She gave him a quick kiss. "In bed."

Brandon smiled at her innocence. The way he ached, he'd be lucky to get the door closed behind them, let alone make it all the way to the bedroom.

The cold air went a long way toward cooling his libido, so that they strolled into the lobby hand in hand. With his free arm Brandon cradled the sculpture; Jess carried the empty picnic basket. Brandon's first thought when he saw the hollow-eyed Nancy at the desk was that he should have known trouble would find him—even today. Then he wondered if he was only imagining the gloom that pervaded the lobby.

Despite his sense of impending doom, Brandon tried to keep his voice even. "You should have been off four hours ago," he informed Nancy.

"George has been arrested."

Brandon shook his head, certain he hadn't heard right. Jessica's grip tightened. "What?"

"For murder." Nancy reached across the desk and grabbed Brandon's jacket. "They say he murdered Stewart and Jacqueline Kendall." She stopped and looked at her own hands, as though surprised to see them clutching her employer's jacket. With great care she folded them on the desk. "And Walter Kendall."

"Where did you hear this?"

"The police."

"They called here?"

Nancy nodded. "George couldn't do that. He just couldn't. What are we going to do?"

Brandon set his burden on the counter. "You are going home," he told Nancy. "And get some rest. Jess, I want you to lock yourself in the apartment. Activate the alarm system and the video cameras. I'm going to the police station."

"No," Jess said softly.

Brandon turned to stare at her.

"I'm going with you," Jess informed him. "We're in this—whatever it is—together."

"I don't know how long this will take."

"It doesn't matter."

"I don't even know what kind of legal mess I might be getting into."

"I know a good attorney I can call any time of the night

or day." When he would have protested again, she said, "No discussion. We do this together or we'll never do anything else together."

Brandon was ready to capitulate when a sudden thought had him turning back to Nancy. What if this was a ruse to get him out of the way so that Jess was left alone? "Did the caller identify himself?"

Nancy nodded. "Carl Mendoza. I recognized his voice."

Brandon tapped the box containing the dolphin sculpture. It seemed like days rather than hours ago that they'd purchased it. "Lock this in my office, then call the police station. Tell Carl I'm on my way." He looked over at Jess, noted the stubborn tilt of her chin and the fire in her dark eyes. "Tell him we're on our way."

The police station was located on the eastern edge of Luz, away from the expensive ocean real estate and tasteful gift shops, as though the local merchants could decree that all crime be kept a safe distance from the tourists. It was a long, low building in the same Spanish style as the Santa Lucia. In fact, most of the public buildings and businesses were built in the same style as the inn, since its proximity was the lifeblood of the little town. When Brandon stepped through the big double doors, he was grateful for Jess's small hand in his own. There was an incredible amount of strength in her delicate fingers.

"I'm glad you're here," Carl said without preamble.

Brandon didn't bother with a greeting. "Why in hell have you arrested George? You're really reaching this time."

"He confessed," Carl explained.

"What?"

"George walked in here and confessed. I had to arrest him."

"He didn't do it," Jess said softly. "He's so gentle. He isn't capable of murder."

"I would have agreed with you about ten hours ago, Ms. Martinson. Now I'm not so sure." Nodding his head toward his office, Carl suggested, "Let's continue this in private."

The door was barely closed behind them when Brandon said, "Okay, Carl, let's cut to the chase. What do you have?"

Carl settled onto the desk chair while Brandon and Jess took the two chairs across from him.

"Well?" Brandon urged when Carl just sat there.

Carl sighed. "George walked in here and told the receptionist he wanted to confess. He's a decent, respected man in the area. My first reaction was to tell him to go home, but when a man known for his honesty and integrity wants to confess to murder, I figure I've got an obligation to hear him out."

Brandon didn't want to hear this. He just wanted to get George and go home. Jess placed a gentle hand over the two he had clamped together.

"That's understandable," she said in her gentle way.

"What do you know about George's background?" Carl asked.

Brandon frowned at Carl. "What background? Hell, he's worked at the inn for close to fifty years. He should retire, but how do you tell someone who loves what he's doing and who's damn good at it that he's through?"

"Did you know he used to be a high school English teacher?"

"You're joking."

Jess strengthened the grip she had on Brandon's interlaced hands. "It makes sense. The way he's always quoting poetry."

Carl shuffled through the papers on his desk. "He taught at a little school back in West Virginia when he was only twenty. Taught almost three years before he was forced to resign. Something about child abuse."

"That's ridiculous." Brandon shook off Jess's hand and rose to glower down at the policeman. "I've known George all my life. He'd never hurt anyone. Hell, when Jason and I were kids we used to take him injured animals we found out in the dunes. He'd bandage them up and show us how to take care of them. He couldn't kill anyone. And he sure as hell wouldn't abuse a child."

"I didn't say he was accused of abuse. Evidently he accused the parents of one of his students. The information that's been faxed to us is sketchy, but he must have tangled with someone influential enough to have him fired. As far as I can piece things together, it took him about eight months to get to the West Coast. He's been here ever since."

Brandon sat back down. "What does that have to do with anything?"

"It made me realize there are things we don't know about George." Carl ran a hand through his already tousled hair. "I'm trying to tell you that we all have secrets. Things we don't want to come to light."

Brandon squirmed at that. God knew he had secrets, things he had hidden. But could George actually have murdered anyone? "I still don't see George as a cold-blooded murderer."

"Neither do I. But I think he's the kind of man who would kill to protect someone he loved." Mendoza ran a hand over his haggard face. "Or confess to murder to protect them. My experience has been that almost any man can be driven to lie—or kill—with the proper motive."

"And what motive did he have for killing Stewart? Or Jacqueline?"

"He didn't kill them. When I questioned him, it was apparent that he didn't. He doesn't know what the deceased were wearing, what type of weapon was used, where the bullet entered the body. Nothing."

"Then why is he in jail?"

"Because I think he killed Walter Kendall. At the very least, he was present when Kendall was murdered."

Brandon was stunned. "How do you figure that?"

Carl sifted through more paperwork. "He knows details that only the murderer—or someone who witnessed the murder—could know. His detailed description of the blow is consistent with the lab reports. His description of the victim's clothing is verified by fibers found on the remains. Hell, he even described how the victim was buried. He gave me too many facts to dismiss his confession."

"And what's his motive for killing Walter Kendall?"

"Self-defense." Carl shrugged. "That's all he'll tell me. My gut instinct says there's more to it than that."

"Considering the stories I've heard about Kendall, it's not so hard to see him attacking someone as gentle as George. Bullies do that."

"Could be." Mendoza nodded. "But why didn't George go to the authorities?"

Brandon sighed. "I don't know. Maybe if I could talk to him, I could make some sense of it."

"Okay." Carl crossed to the door, opened it, and stuck his head out. "Have George Lewis brought in."

"Just like that?" Brandon asked.

"Just like that." Carl heaved a sigh as he sat. "All I want is the truth, Brandon. And the murderer."

"Then we both want the same thing."

"We all do," Jess murmured.

The room was quiet when the officer knocked on the door and escorted George in. Jess wanted to cry when she saw him. He looked old. She couldn't believe anyone could age that quickly. He wore his khaki work clothes without the hat. The sparse hair that covered his head looked grayer than she'd remembered. Between his big, callused hands dangled the handcuff chains.

"Take the cuffs off," Mendoza commanded the officer.

"Chief?" The officer looked startled. "He's a murder suspect."

"He's also in his seventies and without a weapon. Besides, he walked in here and confessed. What reason would he have for running now?"

The room was silent as the officer removed the shackles and left.

George sat on the chair Carl pointed to before he spoke in his usual slow, careful manner.

"I'm sorry they bothered you, Mr. Brandon. I didn't ask them to call."

"I'm not sorry, George. I'm only sorry you're in here. I want to help you get things straightened out, then we'll go back to the inn."

"There's not much to straighten out. I killed 'em. I don't think I'll be goin' back to the inn." He rubbed his big hands on his pant legs. "Everythin' is caught up in my office, and I left a letter of resignation under your office door."

"I'm not concerned with the office or the letter; I'm worried about you."

"There's not much point in worryin'. I did it, and now I have to pay the price."

Jess couldn't believe what she was hearing. "What did you do, George?"

He looked her directly in the eye. "I killed Walter Kendall. Not that he didn't deserve killin', but I doubt the law is goin' to see it that way." His eyes slid toward the floor. "And I killed Jacqueline and Stewart."

"Why?"

"I don't 'spect it matters much. I just did, that's all."

Jess rose and walked to stand before him. He looked up at her. "And then you tried to kill me, too? Why was that?"

His brows came down over troubled brown eyes. "Oh, no, miss. I would never hurt you. Why, that would break Mr. Brandon's heart."

"And killing Stewart didn't?" She struggled to keep her voice calm as she knelt before the confessed killer.

She took his big hands in her smaller ones. His touch was gentle. "George, Stewart Roarke was your friend. I don't believe you could have killed him. And I saw you when you spoke about Jacqueline Kendall. I think you were half in love with her, like almost every other man I've heard talk about her. I don't believe you could have killed her, either." She tightened her grip on the old man's hands. "Why don't you tell us the truth? You may know something that will help the police catch the real murderer—before someone else ends up dead."

George released her hands almost reluctantly. "I killed 'em. I killed all of 'em."

Brandon rose from his chair and came over to kneel beside Jess. He put his arms around her shoulders. "Jess has agreed to marry me, George." His voice, too, was quiet, reasonable. "But I think she's in danger as long as the murderer is free." He forced himself to ignore Jess's wide eyes and continued, "As long as the murderer is free, she'll never be safe. I don't know who you think you're protecting, but I do know that if anything happens to

Jess, it will be on your conscience. If you've never been in love, you can't understand how much I care, but—"

"Never been in love?" George asked. His eyes grew round and wild. "You don't know nothin' 'bout love. You don't know what it's like to love someone so much that you'd cut off your own arm rather than have her hurt again. So much that you'd spend your life slippin' in and out of shadows to protect her. So much that you'd do anythin' to keep her safe—even murder."

George rose to tower over them, but Jess felt no fear. His anger was directed inward. "She deserved better. God knows she did. She was beautiful and sweet and—" His voice cracked, and all the anger just seemed to drain out of him. He sat down heavily and sat staring at his big, gnarled hands.

"And she loved me. Me, with dirt under my fingernails and no prospects." He shook his head. A small smile played at the corners of his mouth. "She saw past the dirt and my plain looks to the man underneath." He turned a bemused smile on Jess. "She said I was handsome. That I was everything she ever dreamed of. When she told me she was pregnant—that she was havin' our baby—I knew we had to leave. We were goin' to run away, where no one would find us. It didn't matter that we would be poor.

"Then he came in. He was drunk and screamin', and he said he'd kill her before he'd let her go." George's hands formed fists. "I couldn't let him do that, could I? I'd promised her I wouldn't interfere, but that was before the baby. I couldn't let him hurt our baby, could I?"

Jess swallowed. "And so you killed him?"

"It was an accident. We fought. He fell back and hit his head on the corner of the fireplace. I checked for a pulse, but there wasn't one. No heartbeat. No breathin'."

"That was self-defense," Brandon said. "Why didn't you call the police?"

The look George turned on him was haunted. "His family was rich. They had power. I had nothin'. I'd learned the hard way that you can't go up against that kind of power. They would have destroyed us. They would have called her a whore. And how would that have been for our child? The bastard was already dead; I couldn't let him hurt her again."

Jess reached out and laid her hands over George's big fists. She felt them turn gentle beneath her touch. "Who couldn't you let hurt her?"

"Walter." The word was obviously bitter in his mouth. "Walter Kendall. He was always hurtin' her. Beatin' on her. He was slowly destroyin' her. The first time I found her hidin' out in the gardens, she had bruises all over and her arm was broken. She said she'd fallen on the beach, but I knew it wasn't true. I'd seen that kind of abuse before. I knew what it was." He closed his eyes as though he could blot out the memories. "And she was scared. So scared." He opened his eyes to look at Jess. "I'd seen that before, too. I'd tried to stop it that other time, but I failed. I wasn't goin' to fail this time."

"You mean when you were teaching?"

George nodded. "They said the girl ran away after I left town, but I never believed that. I always thought there should have been somethin' I could've done for her; she was such a sweet little thing. But I wasn't goin' to let it happen again. So I took her home with me."

Jess wet her lips. "Who did you take home, George?"

George said nothing, just lowered his eyes to the floor with a gentle resignation that was as solid as granite

"Did you take Jacqueline home?" Brandon asked. "Did you save Jacqueline? And then fall in love with her?"

George nodded. "I never intended to fall in love with her. But she was so sweet. So gentle. I couldn't help myself." He shook his head. "The surprisin' part was that she could love me."

Jess strengthened her hold on the old man's hands. "You couldn't have killed someone you loved that much."

"And I don't believe you killed my uncle. You two were friends."

"I killed 'em," George insisted without lifting his eyes.

Mendoza spoke up. "I can't hold you for those murders, George."

George turned a confused gaze on the chief of police. "But I confessed."

"There's no proof."

"You don't need proof. I confessed."

"It doesn't work that way. I need details. The type of weapon. Where you got it. Your motive. You haven't given me any reason to hold you."

"I just forgot."

"You remember details about the death of Walter Kendall. That happened thirty-six years ago. And you expect me to believe you've forgotten similar details from nine days ago? Give it up, George. I'm not buying it, and neither is anyone else." Carl rose and walked to stand beside Jess and Brandon, who were still kneeling in front of the old man. "You know who the murderer is, don't you? Who is it?"

"I don't know." George shook his head. "I don't."

"Then why did you confess?"

"Because you'll think he did it. If you knew, it would look bad for him."

"If I knew what?"

George only shook his head.

Before Mendoza could badger George anymore, Jess spoke. "If you don't think he did it, why are you willing to go to prison for the murders?"

George hunched up one shoulder, still refusing to make eye contact with any of them. "As long as I'm goin' to jail for one murder, what difference does it make?"

"It will make a difference if the killer is still free." Brandon fought to keep his voice level. "It'll make a big difference if the next victim is Jess."

George looked up at that. "I promised Jacqueline that if anythin' ever happened to her, I'd look after our boy." His eyes were brimming with tears. "I promised."

Jess fought her own tears. "Why would we think your son murdered Jacqueline or Stewart?"

"They'd had a big argument, him and his mama. Just before she was killed. They usually got along real good, but just then they were havin' some big arguments. She'd spent the afternoon with me. She didn't tell me what they fought over, but she was real upset. She was on her way back from my place when she was killed." George pulled his hands from Jess's gentle grasp to wipe at the tears that had started to roll down his weathered cheeks. "And Mr. Stewart was on the way to see him when he was killed."

"How do you know that?" Brandon's voice was low and intense.

"'Cause I was the last one to talk to Mr. Stewart. I ran into him out on the grounds. He told me where he was goin'.""

"You should have told the police," Jess chided him.

"I couldn't. I'd promised Jacqueline. Promised her." The tears were falling in earnest now. "And all I had left was my promises. And my boy. That's all I have left."

Mendoza's voice cut into George's tearful confession. "Who's your son, George? Who are you protecting?"

"Jason," he mumbled. "Jason's my son. And Jacqueline's. He's suffered so much already. I couldn't let anyone put him in jail. Couldn't let them lock him up." His gaze went from face to face, then finally settled on Jess's. "He'll go crazy if they lock him up again. I couldn't let them do that."

Jess patted his hand. "Of course you couldn't." But she couldn't help wondering if Jason was already crazy. Crazy enough to kill.

The Watcher couldn't sleep. Couldn't lie in bed or sit still. Could only pace. Step, step, step. Turn. Step, step, step. Turn. Beneath the moon. Under the stars. In the comforting arms of the night.

Too many people calling. Too many people talking to each other. Too many secrets they could be telling. Too much. Too many. Too dangerous. It couldn't be allowed.

Time was running out. The Watcher could see it running out. It was Jessica's fault. Everything had been fine until she'd shown up. The Watcher looked at the weapon. Felt the cold metal. Felt the power. A bullet had silenced Jacqueline. And that fool Stewart. Now it was Jessica's time.

The Watcher laughed. The devil's laughter. Jessica's time.

14

    Jess put her arm around Brandon's waist, settled comfortably against him, and gazed out into the night. Brandon's arm around her shoulder kept her warm as she turned her face into the ocean breeze and inhaled the fresh scent of the sea. Overhead, stars shimmered in the last few hours before dawn, while over the ocean the fog absorbed the twinkling rays that had crossed millions of cold, dark miles.

    She had seen extraordinary things in the night. She had witnessed the introduction of a father and son who had known each other for years. She had seen estranged friends reunited. She had looked, for only a moment, into the hearts of three men. She supposed, then, that she was entitled to this strange combination of fatigue and euphoria.

    Content, she watched the fog shift and change. To her tired mind it looked like an approaching army, soldiers marching shoulder to shoulder, their booted feet kicking up a cloud of dust that obliterated everything in the distance. She snuggled deeper into Brandon's embrace; not even an army could tear her from his arms now. If she hadn't loved him before this evening, she would have lost her heart when she saw him with George. Such kindness and compassion were not what she expected from a man of immense wealth and power. Which proved, she admitted to herself, that she was a snob in her own backward fashion.

Smiling, Jess silently congratulated herself on her good taste in men. "Do you think they're still talking?"

"George and Jason?" Brandon pulled his gaze from the hazy distance and looked down at her. "They have thirty-six years to catch up on. Not that they didn't know each other, but Jason didn't realize that he had his father all that time. I can't imagine what that must feel like."

"Jason was glad, wasn't he?" She gave Brandon an assessing look. "Sometimes it's hard to tell with men. They spend so much time bottling up their emotions."

"Yeah, he was glad." Brandon dropped a quick kiss on the tip of her nose. "George is a good man; Jason has always respected him. Besides, he has to be relieved that Walter Kendall isn't any relation."

"Why?"

"You heard what George said about the bastard. He was a drunk who beat Jacqueline and generally made everyone's life miserable."

"But Jason never knew Walter Kendall."

"This is a small town. People talk. By the time Jason was in high school, he'd heard all the stories. He kept at his mom until she admitted the truth." He pulled Jess closer, as though he wouldn't be content until their two bodies merged. "I think that's one of the reasons Jason volunteered to go to war zones. He was both repelled and fascinated by violence. That's why his captivity was so tough. And the fact that he killed to escape . . ." Brandon laid his cheek against Jess's head. "He must have been afraid that his father's violent streak was showing up in him. He must have been terrified that mindless violence was in his blood."

"But it wasn't mindless."

"I know, but he was in bad shape. Both physically and psychologically. When I first saw him, he was a shadow. I don't mean just the loss of weight. It was as if they'd beaten the humanity out of him. He seemed amazed by simple kindness. Confused when people laughed. I spent years wondering if I could have saved him."

Jess turned in his embrace to look up at him. "It wasn't your fault. You couldn't have fought off an entire army."

"You don't understand. Someone pushed me behind a rock. Someone saved my life. I've always thought it was Jason—then I went off and left him in that hellhole."

Jess smiled; she could at least relieve him of this guilt. "It wasn't Jason. He told me he saw you diving for cover. And as for the time he was held captive, everyone thought he was dead. Their government. Our government. Everyone. How were you supposed to know?"

Brandon's kiss was gentle. "That was a 'thank you' kiss."

"For what?"

"For loving me. For being good for me. You'll always love me, won't you? You wouldn't leave me just because I'd made a mistake, would you?"

Surprised by his insecurity, she framed his face with her hands. "I couldn't stop loving you if I wanted. Satisfied?"

Brandon nodded and gave her the smug grin she was used to. "I knew from the start that I'd be able to charm you. Despite the fact that you were unbelievably rude when we first met, I knew it was just a matter of time."

She gave him a not-too-gentle jab in the ribs. "It wasn't your charm that won me over. It was your heart." She placed a hand over the place it beat. "You have a kind heart. I couldn't resist it."

He gave her a long kiss. "And here I thought you were after me for my body."

Jess stood on tiptoe and returned the kiss. She felt the change in his embrace then, felt the change in his focus as all his senses became centered on her. Just her. His lips became insistent. His hands roamed her curves to settle over her bottom and draw her closer. There was no denying that he wanted her. No denying her answering passion.

It was hard to believe that mere days ago she hadn't known what it was to crave a man's touch. Hadn't known what it was to be so greedy that her hands would be the first to seek heated flesh. That the feel of his skin beneath her fingers could send her temperature soaring, could send her needs spiraling out of control. Her hands roamed the hard planes of his back. Her mouth opened beneath his, and as their tongues mated, her hands edged lower to cover his buttocks, to caress him through the denim that kept her from touching the firm flesh.

She was wild for him, driven by needs that were as violent as they were new. Her hands fumbled to unbutton his shirt; her lips tempted his. When her fingers finally slid the last button free, her mouth trailed down to taste and tease. Her teeth nipped the corded muscles of his neck, and her tongue laved his hard nipples.

When she trailed wet kisses over his flat belly and her fingers reached for the snap on his jeans, Brandon muttered a curse under his breath. The slamming of a door somewhere below them, the quick streak of light from a room several doors down, brought Brandon to his senses enough to grasp Jess's fingers before she could pull down the zipper. With shaking hands, he tugged her to her feet and dragged her inside. There was no time to close the door before she resumed her task. Only the thin curtain fluttering in the breeze hid them from the outside world.

When Jess released Brandon from the confines of his clothes and closed her clever, loving hands around him, his last coherent thought was that they would never make it to the bedroom, that he was thankful she'd agreed to marry him because he hadn't the patience to search for protection. Then they were both on the floor.

The Berber carpet was scratchy beneath his back as the faint glimmer of dawn revealed Jess above him. Somehow she had shed her sweater and bra. She bent down to kiss him, and her breasts brushed his sensitized skin. He trailed kisses along her jaw and down her neck. She answered by moving so that one rosy nipple was offered to his seeking lips. With tongue and teeth, he tormented the delicate bud while his hands worked at her jeans.

The sound of his name on her lips, the way she moaned, drove him wild. He slipped her pants down her slim hips and used his hands to guide her over him. With a cry of joy he drove into her, then his hands were free to cover her breasts as she took control. With her head thrown back, she quickened the pace. He was watching her face when she first convulsed around him. He had never seen anything to compare with the joy and the wonder. The second tremor hit her before her breathing evened. The third had her fighting for her next breath. Wanting to delay his own completion so that he could watch rapture claim her once more, Brandon clasped his hands around her hips to hold her still.

"Don't move," he whispered.

But she was beyond thought as she struggled against his grip. It took all his strength to keep her still until she was able to focus on him. Then, with a smile and a whimper of pleasure, she collapsed across him.

He stroked upward until his shaky hands could brush back her hair. Then he let his fingers glide down her back until they encountered the jeans that cradled the tops of her thighs.

He couldn't manage more than a whisper. "Again?"

"I don't have the energy." Her voice sounded more smug than fatigued.

He smiled and began to move slowly. "Oh, I think you do."

When the tremor hit her, Brandon battled his own need. The next one had Jess struggling to match his rhythm. She whimpered and pushed up on her hands so that she could look at him. He saw ecstasy in her expression, glimpsed heaven in her eyes, just before his body found its own violent release. Still transfixed by the wonder and the love in her gaze, he kissed her once, hard, before she laid her cheek against his chest and they both fell into a dreamless sleep.

The sun was shining in earnest when Brandon awoke. He brushed Jess's hair back from her cheek and kissed her. "Come on, Jess. Wake up."

"It's too early." She swatted at his hand. "Don't want to get up yet."

"We're not getting up," Brandon promised. "But I'd like to make it to the bed before we try this again. This floor is getting damn hard."

Her head came up. Her sleepy brown eyes blinked twice. "I'm sorry."

"No, you're wonderful. But I'm too old to spend the entire night on the floor."

She started to get up, only to find her legs caught in the jeans, holding her like shackles. Blushing, she jackknifed to a sitting position.

"You won't be needing those," Brandon promised as he peeled off her pants and tossed them over his shoulder. Standing, he pulled Jess to her feet for another kiss. There wasn't much time left before he would have to send her home, and he had every intention of making the most of it. So, with a hand on that cute little backside he so admired, he urged her toward the bedroom.

It was almost eight when they woke next. Brandon allowed Jess to head for the shower only because he needed privacy to make a few phone calls. When he'd completed them, he headed for the bathroom. Jess was groping for the faucets to turn off the water when he snaked his hand through the opening to stop her.

"Not yet," he said as he stepped in to join her.

He waited until they'd finished breakfast before he spoke of her leaving. His motives were purely selfish: he needed the memory of these moments to get him through the tough times ahead. He needed the memory of her coming apart in his arms, the memory of her blushing embarrassment after, the memory of her heedless return to his arms to make him believe in the future. For her sake, he needed to bind her so thoroughly that she would understand the necessity for her leaving and believe he would come for her after. He was fairly certain he'd accomplished the first, he could only pray he'd managed the last.

Jess had donned a white terry robe with the green-and-silver Santa Lucia logo while they had breakfast.

Brandon leaned across the table to adjust the gaping neckline before he could be distracted again.

"I know you love me," he began.

Jess gave him a teasing grin. "How can you tell?"

He couldn't smile back. "I need to know that you trust me."

"With my life."

He knew by her sobered expression that she understood he was serious, and he nodded. "That's exactly what I'm trying to protect. That and our future."

"You don't have to convince me. If you tell me to jump, the only question you'll hear is, 'How high?'"

"What if I told you to pack?"

"I'd only ask where we're going."

Brandon shook his head; this was more difficult than he'd imagined. "We aren't going anywhere. You are going home."

The color drained from her face. "I thought this was home now."

"It's going to be. I promise." He grabbed her arm when she would have stood. "But first I have to make it safe. Look at me," he demanded when her gaze slid away. Rising, he grabbed the lapels of her robe, then hauled her to her feet. "Look at me, damn it!"

"You don't have to shout!" Tears swam in her eyes as she glared at him. "And you don't have to make up excuses to get rid of me. If you want me to leave, just say so."

"You little fool," he said. But his voice was a mere whisper as one hand came up to brush the curls back from her face. "I'm not trying to get rid of you. I'll die if you ever leave me." When he saw that his hand was trembling, he buried it in her curls, still damp from the shower. "I'm trying to keep you safe while I see that the murderer is locked away. Locked away so that you can never be hurt." His hand tightened around the curls. "Now do you understand?"

"Not completely."

"I'd tell you if . . ."

Struggling against her tears, Jess placed a gentle hand across his lips. "I told you that I'd ask, 'How high?' if you told me to jump. So now I'll only ask, 'How soon?'"

Brandon smiled and placed a kiss on her palm before it dropped away. "Now. A Greyhound bus stops in Luz in an hour and a half. You're going to be on it."

"Okay."

"It's not the mode of transportation I'd ordinarily choose, but I don't want you on the highway by yourself."

Jess shuddered. "You won't get an argument from me."

"And driving you to the Monterey airport would eat up valuable time." That sounded foolish, he supposed, after dragging his feet for three years. But he couldn't shake the feeling that time was accelerating. That each moment he delayed placed Jess in more danger. "This way you'll be surrounded by people until Marty picks you up in L.A."

"Marty?"

Brandon nodded. "I called while you were showering. She'll pick you up, and she promised not to let you out of her sight until I give her the all-clear."

"I don't need a baby-sitter."

"Don't go stubborn on me now. Please."

He watched while she considered. In the end, he was certain it was his plea that won her over.

"Just this once." She poked a finger in his chest. "But don't ever try it again."

"I promise." Once more, he hauled her up for a long,

hard kiss. She laid her head against his shoulder when he lifted his lips from hers.

"I'll take care of things here as quickly as I can." It was going to be tough, he knew. Especially after the joy of watching George and Jason together last night. "People are going to be surprised. Innocent people are going to be hurt." But hurt was better than dead. That was the conclusion he'd come to last night. "I can do anything as long as I know you'll be waiting for me."

"Are you sure you don't want me to stay?"

He'd considered that. He knew the deed would be easier if he had her to lean on. But that was selfish—and cowardly. The most important thing was to make sure Jess was out of harm's way. If there was even a chance that the killer could get to her, it would make him move cautiously. And caution might make the killer even bolder—and more dangerous.

"You're going back to L.A." He gave her a quick kiss. "Where you will have less than forty-eight hours to resign from your job and pack everything you want to bring back here . . . back home with you."

"But my apartment—"

He cut her off before she could explain. "And start planning a wedding. How long do you suppose it takes to get a license?"

"I have no idea."

"We don't have to worry about a place or a caterer. We'll have the reception in the lobby if need be."

He was warming to the idea. The delighted, bemused look on Jess's face would get him through the rest of this awful day. Would help him deal with the knowledge that he was about to rip apart the only family his daughter knew. But he'd be able to offer Megan so much more now. He ignored the doubt that threatened his ideal picture. He knew—he just knew—that Jess would accept Megan with open arms and heart.

"I'd like to have the wedding in Mother's garden," he continued. "If that's all right with you."

Jess shook the curls back from her face and looked up at him. "It's all happening so fast. I need to think. I need to—" She broke off and laughed. "That's fine. No . . ." She threw her arms around his neck. "It's fabulous."

"In two weeks."

Jess shook her head. "I need a month."

"Okay. You and I have a wedding date—one month from today. You wear white. I'll wear my tux. We'll be the envy of everyone we know." She was laughing when he lifted her off the ground and whirled her around. "Now get packed. The quicker I get you on the bus, the quicker I can come get you."

Jess was halfway finished with her packing before the doubts assailed her. Not doubts about Brandon—her faith in him was complete—but about herself. Was she running again? Taking the easy way out instead of staying to fight her own battles? She would have said she was backsliding except that it wasn't her battle, was it? Whoever the murderer was, whatever had pushed him over the edge, it had been set in motion long before she had set eyes on the Santa Lucia.

As she folded her few items of clothing, her mind fluttered from one subject to another. From love to death. From a wedding to murder. It was enough to make a person crazy, she decided. Ultimately, she focused on the one subject that really mattered: Brandon. She wondered what he knew and who was implicated by that knowledge.

She sighed as she folded the nightshirt Brandon had barely let her wear since he'd purchased it to replace her own. When she thought about everything that had happened, she realized that all she'd heard or seen pointed toward one person as the murderer. George had lied in an effort to protect him, and Brandon had evidently shielded him because of their lifelong friendship and feelings of guilt. Even Jess felt she owed him a debt of gratitude for the way he'd championed her career. But no matter how unbelievable it seemed, all the evidence pointed to Jason Kendall as the killer.

Jess stopped in the midst of adding her newly acquired lingerie to the suitcase. She just couldn't believe it. She couldn't imagine Jason taking a life—and certainly not the life of Stewart Roarke or his own mother. She'd seen only the gentle side of him. She'd been the object of his professional encouragement. She'd watched him with his daughter. How could anyone that kind and loving be a murderer?

But he had killed when he made his escape in South America. So maybe Brandon had hit on it when he'd talked of Jason's captivity. Maybe Jason had snapped in the jungles of San Bernardino and never really pulled himself back together. But Jess had trouble buying that explanation. She couldn't believe that because he'd killed once in self-defense, he'd keep killing. It might—just might—explain his mother's death. George said that mother and son had argued. If it had been violent enough, maybe Jason could have killed in a rage. But how could that account for Stewart's death?

Then she remembered what Amelia had said about Stewart being Megan's father. Could it be true? And could Jason have found out? Could he have been so enraged that he sought Stewart out and murdered him?

Jess had to face the fact that it might be possible, but she couldn't imagine Jason trying to kill her. Could the

man who'd captured such beauty on film, who'd compli-
mented her on her own vision, have turned around and
tried to murder her?

Her packing complete, Jess sat on the bed. How was
Brandon ever going to live with himself after turning
Jason in? How was he going to deal with his own feelings
of guilt, however misguided? God, she wished she had
gotten a clear look at the person driving the other car.
She could have been the one to implicate Jason. She
could have spared Brandon the pain of turning in his
childhood friend.

She rose and snapped her suitcase shut when she
heard a tap on the apartment door. There could be no
retreat now. And when she returned, they'd deal with
this as they were going to deal with everything else:
together.

Brandon stepped back as George entered the apartment.

"I picked this up downstairs like you asked me to,"
George said as he held out the small jewelry box that
looked out of place in his big, callused hands.

Brandon took it. "Thanks."

"This mean what I think it means?"

"I've asked Jess to marry me."

"Where is she goin' to be while we take care of today's
business? 'The grave's a fine and private place, but none I
think do there embrace.'" he quoted. "She's got to be kept
safe."

Brandon nodded in agreement. "We're putting her on
the bus in Luz before we meet Jason. She'll be well out of
it by the time we have to take any action." He jammed
the small box into his jacket pocket and turned when he
heard her enter the room. "You're ready?"

"As ready as I'm going to be." She smiled at George. "Are you going to be with Brandon today?"

He gave Brandon a curious look. "Yes, miss."

"I'm glad. I didn't want to leave him by himself."

"He won't be alone. That I can promise you."

George said his good-bye on the short drive into Luz and remained in the Land Rover when Brandon and Jess went to buy the ticket. In actuality, the bus station was a small storefront close to the police station with a bus stop at the curb. The few people using this mode of transportation stood on the sidewalk. There was a tired-looking woman somewhere in her twenties with three howling, undisciplined children; Jess fervently prayed they were greeting someone. An old man, obviously hard of hearing, leaned on his cane and nodded as his wife shouted in his ear. Two young men—boys, really—stood nearby in military uniforms.

Brandon pulled her off to the side in front of a small secondhand furniture store. He stuffed his hands in the pockets of his jacket and struggled not to look nervous. "The bus should be here any minute."

"You don't have to wait with me," Jess told him. "I'll be perfectly safe right here until the bus comes."

Brandon shook his head. "I'm not leaving till I see you safely on board. Besides, I have something for you."

"Really?"

"This isn't exactly the way I would have chosen to present it to you. I would have preferred champagne and candlelight." He removed the small jewelry box from his pocket. "I should have asked George for an appropriate line of poetry."

"I don't need poetry," Jess said in a breathless voice that hardly sounded like her own. Her hand was shaking so hard, she was afraid to take the small package.

"For God's sake, open it," Brandon said impatiently when she just stood looking at it. "It's hard enough to propose under these circumstances without having to worry that you don't want this."

"Anticipation is half of the joy," Jess explained. But when she looked up to see real nervousness reflected in his gaze, she took pity. After flipping open the top of the satin box, she stood transfixed by the huge diamond set against black velvet. She couldn't believe the size of it. She'd never been the kind of woman who window-shopped for engagement rings. If asked, she would have said she'd rather have a really good camera, but even to her inexperienced eye the stone was enormous. It had to be a carat and a half, maybe two. And when it winked in the sunlight, she was afraid she'd be blinded.

"Did you rob Tiffany's?"

"It's from the jewelry store at the inn. If you don't like it, we can exchange it when you come back. It was the best mounted stone the jeweler had on hand, but he said he could find something bigger if you wanted."

"Bigger?" Jess gave an incredulous laugh. "I'll be lucky if I can hold my hand up under the weight."

He raised one dark eyebrow. "My faith is strong."

When he removed the ring from the box and slipped it on her finger, Jess couldn't resist holding her hand out before her and watching the facets reflect the light.

"I'm not sure it's safe to travel with this. I could get mugged."

Brandon cast a careful look at the people around him. "Do you think I should keep it here?"

Jess held her hand out of his reach. "Not a chance."

"I'd hate to think of muggers following you home from the bus station," he said, but there was a glint of amusement in his eyes.

"I'll keep my hand in my pocket."

"You like it, then?"

Jess couldn't resist holding it out for inspection again. "You could say that."

When she placed her left hand over Brandon's heart, he looked her in the eye. "I love you."

He covered the hand with his own. "I love you, too. And I wasn't about to let you get on that bus without a firm commitment."

Jess looked at the stone that peeked out between his fingers. "I'd say this is real firm," she told him as the bus stopped at the curb with a huge sigh and the slap of opening doors.

Despite his edginess, Brandon took time to give her a thorough kiss before seeing her suitcases stored in the luggage compartment. He gave her another kiss before she climbed the steps. He was still standing on the sidewalk when the bus turned the corner and headed for Highway 1.

Jess lost count of the stops the bus made on its journey south. Even the scenery lost its appeal as she worried about what Brandon was doing. Had he confronted Jason yet? Gone to see Carl Mendoza? And what about poor George? To have claimed his son and then lose him behind bars all within twenty-four hours . . . Jess couldn't imagine what he must be going through. But whenever she thought there couldn't possibly be a way out of the mess, she'd look down at the ring on her finger. It was Brandon's promise. Not just of his love, but of his determination to make a life for them. Her only regret was that others had to be hurt before they could be together.

By the time they reached Santa Barbara, Jess was looking forward to the hour stopover and the chance to stretch her legs. She waited as the harried woman with the squabbling children made her way to the front of the bus; she sincerely hoped they would be exhausted enough to sleep for the last half of the journey. Since she was in no hurry, she motioned for the older couple to precede her. Content simply to be on her feet, she was one of the last passengers to alight from the bus. She was shocked to find Florence waiting for her.

"I was beginning to think I had the wrong bus," Florence said as she grabbed both of Jess's hands in hers.

"What are you doing here?"

"George told me you'd left." Her grip tightened. "I don't know why you're leaving. I don't know what you and Brandon argued about."

"We didn't argue."

"It doesn't matter," Florence said as she dragged Jess through the bus station. "Brandon needs you."

Jess had a sudden vision of Brandon's body lying broken at the foot of the cliff. "Is he still alive?"

"Yes, of course." Florence gave her hand a reassuring pat. "He hasn't been hurt."

"Then why are you here?"

Florence stopped and faced her. "I don't believe it, of course. No one does." She took a deep breath. "They've arrested Brandon for the murders of Jacqueline and Stewart."

The return trip was made in about a third of the time. After several sporadic attempts at conversation, the two women made most of the trip in silence. Jess couldn't believe that Mendoza had arrested Brandon. Her initial hope was that Brandon's arrest had been for something minor like concealing evidence, but when Florence said that Jason had gone to the police station to see about getting Brandon released—when she realized that Jason was free to come and go as he pleased—she knew that something was dreadfully wrong.

"Brandon didn't murder anyone," Jess said after a long silence.

Florence reached a hand across the console to give Jess a reassuring pat. "I know that." The certainty in Florence's voice was more reassuring than her touch.

"We'll get the best attorney. Marty will know whom to hire."

"Jason is already seeing about that."

Jess nodded and fell silent again. She didn't speak until Florence bypassed Luz and took the turnoff for her own secluded home.

"I thought we were going to see Brandon."

"Jason said to go home and wait for his call. He said it's already a zoo at the police station. Reporters. Camera crews. General insanity. When he's made arrangements for you to see Brandon, he'll call."

Jess didn't like it very much, but she didn't know what else to do. She'd give Jason a couple hours. If they hadn't heard from him by then, she'd ask Florence to take her back to Luz.

Sundown was still an hour or so away when they arrived at the Kendall home, but the fog had already begun drifting back toward the land. Most of the Pacific was hidden behind the heavy gray curtain of moisture, and even the sun was reduced to a flat leaden disk.

The house was silent and dark. Jess was surprised by how much she missed Megan's enthusiastic welcome. Her girlish prattle would have been a welcome distraction. Florence explained that the child was having her first sleepover with a friend when Jess commented on the quiet. Florence went through the house, turning on lights. "Nothing on the answering machine," she called from the kitchen. "Make yourself at home. I'm going to make some sandwiches."

Jess dropped her purse and carry-on beside the sofa. "Don't bother on my account." She went into the kitchen, where Florence was already pulling sandwich meat and cheese out of the refrigerator. "I doubt that I could eat a bite."

"You need to eat something." Florence pulled two kinds of bread out of the cabinet. "And I thought that Jason might be hungry when he gets home. Brandon, too," she added after a moment, as though she'd just realized the implication of her statement.

"Let me help."

"No indeed. You go relax." She waved Jess toward the living room. "I'll let you know when it's ready."

Reluctantly Jess retreated to the living room, where she paced until she was afraid she'd wear a hole in the carpet. She moved into the dining room to pace before the picture window.

The fog had all but obliterated the view. It was coming in huge waves. Jess could almost feel it rolling over the house, cutting them off from the outside world. She rubbed her arms against the cold and checked her watch again. Only thirty-five minutes since they'd arrived, and already she was a basket case.

She went back to the living room and pulled out the sweatshirt she'd stuffed into her carry-on. Since it didn't do much to keep her warm, she decided that the cold was coming from inside her. From the place where her heart used to be. Even the diamond on her finger had dimmed. Jess felt as though the warmth and light were being sucked right out of her life.

The old Jess—who still existed deep down inside her—asked what she'd expected: magic? love? happily ever after? She should have known she wasn't special enough for that. The old Jess wanted to sit down and cry. But the new Jess wouldn't have it. Sitting around and weeping wouldn't help Brandon. There had to be something she could do, something that would help prove Brandon innocent. That's when her gaze fell upon the pictures and negatives she'd pulled out of her carry-on when she got her sweatshirt. Maybe there was something there. Something she'd missed before. Jason had a high-powered magnifying glass in his studio. The least she could do was go over the photos one more time.

The Watcher smiled as she watched Jessica through the open doorway. Smiled at her nervous pacing. Smiled at her jerky movements. Smiled as she contemplated Jessica's death. While the Watcher's hands were busy slicing tomatoes and washing lettuce, she contemplated and anticipated.

Not long, now. Not long at all. The tide was coming in. She could hear the ocean creeping farther up the beach. Eating its way to the cliffs. Devouring sand and rock and everything in its path. This time the tide would take the evidence. This time the body would be washed out to sea, and no one would be able to weep over the poor, pitiful corpse. Or to prove that there had been a murder. All she had to do was lure Jessica out into the night.

They'd driven her to it. There was no doubt about that. If George hadn't revealed he was Jason's father . . . if Brandon hadn't reconciled with Jason . . . if Jason hadn't stolen her daughter earlier today, the Watcher might have been content to let Jessica leave—and never return. She could have managed that the way she'd always managed. By holding Megan over Jason's head. He'd do anything for the child who wasn't his. Anything.

She would have used the same weapon on Brandon, but differently. He would do anything to keep his secret hidden. Public knowledge of Megan's parentage would traumatize the child, he always said. And he lived in fear that the truth would destroy Jason.

Love and friendship. Two human frailties that Florence had always used to her best advantage. And secrets. Secrets were the most powerful, because people would do anything to keep them hidden. She'd hinted to Brandon that Jason had killed Jacqueline in a fit of rage. And Brandon's friendship had insured that he would keep the secret. She'd told Jason that Brandon killed Stewart out of greed. And Jason's friendship had prevented him from prying further. Florence knew how to use secrets— how to manipulate people.

Once Jessica was gone, they would know, of course. They would know Florence had killed her, though they wouldn't be able to prove it. They'd cry and threaten and beg. It always amused her when they begged her to get help. She was powerful; she didn't need help. That was the one secret she kept to herself. And with no body for proof, Jessica's death would become just another secret among the three of them. Maybe the most powerful secret.

She laughed when she thought of what the fools would do when they were confronted by the truth. By what they would do to protect Megan from the fact that her mother had murdered. What they didn't realize was that she would murder again whenever it suited her needs. That was the terrible, wonderful secret that would allow Florence to control them all.

15

Jess had gone through her proof sheets four times before she decided to look through the negatives she'd retrieved from Brandon's safe just that morning. Perhaps there was something on a negative—some incriminating evidence—that she'd neglected to include on a proof sheet. It was a long shot, she knew, but Brandon's arrest made her desperate. As soon as she finished, she was going to insist that Florence take her into Luz. She didn't care what anyone else said—she had to see for herself that Brandon was all right, and he had to know that her faith in him was unwavering.

Once she matched the negatives to the proof sheets, Jess discovered that instead of neglecting to make a proof of any of her negatives, she actually had a strip of negatives missing. They were the pictures she'd taken on her walk from the inn to the Kendalls' the day she'd found Megan alone in the house. Florence, she remembered, had been outside working in her garden.

Jess used Jason's most powerful magnifying glass to look at each picture on the proof sheet. There were a couple of Megan with her dolls, a seascape, a close-up of a squirrel, and the shot of the inn that Jason had found interesting but marred by the employee going in the side entrance.

With the high magnification, Jess could see that the figure was dressed in slacks and a jacket—and very familiar. Where before it had appeared sexless and obscure, it now took on a decidedly feminine form. The woman's long hair was hidden under her jacket; that had been an effective disguise when the figure was too small to see details, but now the tilt of the head and the hidden hair appeared furtive. Jess wondered why Florence had wanted to hide her identity.

It was very odd, she thought. First because Florence had no business being at the inn, and second because she'd said she was in the garden. Why would Florence skulk around the inn? And why would she lie about it? And, more important, what did the picture prove?

Jess shook her head. It didn't prove much of anything—except that Florence had lied. And that she'd left Megan unsupervised for long periods of time. And that she knew her way around the Santa Lucia, that she could get in and out of the inn without being spotted—the way someone had done when they'd trashed Jess's room.

Jess's heart stopped. Once it had resumed a natural rhythm, she assured herself that the photo in her hand meant nothing. But if it meant nothing, why was the negative missing? And when had it been stolen?

The negatives had been locked in the safe since Stewart's death, so it had to have been taken before that. And it had to have been taken by someone with something to hide. By someone who could slip in and out of the inn at will. By the someone who'd trashed her room. Someone like Florence.

Jess felt her heart skip into triple-time. She'd always assumed the murderer was a man, but it didn't have to be. A gun was definitely an equal opportunity murder weapon. But what would have driven Florence to murder? Megan had said that her mother and grandmother argued. But was that a reason to kill? Jess smothered a nervous laugh; that would certainly have put paid to the argument. And George had said that Stewart was on his way to Jason's when he was killed, but Florence lived here, too. Maybe Stewart's business had been with the other Kendall. The one in this photo.

Jess told herself she was being foolish. The missing negative proved nothing. Her nerves were frayed beyond belief, and she was making some really stupid assumptions. Then she told herself that she was, quite possibly, alone in the house with a murderer and that the smartest thing to do was get the hell out of there, and she'd better take the photo with her. She took the time to fold it carefully so that the crease wouldn't obscure Florence's identity. She was slipping it into the back pocket of her jeans when Florence's voice floated into the dark room.

"Sandwiches are ready," she called just before she stepped through the door.

"I'm not hungry," Jess replied through stiff lips. She tried to ignore the fact that Florence now stood between her and the only exit.

Florence smiled. "You should try to eat something."

Jess wondered why she'd never noticed the predatory glint in Florence's dark eyes before. "I don't think it would stay down." When she rose from the chair, her movements were unusually clumsy. She caught the chair just before it tipped over. "I'm too nervous to eat. Really." A nervous laugh escaped; she decided she was losing control. "What I really need is some fresh air. You won't mind if I skip the sandwiches and take a walk, will you?" Oh, my God, Jess thought, I'm asking a killer if she'll excuse me from dinner. She clamped down on her growing hysterics.

"It's awfully cold out."

"I have my sweatshirt." Jess looked down to verify that she was wearing it.

"It's getting dark."

"I won't be gone long." Jess had the feeling that Florence was enjoying the cat-and-mouse game. "Maybe by the time I'm back you will have heard from Jason."

She'd never return, Jess promised herself, but she didn't tell Florence. Then she wondered where Jason really was. And Brandon. Could Florence have killed them? And Megan? Where was she?

"Don't wander too far," Florence said as she stepped aside to allow Jess to precede her through the doorway.

"I won't."

"And be careful. I wouldn't want you to get hurt."

Jess stepped through the door, braced for Florence to attack the minute her back was turned. "I'll be careful."

She waited for the sound of Florence's footsteps to follow her down the hallway; when they didn't she turned to look over her shoulder. Florence was still standing in the doorway of the darkroom. Jess resisted the urge to break into a run, afraid that would tip off the other woman. She forced herself to walk to the front door and close it carefully behind her before she gave in to the panic. Once she was out of the light spilling from the windows, she broke into a run.

Florence walked over to the table where Jess had been

sitting. She looked at the photos spread out in front of her. The one where Jessica had caught her sneaking into the inn was missing. So little Miss Goody Two-shoes had figured it out. It didn't matter now, except that she had to be sure to find the picture before disposing of Jessica's body. It wouldn't do to leave that lying around for Jason to find. Florence smiled as she realized that even now Jessica was headed toward the cliff. That saved Florence the trouble of luring her out into the dark, out to where she'd murdered the others. By using a short cut, she should be able to cut Jess off before she reached the Santa Lucia. With a smile, Florence started back to the kitchen where she'd hidden Amelia's gun.

It was time.

It had been a mistake to break into a run, Jess decided only minutes later. A mistake to take off into the fog at breakneck speed when she couldn't see more than three feet in front of her. She was reduced to a walk now. Reduced to sliding her feet along so that she wouldn't trip over rocks and uneven ground. Reduced to groping through the fog with her hands out in front of her so that she wouldn't walk into trees. The ocean sounded like thunder, and she forced herself to step carefully. It wouldn't do to stumble over the cliff and spare Florence the necessity of killing her.

She was doing fine, she told herself. She was headed for the inn, and she'd be halfway there before Florence even realized she wasn't coming back. As long as she didn't get disoriented, she would be in the safety of the Santa Lucia's lobby within ten minutes. That was when she heard the laughter. It was wild enough to send a chill down her spine.

"Jessica . . ." The voice floated through the fog. "I know you're there. You can't hide from me."

Jess froze. She'd almost convinced herself that she'd imagined it when she heard the laughter again.

It was closer this time.

"Come out, come out, wherever you are," Florence called in a singsong voice.

Terrified, Jess looked for a hiding place, but there was nothing big or solid enough to protect her from a bullet. Her best chance was to get to the inn. She hurried forward, taking less care than she had before.

"Are you over here?" the voice called. A shot rang out, and Jess couldn't muffle the scream that escaped her.

"Oh, so you're over this way."

Another shot punctuated the night. This one was closer, but Jess knew better than to give away her location. Silently she continued on. The ocean was louder now, and when Florence called to her, the woman's voice was muted.

With the roar of the ocean to cover any noise, Jess picked up speed, only to trip headlong over a rock. She landed hard on her hands and knees, discovering to her horror that the earth fell away just in front of her. Somehow she'd wandered off the path and close to the cliff. She closed her eyes against the vision of her own body lying broken on the rocks below.

On all fours, she scooted away from the drop, stood, and then plunged back the way she'd come, looking for the well-worn footpath. Once she found it, she picked up speed. She was limping along, favoring the knee she'd scraped in her fall, when she spotted the figure just ahead.

"I told you there was no use hiding," Florence chided, then raised the gun in Jess's direction.

With a small cry, Jess threw herself off the path into the bushes and brambles. A bullet sang of death only a few inches away. She turned and plunged deeper into the brush. The fog was thicker here, as though caught within the low-lying bushes and brambles. Small animals scurried out of her way as she plunged through the underbrush. The sounds of the ocean faded, drowned out by her own labored breathing.

Suddenly the world tilted, and she was hurtling through dark, damp space. She braced herself for the sharp rocks, knew that she would be dead in seconds, then felt herself hit sand and roll downhill. It felt as though she rolled forever—over and over—but she was on her feet again as soon as she stopped. The problem was that she didn't know which way to run. She was lost among the sand dunes, and the fog was so thick that she could barely see her hand before her. The sounds of the ocean seemed to bounce off rocks and trees, seemed to come from all directions. The elements, coupled with her own horrible sense of direction, stopped her as Florence hadn't been able to. If she moved, she was as likely to wander into Florence as she was to find the inn, as likely to stumble into the Pacific as she was to stagger onto the highway.

She was tired and lost and terrified, and she had almost decided to crawl behind a rock and wait for the dawn—or for Florence—when she heard them. At first she thought she was imagining it; then she wondered for one awful moment if she had died. She wondered if she'd lost her chance at love and happiness and been condemned to the dark for all eternity with only the sweet sound of the bells for company.

Then she recognized them for what they were: the bells of the Santa Lucia. All she had to do was follow the sound and she'd be safe. She listened and then staggered toward the sweet song. Up an incline of sand that shifted beneath her feet. Through the brush until she stumbled onto the path. Along the trail toward the inn until she could finally see the English garden and the Santa Lucia in the distance.

She broke into a run then, flying past the garden toward the front of the building, where the guests, in various states of dress, were milling around the lawn. The bells had roused them from their sleep, and their reactions varied from hysterical to indignant. In the midst of the pandemonium, one lanky, khaki-clad figure separated from the group and ran toward her, waving his straw hat and calling her name.

"George," she called as she collapsed in his arms. "It's Florence . . ." She struggled for her next breath. "She has a gun."

"I know, miss. I know." George led her toward a bench, the very one she'd sat on the night she'd discovered Stewart's body.

"She . . . she killed Jacqueline."

"Don't you worry about it."

"And Stewart." She fell silent when she heard a police siren in the distance. "Brandon didn't do it."

George looked almost affronted by the statement. "I know that, miss."

"Where is he?" She grabbed the front of his shirt. "Where is Brandon?"

"He said for you to stay right here until he comes back."

"Florence said he'd been arrested. He wasn't, though, was he?"

"No, miss."

She tightened her grip on the khaki. "Where is he now?"

George's gaze darted back the way she'd come. "He went to look for you."

"No!" she cried. "No!" The tears were falling in earnest now. "Florence has a gun. A gun," she repeated as though the concept were too difficult for George to grasp. She turned, prepared to run back into the fog, but George's grip was surprisingly strong.

"Mr. Brandon said to keep you here."

"Let me go," she cried. "I've got to stop him." She put every ounce of strength into the struggle. Once she broke loose, she didn't look back but plunged headlong into the fog, screaming Brandon's name.

The darkness seemed thicker after the lights of the Santa Lucia. The air seemed colder after being held in George's arms. But she ran headlong into the dark and the cold, calling his name.

"Brandon!" She stopped and listened. Only the waves answered her cries. She ran on, still calling his name until her throat was raw and she could manage little more than a whisper. That was when she heard him.

"Jess," he shouted. "Run!"

So she ran toward the sound as fast as she could in the fog and the night. He was still shouting for her to run when she broke into the small clearing where he stood only a few feet from the edge of the cliff. Crying, she stumbled forward to collapse in his arms.

"Brandon." She smiled up at him through her tears, then laid her head on his shoulder.

"You little fool," he whispered, though his hands were gentle. "Why didn't you run? Why didn't you listen to me?"

"The reason doesn't matter very much," Florence said.

Jess's head came up from Brandon's shoulder. Her gaze settled first on Florence and then on the pistol she held. "Oh, my God," she whispered. The fog shifted and settled around them, giving the whole scene a spectral quality.

Florence smiled. "Nice of you to join us."

"I told you to run," Brandon said. "Why didn't you?"

Jess shook her head. "All I heard was your voice. All I could think of was finding you."

Florence laughed. "Isn't love wonderful?" It was the reasonable, almost friendly quality of her voice that was most chilling.

Brandon turned so that his body partially blocked Jess from the other woman. "What would you know about love?"

"Enough to know that it makes weak people do foolish things. Like you, for instance. Let me ask you again, where is Megan?"

"I won't tell you."

Florence laughed. "I know, that's what you told me earlier. But that was before dear, sweet Jessica arrived." She pointed the gun toward Jessica's head. "Now that she's here, I think you'll tell me anything I want to know."

Brandon slanted Jess a quick look. "Jason took her."

"Tell me something I don't know."

"He didn't tell me where they were going. Only that you'll never find her."

Florence shook her head. "I don't believe you. I don't believe you'd let Jason take your daughter away without knowing where to find them."

Jess couldn't help the small cry of surprise that drew Florence's attention.

"Oh, look, Brandon. I think you've upset Jessica. You didn't know Megan was his child, did you?"

Jess shook her head and looked up at Brandon for confirmation.

He nodded as he brushed the hair back from her face. "It's a long story."

"Not all that long, actually," Florence interjected. Her voice sounded calm and reasonable; it made the hair stand up on the back of Jess's neck. "When Jason was reported dead, I needed someone else to take care of me. Jason had been unbelievably shortsighted and left everything to his mother. Since Jacqueline hated me, I didn't have time to waste. Brandon was very convenient —besides being stupid.

"Men tend to think with that thing that's in their pants. That's how I got Jason to marry me. Brandon was no different."

Brandon looked down at Jess. "Only Jason wasn't dead."

"Too true," Florence agreed. "Though that could have been handled if you hadn't been so squeamish."

"She wanted to kill Jacqueline and blame it on Jason," Brandon explained. "I wouldn't go along with her."

"It was the perfect plan," Florence added. "It would have gotten that bitch out of the way and put Jason in an institution. I could have had Jason's money; Brandon could have had me." She shrugged. "Instead Brandon forced us all into this difficult situation."

Jess looked up at Brandon. "Why didn't you tell someone?"

"Tell them what? That I'd had an affair with my best friend's wife? That she'd wished her mother-in-law dead? Nothing she'd done was really illegal. Besides, it was only my word against hers."

"And by that time I was pregnant." Florence's smile turned to a sneer. "It was the ultimate weapon. He couldn't stand the thought of his child being born in prison or an institution. As I said, he's squeamish."

Brandon brushed the backs of his fingers over Jess's cold cheek. "Try to understand. Once Megan was born, my only thought was to protect her. Jason as well. For the last six years, Florence has kept us dancing on a string. Always holding Megan over our heads."

"But when Jacqueline was killed?"

"No proof." He shrugged. "And half the time I wondered if Jason had done it. He was out of control in those days. He and his mother argued. I could only guess what had happened—and guesses weren't going to do Carl any good." He closed his eyes and leaned his forehead against Jess's. "Now I'm left to wonder if Stewart's death could have been avoided."

"Stewart knew about Megan," Florence said. "Jacqueline had told him, and he was going to tell. That secret was my power. Once that was out, you could have sent me away. They did that when I was little. Everyone sent me away. My parents. My aunts and uncles. The foster care people. They were always turning me out. I won't have that anymore."

Brandon looked at Florence. "We don't want to turn you out. We only want to get you some help."

Florence laughed as though Brandon had told a particularly clever story over dinner. "That's what Jacqueline said. That she wanted to get me help. But I knew what she meant. She wanted to send me away. Wanted to have locked me up. Caged like some animal. Jason said no; he couldn't stand the idea of having anyone caged. He argued with his mother, but I knew that eventually he'd give in. That's why she had to die. Well, I don't want your help. I don't need it." Her voice lost that eerie reasonable quality and edged toward hysteria. "I don't need you or Jason now. All I need is Megan."

"She's gone," Brandon reasoned.

"I have to kill you both." The rapid switch back to a conversational tone made Jess realize how mad Florence was. "I was only going to kill Jessica, you know. I wanted to see you suffer. Like you made me suffer."

Brandon pulled Jess behind him, held her firmly with one hand. "I never meant to make you suffer."

"But you did. You robbed me of my freedom, and you kept me from getting the money that should have been mine. It was your child who was always looking at me with those big blue eyes. Wanting something I couldn't give her. Reminding me of all I didn't have as a child. There was never a day when I didn't suffer because of you."

She pointed the gun at Brandon's chest and stepped closer. She was a creature from Jess's worst nightmare: beautiful on the surface, but evil beneath the facade. The closer she came, the more clearly the evil showed. As Florence emerged from the swirling fog, nightmare became reality.

"This will work out better, I think." Florence sounded like a teacher congratulating a pupil on a particularly clever answer. "With you dead, your daughter will inherit everything. Your precious Santa Lucia and all your wealth will go to Megan. If she should have an accident, everything will pass to her poor, grieving mother. The wealth will be small solace for the loss of my child, but I'll make the best of it."

"Jason will never—"

"Jason won't be able to stop me. After he murders his best friend and his best friend's fiancée, he'll be locked up. He might not be crazy when they put him away, but after a short time he will be."

Jess tore away from Brandon's one-handed grip and came up beside him. "No!"

The hand holding the gun wavered between the two targets; Brandon launched himself toward Florence in a low tackle. Jess watched them both go down as a shot rang out. They rolled around on the ground for what seemed an eternity. There was another muffled shot, followed by a horrible, keening cry. The two figures stopped dead.

Jess was afraid to breathe, afraid that the next instant would reveal Brandon lifeless at her feet. Then he rose— blood dripping from his arm into the thirsty sand, the gun in his hand—to stand over Florence. Jess stood rooted to the spot.

"It's over," Brandon told the mother of his child. "The killing and the vengeance are over."

Turning, he threw the gun over the cliff. Jess heard it clatter on the rocks below as he started toward her. Florence scrambled to her feet the minute Brandon turned away. Her bloodcurdling cry echoed through the night as she bared her claws and started for him.

Jess screamed his name, just once. That was all she had time for. Then Brandon was sidestepping Florence at the last moment. Stepping away from her so that Florence caught only air as she hurtled past the spot where he had stood. A scream lodged in Jess's throat, only to fade away as Florence caught her balance at the edge of the cliff. Turning back toward them, she sent a shower of pebbles and sand onto the beach below.

Brandon extended his arm and took one step toward her. "Take my hand." Blood dripped from his arm to pool between them.

"No." Florence smiled and took half a step back. She balanced on her toes, her heels hanging in the night air. "I won't let you send me away. Not you or anyone."

She turned her head and looked over her shoulder at the rocks below. Brandon used that split second to lunge forward. He grabbed her wrist as she turned back to him. They struggled for a moment, long enough for Jess to fear that the other woman would drag Brandon over the cliff with her. Then, with a laugh, Florence shook off his hands and pushed off with her toes. Graceful as a high diver going for the gold, she disappeared into the night and the fog. For a moment her laughter hung on the wind as her body hurtled toward the jagged earth. Then there was only the whisper of the waves and the keening cry of a far off seabird.

When she could move, Jess stumbled forward like a blind woman, her hand outstretched, not content to see him in the mist. Not believing he was still there until she could touch him, until she could twine her fingers with his and feel the warmth of his body in the chill night air.

Brandon's voice was barely a whisper. "I tried to save her."

Jess strengthened her hold on his hand. "I know you did."

"I really tried." He turned haunted eyes to Jess. "Did I try hard enough?"

"Yes." Jess framed his face with her hands and forced him to look at her. "She chose death. She chose the only way left to hurt you. Don't let her win," she pleaded through her tears. "Don't give her the victory even in death."

He gazed down where her body had come to rest. Jess held her breath, afraid that when he turned back to her she would still see Florence in his eyes.

It seemed an eternity before Brandon brought his gaze back to Jess. "I choose life," he said simply. "I choose you."

Epilogue

With the warm sun on her face and the sweet, cool grass at her back, eight-year-old Megan Kendall lay perfectly still and listened to the gentle lapping of the ocean and the drone of fat honey bees. The song of nature, Grandpa George called it.

She also listened to the tune Grandpa George whistled. Grandpa had promised to teach her to whistle once her two front teeth grew back. Megan giggled; she had a surprise for Grandpa. She'd been practicing whistling in bed at night. She was going to surprise Grandpa pretty soon. She'd whistle for him now if she wasn't so full of the lemonade and popcorn he'd brought her.

Megan was a big girl now and didn't have to take naps, but sometimes when the sun was warm and her tummy was full, she couldn't help drowsing. She was almost asleep when a shadow passed overhead.

She didn't flinch anymore when that happened. She wasn't afraid that she'd open her eyes and see her mommy standing over her. She didn't fear that her mommy would be in one of her mean moods. She wasn't even scared when people argued. Her daddy and Brandon still argued over the campground. Whenever they started, Jess always said something to make them laugh. So Megan wasn't scared of loud voices when she knew laughter followed, just like she wasn't scared of shadows when she knew there was love.

Megan shaded her eyes with her hand and looked up to see a hawk circling on the sea wind above her. She knew it was a hawk because Grandpa had taught her to recognize the wings that looked like fingertips. Grandpa knew all kinds of things like that.

She closed her eyes when the hawk swooped at something in the distance. She felt safe, secure. Daddy said it was because so many people loved her and looked out for her. Megan knew it was because her mommy couldn't scare her anymore.

It was the same at night. Right now Megan was staying with Brandon and Jessica because Daddy was off taking pictures of whales, but she wasn't scared when they came in her room at night. Megan didn't have to lie real still and squeeze her eyes shut so that Brandon or Jess would think she was asleep. When Brandon reached down to brush her hair back or when Jess placed a gentle kiss on her cheek, Megan could open her eyes and smile up at them. And then go right back to sleep.

When Megan confided that to Jess one night, she'd cried. Megan had worried then, worried that the next time Jess came in she'd be angry or mad. But instead Jess sat on the side of her bed and told Megan that she didn't ever have to be afraid again. Then she'd sung a lullaby. Megan would have been embarrassed if any of her friends knew that she had fallen asleep listening to Jess's sweet voice since Megan was already seven then and much too old for lullabies, but Jess had said she needed the practice because someday she and Brandon hoped to have a baby. Megan promised Jess she could practice when no one else was around; that made Jess laugh.

Megan had been almost seven when Jess married Brandon. Megan was a flower girl with a long dress and a basket full of rose petals that Grandpa had gathered right here in the English garden. If anyone asked what was the happiest day of her life, she told them about the wedding. They'd all laughed and danced and drunk punch that came out of a fountain. And Megan hadn't looked over her shoulder even once to see if Mommy was sitting in the shadows giving her that look. The one that said Megan was doing something wrong and that she'd pay for it later.

It wasn't until she and Daddy went home that she'd felt bad. She'd told Daddy that something must be wrong in her since she didn't miss her mommy. Maybe it was the same thing that was wrong with Mommy, she'd whispered, remembering how Daddy had explained there was something wrong in Mommy's brain. Mommy hadn't been able to tell what was right or wrong. She hadn't known the difference between good and bad. Megan had been afraid that the same thing was wrong with her. But her Daddy was so smart that he'd given her a test.

"What would you do if you found a baby bird that had fallen out of its nest?" he'd asked.

That had been easy. "I'd try to put it back, or I'd go get Grandpa George," she'd answered.

Daddy nodded. "And if you had a lot of food and you met another little girl who didn't have any, what would you do?"

"I'd give her mine."

Daddy nodded again. "And if you saw someone drop money out of his pocket, what would you do?"

"I'd pick it up and give it back."

"There's nothing wrong in your brain," Daddy declared. "Everything is connected just right."

She probably had the smartest daddies in the whole world, Megan decided. And she was probably the luckiest girl. 'Cause she had two daddies and Jess and Grandpa George and two bedrooms of her very own.

At first she'd thought it would be confusing to have two daddies. Of course, she knew classmates who had a dad and a stepdad, but this was different. This was two daddies of her very own. But then she'd discovered that it meant twice as many presents for her birthday and Christmas and twice as much love all year. She also got to help Grandpa in the garden and go on long walks with Jess. Not only that, but she got to go on "girl trips" with Jess and Aunt Marty; that's where they bought clothes and ate ice cream and talked about anything Megan wanted.

"Seems you're doin' more dreamin' than workin'," Grandpa said, pulling her back to the present.

But Megan could tell by the laughter in his voice that he wasn't upset. She opened her eyes and smiled up at him. "The lemonade makes me sleepy."

Grandpa smiled. "I'll remember that next time you're runnin' around drivin' me crazy."

"Chocolate-chip cookies make me even sleepier. You might want to keep that in mind next time I'm runnin' around makin' you crazy," she said, trying to talk like him. She loved his soft drawl and the way he had of shortening words. "Grandma made great cookies. I wish she was here."

"'To live in hearts we leave behind/Is not to die.' She's still alive here." Grandpa placed his big, gentle hand on Megan's forehead, then put it over his heart.

"And here. She'll never die as long as we remember her."

Megan nodded. Grandpa was always quoting poetry and saying really important things. He was right, she knew, but it wasn't the same as having Grandma to bake cookies or tell stories. Grandpa knew that, too; Megan could tell by the sad smile. She would have told him so if Brandon hadn't yelled, "Mail call!" at just that moment.

Megan jumped to her feet. "I hope there's a letter from Daddy," she said, even though Daddy was coming home tomorrow.

Jess was sitting on a big wooden chair Brandon had placed under the great, drooping willow. There were pillows under her back, and Brandon was sitting on the arm. His hand rested on Jess's oversize stomach, and he was kissing her. Mushy stuff, Tommy Mendoza called it, but Megan liked it. Jess promised her that Tommy wouldn't always feel that way. Someday he might even want to hold hands with Megan. Maybe even kiss her.

Jess held out a big, padded envelope when she saw Megan. "From your dad." Brandon smiled as she tore into it.

"Look. Pictures of whales." She held it out for Jess and Brandon to see.

Jess rolled her eyes. "Looks just like I feel."

"You look beautiful," Megan assured her.

Brandon smiled. "I agree with my daughter. You look more beautiful than ever."

"Remember that when I need help getting out of this chair."

"Grandpa George and I helped her out before." Megan lowered her voice to a whisper and added, "She had to go potty."

Jess patted her tummy. "The doctor said we're close.

That just proves what he knows; I haven't been able to get close to anything in months."

Megan let the pictures drop to her lap. "Did he say if I'm gonna have a sister or a brother?"

"He didn't tell me."

"Tommy Mendoza's mommy knew he was gonna have a brother. Maybe you should see their doctor."

Jess just smiled. "My doctor may know, but I don't want to. I like surprises." She looked from Megan to Brandon. "The two best things in my life have been surprises. I didn't know when I came here that I'd get you and your father." She looked back at the child. "If all my surprises are as wonderful as you, I'll be the luckiest woman in the world."

Megan rose and went to sit on the other arm of Jess's chair. "Was I really a wonderful surprise?"

A tear slipped from Jess's eye to slide down her cheek. "The very best."

Megan reached up to wipe the tear away. She'd learned not to worry when Jess cried. "And I'm gonna be the big sister?"

Brandon reached over to tug on her braid. "The very best."

"And will Grandpa George be this baby's grandpa, too?"

"Do you want to share him?" Jess asked.

Megan nodded. "Grandpa George has enough love for lots of kids."

"Then he'll be a Grandpa again."

It was Brandon's turn to roll his eyes. "That'll make your mother so happy."

"Why does she say 'gardener' like it's something bad?" Megan asked.

Jess brushed away another tear. "She has the old-fashioned idea that working in the dirt means you're too stupid to do anything else." When Brandon laughed, Jess elbowed her husband. "She'll just have to adjust."

"Grandpa is a terrific gardener. And he's smart, too." Megan frowned in concentration. "Does she have to come?"

"She is my mother."

"Are you sure?" Megan asked. When both adults laughed, she added, "It's just that she always has her nose in the air like she's smelling something bad."

Brandon leaned over and whispered in Megan's ear, "I say we let her handle the diapers in that case. She won't stay long then."

Jess brushed a strand of hair back from Megan's face. "Mom is too busy to stay very long."

Megan nodded, but she thought the real reason Jess's mom didn't stay long was that the laughter bothered her. She'd once asked Megan if everybody laughed all the time. Megan had told her yes, because Jess had chased away all the shadows. Megan hadn't added that even in the dark of the night there was a warm glow now. Because there was love. Then Mrs. Martinson had gotten that "bad smell" look on her face again. She'd left the very next morning.

Jess suddenly laid her hands over her stomach. "I think you'd better call Marty right away."

Brandon tried not to look alarmed. "Why?"

"I think this baby is on its way."

Brandon rose and looked down at his wife. "The baby isn't due for another three days."

Jess held out both hands so that Brandon and Megan could help her to her feet. "I think you'll have to discuss that with the baby later today."

Brandon pressed her back in the chair and whipped the portable phone from the holster he wore at his waist.

"Just sit still. I'll have someone send out the wheelchair."

Jess laughed. One of her husband's most endearing qualities was that he fretted over her pregnancy. Not only had he purchased a cellular phone so that he could be reached at any time, but he'd bought a new wheelchair for the inn and kept it at hand for the last two months. He'd even put in a helicopter pad.

"I don't need a wheelchair. I just need to get to the hospital." Another contraction hit. She glanced at her watch and noted that it was only six minutes since the last one. "Forget the wheelchair," she told them once the pain passed. "Just have George bring the wheelbarrow around."

Just before midnight Kathleen Elaine Roarke was born. She had her father's blue eyes, her mother's curly hair, and her sister's smile. Megan decided Kathleen was the second luckiest kid in the whole world. As she told both her daddies while the three of them stood hand in hand before the window in the hospital nursery, Kathleen couldn't be the "most luckiest," because Megan was.

COMING NEXT MONTH

ONE NIGHT by Debbie Macomber

A wild, romantic adventure from bestselling and much-loved author Debbie Macomber. When their boss sends them to a convention in Dallas together, Carrie Jamison, a vibrant and witty radio deejay for KUTE in Kansas City, Kansas, and Kyle Harris, an arrogant, straitlaced KUTE reporter, are in for the ride of their lives, until one night. . . . "Debbie Macomber writes delightful, heartwarming romances that touch the emotions and leave the reader feeling good."—Jayne Ann Krentz

MAIL-ORDER OUTLAW by Millie Criswell

From the award-winning author of *Phantom Lover* and *Diamond in the Rough*, a historical romance filled with passion, fun, and adventure about a beautiful New York socialite who found herself married to a mail-order outlaw. "Excellent! Once you pick it up, you won't put it down."—Dorothy Garlock, bestselling author of *Sins of Summer*

THE SKY LORD by Emma Harrington

When Dallas MacDonald discovered that his ward and betrothed had run off and married his enemy, Ian MacDougall, he was determined to fetch his unfaithful charge even if it meant war. But on entering Inverlocky Castle, Dallas found more pleasure in abducting MacDougall's enchanting sister, Isobel, than in securing his own former betrothed.

WILLOW CREEK by Carolyn Lampman

The final book in the Cheyenne Trilogy. Given her father's ill health during the hot, dry summer of 1886, Nicki Chandler had no choice but to take responsibility for their Wyoming homestead. But when her father hired handsome drifter Levi Cantrell to relieve some of her burdens, the last thing Nicki and Levi ever wanted was to fall in love.

PEGGY SUE GOT MURDERED by Tess Gerritsen

Medical examiner M. J. Novak, M.D., has a problem: Too many bodies are rolling into the local morgue. She teams up with the handsome, aristocratic president of a pharmaceutical company, who has his own agenda. Their search for the truth takes them from glittering ballrooms to perilous back alleys and into a romance that neither ever dreamed would happen.

PIRATE'S PRIZE by Venita Helton

A humorous and heartwarming romance set against the backdrop of the War of 1812. Beautiful Loire Chartier and dashing Dominique Youx were meant for each other. But when Loire learned that Dominique was the half brother of the infamous pirate, Jean Lafitte, and that he once plundered her father's cargo ship, all hell broke loose.

Harper Monogram **The Mark of Distinctive Women's Fiction**